Discovery

Ship Series
Book One

By
Jack and Sue Drafahl

© 2019

"Today the human race is a single twig on the tree of life, a single species on a single planet. Our condition can thus only be described as extremely fragile, endangered by forces of nature currently beyond our control, our own mistakes, and other branches of the wildly blossoming tree itself. Looked at this way, we can then pose the question of the future of humanity on Earth, in the solar system, and in the galaxy from the standpoint of both evolutionary biology and human nature. The conclusion is straightforward: Our choice is to grow, branch, spread and develop, or stagnate and die."

Robert Zubrin, *Entering Space*, 1999

Jack Drafahl

Sue Drafahl

i

Discovery

Published by

Earth Sea Publishing

Copyright © 2019 by Jack and Sue Drafahl

All Rights Reserved

ISBN: 978-1-938971-30-3

10 9 8 7 6 5 4 3 2 1

April 2019

This book is dedicated to all the men and women who work for NASA. Thank you for all your efforts to discover what is beyond Earth's boundaries and share it with the rest of the world.

Chapter 1

Earth, 175,000 years before the end of the last Ice Age

The northern offshore breeze brought a cold and damp morning to the large grassy meadow. The field spread out for miles, and heavy dew was forming on the thicker blades of grass, forcing them to bend and droop. Prismatic colors pierced through the center of each drop, forming thousands of inverted images of the surrounding area. The cloud cover was rapidly moving inland as a mastodon herd started to migrate from the tree line to the grasslands for their morning grazing. The herd now numbered more than fifty with the recent addition of a half dozen new calves. The three bulls had placed themselves on the outskirts of the herd, keeping watchful eyes as the young mastodons were extremely vulnerable to predators.

To the distant south, just out of the herd's view, lurked the saber-toothed cat, the second most dangerous predator of the era. The mother cat and her two cubs had picked up their scent an hour earlier and had been lying in wait for the herd to approach. The cats began slowly crawling along a shallow sandy gully, careful to stay downwind from the herd, yet hoping to get a running start on one of the calves as it passed.

Just behind a small hill to the west hid the pre-humans, the most dangerous predator to the mastodon herd. Their appearance was a cross between the Neanderthal of the past thousand years and the Homo sapiens that would appear 150,000 years later. They had no language yet, so grunts, groans, and threatening moves constituted their communication. They wore no clothing, but a large amount of body hair kept them adequately warm in their mild climate. Their weapons were primitive spears, which were ineffective for the massive task. Although they didn't yet stand fully erect, they could outrun several species of small game and the younger mastodon herd members.

The band of twenty-five pre-humans split into two groups. The key to hunting the mastodons was to yell and run off the saber-tooth cats while the other group charged the herd. The protective mother cat would pass on the hunt if there were any risks to her young. The group would then attempt to take down one of the mastodon adults but would settle for one of the young ones.

All the predators sat in wait as the herd started to graze in the deep wet grass. The mastodons would eventually work their way toward a local stream, but for now, they were content to capture the moisture from the dew-covered grass. A few small birds chirped in the distance, as the sun finally poked its way between two clouds. It was only minutes before the attack began.

An object with a piercing light brighter than the sun appeared from the north and moved slowly over the distant mountain range. The bull mastodons turned their heads to look at the source of the new light. So did the two groups of predators. Hunting was now a secondary thought to understanding this new threat. As the object continued to get brighter, a pulsating light emanated from the polished surface as it quickly moved through the sky.

The herd started to scatter for the nearby trees, and the saber-tooth cats made a hasty retreat to the underbrush. Only the pre-humans bravely remained, trying to make sense of it all. The large object slowed its movement, and the brightness dissipated as it hovered just a few hundred feet above the treetops.

As the mother saber-tooth and her young moved away, she took one last look at the strange object, and suddenly felt a sharp pain in her rump. Startled, she stopped for a moment and looked at her rump, but saw nothing. She and her cubs continued away from the meadow, as her only concern was to get her young to safety.

As the herd of mastodons moved away from the meadow, a bull noticed that one of the calves was struggling to keep up. As he shadowed the youngster until it could catch up with the herd, he felt a sharp pain in his hindquarter. He had no time to consider the source of the pain and continued to guide the young mastodon to safety.

The dark object now blocked the remaining sunlight and hovered over the pre-humans. The tribe leader stepped up front and took a stand against the alien-looking object by shaking his spear into the sky in protest. Suddenly, he felt a sharp pain in his arm. When he looked down, he noticed a small piece of his skin missing, and blood was now running from the open flesh. As his pain receded, the dark object moved toward the west and quickly disappeared from sight.

After completing its sample extraction from the pre-humans and Earth creatures, the object now headed toward the island of Santa Rosae. Over the next 100,000 years, this island would eventually break apart and become the Santa Barbara Channel Islands. It hovered over the island for more than two hours, sending sensor beams in all directions analyzing every aspect of the island. Suddenly, it stopped because it determined this island was unacceptable for its purposes and must now continue searching elsewhere.

The object moved another forty miles to the west and hovered over what is now known as Santa Barbara Island. It fit all the phase two requirements, so a circular boring device descended to the surface of the island. It started to cut a large hole, deep into the ground causing dust and debris to fly in every direction. Once the device reached its required depth, the boring stopped and using an advanced gravity technology, the massive rock core was lifted out of the ground.

The object then started a slow descent into the newly bored hole, stopping only a few feet from the bottom of the pit. A thick liquid started to ooze from the bottom plate on the object until the liquid solidified and became a platform comprised of a unique alloy of plastic and metal. The object rested itself on the platform, and additional ejections were sprayed on the pit walls until none of the rocky surfaces were exposed. The rock core was then moved back over the object and lowered partially into the hole. Hundreds of small laser beams cut the rock into very small gravel pieces, which fell around the object until it was completely covered with pebbles and no longer visible.

The object's operating systems powered down and went to a standby mode. Everything was accomplished in one Earth day. Phase 2 was now completed.

Chapter 2

It was built for speed. Dropping down to a few feet above sea level, it gently skimmed the shimmering surface of the crystal-clear water, riding on the air below its fragile wings. Maneuverability was not a problem, as it could accelerate from a quiet hover to maximum speed in less than a second, and then immediately make a complete 180-degree turn. The variable wing angle changed slightly to accommodate the straight-ahead approach to its final destination. Santa Barbara Island, located 63 miles west of Santa Barbara, California, rose more than 600 feet above the Pacific Ocean and covered one square mile.

As it approached the island, steep rocky beaches came into view. Its visual scanning systems locked onto several projections directly in its flight path, so it quickly made navigational adjustments around the shoreline outcroppings. Moments later, the island's main harbor came into view, and its massive kelp beds became visible below its transparent wingtips. As the glass-smooth blue surface rose to meet its small fragile body, its hairy legs extended for landing.

SPLAT! "God damn kelp flies," grumbled Jake McDonald as he lifted the month-old newspaper off the fiberglass edge of his lobster fishing boat, the *Razor Tail*. Jake hated kelp flies, and the only thing he hated worse was the way his miserable life had turned out but was his own doing.

Jake was 210 pounds and a couple of inches over 6 feet, but he was still in great health for a man who just turned 40. He sported a short, scraggly beard, which had recently been added at the onset of his fishing career. His hair was slightly greyed in places but was mostly sun bleached from working outdoors. His hard work on the old fishing boat had helped get him back into shape, which was probably the only good thing to happen since he'd left his comfortable job at the local bank. He was dirty and didn't smell great either, but there was no one around to notice.

He looked down at his hands and shook his head in disgust. They had gone through more abuse than the rest of his body. Instead of well-manicured banker's hands, he now had dirt under his fingernails, cuts, calluses, and severely cracked skin from working in the salt air.

His evolution from a banker to lobster fisherman had taken its toll. Jake had no friends, except maybe a few sea lions, and even they were a bit standoffish. He'd almost run out of money, and when in town, he had to avoid bill collectors by ducking down alleys and entering businesses through the back door. He could hardly afford a bottle in which to drown his sorrows. His wife, Beth, wouldn't let him see the kids anymore and even threatened to divorce him. Jake put his head in his hands and muttered, "My life really sucks."

When Jake left his father-in-law's bank, the man was livid and felt Jake was an ingrate. He loudly let it be known that Jake needed to be out of Beth and the kid's lives. He gave Beth money for living expenses, demonstrating that Jake was unfit to support them.

Jake tried to find work but to no avail. He then decided to pursue his boyhood dream of becoming a lobster fisherman. If truth were known, he should have left it as a dream, because it was quickly becoming his worst nightmare. The problem with boyhood dreams was that they were usually glorified, but now he couldn't turn back the clock.

Everything had started out fine. He acquired a boat and a license at a good price and even hired a crew member. Then all the problems started. The engine was continuously breaking down, and the main seal on the drive shaft failed on one trip, almost sinking the boat. A local fisherman had been a great help to save the boat, but the damage caused him to draw upon his remaining financial reserves. If those weren't enough problems, the poachers moved in and cleaned out his lobster traps.

Eventually, his last crew member quit and for the past four weeks, he'd been trying to do it all himself. A lobster fishing boat really needs two people to handle the work properly. He tried to jerry-rig the engine controls so that he could do it all, but after losing several traps, he was looking at a dire situation. A new direction had to be made, and things could only get better...right?

Bill Walker had been the skipper of the research vessel, *New Species* for many years. His young crew was predominately male, in extremely great shape, and actively involved in marine biology studies on Santa Barbara Island. A couple of boats conveniently anchored next to his, displayed several bikini-clad beauties that were a distraction to his crew. He had no time to worry about horny guys who often spent weeks at sea. It was times like this that he prayed for bad weather, or at least some warm gentle rain to cool them down.

Bill's love of the sea began when he first ventured out on his father's small fishing boat. His only regret was that he hadn't gone with him the time that his dad's ship went down with all hands. He always felt that if he'd been there, he might have been able to help. Those oceanic trips had taught him that the sea could be gentle, and then turn cruel the next moment. His unrelenting respect for the ocean had made him one of the best skippers in the islands.

All his years at sea had been tough, and although he was still in his forties, he resembled the old man of the sea. His hair had turned white, his face was weathered from the sun and wind, and he sported a limp from a previous boating accident. His looks were deceptive, as he was still in great shape, and could keep up with the best of his crew.

He'd been at this Santa Barbara Island anchorage for more than three days and was ready to move on. He'd just relieved one of his crew members on watch and noticed the lobster fishing

7

boat close to shore. He picked up the mike and said, "*Razor Tail, Razor Tail,* this is *New Species.* Come back on channel 6." He waited and was about to retry the call when the small speaker squawked out the voice of Jake McDonald.

"*New Species,* this is *Razor Tail*. How the hell are you doing, Bill?"

"Same old shh-stuff. We are finding sea lions, nudibranchs, holdfasts and lobsters. You do know what a lobster is don't you?" Bill laughed.

"Not so funny. I've just had a bad month."

"More like a bad year. All kidding aside, why don't you come over and get a good meal? We've got plenty of room and food," replied Bill.

Jake thought it over a few moments. He looked around at the steep rock walls, and the boats swaying in the gentle waters next to him before he responded. He didn't want people feeling sorry for him, and even though he got along great with the skipper, he knew the crew would make fun of him. Besides, he was having trouble tolerating his own smell, let alone subjecting it to anyone else.

"Thanks, but I think I'll pass this time. I have a meal prepared," he replied.

Bill knew Jake was lying but didn't want to push the issue.

"Okay, but the offer stands anytime we're around. By the way, our weather fax shows a small storm front coming in tonight. It might get a little rough." Bill didn't want to blurt out over the speaker that the *Razor Tail* was too close to the sharp rocky shore, so the weather fax was the best he could do to warn him.

"Thanks for the info, Bill. *Razor Tail* out," replied Jake.

Jake wished he hadn't left Santa Barbara in such a hurry. He was so angry with everybody, including himself that he forgot to shop for trip food before he left. All he had on board was a couple of cans of beans, some moldy bread, and warm beer. He sure wasn't going to eat any of the lobster he caught earlier in the day. He was sick of lobster.

His only solution was to make a quick dive for some fresh fish. The problem was that this was a game preserve with fishing restrictions, and the park ranger always had her binoculars scanning the area. He would have to hide a small power spear gun under his BC jacket, spear a couple of fish, and then hide them under his vest with the spear gun. He could clean the fish in his cabin, and fry them up on his old rusty barbecue. It sounded like the best plan.

He went into the cabin and changed into his swimsuit. Once back out on the deck, he put on his beat-up wetsuit for the second time that day. Jake checked the pressure in his tank and saw he had 2800 PSI, which was more than enough to spear a dinner. He looked down at the rest of his sad-looking dive gear and shook his head. He'd sold all his belongings six months before to buy this scuba gear, and it already looked like a diving death trap. The gauges were so scratched that he could barely read them, and his BCD had more repair material than not. Oh well, it would get him through another dive.

He grabbed the tank and threw it over his head and into place on his back. Divers didn't on put tanks that way anymore. In fact, divers did almost everything differently these days, but he still preferred the old-fashioned ways.

He sat on the gunnel of the boat, put on his fins, and looked toward the rocky shoreline. He didn't see the park ranger, so he reached over for the small power spear gun and slipped it into his BC. He picked up his facemask, spit into it, and rubbed the spit around to clean the glass. He reached over, dipped up some seawater, and rinsed out the mask.

Oh well, he thought. I *might as well get this done.* He rolled over the side and into the water, hoping nobody would be watching. Then again, who would be watching an old washed-up lobster fisherman?

The water was clear for this time of the year, even though it was low tide. He swam quickly to the bottom and looked around at the gentle swell moving small pieces of debris across the sandy bottom. He was in about 30 feet of water, but there wasn't a fish in sight.

He was wondering why all the fish had disappeared when a couple of sea lions circled around him and wanted to play. *Great, that's all I need now is a couple of sea lions to scare all the fish away.* Then he remembered that many of the fish hid in the rocks along the shoreline when the sea lions were in playful moods. He'd been diving in this area many times before and remembered several small openings about 25 feet down along the face of a sheer wall. He started to kick in that direction and the sea lions followed for a short distance, before getting bored and deserting him.

Jake looked at his gauge and saw he was down to 2000 PSI, which still gave him plenty of time. He looked into several algae-covered rock openings, and found a couple of small fish, but nothing worth putting in his empty stomach.

As he rounded a corner, the steep wall looked different than it had on previous dives. Some of the dark-gray granite-like rock had broken away, and the opening was larger. He looked in, but the passage went so far in that he couldn't see the back wall of the small cave. He reached down hoping he'd remembered to put the flashlight in his BCD pocket and praying the batteries were still working. He undid the Velcro pocket, turned the flashlight switch, and a small beam of light pushed its way into the dark water. The batteries were almost dead so it only produced a low-intensity beam that would fade soon. He pointed the beam into the opening and panned the walls of the cave.

The front of the cave was covered with a thin layer of algae that was being gardened by a couple of Garibaldi fish. As soon as they saw the light, they darted away for a couple of seconds, only to return and nervously move back and forth.

Jake turned the flashlight away from the front edge toward the center blackness of the cave. As the shaft of light reached the far end of the long passage, a slight reflection bounced back at him. It looked like smooth metal, possibly manmade, but was too far away to see any fine detail.

A wise diver never enters a cave without a buddy or a guide rope, yet he was considering doing both. Now wasn't the time for Jake to do something stupid, but curiosity was getting the best of him. The cave opening wasn't big enough for a diver wearing a tank to fit through, so he removed his scuba tank, and set it down on the sandy bottom in front of him while continuing to breathe through the regulator.

Oh, what the hell, he cursed into his regulator, and pushed the tank in front of him and swam into the smaller part of the cave. His hunger seemed to subside as his curiosity was taking control, even when it meant taking chances with his miserable life.

As he pushed the tank in ahead of him, he was able to slide it into a side pocket near the back of the cave. Finally, he could get a closer look if his luck and the flashlight held out. He could see the newspaper headlines now - *Lobster diver dies in a small cave in 25 feet of water.* Then he realized that he wouldn't ever make the headlines. His death would be on page eight, under a plumbing ad.

The metal wall was not a bright shiny metal, but rather had a flat finish like pewter. There was enough reflectance to mirror the light back, but not in any specific direction. The metal surface had no visible marine growth on it, and the rock around it looked as if it had been burned with a hot torch.

As Jake moved his light beam back and forth, the light's shadow caught several small indentations in the metal. He backed the light up a couple more feet to reveal a large engraved circle with eleven smaller circles inside. The circles were arranged like the numbers on a clock, but there were only eleven, not twelve. Inside each of the smaller circles, Jake could see small indented dots. He discovered that each of the smaller circles had from one to eleven dots, but not in consecutive order.

As he reached out to touch the dots, something clicked in his slightly compressed brain. He quickly grabbed his air gauge and saw 1000 PSI air pressure remained in his tank. At this point, even if he ran out of air, he could back out of the cave and still make a free ascent to the surface.

He looked back, analyzing the circles. They looked like some kind of lock on a door, but why would a door be at the back of an underwater cave? He decided to touch one, but nothing happened.

Then Jake made the most obvious move possible. He touched the circle with one dot, followed by the circle with two dots until he reached the circle with eleven dots. As he pushed the final one, all the dots lit up producing a red glow, and the outer circle started to flash. The rock around the metal seemed to melt away creating an area that was now twice as large.

He looked back at his gauge again, and it now showed 750 PSI. He was still okay, but it was getting borderline. Nevertheless, he looked back at the metal wall, and the red glow was gone. He looked at the circles again and noticed that the dots inside the smaller circles were now in consecutive order. He reached out and pressed the circles in the same order. Nothing happened. He tried a reverse order with no luck. He tried pressing in an odd order, even order, and still nothing.

Jake spent the next 400 PSI of air racking his brain trying to figure it out. He tried to remember his entire high school math in hopes that it would help. He couldn't believe that a simple dinner dive had turned into an irrational underwater puzzle. By this time, his stomach was starting to take control of the situation, and his mind began to drift toward a delicious prime rib dinner.

Then it clicked – prime rib – prime numbers. He looked down at his air gauge again, and it read a little more than 200 PSI. There was just enough time for one final try. He reached out and pushed the numbered sequence of 1, 3, 5, 7, and 11. As he pressed the circle with eleven dots, a bright blue beam of light came from each corner of the exposed metal edges and struck Jake. Before he could remove his hand, his body became rigid, and his mind became fuzzy. His last thoughts were about some stupid circle of dots that had just gotten him killed.

Chapter 3

Deep inside the massive ship, electrical impulses from the sensor system in the intelligence trap were sent to a sub-processor system. This system then initiated more bio-support systems inside the trap. A quick analysis of the life form's needs was transmitted to the main feed, and the correct gas mixture was distributed into the capture chamber. Simultaneously, a diagnostic system activated to keep all the bio-systems in proper working order. When all the systems seemed to be functional and the subject was stabilized, it sent an awakening signal to the main maintenance and diagnostic processor for the lower memory core functions.

The ship was so large and complex, that it could not merely turn itself on, but had to be awakened in a series of steps. At each step, a set of tests were performed, and any necessary repairs were made before the next step was taken. Most repairs could be made through electrical impulses, but the more complex mechanical operations were done with the repair drones that were located throughout the ship. The first diagnosis indicated that damage to the ship was minor considering that it had been locked deep in the mountain of rock for more than 188,137 rotations of this planet around its star.

Jake's wife, Beth McDonald, was a strong-willed woman who took charge when the going got tough. When Jake left the family, she had immediately taken over all of his responsibilities. She already worked in the real estate market but expanded her workload after he left. Raising the kids was hard without Jake, as they needed a father. Truthfully, she needed Jake, but not the way he was now. She could easily forgive him if he came back, but it would have to be Jake's decision.

He had a mistress, but the sea was tough competition. She felt that his leaving was her fault because she pushed him into the banking job. She'd tried to mold him into the person she and her family thought he should be. What no one realized was all that was accomplished was to break a man who had a free spirit. Of course, he didn't have to give up so easily either.

When she first met him, he was clumsy and rough around the edges. No one in the family encouraged the relationship and even tried to torpedo it a few times. Even so, Jake was persistent, and she welcomed him. She knew after their first date that he was the one she wanted for the rest of her life. Now all of that had been lost because Jake had been so stubborn. If only she could turn back the clock.

As she traveled to her next house showing, she looked out over the ocean and sighed. *Jake, I really hope you know what the hell you're doing. The sea can be such a dangerous mistress*, she thought.

When Jake first looked for a boat for his fledgling lobster fishing business, he struck up a friendship with Charlie Worth. Most people who worked with Charlie called him "Shorty," not because of his height, but rather because of his very short temper. For some strange reason though, Jake and Charlie hit it off. They both were very forthcoming and often said their piece without completely thinking things through. Charlie had a good heart, and not only helped Jake get a boat but made special arrangements for Jake to get his lobster-fishing license.

When Jake needed help onboard, Charlie scoured the harbor and found Jake a reliable crewman. He heard Jake talking to the *New Species* on the radio, and Jake seemed pretty down. Charlie wished he could help Jake more because he was like the son he never had. When Jake was in trouble, Charlie took it hard. That's why he'd skipped checking his traps today, and decided to head to Santa Barbara Island. His crewman was having a fit, but Charlie barked out a few choice words, and they were on their way.

The island was now in sight, and Charlie scanned the main

harbor hoping to spot Jake's boat. When he finally spotted the *Razor Tail*, he picked up the mike.

"*Razor Tail, Razor Tail,* this is the *Spiny T.* Come back on channel 6." There was no response. He tried again, but still nothing. Charlie remembered that Jake loved to dive his problems away, so maybe he was on one of his "Get away from it all dives." Charlie tried another call but still got no response. Something in his gut told him things were very wrong. He didn't want to ask about Jake on the radio, so he'd have to wait until he arrived in the Santa Barbara anchorage.

In about fifteen minutes, Charlie pulled up near the *New Species* and took his dingy over to talk with Bill. As he approached, Bill came down and welcomed him aboard with a strong handshake. As Charlie moved toward the ship's lounge, he started to talk about the weather and fishing but motioned with his eyes that he wanted to talk privately. There were a couple of crew members sitting at tables, but a few hand movements from Bill and they quickly vacated the area.

Bill started the conversation, "Okay, what's going on? Are you in trouble with the ranger, or is that new crew member driving you crazy?"

Charlie gave Bill a "Something's wrong" look and said, "Have you seen Jake, lately? I called him on the radio and got no answer. Before I go over and intrude on his domain, I want to verify what you know."

Bill started to pour a cup of coffee, and answered, "I talked with him earlier about coming over for a meal, but he refused. Then about 45 minutes later, I saw him suit up and start a dive. That was more than an hour ago, and I haven't seen him come up. I'm a little worried."

"That makes two of us. I know Jake has been depressed lately, and he goes diving to relax, but it still bothers me. I think the two of us should go over and make a friendly visit and hope that he doesn't bite our heads off."

"I thought that was your specialty," laughed Bill.

16

"It is, but I think Jake picked it up from me," Charlie returned.

Bill started to get up from the table and said, "Give me a couple of minutes, and I'll meet you on your dingy."

Charlie got up and moved to the back deck, as Bill climbed up top to talk with his crew. Moments later, both men were on the *Spiny T's* dingy, motoring toward an unknown. As they approached the *Razor Tail*, they both noticed how it had seen better times. The deck was strewn with various fishing gear and looked almost abandoned. They tied up to the side but didn't take that first step into Jake's domain.

They barked out hello but got no response. Both looked at each other, and Charlie spoke the first words. "Maybe we're overreacting because Jake can stay down for more than an hour. We're going to look pretty funny when he comes up in a few minutes."

Bill was scanning the condition of the boat as Charlie spoke, and after a hesitation said, "True, but what if Jake is really in trouble? We need to be here if he requires help. We have nothing better to do for a while. Let's just relax and see what happens. I'll bet Jake came out of the water earlier and is either ashore or asleep in his cabin."

"I don't think he went ashore, but he might be in his cabin," answered Charlie. Deep down, he sensed something was very wrong. Jake was unsociable, but not to his friends. He just wasn't here, and there was no other place for him to be. Then another feeling started to surface. What if Jake really hit bottom and was looking for a final way out?

Charlie couldn't stand it anymore. He started to yell, "Jake, come on out and greet your friends. We know you're in there."

There was no answer. Charlie looked at Bill, and before Bill could say anything, Charlie jumped over the railing. He opened the cabin door, turned, and then looked squarely at Bill.

"Now I'm really worried," he said. "Jake isn't here, and

17

neither is his dive gear. He's still down and should be out of air by now. We need to do something."

Park Ranger, Dana Leffler, looked through the front window of her small island home. Down in the safe anchorage was a hodgepodge of both business and pleasure boats. She loved this assignment, even though she'd been there more than two years. It was far enough away from the California mainland to give her the peace and quiet she relished. She started this job on her 25th birthday and felt lucky to have such a great position with the National Park Service.

She was still single and only had a few romantic encounters when she was on shore leave. Nothing was very permanent, and she wanted it that way. She was pretty and had what it took to attract a man, but a relationship just wasn't a priority in her life right now. She'd worked hard to get where she was and wasn't going to give it up for some nine-to-five executive who wanted her as a baby maker.

She was just about to make the trip down to the dock when something caught her attention. She saw a man boarding the *Razor Tail*. A minute later, a second man boarded, and the two men seemed to be searching the back deck and cabin. Something didn't seem right. She reached down, grabbed her radio mike, and made the call. "*Razor Tail, Razor Tail*, this is the park ranger. Is there a problem on your boat? Can I be of any assistance?" She watched the two men talking to each other, and finally one of them picked up the mike.

"Ranger Station, this is Charlie Worth from the *Spiny T*. The captain of the *New Species,* and I are here looking for Jake McDonald. This is his boat. We're a little concerned about his well-being. Bill Walker saw him go diving over an hour ago, and he hasn't returned to his boat. We think he's still down."

Dana pulled away from the binoculars, and thought, *this wasn't what I needed today. I haven't had any deaths on my watch, and I don't want to start now.*

18

She pulled the mike back up near her mouth and pressed the transmit button. "This is Dana at the ranger station to the men on the *Razor Tail*. Can you do me a favor? It's going to take me twenty minutes to get down to the dock and put a boat in the water. Can you two go around and make sure Jake isn't on one of the other boats? We don't want to panic until we're sure Jake is really missing."

"*Razor Tail* to the ranger station. We'll start right away, but we don't think he's on any of the other boats. It's not his style."

Dana quickly responded with, "I agree, but it's the first part of the process we have to go through before we call in the troops. I'll see you in a few minutes. By the way, can either of you dive?"

Bill and Charlie looked at each other with the realization that one of them may have to look for a body. Bill then spoke into the mike, "I'm a certified diver, but haven't been diving in several months. I have all my gear on my boat. If we don't find Jake on any of the boats, we'll go back to my boat, and I'll get suited up. *Razor Tail* out."

As Dana took one last look through the binoculars, she saw the two men board the skiff and start for the first sailboat. She grabbed a few emergency items, stuffed them in a backpack, and headed out the door.

Chapter 4

In another twenty minutes, Bill and Charlie had checked with all the boats and there was still no sign of Jake. Dana was now in a position where she was going to have to make some serious decisions. Sending non-professional divers on a body search was not a good idea. However, at this time it was the only choice.

She looked at Bill and said, "I'll let you look for Jake, but come up every fifteen minutes, and make sure that Charlie will be above you at all times. I want him to keep track of your bubbles. Make sure you make three-minute safety stops for each bounce dive. I'm going to call headquarters, and inform them of the situation, and request a search and rescue team. If they want me to pull you out, I'll give Charlie a signal, and you'll stay on the next surface check-in. Okay?"

Both men shook their head in agreement. Dana went back down to her boat and sped away toward the dock. Bill went over to an equipment locker and started to pull out dive gear.

Charlie looked at the old beat-up diving gear. "Are you sure you want to do this? That gear looks pretty old, and even if it does work, are you going to be able to use it?"

Bill started to pull on the very tight-fitting wetsuit. "The dive gear and I may be old, but we both can still function as required. Besides, Jake's life may depend on it. Why don't you grab the rest of the gear, and I'll put it on when we get over near Jake's boat."

Charlie grabbed the tank and regulator as Bill finished squeezing into his wetsuit. He reached down for his mask and fins, and they both moved quietly toward the skiff. Within minutes, Charlie had the engine going, and they were back near Jake's boat, just as the sun crept behind the island, leaving only one more hour of daylight.

Charlie sat back and watched, as another one of his

friends prepared to challenge the sea. Charlie then broke the somber silence. "Make sure you come up in 15 minutes. We don't want to lose you too. Do you have a watch? Is there enough air in your tank?"

Bill didn't even look up at Charlie as he broke into Charlie's rambling. "You sound like my mother if she were a dive master. I'll be okay. I went diving last year in much worse water than this. Just be here when I come up."

Before Charlie could say any more, Bill flipped backward into the water and was gone. Charlie watched as the bubbles started to move away from the skiff.

Bill decided that the best way to search was in an increasing circle. He would loop the boat at a distance where he could still see the entire bottom. As each circle was completed, he would then expand the circle to his maximum horizontal visibility. He would use the sand ridges on the bottom to keep his bearings.

On his third circle, he approached the rocky wall near shore and spotted an unnatural dark object ahead. It was a dive fin, and that surely wasn't good news. Then he found another fin, a facemask, and finally, he spied a BC with the tank attached. The tank still had 200-PSI air. It looked like Jake had taken all his gear off, but that didn't make any sense.

Then he caught a glimpse of a wetsuit floating at the top of a small underwater cave. He took out his light and shined it toward the back of the cave. It went back only a couple of feet and ended at an irregular-shaped wall. A small sparkle of light gleamed from between two rocks. When he pushed them aside, he discovered a wedding ring. He put the ring up his wetsuit sleeve and reached for the wetsuit at the top of the cave. It was still fully zipped up and when he unzipped it, there was a pair of swim trunks inside. He'd never heard of any diving accident like this before. He bundled all the gear together and started toward the surface.

By this time, Dana had returned to the dive site and was waiting for Bill to come up. As Bill surfaced, she reached down and helped Charlie bring all the loose dive gear into the boat.

Before either man could say a word she said, "Headquarters wants you out of the water. They're sending the Coast Guard and a special search and recovery team out to the island by helicopter. They'll be here in a few minutes."

Bill was very depressed at this point and looked at Charlie. They both knew that Jake was dead. Even worse was the fact that it was looking like he did himself in. That just wasn't like Jake, but it was the only thing that made sense.

Charlie spoke first. "It looks like your people will be too late. It's just a matter of finding the body now. It sure is weird finding all his gear like that. It's like he just swam out of it."

The ranger and the two boat captains sat there in a trance for several minutes looking at the dive gear. Just then, the roar of a large Coast Guard helicopter flew overhead. It hovered near their boat, and two fully geared divers jumped out of the side door. The helicopter then rose and moved toward the heliport on the cliff near the ranger station.

The two divers surfaced, got instructions as to where Bill found the dive gear and then submerged. Minutes went by and everyone was silent because there was nothing more to say at this point. When the two divers surfaced, they had more equipment in their hands.

The one that seemed in command spoke first. "All we found is this spear gun, and a dive watch. It looks like you found most of the gear. There was no sign of a diver though. More divers are on their way, and will help us widen our search pattern."

Charlie quietly added, "The currents at this time of day will drag stuff around the corner and then out to sea. If you want to expand your search that would be the direction to head."

Chapter 5

As the ship became more aware of its surroundings, it activated more of its sensor systems. Communication was through a thin layer of plastic metal on the surface of the walls and floors. In essence, it was like a massive circuit board with runners throughout the ship.

Each communication circuit had at least eleven distinctive paths it could take, so in case of system failure, it could reroute through another circuit. Booster cells were located at each junction, which allowed signals to transmit over short distances through the air. If a circuit needed repair, it could literally grow a new path between the broken runners. Communication could be restored to one hundred percent very quickly.

The alien craft had gained more control of itself, so it started its chemical analysis of the outside environment. Probes were extended a short distance in several directions. The lower sensors checked the rock and soil that had formed around the base of the ship. Core samples of the rock were taken, analyzed, and stored in the ship's massive databank. Water was sampled and analyzed from the moisture found around the ship. Each of the sensor movements was quick and precise as they gathered external data.

The upper sensors moved more slowly until they pierced the surface and then stopped when it indicated they were in the exterior atmosphere. Motion detectors made a three hundred sixty degrees sweep for any movement of animal life on the surface. The creator's instructions were quite clear - the ship was to stay undetected by the outside environment.

When all the system checks were completed, a comprehensive diagnostic of the surrounding area was stored along with the original data collected upon landing on the planet. A signal was sent to the communications system to start scanning all frequencies for possible signals created by sentient beings. As it scanned through the frequencies, sensors started to pick up thousands upon thousands of streams of data sent on a wide range of frequencies. Initially, the data meant nothing to the ship, but as the translating system started to analyze each frequency, it discovered that both sound and visual communications were being transmitted via systems called radio, television, and telephones.

Once a translation protocol had been accomplished, the ship started to compile data extracted from the data streams. Initially, the ship assumed that all the information transmitted was factual, but soon learned that the television data stream was called entertainment. Once the ship had learned the difference, it began to search stored databanks, only keeping the basic concept of each transmission.

The data were sorted into various sections so that when enough was collected, it could create a clear picture of what existed in this strange world. Facts were classified into history, geography, weather, biology, chemistry, physics, language, and social structure of the sentient beings living on this planet. From this information, the ship learned that the creature that had set off the intelligence trap was a male member of the species. The ship also discovered that it needed to learn more before initiating interaction with the species called Homo sapiens or humans.

As the alien craft continued to scan the data streams, it ran across a system called the Internet. This complex system of information was transmitted via metal and fiber-optic lines on the surface of the planet, and through a telephone communication system called a satellite. Once it comprehended the purpose of this system, it stopped monitoring of other data streams and concentrated all its communication power on this single data source.

As the ship investigated the Internet, it learned that each Internet connection required an encryption code called a password. It further discovered that a social structure called an Internet server controlled the passwords, and gave out temporary passwords to humans. Many of these passwords were not used by humans, so the ship began the process of discovering and collecting as many unused passwords as possible. It could have just broken into the system, but that would have caused the humans to investigate the break-in source. Their orders clearly stated that they were not to be discovered.

In two human time units called hours, the data processor deep in the ship began logging onto the Internet using the temporary passwords. At first, one hundred connections were used, but as it learned how to "surf," additional connections were added until more than five thousand simultaneous connections were being used.

John Travers had spent most of his life working with computers. He graduated from college with a degree in computer science, with expectations of working in software development. Unfortunately, so did several thousand other graduates, which left him very few options. Eventually, he worked his way into an Internet server company. The work was pretty straight forward and didn't provide him much of a challenge. It was at least in computers, and maybe someday he could find his niche.

His duties at US Online Systems were to watchdog new Internet log in efforts. He kept track of how many and where they came from, as well as helping those having trouble logging on for the first time. His terminal kept a running count of new customers and constantly added them to his database.

It was 4 a.m., and he was busy working on his schedule for the rest of the day. He glanced at his monitor and saw that ten new login attempts had appeared in the past fifteen minutes. He turned his head away from the screen for just a second and when he looked back at the screen again, it read one thousand more. In the next sixty seconds, the number went to two thousand and then jumped to five thousand.

"Shit, what the hell is going on?" he yelled to an empty room.

25

He knew there was no way so many new users would sign on at the same time. There had to be a bug, hacker, or unknown virus in the system. He started to check out a few of the new users, and as he scrolled down the list, he found that they all seemed legitimate. Each had a valid password, and correctly filled-in information blanks. However, he knew something wasn't right.

Even though he knew he was alone, he looked around to see if anyone was watching, because he was going to break the privacy law. He tapped into one of the user's connections and was surprised to see they were going from screen to screen, and page to page at a rate beyond speed-reading. He also noted that the speed of transmission was considerably higher than any standard PC system could receive.

He tried several newer users, and each story was the same, except each user was concentrating on a specific subject. One search was on electronics, another on global economics, yet another was learning French. John also noted that the language barrier didn't hamper these users as they searched a variety of pages in every language. He picked up the phone and started to dial the department manager on the next floor when all five thousand connections stopped.

The ship was aware that this Internet was the fastest way to gather information about the development of this planet. It also realized that a human had discovered its multiple attempts to log on to the system. It knew that the next time it would log on with fewer concurrent connections so that the humans wouldn't detect the ship's access. It would have to abandon the five thousand passwords and use brand new ones. Each time it accessed the Internet, it would also use new connections, which would make data access slower, but should avoid detection.

One of the last connections made during this first session was to access the company's employee records. Using its computer logic, it quickly located the name of the human that had monitored its activities and noted his work schedule. Once it was determined that this human wasn't near the Internet system, the ship logged back on and discovered an extremely complex website called the Pentagon.

Chapter 6

"You promised," complained Brad. "You said you would take me fishing."

Jake turned around to see his son holding a fishing rod and tackle box. His head was spinning. What was going on? The last thing he remembered, he was diving in a cave. Now he was at a lake having a picnic with Brad and Beth. Was he dead, and this was heaven, or was this real and the diving a dream? Everything was so confusing.

"Are you all right, Honey?" said Beth in a sweet tone that melted Jake's heart. "Be a good father and go. You did promise to take him fishing. Lunch will be ready in less than one hour."

Jake looked back at Beth and saw the smile he remembered from when they first met. What's going on? Brad was running toward the lake yelling that he was finally going fishing. It felt real, not at all like a dream. What if this was real, and all the rest was a dream?

Then out of the sky, a bright light came straight at him. Jake tried to hold his arms up in a useless motion but found he couldn't move. Then everything went black.

He knew he was breathing, but he couldn't move a muscle. Jake realized that he was flat on his back, and on a very cold, hard surface. He was naked, yet still felt like he was somehow covered. His eyelids were frozen shut as if they were paralyzed. Then as the Novocain-like effects wore off, he started to feel the muscles move in his arms, his eyelids, and some twitching in his legs. He started to hear faint sounds and struggled to open his eyes. As his eyelids opened, the bright light became a soft blur and the image of his surroundings began to focus.

He was in a room full of walls made up of very complex computers. He'd never seen equipment like this before, but it looked very high-tech. Most of it was marble black and had small slender lights repeatedly moving up and down the wall. Circles of light appeared in various places, but none of it made any sense to him.

Then it caught his eye. In the middle of the room was the same large circle with eleven smaller circles inside. So, he had not dreamed about it after all. He sat up slowly and maneuvered his legs to the edge of the table. He was weak but determined. He started to stand, but fell and caught himself by grabbing the edge of the table. He righted himself up again. The floor was extremely smooth but seemed to have enough traction, so he would not slip or fall.

He shivered a little as he looked down. He was a naked man standing in a room full of computers. He no longer had a wetsuit, mask, fins, wedding ring, or anything. He then realized that even the two fillings in his mouth were missing and replaced with normal teeth. He had nothing left that could identify him as Jake McDonald. Someone was going to a lot of trouble to strip him of his identity.

He sighed and looked at the circles again. He needed to get out of this place and try to get his life back together. It was time to work his way back up the ladder of life, or at least die trying. He reached out and pressed the first circle, the second, and nothing happened. He tried the prime numbers, but no response. He tried it in reverse order to no avail.

"Damn," he said in a scratchy voice. A second later, a small beep similar in sound to his voice echoed across the room.

What am I doing wrong?

He leaned back against the edge of the table and looked at the circles. They had to be the key. Maybe he wasn't looking at the numbers correctly or pushing them in the wrong sequence. If he talked himself through it, something would work. It was certainly worth a try.

He held up one finger and then said "One" as he pushed the first button. The retort came from the wall in a female voice,

"One." He jumped back. Someone was playing games with him.

He held up two fingers, said "Two," and then pushed the second circle with two dots. The answer from the wall was "Two." The voice wasn't human, but maybe someone was using the computer to mask their voice. But why play this game? Then it occurred to him, that maybe he was actually dealing with a computer.

He continued using three fingers and received a matching response from the wall. *Let's try something different.* He held up five fingers and said, "Four" as he pressed the fourth circle. There was no answer from the wall. He held up four fingers, and said, "Four," and a "Four" returned from the wall before he even had a chance to touch a circle.

"This could take forever," he finally said aloud.

"Depends on you, Jake," came the report from the wall.

That was it. Jake had enough of these games. "Who are you, and what do you want from me?"

"I am, who I am," was the reply.

"WHO ARE YOU?" yelled Jake at the top of his lungs.

"Who do you want me to be?" was the next response.

Then Jake rephrased the question. "What are you?" There was complete silence.

"Can't answer that one, can you smarty?"

This time the voice from the wall sounded more human. "In your world, you would probably call me a computer. Actually, I'm a very large computer, with more capacity than any on this planet."

Jake was awestruck. He was standing in a room naked, talking to a computer, in who knows where. "Exactly where am I?" came the next desperate question.

"You are inside me," was the response.

This was still getting nowhere fast. "We could go at this all night or day, whichever it is, so can you just tell me what's going on without me asking 20 questions? And by the way, where do I direct my voice when I talk with you?"

"You can talk to me in any direction you wish. I'll be able to understand you from any position within my structure. I was directed to bring you here. I am a probe, but you may think of me as a spaceship. The fact is that you are inside me, and I am inside what you call Santa Barbara Island. I have been here for more than 188,137 of your years. I was sent by another highly intelligent sentient race. I do not know my original purpose for coming here, but do know that an intelligence trap was set to wake me up when a sentient species, such as you, was trapped in it."

"What do you call yourself?"

"I do not have a name. I am."

"You need a name, and I think it should be simple. From what you tell me, you're a large computer inside a sizable spaceship. Let's call you Meg, which is short for MEGA. Now tell me why I'm inside you and what you want with me."

Chapter 7

After searching for Jake's body for more than 12 hours, the situation was considered hopeless. The budget for search and rescue was limited, and the fact that he was a down-and-out fisherman didn't help either. Eventually, the notice was posted, and the search was officially over. The *New Species* planned to hang around for several days, more out of respect, than hoping his body would be found.

Charlie and Bill met one last time, and it was decided that Charlie would be the one to tell Beth. The *Razor Tail* would be returned to Santa Barbara harbor, and Charlie would help her deal with Jake's few remaining assets.

While Beth was showing a house to a newlywed couple, her beeper went off, but she ignored it. Her priority was selling this home, and it was good as sold, but she never knew for sure until they signed on the bottom line.

This happy couple triggered a memory of when she, and Jake had bought their first new home. Jake insisted that he handled all the details, but in the end, Beth was the one who took care of all the business. He was so excited about getting their own home that he insisted on staying overnight the day they signed the papers. The furniture hadn't been moved in yet, but that didn't stop Jake.

She remembered him picking her up from work with a big grin on his face. When they got to the house, he opened the trunk, grabbed a sleeping bag, candles, glasses, and a bottle of wine. He was just about to close the trunk when he reached in for a small CD player. That night they stretched out on the sleeping bag drinking wine under candlelight, listening to music, and talking of their future together. They made love into the early hours. She wished she could go back in time and capture the way life used to be.

She was interrupted from her thoughts when her beeper went off again. The number was from a cell phone number she didn't recognize. When she called it back, she found Charlie was on the line. Immediately, she could tell it was bad news, as Charlie was never short for words. His words were soft, but the message was hard. Jake was dead, lost to his mistress, the sea.

Beth was devastated. She thought she was over him, but when it came down to it, she was still madly in love with him. She always assumed that, in time, they would get back together. Why had he been so bullheaded? Why did he have to go out on that stupid boat? She hated him and loved him at the same time. The sea had won, and it wasn't fair. Beth wanted another chance, but she knew that was impossible now.

When she arrived home, she told her family, and they tried to console her, but no avail. The kids stayed with her parents that night to give her some space. She spent hours walking the breakwater, wondering what she had done to deserve such a fate. As the moon rose over the ocean, she rested against the sea wall as the surf pounded below.

Behind her, a familiar voice rang out. "Beth, I'm so glad to see you."

She turned around to see Charlie with tears in his eyes. He reached out with open arms, and she ran to him and gave him a big hug. She held on, and said, "I miss him so much."

"I know," said Charlie. "We all do."

Chapter 8

Jake stared at the black monolith wall of a supercomputer. If he wanted to get out of this ship, as it called itself, he would have to think things through slowly. Although that was difficult after dying, waking up stark naked, and now facing the unknown. Emotions started to get the best of him.

"I've had enough of this. I want out of here, and you need to let me go. Why did you take all my clothes?" By the way, it's freezing. Can't you warm this place up?

Before he could say any more, a small opening appeared to the right of him. Inside was a neatly stacked pile of men's clothes.

"That's better, now we are getting somewhere," he said with a slight chuckle.

He picked up the clothes and started to put them on. They all fit perfectly. How would a computer know his exact size? Someone must be behind the wall.

"Who's back there? Come out and face me, and quit hiding behind the wall."

The answer was quick, "There is no one behind the wall, Jake. I am as I told you. You are the only human on the ship. I had to beam you on board without your clothing as I was unsure of any contaminants you might bring. It was my way of quarantine. I can now tell from your voice that you are afraid of me. I mean you no harm."

Jake was getting very frustrated. "Then let me go."

The black wall answered. "I cannot do that, Jake. In time you will be free to go, but my directives will not let you go now. You must learn about future considerations."

"Your directives can go to hell and bullshit future considerations. Don't talk in riddles. Just tell me what's going on, and what you want with me. I'm really getting sick and tired of talking to a machine, and getting nowhere." Jake sat down on

34

the table and sulked. He was good at that, which is one of the reasons he wasn't with Beth anymore.

There was more than a minute of silence, and then Meg answered. "As you humans say, I will lay it on the line for you, step-by-step. When I am done, you can ask questions, and I will do my best to answer them."

"Now we are getting somewhere. By the way, I'm hungry. You don't by any chance have a ham and cheese sandwich stashed away somewhere," he joked.

Before he could say more, a sandwich appeared from the same section of the wall where his clothes had revealed.

"I'm impressed," said Jake as he reached down and grabbed the hot sandwich. "Oh, and what about a bee---."

A beer appeared before he could get the word out.

"Not bad for a condemned man. Meg, continue with what you were going to tell me while I eat."

Meg's voice was sounding even more human as it started a lengthy conversation about this spaceship lodged inside an island.

"There is much to tell you, but I can only disclose part. It is vitally important that you help me move from this location."

Before Jake could interrupt, Meg continued. "You have to understand that the ship you are in is very large, and has several sections. I will describe different parts of the ship using descriptions from your human science fiction stories.

"First, you are in the medical lab. This is where I will treat your injuries if necessary. There is a bridge for command control of the ship, an engine room, cargo bay, repair section, dining room, communication center, navigation array, transportation system, living quarters, and a very large garden."

As Jake started to say something, line drawings started to appear on the wall. Meg continued, "Each section of the ship is now displayed before you."

Lines designating each section of the ship began to appear on the black wall. Jake reached out and touched the section where he was standing. There was a small red dot in that section.

"That is you, Jake. Life forms aboard this ship will register in the drawing anytime you ask for directions. Just say the word *directions*, and then point to the section you want to go, and precise instructions will be provided to get there.

"Before I captured you in the intelligence trap, I had been studying your world through several methods of communication. Your Internet has been especially useful. Even with all that information, I cannot solve a problem that would eventually allow me to let you go. My directives tell me that I must move to a high orbit around this planet without being detected by the planet's sentient population like the prime directive in a TV show you call *Star Trek*.

"When I get into a high orbit without being detected, I will send a message back to my creators telling them that intelligent human life now exists everywhere on this planet. To complicate matters, my power supply is very low, and cannot be regenerated until I am in orbit. Even more problematic is the fact that I must blast the upper rocks off the ship before I can move into orbit. This would kill several humans in the process, which is not allowed by my directives. So, Jake, you can go free if you can help me achieve this next directive."

Jake was more frustrated than ever because there seemed to be no way out. He thought about his options and decided he had to deal with one problem at a time if he had any hope of finding solutions.

So, with a calm voice he stated, "You mean to tell me that with all your brain capacities, you can't figure out how to get out of here?"

There was some delay before the answer came back.

"The problem is more complex than you think, and my logic has not produced any solution. My system has run several scenarios, and each has resulted in someone discovering me, or several humans being killed in the process. If I cannot find a solution to the problem, my directives tell me that I must self-destruct. My self-destruction is not explosive, but rather dissolving of all materials on the ship. Jake, if I do self-destruct, you must die with me. That way no trace is found by humans."

Jake's anger returned when he heard the last part but quickly realized his fury would gain them nothing.

"So you're not as smart as I thought. Maybe your problem is that you're using logic to solve the problem. Have you tried illogical solutions?"

The answer was quicker this time. "That is why I am asking you for help. My research has shown me that many difficult problems in human history have been solved using illogical methods. I have stored all the scenarios that I have investigated so far, and they can be displayed anytime for you to study. If you have any questions, feel free to ask as I am not going anywhere."

Jake laughed because it seemed that Meg had a sense of humor. That was a step in the right direction. He turned to his right, and a computer desk and monitor had now appeared in the room. He shook his head and wondered how things appeared so quickly. If he were going to get out of this place, he would have to sit down and examine what the silicon brain had discovered.

As he looked at the first item on the screen, his mind drifted. When he first met Beth, he was a different man. He was excited about life, self-confident, and ready to conquer the world. Beth brought out the best in him. She was intelligent, beautiful, and for some strange reason had picked him. She had gorgeous long brunette hair, hazel eyes, and a figure that most women envied.

Although she looked a bit fragile, she was actually very strong. She had great physical endurance and had no problem keeping up on their hiking escapades. After they met, they had dated constantly for two months, and before long, they were married.

Her father, Bill Travis, was a short, balding man, who owned several lucrative businesses in the Santa Barbara area. He was adamantly opposed to their marriage and made it loud and clear that Jake wasn't welcome in the family. Over time, he relented when he realized he was going to lose his daughter if he didn't accept her husband. In order to keep peace in the family, Jake was offered a job at Bill's banking firm.

Jake gladly accepted the job, but it didn't take long for him to become restless. He felt useless, but he should have left well enough alone because then he wouldn't be in this fix. He stuck with the job as long as he could tolerate because he loved Beth, and had two wonderful kids to prove it.

Kathy was 16 and just starting to date. Thankfully, her busy school activities were helping keep her out of trouble, at least so far. She was a pretty, blonde-haired gal, who was very popular and constantly getting calls from boys. She'd once been her daddy's girl, but that all changed after Jake left. Her father was no longer in the picture at a time in her life when she really needed two parents. Kathy had started to rebel by wearing strange clothing, spending odd hours at school, and developing a hostile attitude.

Brad wasn't necessarily a bad kid, but 12 isn't an easy age. He always seemed to be getting into small pockets of trouble at school. He was heavily into computer science, games, and viewing science fiction movies. Brad had a great imagination, but this seemed to get the better of him when asked to answer questions in class.

One of the favorite pastimes Jake shared with Brad was performing magic tricks. Jake loved magic as a child, so when Brad was old enough, Jake taught him the ropes, just as his father had with him. Jake took him to an upscale magic shop and purchased several of the more expensive tricks. They worked together perfecting their skills, and then Brad would give performances for the entire family. Kathy always tried to sneak out of these events, but Beth made sure they all stayed for the presentations.

Brad eventually became proficient at magic, and ultimately

expanded his expertise into some very elaborate practical jokes. Many of his groundings were based on practical jokes he played on his school classmates. Beth wanted to restrict Brad's magic tricks but knew that was a sacred father and son bond. She had several conversations with Jake on the subject, and they finally came to a compromise that seemed to limit Brad's antics.

Jake shook his head. Why did he have to be so independent? Because of his stubbornness, he'd lost almost everything, including his family. Now, he was trapped on an alien ship with no way out. *Mulder from the X-Files would have loved this one*, he thought

He refocused his thoughts on the first item labeled, Ship Specifications. There were more than a dozen listings under that heading showing the capabilities of the ship. As he scanned the first few pages, he noticed the page number at the bottom. It read page 7 of 1,500. It was then that he realized that it would be impossible for him to read and understand all this information in one sitting. He scanned a few of the specs he thought might be useful and was amazed at the potential applications of the ship.

He scanned the pages of Internet research that Meg had gathered, and was amazed at the various scenarios that the computer had analyzed. In all cases, it resulted in the discovery or death of humans. More interesting was the method for achieving each scenario. The ship had technical advancements that could create just about any physical condition possible, yet it couldn't seem to solve the problem.

After scanning more than a hundred of the best of the scenarios, Jake realized that the ship was smarter than he'd given it credit. There really seemed to be no solution.

He saw a section on the computer screen called military research and decided anything was worth a try. He started to scan through the thousands of web pages that the computer had collected. Jake was just about to give up on this section when he ran across a web page called "Mushroom Gallery." He scanned through several pages, and then bounced back to the ship specifications, before going back again to the military web pages.

"Bingo," was his loud determined response. He touched the shutdown button and lay back on the uncomfortable cot that the computer had produced while he'd been working on the computer. Within moments, sleep followed.

Chapter 9

Henry Winston reached out and picked up his second cup of coffee, and scanned around his perfectly organized office. Everything was in its place now that Jake was dead. Henry was a small thin man, with a receding hairline. In an effort to improve his appearance, he replaced his thick glasses with contacts, even though they were harder to wear. He was introverted but had been working on gaining a more outgoing personality. He thought he had a chance with Beth until Jake interfered years ago.

Henry had great plans for his own future and decided that Beth would make his perfect wife. She was in line to get the entire banking estate when her parents passed away, and her husband would be equal partners in that banking fortune. Neither parent was in good health, so he figured it would just be a matter of time before he gained control of the bank.

His first date with Beth had been canceled at the last moment, and he was never able to arrange another. He later learned that she'd met Jake earlier that morning, and accepted a date with him instead. Not long after that, Jake and Beth were married.

The strangest part of it all was that Beth's father actually liked him better than he did Jake. Henry was offered a promotion to lead bank teller and later worked his way up to bank manager. He became Bill's, right-hand man. He never married, because, in the back of his mind, he hoped that eventually, his future would include Beth. He hated Jake and everything for which he stood.

That was all about to change because Jake was dead. Hurray! Beth was now available again, and his plan was going to work this time. To be sure, he didn't screw things up, he would have to take it slow. He would offer his help to Beth in her time of need, acting like a perfect gentleman. He would bypass opportunities to make physical contact until the time was right.

Then he would slowly work his way into her life and marry her, despite the kids. He could probably ship them off to a boarding school when he could no longer tolerate them. He'd get control of the bank, and no one would get in his way. His thoughts were broken by the sound of Beth at his office door.

"Hi, Henry, have you seen my father? I need to see him right away."

Henry was very careful about how he approached his prey. "Hello, Beth. I think your father went to a late breakfast meeting with a German investor. He should be back anytime. I know everyone is asking, but how are you doing?"

Beth, with her mind going in many directions, stared at Henry for a second, before realizing Henry was waiting for a response. "Okay, I guess. Everyone tells me that I should just go slowly from day to day. Somehow that really doesn't make it any better."

Henry swallowed hard and struggled with his next words.

"Jake was a good man, and I'm very sorry for your loss. If there's anything I can do to help, just let me know. You can call me anytime you need to talk with someone."

"That's very nice of you to say, Henry. I may take you up on it sometime. I think I'll run a couple more errands, and come back later. Can you tell my father that I need to see him?"

"No problem. I'll let him know as soon as he returns. If you give me your cell number, I can call you as soon as he arrives."

Part of his plan was to get her number, and when the time was right, he'd call her. The problem was that when Jake died, Beth stopped answering the house phone and all calls went to her unlisted cell number. Only clients and certain friends had that number, but he now had an opportunity to rectify the situation.

Beth forced a smile at Henry and thought that maybe she had misjudged him years ago. He seemed to be very nice. He was polite and didn't try to hit on her. Then her mind went back to Jake, and she shook her head a little.

42

"Sorry, Henry, I'm not all here today. This is my cell number, but don't give it to anyone. I've got to go."

She rushed out the door, and Henry smiled and thought, *Phase 1 accomplished. Soon it will all be mine.*

Beth thought she should be handling Jake's death better than she was doing. She was starting to lose it. Her mind drifted, she couldn't concentrate, and she was losing all her real estate clients. The kids had been devastated about Jake's death but they were already back in school. Brad had gotten into a couple of fights when some kids made off-color fisherman jokes about Jake. They both missed their dad, but each dealt with it in their own way.

She felt she needed to get out of town to grieve, and needed her dad's help. She asked Brad and Kathy if they would mind if she went away on a trip for a week or two. She was a little surprised when they both encouraged her to go away to help sort things out.

Her future was so cloudy. If only she could go back in time, and do it over. She wasn't sure what she would've done differently, but maybe it wouldn't have turned out the way it had.

Just then, a blaring horn stopped her from stepping off a curb in front of a car. Someone from behind grabbed her and said, "Are you okay?"

She turned and looked at the older gentleman who reminded her of her dad and said with a shaky voice, "Sorry, I got distracted. I'm okay. Thank you for your help."

She forced a smile again, shook the man's hand, and walked away. She needed to get away, soon.

Brad McDonald closed his locker door and came face-to-face with the class bully, a tall burly football player nicknamed appropriately, Bull. He tried to walk around Bull, but the size 12 tennis shoe blocked his way.

"Where are you going, featherbrain? I didn't give you

permission to pass me."

Brad knew he was in trouble as he'd already been in several fights and needed to get out of this one. The big chest facing him said differently. It was becoming a daily event for Bull to corner him, and rough him up a little before class. He fought back, but always got the worst end of it. He wasn't doing well in school since his dad died, because he had trouble concentrating. Dealing with Bull was just one more problem than he could handle. He didn't care if Bull beat him to a pulp because today it was time to do something.

Bull started to push him up against his locker, so Brad made his move. He pushed Bull back just enough, and then kicked up as hard as he could between Bull's legs. His foot hit Bull's balls dead center, and Bull fell to the floor, whimpering. Brad knew that as soon as Bull was up, he would be dead, but seeing him squirming on the floor was worth it. All the other kids in the hall were laughing.

Just then, a large hand grabbed his shoulder. He turned, and found the principal glaring at him, pointing toward his office.

Brad was having another wonderful day at school. He only hoped his sister's day was better.

Chapter 10

The blast from one spaceship ship firing at the other rattled their home speakers. He and Brad were enjoying a movie the two had seen together a dozen times. The loud detonations continued as Brad downed his Coke, and Jake polished off his beer. He and Brad both loved action and Sci-Fi movies, which made it the perfect way for them to spend time together.

Beth and Kathy were away at a local shopping mall, and promised the guys they would give them at least four hours of uninterrupted movie viewing. If they skipped through the credits and got to the good stuff, they could squeeze two movies in before they returned. As they lounged together on the couch, another massive discharge from the ship erupted on the TV.

"Are you having another bad dream?" said a voice from the wall.

"Yes and no," was Jake's groggy response.

"I have scanned all the human literature on dreams, but still do not understand them. Can you explain your dreams to me?"

"All I can tell you is that it's much like an alternate timeline that really doesn't exist. The mind sometimes likes to explore areas that it can't normally do in the real world. It may be a visit to the past, or a mixture of the present and future. It's a way for the mind to cross between the subconscious to the conscious. The point is that it isn't real, and I don't want to talk about it anymore.

"If you gave me better sleeping quarters, I might be in a better mood. That cot that you gave me to sleep on is awful. If you can create just about anything, can't you at least make me a small bedroom that isn't so sterile?"

Meg's response seemed puzzled. "Do you want a sleeping area that is not clean?"

45

"Meg, you're taking me literally. I meant that the sleeping area should be homey. You could add a lamp, maybe some carpet, a bathroom with a shower, and maybe even a kitchen."

"I understand now and will try to accommodate your request. First, I must know if you have solved the problem."

"Since the computer is part of your system, I assumed that you already knew what I found."

"The systems in me are vast and require a lot of monitoring. Your computer terminal is separate from my systems, so I don't always have knowledge of everything going on in the ship. If you want me to tap into that computer I can, but I would prefer to hear any solution directly from you." Meg was sounding more and more human.

Jake knew this wasn't going to be an easy sell and Meg might not go for his idea. The problem was that it was his only solution and his life depended on it. His presentation had to persuade his electronic keeper.

"Before I tell you about my idea, I need to know a couple of things about your capabilities. Much of my plan depends on your abilities. I know that you are more advanced than the human race, so I assume that you can control our surroundings. I need to know if you can create a very bright burst of light. So bright in fact, that it will almost blind someone.

"Next, I need to know, can you control the force of the wind? Can you make it move like the wind in a hurricane, but maybe a little more like a wind wave? Finally, and most importantly, can you alter and modify electronic signals in human inventions from a distance? In other words, can you turn something on, operate it, and override operating systems from a distance? If you can do all these things, I have your solution. Although it's a little crazy, it should work. The only other problem I see is that once you are up in space, the military will still be able to spot you with all its tracking systems."

Meg didn't respond for 20 seconds before offering an explanation. "I apologize for the delay in responding to you, but the main subsystem failed, and I was busy rerouting signals to the repair drones so that they could repair the damaged system. Since the system affected was the communication system, it needed immediate attention. The answer to all your questions is affirmative, but I fail to understand how these functions will allow me to get into space unnoticed."

Jake was starting to feel better now because he just might have a chance of survival.

"In all your research, have you ever run across a statement that indicated that sometimes the best place to hide is in plain sight? That's what I'm proposing. I don't want to screw up my presentation, so I want you to read the file I created on the computer. It gives a step-by-step approach to the problem. I call it Operation Mushroom."

Before Jake had finished his last statement, Meg had already pulled up the file and was scanning its contents.

"The idea is illogical indeed, but I agree it has a chance of working. I agree with your solution. Just know that if at any time it fails, I will self-destruct."

"If that's the best I can hope for, then so be it," Jake answered.

Just then, a door opened revealing a long hallway. Until now, Jake had been restricted to a small area in the medical lab, but it appeared that he had acquired new freedom. He moved out into the hall and walked down to another doorway. He turned the handle and viewed his new fully furnished apartment.

"Now we're talking," he said as he closed the door behind himself. Once inside, it was as though he was no longer on the ship. A light came through the windows, and he could see normal street activity outside which was obviously just for effect. When he opened the refrigerator, he discovered it was stocked with a whole case of Heineken beer.

"This is fantastic." He sat down and turned on the TV to a football game. "This is almost like home." In his mind, he knew that it wasn't home, and he wished he could be back with Beth and his family. He made up his mind that he was going to do whatever was necessary to get them back. Fishing be damned; he was going to be a husband and father again. He just had this one little problem to deal with first.

Chapter 11

Colonel Jack Mitchell was happy that this was the last flight of his military career. He loved the Air Force, but it was time to move on, much like the B-52 he was flying. Both were making their last flight as he was ferrying it down from Travis Air Force base to the Air Force boneyard in Arizona.

His flight plan included the transport of one nuclear-tipped cruise missile to a storage facility just outside of Los Angeles. Normally, weapons of this type are transported on the ground, but a report from the FBI and Homeland Security had indicated that a terrorist cell on the West Coast was planning to hijack any WMD that were transported on the ground. Transport by air over the U.S. had been banned years ago, but that order had been reversed when this new threat had surfaced.

His base commander was due to retire in a couple of weeks and wanted all the weapons moved before he retired. It was a risk, and everyone was told to keep a tight lid on the operation, or they would be assigned to the North Pole. A special runway was located in the facility for aircraft to land and unload weapons for permanent storage.

His copilot, Dwayne Stillwell, had only five years in the Air Force and had no real combat experience. Jack doubted that Dwayne could handle a stressful situation if it ever came to be. It didn't really matter, as it would be the Air Force's problem after this flight. As a senior pilot, he was still in command.

They had just taken off and were in level flight. The flight crew was minimal for this flight, and most were resting as soon as the bird was airborne.

He looked over to his copilot who was busy going over the checklist.

"Did you verify that the weapon was locked down and all safety devices enabled?"

Jack knew they were, but he wanted to make sure that

Dwayne knew they were.

Dwayne seemed to resent the question as he'd already gone over the checklist.

"You don't have to worry about a thing, I went over it all. Relax, this is your last flight. You're a short timer. You have better things to worry about than one nuclear weapon. The weapon's console is all locked down."

The Colonel answered with such authority that Dwayne realized he better take him seriously.

"When it comes to nuclear weapons, there is no time for taking it easy. I want you to check that panel every fifteen minutes, even if it is locked down. I'm not sure why the base commander is in such a hurry. We just need to do what they say and get this thing on the ground."

They were more than an hour in the air and the old B-52 had already passed several checkpoints along the California coast. It was standard procedure to ferry older aircraft over water whenever possible, especially if transporting weapons. Jack contacted the military control tower, and they gave final instructions to turn inland toward the storage facility.

As Jack was about to make a confirming transmission to the tower, he heard an alarm go off behind him. He turned and noticed a flashing red light on the weapon's panel.

"What the hell is going on? Dwayne, the plane is yours. I need to see what's happening."

Dwayne looked over with a worried look.

"Yes, Sir, do you want me to inform the tower that we have a problem?"

Jack was not ready to end his career with a big mistake, so he wanted to make sure.

"Not yet, let me find out what the issue is first. Just keep us straight and level, until I figure this out."

He looked at the panel. He couldn't believe his eyes. The power light indicated that the weapon had been turned on, and the launch sequence had started. He reached down and tried to shut the system down, but none of the switches or controls were having any effect on the weapon's system. This wasn't looking good.

"You better notify the tower that we have a problem. We could be looking at a Broken Arrow real soon. Don't mention the Broken Arrow yet, just tell them we have a weapons issue. They'll check their records, and immediately know what we're saying. We don't want someone listening in getting the wrong idea. Do it now!"

Dwayne was nervous and his hands were shaking as he clicked on the mike.

"Victor Alpha One, this is Air Force TAV234. We have a problem with our weapons control system. It is powered up, and we have no access to the system. Please acknowledge and advise."

Ricky Trent had it easy today with only three flights bringing in old military bombers, and this was the last one. He had a hot date tonight and really didn't need a problem that would keep him on base.

"Air Force TAV234, switch to channel 34E, and repeat your problem in more detail."

Channel 34E was a new encrypted channel that allowed sensitive military communications. Ricky knew that the answer back might have sensitive material, and he didn't want to take any chances.

Jack looked at the panel again and returned to his seat. He reconnected his headset and turned to channel 34E.

"We don't have a lot of time here, so listen carefully. Get your base commander down there right away. We have a weapon panel that is hot and about to launch a nuclear-tipped cruise missile. The missile has no arming system, but it is in a pre-launch mode. We have no control over the panel. We need help from a nuclear weapon's tech, and a decision by your commander."

Just then, another alarm went off. "Hold a second, we have another alarm."

He went back and looked at the panel. The launch sequence had been initiated. In 45 seconds, the bird would be out the bottom doors of the B-52.

"We have a real serious problem here. The missile is set to launch in 45 seconds, and we seem to have no control over it. Get ready to call a Broken Arrow."

"I've called the base commander and the weapons people, but they won't be here in time. Keep me posted, so I can update my people when they arrive."

Ricky knew they were in deep shit now. If Colonel Mitchell was right, a big chunk of the good old USA might become contaminated minutes from now.

As the timer counted down, Jack continued to try to shut the system down. At the 10-second mark, the doors opened.

"We are screwed now," he yelled to the copilot. "Tell them the doors are opening and the missile is going to launch."

He listened as Dwayne relayed the message, knowing that it wouldn't do much good. As the counter hit zero, the big jet surged as the cruise missile dropped from the bay, unfolded its wings, and fired its engines. It made a quick 180-degree turn and headed back over Los Angeles toward the Pacific Ocean. Jack knew he was in big trouble now, but had to make the call himself.

"Victor Alpha One, we have a bird on the loose. It's headed due west, but we have no other information on where it's going. Please be advised."

He knew the answer would be to stick your head up your ass and kiss it good-bye.

Chapter 12

General Wendel Stone wasn't in the mood for some airman screw up in the air-traffic control tower. He had interrupted his officer's party and would pay dearly for this intrusion. He burst through the door and yelled at Airman Ricky Trent.

"What the hell is going on? This better be good, or you can start buying winter coats for your next assignment." He glared at the airman.

"Sir, we just got a call from TAV234 with a weapon's problem. They just launched a nuclear-tipped cruise missile, and it is headed west."

It took a second for that statement to sink in and the General realized the gravity of the situation.

"That's impossible. We don't transport nukes by air. Besides, they need a code to launch from the plane or turn on any of the weapons systems. Did you ask them to verify the problem?"

Ricky's response was broken, "Sir, they reported that the system turned on by itself, and they couldn't shut it down. They also said that the doors opened on their own, and the bird left without a command from either pilot."

The General was now looking over the airman's shoulder at the radar screen.

"First, tell that idiot B-52 pilot to land immediately and report to me. Where is the missile now?"

Ricky pointed to the radar screen, "It's about halfway between Los Angeles and Santa Barbara Island. It's dropping in altitude, and soon will be off the screen. I can estimate that the target area is the island."

"Call the flight line and scramble a couple of fighters to go after the damn thing. We need to call the Pentagon, and hopefully, they'll be able to tell us how to handle this."

Ricky again pointed to the screen. "Sir, it just disappeared off the screen, about a mile on this side of the island, but there was no explosion."

The General knew he would take some heat for this.

"Connect me to the Pentagon. I'm calling a Broken Arrow."

Major General Baur had just finished the daily briefing when the call came in from the weapons depot. He listened as General Stone informed him on the events that had transpired in the last hour. He couldn't believe what he was hearing. How could this happen? Just when things were beginning to settle down again.

"First, I want no one talking to the pilot. Second, I want your base locked down. No one in or out without my permission. Now, what have your fighter jets found?"

General Stone looked out over the flight line to see several choppers leaving for a search for the weapon.

"Sir, the Jets have found nothing yet, so I just authorized six choppers to the site to see if they can find anything. I'll hold all other aircraft for your orders. The B-52 pilot could make no sense of what happened. He keeps saying that it launched itself. As stupid as that sounds, I think he's telling the truth."

General Baur's reaction was furious. "Well, General, weapons just don't take off on their own. Someone is at the bottom of this, and your pilot is our only lead. I'll be there in a few hours to oversee the operation. Until then, everything is locked down and under high security."

"Can you pipe a transmission directly into their system so that they can simultaneously see the weapon and me?" It was a question, although Jake already knew the answer.

"Yes, I can direct a video and audio signal to any TV system you want. Would you like it in normal screen format, wide format, or high definition?"

"Don't go Hollywood on me, Meg. I just want a nice clear

signal that gets my point across. Make sure you blur my face so that they can't see who I am. Although I have a feeling that no matter how well I hide my voice or face, they'll find out who I am. My only question is when can we get the show on the road?"

"Major General Baur is on a military jet in route to a weapons depot just outside Los Angeles. He will get there in about two hours and we can transmit your message then."

The two hours seemed like forever to Jake and General Baur, but it was exactly two hours to Meg, no more, no less. When General Baur burst into the base communication center, everyone jumped to attention. "No time for that," stormed Baur. "Bring me up to date. Tell me everything that has happened since I last talked to you."

Jake wasn't sure he was ready because this was his first time speaking in front of people. He needed to get his message across and they had to believe him, or all was lost. He gave the signal that he was ready, and his blurred image appeared on the TV screens in the base's communication center.

While General Baur was listening to a rundown of the last two hours, suddenly all the monitors in the room flickered and then displayed a blurred image of man.

"I would assume that I have your undivided attention. I have a statement which I will read, and then you can ask your questions."

The image on the screen changed to show a close-up of the missing cruise missile. The control panel display inside the missile indicated that it had been armed.

"Yes, that's your lost cruise missile you now see on your monitors. I want to assure you that I don't want to detonate it any more than you do. I also know that you don't negotiate, so I'm not asking you to do so. I'm just trying to make a statement using this weapon. I want no money, no prisoner released, or any other type of terrorist demand. I just want you to see the stupidity of having such weapons around. I want you to feel what it is like to have a weapon of this type pointed directly at you for 36 hours. At the end of that time, I'll give it back to you, unexploded.

"I only ask one favor. I want you to evacuate all the people within twenty miles of Santa Barbara Island. You have to understand that I don't know anything about these devices and had a friend arm it for me. She knows about such things, but I'm not sure if it's very safe. In 36 hours, you can come in and pick up the weapon. It's just that simple. I know you have questions, so speak and I can hear your voices through your TV monitors."

General Baur released the breath he'd been holding.

"I don't know who you are, but this will NOT work. We want the weapon back now, and you're right, we won't negotiate. We don't know what your game is, but it doesn't work with me. I don't bluff."

Jake had expected the General's response and was prepared.

"General, you need to take a closer look at the weapon."

The TV image jumped back to the weapon section of the missile. Jake took a deep breath and continued.

"If you look closely, you will see that it's armed. I was able to build an arming device and get around your arming codes. You have a win-win situation if you back everyone up to twenty miles and wait for me to give the weapon back. You don't have anything to lose except a little pride. I have no ulterior motives, but I can't guarantee the safety of the civilian population inside the twenty-mile radius. It's now all up to you. I'll get back to you once you have cleared the area."

Jake had Meg cut off the transmission, and let the General stew a little. As Jake entered his apartment to get a beer, Meg spoke through the ceiling.

"I am not sure the General believes you. I don't know if the plan is going to work."

Jake took a couple of swallows and joked, "In all your

56

research, have you never run across a game called poker? I suggest that you look into it because a big part of the game is called bluffing. In this case, we see all their cards, and they only see a couple of ours, so we can bluff. The secret is to bluff adequately so they believe it to be true. By the way, I think the talking ceiling is cool. Whatever happened to the talking wall?"

Meg programmed the next voice to come from the floor. "I understand poker, but are you sure that it is going to work?"

"With the voice coming from the floor, does that mean that I'm walking on you now?" Jake laughed. "Poker is part art and part science. You play the odds, and the rest is skill and bluffing. So far, it has worked, but the most difficult part is next."

Chapter 13

Over the next few hours, the Coast Guard and Air Force were busy removing everyone from the Channel Island chain. They increased the quarantine area to a fifty-mile radius around Santa Barbara Island using the explanation that there was a possible chemical weapon accident. Within minutes, all the news stations had picked up on the story with speculation as to what had happened.

The keywords causing havoc were "possible chemical weapon." The mere mention of such a weapon made everyone leave the area quickly. Boat crews that required longer than six hours to vacate the area were evacuated by helicopter, willingly or not. Within five hours, the area was clear. Both sides just waited to see what happened next.

It was now time for Jake to play his next card in this high-stakes poker game. His blurred image reappeared on the TV monitor.

"I see that you've moved everyone to a safe distance. Great job, General. Now we just wait thirty-one hours, and the weapon is all yours. There's one more thing you should know. The one who helped me steal and arm the weapon didn't trust me, so she installed a safety device so that I can't detonate it."

"We're not going to wait for thirty-one hours for the return of the weapon. If there's a safety device on it, what's to prevent me from coming in and taking the weapon?"

If his poker skills ever had to come into play, now was the time.

"General, the safety device I told you about has what you might call a double edge. I can't detonate the weapon, but you can. All you have to do is send any of your troops inside the twenty-mile radius, and a two-minute timer triggers on the weapon. This feature was activated when the last person left the

58

twenty-mile radius. You see, General, the one who helped me didn't trust either of us. So you stay your distance, and we'll all stay alive."

Jake put his hand up to his throat for Meg to cut the transmission.

General Baur was fuming. "That son of a bitch. He sucked me in. He wants something, and I'm not going to wait for the other shoe to drop. Get a penetration team together, and put them on our best submersible. Have it ready in two hours."

Everyone scrambled in preparation for his orders. The General wondered what was next in this bizarre set of events.

"Jake, I don't understand. I have researched the General, and he will not wait the thirty-one hours as you have stated."

"I know, Meg, that's part of my plan. I expect him to try something within the next two to three hours. When he does, we'll activate the next part of Project Mushroom. I love that name. I know, computers don't have patience, but try anyway."

He laughed as he turned the TV on to wait for the next series of events. A rerun of *JAG* had just come on, and Harm was in trouble with Mac again.

The Navy SEAL team readied their fifteen-man submersible. It was equipped with the Navy's best underwater technology. The sub had extreme stealth capabilities, and the ability to turn on a dime. Special high-speed underwater rockets had been attached to the sides of the vehicle to enable speeds up to 90 knots underwater.

The command was given, and the SEAL team was on their way to Santa Barbara Island. The sub captain kept his boat at the 100-foot depth most of the way, to help avoid detection. Once they breached the twenty-mile limit, they had orders to approach the island and hide in a kelp forest where divers would exit the sub and go ashore at night.

"Jake, I have sensed a group of divers in a small sub crossing the twenty-mile line. At their rate of speed, they will be here in less than forty minutes. I am ready to transmit your next message."

Jake had fallen asleep, and Meg's voice startled him. He rubbed his eyes and moved to the location Meg was using to transmit his image.

Back at the Air Force communication center, the TV screen again filled with Jake's blurred image, and then a close-up of the timing device starting to count down from two minutes.

"General, you disappoint me. Look at the timer. You have less than ninety seconds to turn the sub about. If you don't, you will have to post a Do Not Enter sign out here for the next one hundred years. General, this is no joke. The timer will stop once you turn the sub around, and will reset once it's clear of the twenty-mile limit. We can see each of your fifteen-man team in the sub, so don't try to leave anyone behind."

Jake left the transmission of the countdown timer on the TV screen for the General to watch.

The General was in a bad spot. He couldn't take a chance that the weapon was armed. The fallout from such a blast would cover all of Los Angeles.

"Turn the sub around," he ordered, as the timer hit twenty seconds.

The command took a few seconds to reach the sub, and the sub's change of direction took another ten seconds. The timer stopped at two seconds. Sweat was now rolling down the General's forehead.

Jake got ready for the next part of a very dangerous game of nuclear weapons.

"General, you were lucky this time. The timer you see set at two seconds will reset to two minutes. The next time someone crosses the twenty-mile line, it will count down to zero with no chance of resetting. This is your last warning. If you obey my rules, then you will get the weapon back."

Jake lay back on the bed and thought about the happenings of the last few hours. Up until now, he had a good idea of how things would work out, but now he was in an area he knew little about. He could no longer predict what the General would do. He could only hope that the General would try again. Then this game would be over, and he would be free to go back to his family.

The General had been in contact with President Gordon, who had agreed with his decision. They both decided that the best option was to wait the situation out. The President's orders were clear - No military approach within thirty miles of the island. The General would just have to sit and wait.

Chapter 14

Back on the ship, Jake was getting restless. Twelve hours passed with no movement from the General. The plan wasn't working the way he'd planned. The General should have tried something by now but was obviously doing as he was told to do by his superiors. Jake would now have to take action on his own.

"Meg, can you take a look and see if there are any fighters near the twenty-mile radius?"

"There are two F-22s on patrol at thirty-one miles from our location. Both are flying in a southerly direction."

Jake knew that the time was now. "Meg, I have a little favor to ask."

Captain Art Miller had been a military pilot for more than twenty years and was looking forward to his new job offer from the airlines. He'd flown just about every type of aircraft made and that's why he was in command of the no-fly zone around the island. He had strict orders; approach no closer than thirty miles, and communications every five minutes. The communication was annoying, but considering the problem, understandable. He reached down to flip a switch on his communication system, and sparks shot up from the console. Communications went down. He tried all the channels, but nothing worked.

He looked out the window and realized that the other pilot was indicating that his communications were also out. He indicated to the other pilot that they needed to return to base. It was then that he realized that all his flight controls were frozen, and he had no control. He looked over at the other pilot, and he indicated he had the same problem. Then terror entered the cockpits, as both planes turned ninety degrees directly toward the island. In seconds, the ten-mile distance was covered.

The General was screaming. "What the hell are they doing? Get them back. They're going to kill us all."

The control tower tried every frequency to call the fighters back, but it was soon obvious that the fighters couldn't hear them. The General closed his eyes, as he knew what would happen next.

Jake's blurred face reappeared on the screen. "I don't believe it, General. You couldn't wait, could you? You just had to try. Well, now you're going to pay. In two minutes, this whole island and much around it will cease to exist. There's no stopping it now. I do have a suggestion. Since this weapon generates a large Electro Magnetic Pulse, you might consider turning off all your electronic equipment for a few minutes. That way you don't fry all your precious electronic toys. You'll need them afterward to prepare the population for the aftermath of the explosion. Let's see, thirty seconds to go. That's hardly enough time for a beer. Goodbye, General, and have a nice day."

The TV monitor remained on the counter as it counted down to zero. Jake was almost home. He grinned as he spoke to the air in front of him, "Eat your heart out David Copperfield."

A lot was about to happen in the next few seconds. In the communications center, everyone waited for the inevitable. They had put on special glasses so they could witness the explosion. All electronic devices were shut down to avoid any damage by the EMP from the blast. A cover story was created about an out-of-control missile launch heading toward Santa Barbara Island. Now it was just a matter of waiting.

The two F-22 pilots were now in a major panic mode as their planes descended to ocean level heading directly toward the island. Both pilots knew they only had seconds left before the blast vaporized their aircraft. They both looked at each other and waited.

Thirty seconds before the counter hit zero, a small probe extended itself thirty feet above Santa Barbara Island. This wonder of visible light was about to start a chain reaction that couldn't be stopped. At zero seconds, the probe started to produce light similar to a camera flash, except that it increased in intensity until it was too bright to look. In milliseconds, the light was at full power and held for at least fifteen-second duration. At the same time, a huge blast forced the rock on top of the ship upwards and massive boulders began dropping into the ocean, creating new underwater reefs.

Then for the first time since it had landed on the island, the ship started to move upwards and used a magnetic force to create a gigantic wind wave toward the California coast. Simultaneously, a funnel of thick dust and wind was created around the ship as it rose toward its destination in space. The concentration of dust was just larger than the ship, which hopefully would be enough to confuse any functioning radar system.

The force knocked Jake off his feet, so he crawled over to a chair. Once he did, straps magically appeared and wrapped around him. There was nothing to do now but enjoy the ride. As a final touch, the ship created a mushroom cap of dust, light, and wind above the rising ship. The combination of all these effects would give the illusion of a nuclear weapon exploding.

The pilots of the two F-22s knew they were toast. The power systems in their plane went offline at the same time as the bright light appeared. In a last-ditch effort before the blast hit them, they both hit their ejection seats. When the blast of wind hit them, they were carried miles from where their two planes disappeared.

In the communications center, when the timer hit zero, everyone heard the General as he spoke an undignified, "Oh, shit."

He turned around to the technicians and quickly asked, "How long before we can turn the electronic gear back on? We need to be up and running as soon as possible."

The tech looked white with fear and was slow with his answer.

"Sir, I'm not really sure, as I wasn't prepared for this type of situation. My guess would be 1 to 2 minutes before we can safely go back online."

The effect along the California coast was stunning. Most people had seen a nuclear blast in Hollywood films, but never for real. The military had decided not to warn the public, because there wasn't enough time to do anything. The panic would be worse than the blast.

The first indication of the blast was the blinding light, which drew everyone's attention to the western horizon. They were hypnotized by the light. The blast and mushroom cloud followed and most were starting to realize they were in big trouble. Some didn't move as they were mesmerized by the blast, but other frightened people ran, figuring they still might have a chance.

The General turned back around to see the massive mushroom cloud climbing toward the sky. He wondered what kind of job he could get in the private sector after his court-martial.

"Okay, everyone, things are really bad, but we need to maintain order. I'm still in command. At zero plus two minutes, I want all electronics back online. I need to know what's going on out there."

Chapter 15

The ship was rattling back and forth, as it rose into the sky. It used maximum power consumption to lift itself while simultaneously maintaining the illusion of the blast. Systems started to overload and fail all over the ship. It became obvious to Meg that there wouldn't be enough power to complete the task. All internal lighting systems were turned off, and environmental systems in all rooms were shut down except Jake's section.

It was still not going to be enough power. Meg then decided to cut the illusion of blast light to 10%. Most people watching, including those versed in nuclear fission, would see the change, but wouldn't understand what happened. Meg knew that human confusion was also a good deception.

Even doing all that, the power levels were still not acceptable. Meg terminated the energy used to create the wind wave and new computations were made. There was just enough power to achieve orbit, but the ship would be visible briefly to radar before the stealth mode could come online.

Jake knew there was little he could do at this point, but wanted to know what was going on. The ship was vibrating violently as Jake got the words out.

"Meg, I don't mean to bother you, but how's it going? I would assume that with all the systems being shut down, that you are having problems. Is there anything I can do?"

There was no response from Meg. This wasn't good. The only light in the room was from a viewing screen. All he could see on the monitor was a blue sky. Change that. Now it was turning black with stars! She'd done it. He was now in space. Now, what was he going to do?

"Jake, I am sorry that I could not talk to you, but I had some problems to deal with. We are almost in space, but we have one last problem. We do not have enough power to operate the stealth systems. Without them, I will be visible to the radar systems on the ground. I should be able to have them online in less than a minute. What do you think the military will think the large object is on their radar systems?"

"I think they'll see you, but with all the confusion, most will think it is some kind of glitch. We can only hope for the best. The point is that you accomplished your objective. We can only hope they'll ignore the blip on the radar and be more concerned with the other problems, especially when they find out what really happened. By then it won't matter."

Two minutes seemed like forever to the General. What seemed strange was the way the explosion happened. He'd seen several tests in Nevada, and none of them resembled this explosion. Something wasn't right.

"I want a chopper out there as soon as you can get it off the ground. I want readings from that blast, and I want them right now. Make sure all the men are in suits, and they have dosimeters. I don't want to have to explain any unnecessary deaths. Now get me the President back on the line."

The communication center was as active as a beehive. All communication lines and radar systems were now back on. The airman in charge of high altitude radar readings was confused. His system was picking up a very large object above the explosion. He tested his equipment and confirmed it was working perfectly. He reset the system, tried again, but then the object disappeared.

The airman handling the President's call handed the phone to the General.

"Mr. President, I'm sorry to inform you that it appears that the weapon detonated. Two of our fighters strayed into the restricted airspace and triggered the explosion. I take full responsibility for what has happened."

The President knew that this was not the time to place blame. Now was the time to regroup and get the situation under control. The General was still the man to do the job.

"General, right now I'm not concerned about blame. Containment is our highest priority. We need to know just how much danger our coastal population faces. We need facts as soon as you can get them. I'll need to address the nation soon, and I want my information correct. You have fifteen minutes, General."

"Yes, Mister President."

Another airman operating the communication lines to the chopper motioned to the General.

"Sir, the chopper pilots report no blast wind, and no radioactive readings at fifteen miles out. Sir, they now state that there are still no readings, and they are ten miles out."

The General moved over to the airman's workstation.

"Put one of the pilots on the speaker. I want everyone to hear this. If anyone has any ideas, let's hear them now. Something isn't right with this blast."

The airman turned on the speaker, and silence came over the room. The pilot cut in.

"We are five miles out and there are still no readings indicating a nuclear blast. We can see the island. Most of it is gone. There was a blast, but it seems to be isolated to just the island. We are three miles out and still no readings. Now we are one mile out. General, we are over the island and there are no radioactive readings. There is a large crater in the middle of the island and several objects at the base. We are going down to investigate."

There was a scurry of excited voices in the communications room.

"Sir, the cruise missile, and the two F-22 fighters are intact at the bottom of the crater. It did not detonate. I repeat the cruise missile did not detonate. The fighters look undamaged as well."

The General stood back for a few seconds.

"What the hell is going on? I want the no-fly zone expanded to forty miles. No one comes near that island without permission from me. Get me the President back on the phone."

"Mr. President, we have an unusual situation here. It appears that the weapon didn't detonate as we thought. The explosion was not the weapon, but some type of non-nuclear device that destroyed the island, but nothing else. You can tell the public that it was not a nuclear blast. For now, we can tell them that it appears a large, unknown explosion occurred on the island, and we are investigating. We should also state that there is no danger to the public, but that Santa Barbara Island is off limits during our investigation."

The President felt relieved. "That sounds good, General, but very confusing. I'll go on TV in a few minutes and explain what we know. Then we need to sort this out. I have called in the FBI, CIA, and all the agencies to assist with your investigation."

Chapter 16

One of those other agencies the President hadn't mentioned by name was simply called TF, or Technical Forces. This group of secretive black ops agents worked to help protect the military defense systems in the U.S. They had their own manpower, special electronic equipment, and objectives not necessarily revealed. They would protect the military at all costs, even if murder and assassinations were necessary to hide the agency's existence. The agency was born in secrecy, and even the President didn't know of its existence.

Over the years, members of various high-tech companies and adept members of the military were secretly recruited to this clandestine organization. When Tech Forces found out about a proposed technology, that had been abandoned either military or public because of expense, they would secretly pick it up and continue development. Funds were secretly funneled into the TF from various companies and covert military budgets. Money was used to buy or steal every secret technology TF could discover from every country on the planet.

In the last couple of years, Tech Forces had become the most technologically advanced organization in the world. They even had their own sophisticated radar tracking systems along the U.S. coastlines. They too had picked up the same object above the mushroom cloud but didn't dismiss it as a glitch in the system. They saw it as a threat to the security of the United States. They were already processing the video data of Jake and the mysterious object to piece together answers.

The head of the TF main office, James Randel, had assembled a staff of computer operators who could tap in unnoticed to all the other government agencies. It wouldn't be long before they ferreted out who owned the unknown voice on the island. They knew that new super technology had caused the event off Santa Barbara Island, and they wanted it. Randel had informed the TF committee that he required unlimited resources to obtain this new mysterious technology. The committee had agreed that this new technology would supersede all that they had collected so far, and it couldn't fall into anyone else's hands. They gave full blessings and carte blanche to Randel's plan of acquiring this new technology.

After hanging up the phone with the committee, Randel leaned back in his chair and surveyed his office located more than three hundred feet underground. He needed to talk with his most trusted member of the group, so he grabbed the phone, and punched in a number.

"Pete, I need to see you right away. We have a special ops project that may change the whole way TF operates in the future. Pick out six of your best men, and meet me in four hours."

As with most of the phone conversations at Tech Forces, the answer was only a series of numbers, which indicated that Pete Killian, head of Special Operations for Technical Forces had received the message. Randel hung up the phone, picked up his coffee cup, and started to plan what would be the biggest change in political history. Tech Forces planned to overthrow of the U.S. government.

It had always been his belief that the U.S. government was on borrowed time. Eventually, someone would take out several U.S. cities with nukes, and the country would be in chaos. When the people of the U.S. had lost all faith in their government, TF would then announce its existence and its plan to save the good old USA. Once Tech Forces came into control of the government, there would be no limit to what they could do. They would disarm all other countries of the world, and if they did not cooperate, they would be destroyed. The technological advancements of TF would ensure victory, Randel was sure of it. Nothing was going to stop them now.

Chapter 17

Once the ship was in space, the rocking and rolling stopped. The straps holding Jake in place disappeared.

"We need to talk. You keep talking about stealth capabilities. Are they good enough to hide this ship from radar? Since I have helped you get here, isn't it time you to hold up your part of the bargain? In other words, can I go now?"

"Jake, first I want to thank you for the help. That is what I am supposed to say, is it not? I try to be more human, but it is still difficult. As you humans like to say, let's get down to business. First, the stealth mode is not like your stealth fighters. All electromagnetic frequencies such as visible light, infrared, ultraviolet, gamma, and X-rays are picked up by a sensor grid on the surface of the ship and transmitted to the opposite side of the ship. More than a million small plates composed of elements your scientists have never heard of before cover the outer skin of this ship. Each plate alternates in function with one receiving electromagnetic waves and the other transmitting the waves. Each has the ability to transmit the data it sends or receives to the opposite type of plate on the opposite side of the ship. This process takes more than 75% of my power and computer memory to function, so I am limited to other tasks when I am in stealth mode."

More vibrations forced Jake to hold on to the side of his chair as Meg continued her explanation of what was happening.

"Since there are no reflections, I am not visible to any optical systems or radar screens. The star cluster formations that I block from view are captured and transmitted back to the ground. If anyone gets within a 1,000-foot distance, I become visible because of the angle of coverage on each individual plate.

"Now before I let you go, I have a proposal for you. Take time carefully considering your answer, as it could have a great effect on your life."

Jake's face twisted a little, "You know when I asked you about your stealth mode, I just wanted a simple answer, not a full dissertation on quantum physics. I just want to know when I can go home. I held up my part of the bargain. So, how do I get back down on Earth?"

"Jake, it is going to take some time getting all my systems back online, so why don't you shower and I will cook you a meal. Will steak and beer be satisfactory?"

"That sounds great, but you're not going to change my mind about going home."

Jake opened the apartment door and turned on the TV. He watched as all the Networks were tuned to the explosion on the coast. They would go crazy if they only knew the truth.

The warm shower felt so good. So, how is a shower possible with no gravity in space? There was no end to what Meg could do. When he emerged, new clothes were lying on the bed.

"I could really get to like this," he half-heartily joked.

The table had been set, and the hot food was waiting. He took his time eating, with no conversation from Meg. He finished off the beer and moved the chair back. "Okay, Meg, I'm ready."

"First, I want to tell you that I have sent a message to my creators telling them of this world. I have accomplished my mission, and my last act is to give you control of the ship. You can do with it as you wish, but with a couple of restrictions. You cannot use it as an offensive weapon or cause any bodily harm to anyone. You must leave world affairs alone. You cannot give this ship to anyone for inspection or use. You must keep the ship hidden from view. You can have visitors if I approve of them. If any of these conditions are broken, I will self-destruct."

There was a short electronic pause from Meg as she waited for Jake to absorb this information. When she was sure he understood, she continued.

"You can travel to other planets if you desire, or return to Earth and send me into deep space. If you want to take control of the ship, I will instruct you on all its inner workings. I will only respond to your commands. Most importantly is that if you are ever put under duress to give up the ship, you will lose control of the ship, and I will self-destruct.

"If you do decide to take control of the ship, you can still go home. I am automated and can operate on my own for years. My power is recharged from the sun, and I am almost back to 100% capacity. The maintenance drones have repaired about 80% of the damage and will be 100% in a couple of days.

"The people on the ground are confused, and it appears that we were undiscovered. I can tell you more if you decide to take control. The decision is yours. I don't want an answer right now so take time to think about it. I'll get back to you in four hours."

Jake mulled over one idea after the next. If he did take Meg up on her offer, he still could go home and be with his family. It sounded like he could have his cake and eat it too, so why not keep his options open. There was nothing to lose, or was there? He must be missing something. The bottom line was he could go home to his family. As hard as he tried, he couldn't seem to find any reason not to take Meg's offer.

Jake decided to watch some TV while he formalized his decision. Most of the news channels were still covering the blast, but the movie channels were loaded with options. As he scrolled through the channels, he landed on the original *Star Wars* movie. It would be a strange twist of irony to watch a space movie while in space.

As the credits rolled by, Meg spoke. "How would you like to experience it for real? Just say yes to my proposal."

"Meg, you don't have to convince me anymore. I agree to your terms. I want to learn all about you, but first I want to go home. It's not fair to my wife and kids because they think I'm dead. So, how do I get down to the ground?"

"Jake, a lot has happened in the last few hours. You have been a great help, but my memory banks tell me that humans need more time to make such important decisions. My sensors tell me that you are physically exhausted. As humans say, sleep on it, and we will discuss it in the morning. I will then brief you on how you can return to Earth."

Jake frowned at the wall and stifled a yawn. "You may be right about my physical condition, and I'm willing to wait until tomorrow to finalize my answer."

A couple of minutes later Jake was getting the best night's sleep he'd had in weeks.

Chapter 18

The military had declared Martial Law in all the cities along the California coast. The governor had made a broadcast explaining this was only a precaution, which would only last a couple of days. Meanwhile, the news media was having a heyday with speculation and conspiracy theories of what may have happened. Several retired military and intelligence officers were solicited to give interviews and their perspectives on what transpired today.

The news media had preempted all TV shows and were running around-the-clock specials. Each station was claiming to have exclusive information only found on their network. People were glued to their TV sets wondering if this was the prequel to a much bigger event. Terrorism was at the top of everyone's list, and people were in a panic mode worried about what was next. Police departments were in overload from the never-ending calls as chaos and confusion grew.

The Technical Forces staff had been busy for the last few hours to match the unknown voice with voices illegally captured over the public phone system. The agency had tapped into a telephone database that had millions of conversations, and their sources. They were determined to match the voice to the instigator of the explosion. The object in the sky would soon become part of their ultra-secret hardware.

A beeping sound under James Randel's desk indicated that Pete Killian had arrived. Randel pushed a button and a special door at the side of his office opened. Killian walked in and spoke hurriedly.

"It sounds like we've got a good one coming up. I've been watching the news about the Santa Barbara incident. That's what the ops are about, right?"

Randel motioned for Killian to sit down and spoke in a

military manner.

"Mr. Killian, we have a very special operation coming up. First, let me explain, and then you have permission to ask questions. We think there is new super technology behind the Santa Barbara incident, and the object responsible is now in space above southern California. We want that technology, and if we can't get it, no one shall. I have a team trying to match the voice to the fellow who had General Baur in such a quandary, as he seems to be in control of this high-tech device. Once we find out who he is, you will go to work. He must have family, friends, or someone we can threaten to kill if he doesn't turn over the technology. Have your team ready for immediate action."

Killian absorbed this information for a couple of seconds, and then returned a response.

"Sir, I've located the men you requested. They're the best we have and will follow my orders explicitly. They'll die trying if needed. When we find out who this guy is, how far do you want us to go?"

Randel's answer changed from military to a more personal approach.

"Pete, we've known each other for twenty years. We've gone through all kinds of backwater wars, and what for. We now have a chance to change the whole world. If this technology is what I think it is, we can control the world from one single location. The stakes are high, so use whatever means necessary to obtain our objective. You have unlimited resources at your disposal. Get your men to a central location and have them ready for immediate action."

"Yes, Sir, I'll have the men ready by 0800 tomorrow morning at our location in the Santa Ynez Valley just north of Santa Barbara." Killian stood up and exited the office.

Randel leaned back in his chair. He felt good about this new development. He knew his superiors would have an upgraded position for him when the new Technical Forces government was installed.

Chapter 19

The smell of bacon and eggs drifted down the hall and under the door to Jake's room. Jake's eyes blinked open quickly. Was this all a dream, or was he really in space on a weird ship? The smell his nostrils inhaled made him feel as if he were home. His memories from the last few days told him that he couldn't have dreamed it all as it was too real.

The home-cooked meal caused his mind to back to his family. He'd screwed up so much, and now fate had played a very strange joke on him. He'd been in difficult scrapes before, but this was almost too much to comprehend. His mind started to drift again when Meg's voice came from the ceiling.

"Breakfast is ready. It is time to get up. We have a lot to do today."

Jake waited for more information but received none. He called back to Meg, but there was no response. He looked over to his right, and there sat a perfect breakfast. He wolfed down three eggs, several slices of bacon, toast, and washed it down with a steaming cup of coffee.

"This is great, Meg. You can make all my breakfasts from now on. What I want to know is how do I get to the ground? I have a bad feeling that it's not going to be easy."

"There are two methods for transportation from this ship to the planet. With the first method, you would take a small flight vehicle to the ground and land near your intended location. The problem is that I have no such vehicle, and would have to build one. Since most of my resources are required to maintain my invisibility, it would take time to build a small ship that would duplicate my stealth capability. I estimate that the time to build one would be at least two of your weeks."

Meg refilled Jake's coffee cup before she continued.

"The second method is a little more difficult to explain. There are no words in my creator's language to translate it, so the closest I could come up with is a 3-D scanner. On Earth, you have computer scanners that scan papers and photographs and transmit them through a computer system. You can then send them via phone wires or satellite to other locations. Let's take this concept one step further. What if you could take a 3-D object, scan it, and transmit it to a new location. The difference is that the actual object is transmitted, not a copy. A special locator device is transmitted with the object so that it can be reinstalled at the new location. If you want to compare it to something similar, it is much like the transporter beam in *Star Trek*. The difference is that I am very limited on how much data I can send."

A diagram appeared on the wall in front of Jake illustrating what Meg had explained so far. As the drawing started to animate, she continued with her explanation.

"Objects made up of one material are easy to send. Instead of assigning data to every molecule in the object, I can compress the data stream by giving the outline of the shape and transmit one set of instructions for all the molecules in the object with one set of information. The more materials in an object, the more difficult it is to send. If I use almost all my extra data memory storage for transport, I can transport one human at a time. That is assuming that I assign new data sets for each new set of molecules in the human that I am transmitting. However, many of the cells in the tissue structure in the human body are almost identical. If I use the same data compression on the human body, the data stream is much smaller. Similar muscle cells would be in one group, blood cells, and bone cells in others. I would do this for the entire body, except for the brain cells. They are so unique that no compression could be used in that area."

After a brief pause, Meg continued.

"There is a side benefit to this option that you might like. Since this process can group cells, it can eliminate diseased cells. If you have cancer cells, they disappear during the scan. I have estimated that your life span can be increased over ninety years if you go through this process a couple of times. You would be in perfect health. The downside is that you cannot be transmitted with the compressed method more than a dozen times in your lifetime, or your cell structure will start to degrade. A few times can improve your quality of life, too many will kill you. If I were to transmit a human body in an uncompressed state, I would have to shut down my stealth mode during transport, which would make me visible for about fifteen seconds."

Jake's mind was reeling with the overload of technical information that Meg had just provided. The idea of being in an alien craft was a little scary, but less than having his body disassembled and reassembled.

Then it dawned on him that with all that was going on, he'd never looked out any of the windows to see where he was in space.

"Where can I get the best view of Earth, Meg? I want to see how far I have to go to get home."

"If you go down the hall behind you and take a left, you will be next to the main dining room. There is a large viewing port along the side of the wall."

Before Meg could continue, Jake was running down the hall past a spacious dining area that looked vaguely familiar. Then he realized that it looked like Denny's restaurant. Meg had just copied what she thought he'd like for a dining area. He laughed as he moved toward the large clear port overlooking the Earth.

He felt his breath freeze, and he grabbed the edge of the window. It was overwhelming. Now he understood why the astronauts found it so hard to explain space. You just had to be there.

He was slightly afraid of heights, but this was different. A wonderful tingling feeling came over him as he saw the small size of the Earth. This made him even more eager to see his family.

"Meg, I want to see my family now, but do I really have to use your 3-D scanner to get home?"

"Relax, your family is fine. They are all home right now because of the explosion on the island," Meg answered.

"You have information on my family? How do you know where they are?" Jake exclaimed with excitement and anticipation.

"Jake, the answer is again complicated. As you now know, much of the technology in the ship, or Meg as you call me, is far beyond that on Earth. You have already seen how I can manipulate and modify electronic and mechanical devices from a distance. I can send a signal to any TV or computer monitor on Earth and turn it into a camera. In effect, I can see anything in front of any monitor on the planet. I can beam a signal to a specific monitor, and it will show me whatever is in front of it. It does not even have to be turned on. I am guessing that you would like to see the TV in your house?"

Before Jake could say anything, a large screen appeared on the wall to his right. At first, he saw no more than the living room in his house. Then Brad walked by and sat down on the couch. He grabbed the remote and started to surf through channels. He seemed a lot older, even though it really hadn't been that long. What mattered was that Brad was safe.

Brad looked back over his shoulder, "Mom, there's more on the explosion. It looks like an H-bomb, but the news guy says it's not. It looks really awesome."

Just then Jake's heart stopped. Beth had come into the room. She was frazzled, but nonetheless still looked beautiful. Why had he been so stupid? Beth looked at the TV, and then grabbed the remote from Brad and turned it off.

"We've heard enough about that bomb and Santa Barbara Island. I don't want to think about that right now. You and your sister aren't going anywhere tonight. I want both of you to stay home because I don't like the way things are going."

"Mom, that's not fair. The guys are meeting at the Game Zone this afternoon. We have a tournament of *Space Wars*. I have the leading score so far. If I don't go, they'll call me a mama's boy. It's not fair. Dad would've let me go."

As the last words came out of his mouth, Brad realized that he had gone too far. He knew he'd lost the argument because of his last comment. The look on Beth's face told him that he needed to go to his room and study. He hated studying, but it seemed the safest bet.

Beth's face was pale and sunken. It was obvious that she still cared about Jake. Maybe he still had a chance to put it all back together. He needed to get home but wasn't impressed with Meg's plan on how it was going to happen.

"Okay, Meg, I'll try your 3-D scanner. I need to send a message to Brad first, and then you can beam me down, or whatever it is you do to my molecules."

"Jake, I do not understand why you are so worried about the 3-D scanning to the surface. You have already done it once when I brought you aboard, so this will be your second time. Your life span has already been increased by at least 40 years. The procedure is painless but can be a little uncomfortable. When you are ready to go, let me know, and I will instruct you."

Jake went to the computer terminal in the medical lab and sat down to compose his first email from an alien ship. Now, what was Brad's email address? He started to type what he thought it was, and then stopped knowing that it didn't look correct. He backspaced and started to type again when suddenly the address started appearing on the screen by itself. Meg was anticipating his needs again, which was nice, but a bit unnerving. The page remained empty for more than two minutes before Jake typed his first words.

Son,

This is really going to be hard for you to believe, but I'm not dead. I didn't drown at Santa Barbara Island. If I told you where I was, you wouldn't believe me. You may not believe this message is real, so I have the following proof that I'm your father, Jake McDonald. Do you remember when you and I went fishing last year? We caught all those fish and then burned them to a crisp on the fire. You and I sat under the stars and talked about what we'd do if we could go to other planets. You said that you wanted to visit Mars and ski on the polar ice caps. That night we saw two meteors that appeared to crash into each other. If you believe I'm who I say I am, please reply.

Love always,
Dad

Jake punched the send button and hoped that Brad's study time included computer time. If anyone understood and would forgive him for all that had happened, Brad would be the one. Beth would take more time, but Brad might be able to help.

Brad sat in front of his computer screen contemplating his dilemma. He really wanted to go to the Game Zone and win the competition. He'd really pissed his mother off this time, and would probably be grounded again. He better email his friends and make up some story as to why he isn't coming.

He checked his messages first, and the third one caught his eye. It was from razortail7@hotmail.com. That was the name of his dad's old boat. Someone was making a sick joke. He was just about to trashcan the message, but something in the back of his mind told him that something was amiss. He opened the message, started to read down the page. He froze, and a shiver went down his spine as he read the full message. He'd told no one about the camping trip and the references in this email. Could his dad really be alive? He wanted to go down and tell his mom but decided it might not be a good idea.

Instead, he replied and asked his dad what to do. He pressed the reply button, and a blank message appeared, ready for an email Brad never dreamed he would have the chance to send.

Dad,
It is hard for me to believe you're alive. Where are you? What happened to you? Why did you disappear? Mom hasn't

been the same since we thought you died.

Brad

He pressed the send button and waited for what seemed an eternity, but actually were just a couple of minutes.

Meg had piped in the images of Brad typing a reply message. Jake read the message as Brad typed, and prepared a return almost as fast as Brad composed his message.

Brad,

You have so many questions. How about, how are you, DAD? Anyway, I'll try to answer your questions, but not through the computer. Can we meet at Game Zone? I know your mother doesn't want you to leave the house, and I don't like to counter her wishes, but we really need to talk. Can you get out of the house without her knowing? If so, meet me at 3 p.m.

Brad looked at the response and sent a quick *OK* reply. Now he had to figure a way out of the house. He closed down his computer and crept down the hall. His mother was lying on the couch, apparently asleep. He headed out the back door, and over the fence in the back yard. He would have to walk, as his bike was too close to where his mother was sleeping. No problem as he had plenty of time to make it to the Game Zone. When he arrived at 2:30 p.m., his friends were pleased to see him and started discussing gaming strategy.

He looked around to see if his dad had come early, but there was no sign of him. While he waited, he decided to practice some of his gaming skills before the competition.

Chapter 20

Jake swiveled his chair away from the computer. He was dreading the next step, but there was no more putting it off.

"Meg, I'm ready to go down now. What do I do?" Jake was sort of hoping he wouldn't hear an answer, but it came in just a few seconds.

"Go to the transport room, which is a small area adjacent to the medical lab. When you get there, lie down on the table, and try to be very calm. Unlike your science fiction movies, you cannot stand up, as you will be very faint during the process. It will be painless, so do not worry. Just think about seeing your son. The procedure takes a few minutes of preparation, so you need to get going."

Jake walked down the hall and entered a room he hadn't seen before. This ship was like a computer game with things appearing where they weren't before. The room had smooth walls and was barren except for a circular disk rising from the floor in the middle of the room. When the table stopped rising, he got up on it and lay down.

"I have picked a transport location behind the Game Room in an alley. My sensors cannot find anyone near the area, so it seems safe. If you agree and have no objections, I will transport you in ten seconds."

The location sounded good to Jake. He watched as the numbers counted down on the wall in front of him. His body started to tingle all over just like before. He couldn't breathe or move and then he started to black out.

Transport systems on the ship checked and rechecked before initiating the final scan on Jake. His body data was compressed and stored into the huge onboard memory system. The data was then transmitted into a very tight electromagnetic pulse and fired to an exact position in the alley. Within seconds, Jake reappeared, but now he was resting on day-old newspapers, oily rags, and garbage.

"Meg, next time you need to find a better transport site than this. Now I smell like my boat again, but I'm not complaining. It's so nice to be back on solid ground. I have one last question before I find my son. How do I get back up there?"

Jake stood for several seconds realizing he was talking to no one, and maybe he was supposed to communicate with Meg another way. Then a voice came from the new watch he had on his wrist.

"I can hear everything you say, so when you are ready, just tell me. Just make sure you are lying down, and you are in a secure location. Have fun with your son."

Jake took a closer look at the watch. It looked exactly like one he'd seen in a *Dick Tracy* comic book. Meg had a sense of humor indeed.

He walked down the alley and entered a world his son loved called the Game Zone. Deafening sounds of blasters and explosions were enough to disable anyone's hearing in no time. He looked around, knowing Brad would be watching for him. His eyes scanned the noisy crowd of space cadets as they killed aliens. If these kids only knew what he now knew. Then his eyes caught Brad's as he turned around, and stopped in a stare. They walked toward each other speechless.

Jake knew Brad wanted to give him a hug, but not in front of the other guys, so he diplomatically held out his hand. Brad surprised him by putting his arms around him in a big hug. The noise level in the room diminished, and they both realized everyone was looking at them. Jake heard muffled comments about Brad's dad being dead.

Jake spoke first. "Let's go outside where we can talk. It's so great to see you."

They turned and quickly headed out the back of the Game Zone. They were but just a few feet outside the door before Brad started questioning.

"Dad, where have you been? Mom is going crazy about all

this. I'm not sure what she's going to say when she hears you're alive. Why haven't you called us?"

"Whoa, Brad, you have too many questions. I wish I could tell you where I've been, and why, but you wouldn't believe me. In time, I'll tell you, but not now. The most important thing is we have to break the news to your mother. I know she's not happy with me, dead or alive, so we have to take it slow and easy."

"Dad, you can tell me where you have been. I'll believe you."

"Sorry, Brad, but you probably wouldn't. Besides, telling you might complicate things right now. We need to go home and tell your mom."

"Okay, but I'm going to keep asking you."

"You'll find out soon enough, so let's get going."

As they walked down the street, Jake asked Brad how things were in school. For a few minutes, everything seemed back to normal until Brad described his schoolyard fights defending his dad. Jake was proud of him, yet upset for causing him undue harm.

Jake stopped at a small shop along the way and bought a few things with Brad's money and they were on their way home.

Chapter 21

Henry Winston decided it was finally time to make his move and headed toward Beth's house. He wasn't sure what excuse he was going to use to explain his appearance but figured he would come up with it on the drive over.

As he turned the corner, he saw Brad walking with an older man. He slowed down. The man looked familiar. Shit! It was Jake. He couldn't believe his eyes. How was this possible? It looked like his plans were lost again, but maybe Beth wouldn't take him back. He parked along the curb and waited as Jake and Brad made their way toward their house.

Kathy McDonald came into the room and accidentally bumped the light near the couch where her mother was sleeping. Beth awoke and looked around at Kathy.

"How is school going, Honey?"

"Just fine, if you don't mind all those stupid boys constantly making idiots of themselves. What gets into them, Mom?"

Beth became more awake as she composed her answer.

"They say 'boys will be boys'. Unfortunately, it never changes from when they are born, until they die. At your age they are 97% hormones and 3% brains."

They both laughed and Kathy said, "Tell me about it."

Beth smiled, "I just did!"

Kathy looked around the room. "Mom, I can't find Brad. I wanted to talk to him about one of his friends that I like."

"Did you look in his room?

"Yes, and he's not in the house."

Beth's face turned from her normal light complexion to bright red.

"BRAD!" There was no answer. "Brad! You better be in the house, or you're grounded for life." There was still no sound.

Just then, the front door opened, and Brad walked in with his backpack and something folded under his arms.

"Where in the hell have you been? You know I told you not to leave the house. Did you think I wouldn't find out? Answer me."

"Mom, I know you're mad, but you have to listen to me. Dad is alive."

That statement shook both Beth and Kathy. They looked at each other not understanding, and then back to Brad.

"What are you talking about? Are you crazy?"

"Mom, Dad contacted me through email, and I went to see him."

"You did what? Do you realize how many crazies there are out there on the Internet? One of them took advantage of the fact that your dad died. I don't want to hear any more about it. Get up to your room NOW, and no more computers."

Brad looked over his shoulder as if someone was behind him. He set the folded plastic on the counter and stood staunch with no intention of going anywhere. Beth looked up at the ceiling in anger, and then down at the object on the counter. She picked it up and found six red roses with one white one in the middle. Only once before had she seen that combination and that was on her first date with Jake.

A tingle started to run down her back and she wondered if it could be true? Something told her that he was waiting at the front door. Even though that was a stupid thought, she slowly opened the door to see a sheepish Jake standing before her.

Henry Winston could stand it no longer. He had to find out what was going on. He got out of his car, and slowly walked toward the McDonald house. Jake and his son had just gone inside. He noticed that there were several bushes near the side of the house. He moved quickly toward them and slipped between the largest and the side of the house. He was near one of the windows that gave him a direct view of the action inside. He couldn't hear what was being said but hoped he could tell enough from what he could see. They seemed so intense with their conversation, that they didn't look in his direction at all. His hope was that she would throw Jake out, and be even more pissed off at him. That would leave room for him and all the money at the bank. He watched as Beth stared at Jake.

Inside, Beth took a long hard look at Jake, and Jake returned the favor. In the background, both heard Brad's excited voice.

"See, Mom? I told you he was alive. No one ever believes me. Isn't this great, Mom? Now we're all back together."

Both Beth and Jake spoke in unison. "Be quiet, Brad!"

Beth looked Jake over. He looked better than he had in a long time. Then she realized she was still pissed at him for leaving her and dying.

Jake decided not to say a word and let Beth vent and say the first words.

"Jake, I don't understand. We all thought you were dead. Do you have any idea what that did to your family? Where have you been all this time? Why did you let us think you were dead?"

The first volley had been fired, but Jake had to be very careful with his words. He wanted his family back, and the slightest incorrect word choice might be his end. He had to tell them the truth, but slowly, so that they would believe him.

"Beth, it's so good to see all of you. I can't even begin to tell you how sorry I am about this mess I've created. I was so wrapped up in my own needs, that I forgot about family first. I failed all of you, and most importantly, I failed myself."

Jake stopped because he knew that the conversation had to be a balance between the two of them. A little bit of information from each side would keep the tension low.

"Okay, Jake. So, why did you come back? You still haven't explained where you disappeared to and why. No more secrets, Jake."

Jake was surprised that Beth hadn't thrown him out, and they were having a good discussion. Even though he was in a tight spot, there was no other place he wanted to be. He considered his next few words carefully.

"The reason I came back is to let you know that I'm alive and that I'm a changed man. An Earth-shaking event has changed my life completely. I now realize that being a member of a family and making it work successfully means compromises are necessary. I know I really screwed up by thinking only of my happiness, and not all of yours. That has all changed and what I really would like is a do-over.

"I know that's impossible, so I have a proposal for this family. I want to try to become a good father and husband again, but on your terms. If it means seeing you for only a few hours a week while you judge if I've really changed, then so be it. You set up the rules and we'll see how it goes from there. If you don't like what you see, terminate the relationship, and I'll give you a divorce if that's what you decide. That's the very last thing I want, so think it over and I'll come back whenever you say it is okay."

Beth was stunned as this wasn't the Jake she'd recently known. It was the Jake she married, and the reason she married him. His proposal sounded reasonable, but before she agreed, she wanted more answers.

"I'm listening, but you still haven't told me where you've been and why. Until I hear a good answer, your proposal isn't going to fly."

Jake knew this was going to be hard, but he also knew she was one tough cookie. That's why he loved her so much. How was he going to tell her where he'd been? His mind was reaching for a solution.

"Beth, I would love to tell you where I've been, but if I do, no one here will believe me."

"Jake, that's one of your problems. You don't have enough faith or trust in your family. If you tell us the truth, we'll believe you."

Brad spoke from behind. "Yeah, Dad, where have you been?"

Beth turned around and glared at Brad. He instantly knew that this might be a good time to be a listener rather than a talker. Beth turned back around to hear Jake's answer.

"I want to tell you, but it would be like telling you I was swallowed by a whale, or abducted by an alien spaceship. If I told you that, you wouldn't believe me. I will guarantee you that the last thing I do before I leave again is to provide you with an answer to that question. Right now all I can tell you is that I have a new job as Captain of a large ship."

Beth interrupted his carefully planned speech with something he hadn't considered.

"Jake, I know the difference between a boat and a ship. A ship is hundreds of feet long, and a boat is something you pick up and put on a ship. You have a license for a boat, but not a ship. That takes a long time and plenty of experience. Who would be stupid enough to hire someone without a proper license? What are they going to do the first time you hit port? You would be arrested."

This was getting tricky. Jake knew he had to tell them more, but a little at a time.

"I really am a ship's Captain, and I don't have to worry because the ship never comes near a port. In fact, it is in open space all the time. It's a long way from any city or anyone who would check my credentials."

Beth was slowly warming up but did not want Jake to know that just yet.

"Okay, Jake. I'll go along with your story. How big is this ship, and how many crew are under your command?"

"I am told that the ship is six hundred feet long, and I don't have a clue about crewmembers because I haven't met them yet. In fact, when I leave here, I'll be having my first official tour of the ship. I'm sure that the crewmembers will be alien to me."

Brad couldn't resist piping in with this statement.

"Dad, don't you know anything? You should watch the news. They're called illegal aliens, and they are usually from south of the border."

"Actually, Brad, I don't think they're illegal, but I'll let you know what they look like when I come back. That is if it's okay with your mother."

Jake was having difficulty judging Beth's reaction to all this. The look on her face was hard to read.

Beth was having a difficult time with this conversation because she knew she had to make a decision soon. One second she wanted to tell him to leave, the next she wanted to wrap her arms around him and give him a big kiss.

"What the hell. Life is too damn short to let it go by so fast. Jake, you have your chance, but don't screw it up. You also need to tell us where you've been before you leave again."

Jake was ready to explode inside with joy. He smiled so big, his face almost cracked. He couldn't resist and reached out to give her a big hug before stepping back.

"That's great. You won't regret it. You remember all those magic tricks that Brad and I worked on mastering. I hope that my next trick will answer your unrelenting question. Just think of this as one of the best tricks I've ever done. Don't laugh when I lay down on the floor either."

Beth and the two kids looked at each other with puzzled looks on their faces. They stepped back when Jake started to lie down on the floor. This was weird. They were all starting to have second thoughts when they heard Jake say something very strange.

"Okay Meg, I'm ready to come back."

Beth looked at Kathy and Brad, "Who's Meg?"

Before anyone could say more, Jake's body started to glow with a bright blue light. They began to see the rug right through his body, and then he vanished. There was complete silence among them for almost twenty seconds.

"Mom, that ship Dad mentioned, I don't think it's a ship that goes across the ocean. I think that it's ....."

"I know, Brad, I know," said Beth. She thought to herself, *Jake, what the hell have you gotten yourself into this time?*

Henry Winston couldn't believe his eyes. For more than twenty minutes, Jake and his family had been in a heated discussion. Then Jake lay down on the floor and disappeared like a character in *Star Trek*. Henry's head was spinning. His careful planning had taken a twisted turn. It was time for him to find out more about this new Jake, and come up with an updated plan. He wasn't giving up that easily.

Chapter 22

Jake, what gives with the candlelight dinner, flowers, and music? Jake, are you there?

Everything in front of Jake was a blur. As his eyes started to focus, he realized that Beth was sitting across the table from him. She was so beautiful and he was confused. It seemed so real, and not a dream. Yet, here he was on the night he proposed to Beth. How could that be?

Jake, where is your head? You look like you're in another world right now. You said you want to say something to me. I'm waiting.

He tried to talk, but his mouth wouldn't cooperate. Somewhere in time, he'd forgotten the reason he was so attracted to her. Was he getting a second chance or what? Finally, he was able to speak.

Beth, I brought you here so I ... The candle on the table started to get brighter and brighter until he could see no longer tolerate its intensity.

"Welcome back, Jake," said a female human-sounding voice. "How is your family?"

Jake's vision started to clear, and he realized that he was back on the ship.

"My family is great. Thank you for the chance to make things right with them. Of course, you already know everything that happened. Can you tell me why I have these extremely realistic dreams when you transport me back and forth on the ship?"

A visual display appeared on the sidewall that undulated with colors at the sound of Meg's voice.

"I asked about your family because I knew from your voice and facial expressions that the visit was good for you. I wanted to understand human emotions by comparing your actions with

95

your verbal responses. Your dreams are something I still do not comprehend at this time. They are beyond most technical aspects of my internal systems."

Jake sat up on the table and looked at the colorful movement on the black wall.

"Why the change in how you speak to me?"

The answer was again answered with bright colors. "My research into human communication tells me your species communicate better when they have someone visual with which to interact. This was the best I could do for the moment. I can create a 3-D model of a person who could interact with you directly if you prefer."

Jake thought the concept over for a few seconds.

"The ideas sound great, but let's take one step at a time. The color visual sounds are fine for now. Maybe later we'll concentrate on the 3-D model.

"Everyone has a different dream interpretation, but I see them as an alternate unreal universe. Most people have no control over their dreams, and go wherever they lead them. In many cases, they can be terrifying or provide extreme pleasure. Some people have such vivid dreams that they experience an entire book and can then transcribe it the next day.

"I have to admit though that I cannot understand why each time I transport, I revisit the best parts of my past."

Bright red colors started to appear on the wall.

"Would you like to tour the ship now? There is much to see, and crewmembers to meet. Would you rather I prepare a meal for you first?"

Jake's eyes widened.

"What exactly do you mean by crewmembers? Are we talking about other humans, aliens, or what?"

The colors changed from red to yellow with shorter peaks.

"Maybe the terminology is not correct. There are many droids or robots, as you might call them, which keep me functioning. Most have simple intelligence but one is on the level with humans, and is used to directly help the sentient beings onboard."

Jake shook his head from side to side. "I have the feeling that I've just scratched the surface on how this ship works. By the way, I still don't have any idea about the shape of the ship. When I looked at your specs, I was so wrapped up in the internal structures and the capabilities, that I forgot to look at the shape. Are we talking about a flying saucer, *Millennium Falcon, Battlestar Galactica, Bird of Prey,* or what?"

Meg absorbed this information, before answering.

"Do I understand that you want to know the shape of the ship in comparison to a science fiction spaceship?"

Jake smiled and was finally relaxing. He had a good time with his family, even though it was too short. Hopefully, he would be able to go back soon. Right now, he had to get his bearings, to see where he was going.

"Okay, I'll tell you what. Let's play a little game that my son and I used to play all the time. You give me a difficult clue about a movie that has a ship that resembles the shape as this one. Make it difficult, and give me a second clue if I can't guess it."

There was silence in the room with no response from the wall.

"If you're such a brain, why's it taking so long to devise a clue?"

Finally, the colors started to move on the wall.

"Working on the ship's technology is easier than interacting with a human. The clue is as follows: It will take crossing only one of many bridges to find the shape of this ship."

Jake shook his head in disgust.

"I told you to make it hard. It's Jeff Bridges in *Starman.* I've seen it a half dozen times with my son. Are you telling me the ship is perfectly round just like in that movie? Is that the best shape your creators could devise? How do you know if you are coming or going? When I'm done with your tour, I would like to arrange to go back to the surface for a date with my wife."

"Jake, I underestimated your knowledge of Science Fiction movies. I was going to refer to the movie *Sphere,* but I thought the older *Starman* would be harder to guess. I will try to make it harder next time.

"Regarding your return to Earth; there may be a small problem. When I told you a person could transport back and forth a dozen times before incurring any physical damage, I did not give you all the facts. The assumption was that these transports would be spread out over months or years, not within a few days or weeks. Transporting so close in time is dangerous, as your body has not had time to adapt to the compressed cell structure created during transport. Three times in less than seven days is all that you can safely do. Another transport in less than a couple of weeks would be dangerous. After that, it would be weeks before it is safe. Eventually, you will only be able to transport in emergencies.

"The only safe way I can send you back to the surface again is on a flight vehicle. As I mentioned before, it would take me several weeks to create a smaller version of myself for transport. Most of my energy is used to keep the ship in stealth mode, so it takes time to create such a vehicle."

Jake started pacing back and forth in front of the wall.

"Now you tell me. Why didn't you tell me this before I left the surface? There has to be another way for me to go back. With all this high technology, that's the best you can offer?"

"Again, I am sorry for not communicating correctly about the transport system. There might be another way to get to the surface. I can create a less technical flight visible vehicle, with only enough features to get you there and back. All you have to do is decide what type of flight vehicle you want."

Jake's pacing became even more nervous.

"You forgot one small detail - I don't have a clue how to fly an aircraft, and I don't have the time to learn. Can't you have one of your robots fly me down?"

The colors on the wall now turned to a swirling motion of yellow and orange.

"Jake, you have the necessary experience to fly. The flight vehicle I can build for you will be lighter than air. This is possible with technology much like two magnets held at opposite poles against each other. A computer onboard the aircraft will keep the magnetic forces of the Earth and your aircraft in perfect balance. All you have to do is go forward, up, down, or stop. There would be no worry about the lift. It is very much like all those space computer games you and your son have been playing all these years."

Jake's pacing slowed now that he had been given an option to return to earth.

"What if I get into trouble flying this thing? I crashed a lot in those computer games, and when I died there I just played another game."

"Jake, there is nothing to worry about. It will be very safe. I will build a voice command system that will automatically land the ship and return it here. All you have to do is tell it where you want to go. The computer will not let you get into trouble. You just have to decide what type of aircraft you want, so I can have my crew build it. It will still take more than a week to build even with the limited functions of the aircraft. Now, can I give you a tour of the ship?"

Jake wasn't budging.

"Not yet, because you're in a big hurry to have me tour the ship for some reason. You still haven't explained why it is round and how it works. Please avoid the highly technical explanations and simplify it to friendlier terms. After that, I'll take this tour you seem so determined about."

The ship's processors extracted all the information on the design of the ship and the data pertinent to the shape of the ship. It then calculated that it would take hours to explain it. The computer reasoned that a lengthy explanation was not going to work as Jake too impatient. The computer reduced the information to a workable format before continuing.

"Sorry for the delay, but I wanted to keep the explanation as short as possible without losing too much content. The round shape of the ship is perfect for both space travel and stealth modes. As I mentioned before, the diameter of the ship is about 600 of your foot measurements. The surface of the ship is covered with more than 1 million sensor plates that alternately absorb and transmit all parts of the electromagnetic spectrum as it strikes the ship. This is what makes it invisible.

"When the ship needs to move into a gravity-controlled environment, it becomes magnetic on the base and repels much like the concept on the small aircraft that I explained before. Flight in space is accomplished by transforming several of these plates into a type of rocket engine that uses solid matter converted into pure energy. A few particles of solid matter can produce enough energy to push the ship out of the solar system. Travel between stars is accomplished with a more complex technology that I can explain to you when and if you decide to go to other star systems."

The information was mind-boggling, and it took Jake some time to realize the ramifications of what he'd just been told.

"You mean to tell me that I can go to other planets and star systems in this ship?"

"Yes, you can, but a tour of the ship might be in order first."

Jake chuckled as he ran his hand across his chin.

"You keep coming back to this tour. Do you get special points or space miles for this tour, or is there a little bit of human pride coming through all those circuits?"

A soft blue soothing color was displayed on the wall.

"The truth is that one of my final directives is to make sure that the sentient being running the ship has a good working knowledge of the ship before I can transfer control. I don't get any space points; it is just what is required of me. I understand the concept of pride, but it is not necessary since I am perfect."

Chapter 23

Frank Mendol had painstakingly worked his way up through the ranks at NASA and had finally achieved his ultimate dream. He was now in command of the entire space program. His Air Force career began flying fighter jets, and because of his proficiency, he was transferred to become a NASA astronaut. He made several trips to the International Space Station and eventually became its commander.

The present director of NASA decided to step down. When the call came from the President asking him to be the replacement, he was shocked. He boarded the next shuttle back to Earth, and the rest is history.

He worked diligently to get the most lucrative space budget possible, but he was competing with the military and had to be selective with his proposals. One of the reasons the previous director had stepped down was the imminent demise of the space shuttle program. It had successfully served NASA for more than a quarter of a century. Now because of budget cuts and the age of the shuttles, NASA was forced to step backward using capsule and cargo technology similar to the Russians.

To complicate things further, the military had started its own unmanned mini-shuttle program that concentrated on space defense projects. Then unexpectedly, General Markus Dugan, the Air Force Chief of Staff, submitted a proposal to extend the life of the space shuttle program by another five years. He proposed that NASA construct a new manned shuttle that would be jointly shared between the military and NASA. This new shuttle would be half the size of previous shuttles, take smaller payloads, and a seven-man crew.

Over the years, NASA had stored backup engines, booster rockets, computers, and other critical components designed to repair the older shuttle fleet. Since the deactivation of the three shuttles, spare parts and technologies could be used in creating this new military shuttle. Newly designed parts had been farmed out to military contractors and were already in place. A smaller unmanned test shuttle was built and taken up with one of the remaining NASA shuttle flights. It was in orbit for several months before the final decision was made to build a manned version.

The shuttle's name came under heated discussion before the Air Force decided on the name *Excalibur*. NASA agreed to secretively build *Excalibur* at Edwards Air Force Base and then run two manned test flights before turning it over to the Air Force.

The next problem was hiding the launch facility. The Air Force found a large sloping hill at the base of a mountain range. They dug a mile-long road that was cut through the valley so that it resembled a large riverbed with curves and uneven hills. The level transport tracks were hidden in a recessed part of the road as it led to the launch tower. Deep blast holes were carved out of the rock below the launch tower that angled alongside the road. This created two tunnels for the exhaust fume venting during the launch.

It took less than a year for NASA to build *Excalibur*, and now it was ready to launch. Frank wasn't initially happy with the agreement, but the General assured him that the Air Force would piggyback some of NASA's experiments along with the military projects. The General had also assured Frank that if there was ever an emergency with the space station, that the Air Force would lend a hand with *Excalibur*. Frank found it somewhat ironic that space exploration had come full circle. It started with the Air Force, then evolved to NASA, and now returned to the Air Force.

One of Frank's best radar men had picked up an anomaly in space directly over southern California. As they analyzed the data, the technicians became excited at the information, but no one could figure out what they were seeing. Most of the stars in the area appeared normal, but there seemed to be a slight circular displacement of the stars as the Earth rotated on its axis. They agreed that the only way to find an explanation was for *Excalibur* to take a side trip on its first launch.

This would mean priority changes for the launch because the plan was the inclusion of a Mars probe as *Excalibur's* cargo. Now this package would have to be replaced with a special sensor satellite designed to investigate the anomaly. He would have to smooth over some ruffled feathers, but the potential discovery rewards would be worth the substitution.

The Tech Forces communication systems were directly tapped into NASA, and the changes for *Excalibur's* flight were already on James Randel's desk. This wasn't what he needed. Something had to be done quickly, and the TF committee may not like his solution. They couldn't change NASA's mind for exploring the anomaly, so the only solution was to disable *Excalibur* during the launch. Disable was such a nice and fuzzy word for murder, but it seemed the only option. He picked up his phone and called the special weapons division of TF.

The head of this division was a small man with large thick glasses that went by the name of Brent Tolian. Although that was not his real name, all that really mattered was that his IQ was through the roof. If given enough time, he could figure out just about every technology known to mankind.

His most recent project was the TF acquisition of a high-tech company called Extreme Elements or XTE Industries. It specialized in military applications for working with rare elements. Many of their weapon ideas that they proposed to the military were too expensive to produce. Tech Forces had a different plan for XTE Industries and could see the weapon's potential.

Any project proposed to the military required extensive red tape and numerous steps to receive for approval. Many times the squandered time and money defeated even the best projects. Therefore, Tech Forces bought XTE Industries and gave the employees huge raises that provided the venue for pure weapons research.

At the time of the acquisition, the company was nearing a

breakthrough researching a newly discovered element near the North Pole. In its natural state, this element gave off radiation that shifted the electromagnetic spectrum, which in turn disrupted most electronic devices. In addition to shutting down all electronics, the element also shifted the visible-light spectrum so anyone viewing it became blind to the visible spectrum and could only see infrared.

The original plane that had found the metal crashed because this very rare element had shut down the aircraft's electronics. Even when the pilot tried to glide in, he became confused with only infrared viewing.

Once the effects of the element were understood, efforts were made to acquire the small amount that had caused the crash. After extensive research into other similar accidents, the company speculated that there was a high concentration of the element in an area called the Bermuda Triangle. If the research proved encouraging, the company planned to send salvage vessels to that area with special protection against the effects of the element.

The new element was eventually dubbed Spectronium for the lack of a better name. The company had built a special pressure chamber with ten-foot-thick walls that could withstand incredible pressures at high temperatures. This process could change the Spectronium metal into a gaseous state, which was then slowly cooled so the gas would transform into a unique crystal form.

These crystals could then be mounted in a special non-conductive apparatus in a vacuum chamber. When a very high electrical charge was sent through the crystalized metal, a laser beam resulted that would disable all electronic devices in its path. The problem was that they hadn't figured out how to control the direction or intensity of the beam. In the first few trials, the lab's equipment became disabled and required replacement.

The military deemed the technology too expensive and unreliable. That was too bad for them, but great news for Tech

Forces. Brent Tolian figured out the problem within a few weeks of the acquisition. They had purchased another high-tech company that built software/hardware for high-energy lasers. It was a simple matter of combining the two technologies into one high-tech weapon.

The new computer control system controlled the power level, angle, and distance of the Spectronium crystal discharge. The result was a weapon that could fire a short pulse beam at any object up to five hundred miles away. It would completely disable all electronic systems, much like the EMP, Electro Magnetic Pulse, from a nuclear weapon.

Tolian was surprised when the call came from James Randel. He hadn't heard from the head of TF for some time and was concerned that Mr. Randel was calling because progress wasn't going at the speed demanded.

"Brent, this is James Randel. I don't have a whole lot of time, so listen carefully. How soon before you'll have the new Spectronium laser weapon online?"

Tolian knew it. He was in hot water now. He'd worked day and night to get the weapon ready, but it still wasn't there.

"Mr. Randel, I'm sorry to report that we still have probably two weeks before the weapon comes online. We've been working around the clock. If we rush it too much, it could literally blow up in our faces."

Tolian nervously held the phone in his hand waiting for the other shoe to drop.

"Brent, I know you guys are doing the best you can. My problem is that I need it sooner. If not, I need another solution to a problem that has come up. It seems that NASA changed the itinerary for the next shuttle mission and plans to investigate that object we spotted over California. We can't let that happen, and the launch is in two days. I was hoping that you might be able to put a rush on your project."

Tolian relaxed and sat down. He didn't know why he'd stood at attention. Maybe it was because he knew people who failed TF almost always disappeared forever. He took a deep breath before continuing.

"If we remove all the safety features, and skip several stages in the testing, the best we can do is 3 to 4 days. Even then, it would be very risky, and could set us back several weeks if it doesn't work."

Randel contemplated his response. If the weapon didn't work, *Excalibur* could still investigate the object, and TF couldn't do anything about it. He needed another plan.

"Brent, as much as I have faith in your success, I still have to guarantee the committee that *Excalibur* won't get to the object. Do you have anything else in your bag of tricks? I'm open to any idea at this point in time."

Tolian knew he had to come up with something fast, so he started to rack his brain about his previous projects. Then it came to him.

"Sir, I remember we had a project a few months ago that worked with miniature shape charges. They used a new type of explosive 100 times more powerful than C-4. The final design was in the form of a flat sticker that could be overlaid on any label in a car, bus, or plane. We have a man inside NASA that works on the launch tower. We could have him place a couple of these labels on one of the booster rockets. When the launch reaches a specific altitude and they are triggered, it would look like a shuttle accident. With NASA's previous accidents and this new one we create, it will put them out of commission forever."

Randel had a good idea what the committee's response to this new idea was going to be, but he didn't think he could get them to abort the mission.

"Brent, I see no other choice at this time. Get the devices to your man on the inside. Continue to get the beam weapon online as soon as possible. I would rather disable the ship in orbit, and have NASA go into a rescue mode. That would keep them away from our objective for a long time. Keep me up to date on the progress of both solutions."

Tolian responded with a short thank you and hung up. Randel really didn't like that solution. Sure, they wanted to keep NASA away from the object, but he wasn't sure about taking out a shuttle in the process. It would be a big loss to TF too as they would have used the mini-shuttle after they overtook the government. Odds were that the military had a second shuttle in construction, so TF could still finish what NASA had started. He seemed satisfied with his decision and made the call to the committee.

Chapter 24

Jake stood in front of the black wall with which he was now accustomed to communicating.

"Meg, I give up. Let's take this tour of the ship that you keep bugging me about."

As the last word came out of Jake's mouth, a drawing of the ship appeared on the wall. A few seconds later, the drawing moved off the wall and took on a 3-D shape in the middle of the room. Jake sat and listened as Meg carefully explained each section of the ship. He decided not to interrupt and listened in bewilderment as Meg described the most incredible device ever seen by man.

"As you know, my outer skin is made up of small plates that are used to cloak the ship, negate gravity, provide protective shielding, and can be used for propulsion. These plates are only about 6 inches thick but are made of composite metal foam that can withstand extreme outside forces. The memory core at the center of the ship is over one hundred feet in diameter and uses a network of surface connections to communicate with all parts of the ship. Any connection that breaks is regrown much like your crystal growth.

"The ship itself is divided into two distinct halves with the top half for living quarters, and the bottom half for maintenance, robotics, landing bays, solid matter storage, and the propulsion system. The two halves are separated by a ten-foot thick metal plate that is impervious to everything known to my creators. If a shock wave, weapon, or meteor is directed toward the ship, the living quarter's portion of the ship immediately rotates in the opposite direction. Even if the lower section is destroyed, the upper section can be used to rebuild the lower half."

The 3-D drawing rotated, and more detail started to appear as Meg continued.

"The memory core on the top half of the barrier is

constantly updating and transmitting to the lower half as a backup of my memory. In extreme emergencies, I can dump the memory from the lower half of the core and add it to the upper half. Access to the lower half is through a special passageway that goes directly through the core of my memory. Security between the two halves is controlled by hand scanners.

"Gravity in the upper half is 1/2 Earth standards, but the bottom half has none. You will have to use special shoes to keep your feet stuck to the floor. They work very much like your Velcro. If you jump off the floor, you will float above it and have to grab onto something to get back down. There is no gravity on the lower half because it uses less power, and is easier for the maintenance drones to work."

There was a pause in the explanation as though Meg was expecting a response from Jake.

"Actually, what you've told me so far makes sense. I'm not exactly sure why, but it does. Maybe some of your computerese is rubbing off on me."

Meg continued to explain the inner workings of the ship by explaining the large hemisphere structure in the top half that rose above the memory core two hundred fifty feet. The hemisphere was six hundred feet across leaving a two hundred fifty-foot-wide donut-shaped area around the one-hundred-foot center memory structure. The open area was filled with trees, plants, streams, rocks, soil, and just about everything else you would find in a fancy backyard garden. The outside plates on the top of the ship allowed sunlight to pass through so the plants in the garden could grow without artificial light.

Above the center structure of the ship, several levels include a mess hall, living quarters, medical facilities, recreation room, and exercise room. The main bridge was located at the top of the structure. An elevator system connected each of the levels together. After the brief explanation, Jake informed Meg that he was going for a walk and see things for himself.

As he went from floor to floor, Jake realized much of the

structure was unfinished. When he asked Meg about it, she informed him that she only built what he needed for survival, but had adequate space for a hundred people to live very comfortably.

For the next three hours, Jake moved from floor to floor until he reached the center of the memory core. Next to the hatch was a small camera, and a hand scanner. He wondered if Meg had modified the security to mimic Earth's so that he would be more comfortable with the system. Whatever Meg's reason, he looked directly at the camera and placed his hand in the correct position. Soon the door opened, and a small, lighted passageway appeared with a ladder running through the ten-foot-thick protective floor.

He went down the ladder, to the floor below. As he passed through the section that separated the ship's halves, Jake could feel the lack of gravity. By the time he was through the other side, he was floating as if he were in a swimming pool. Stuck to the underside of the opening was a pair of strange-looking slippers. He grabbed the pair, and with much difficulty, put them on in zero gravity.

He could now place his feet firmly on the floor and continue the tour. As his feet touched the floor, the ladder retracted, and the door above him closed. He was now in the lower bowels of the ship.

"Meg, so far, so good. Now, where do I go?"

"You are in the storage area, Jake. This is where all the raw materials are stored. Almost every element known to man can be found here, along with some that humans do not know about. I can use our technology to create an object from a single element like a pair of scissors or combine them to make computers that are more complex.

"If I want a template for a car engine, I would transport one onto the ship, scan it, and then transport the engine back to its original location. The template is then saved into my memory banks, and I can re-create it anytime in the future using the raw material stored here. I can also approximate objects from drawings or models, but they are not as exact.

"If you go down to the next level, you can meet most of the crewmembers."

"Do they know I'm coming, and how safe are they to be around?"

"Don't worry, Jake, I control most of them directly. Only one operates on its own, and you will meet it later."

"One question before I go down to see them. What are they called? Do they have names or what?"

"The creators did not use names for them. Each unit actually has a numerical reference I use to direct their working tasks. The best reference for a name I can find in my collection of human knowledge is droids. To make things easier, all the units will now be referred to as droids."

"That sounds fine to me, but is that going to upset them?"

"Jake, they don't have feelings, so do not worry. They will know when you are talking about them if you use the word Droid."

Jake seemed satisfied with the explanation but was still worried about the one crewmember that Meg didn't control. He had an uneasy feeling about it.

He moved down the hall past endless stacks of raw materials that he couldn't identify. Some were in special containment areas, and Jake assumed those materials were more dangerous but didn't want to ask at this point.

His head was spinning as he got into the elevator and entered the next level. Everything was so overwhelming. What would the guys at Area 51 do with something like this? Even knowing what was on the next floor, he wasn't prepared for what he saw when the doors opened. Meg's explanation of a few droids was a bit lacking. In front of him were endless rows of droids. There were hundreds of them. Every size, shape, and color you could imagine. Most were motionless, but a few small units were quickly moving up and down each row of droids performing some kind of task.

Jake couldn't stand it any longer.

"Meg, can you tell me what's going on? You also need to study up on what the word "few" means."

"I'm sorry about my explanation of a few crewmembers. In this case, it means 311 droids. The little droids moving around are checking the ones at rest to be sure they are ready to go at a moment's notice.

"If you go to the back of the room, there is a repair facility. I have special droids there that check and repair any crewmember found to be malfunctioning. If they need new parts, I make the parts from templates in my memory banks. Many of these droids remain idle, but can quickly repair ship damage when necessary. The walls in the droid resting areas are protected with an additional shield similar the one that separates the two halves of the ship, but thinner. The worker droids here take commands from the maintenance computer, or from you. I have programmed in your voice so that the only human voice they respond to is yours."

Jake walked down the row of droids nearest the elevator. Some of them were actually cute. Some even looked like they'd been created by Disney Studios, while others were just plain ugly.

Jake looked at the directional map on the wall and saw the landing bay was next on their tour. Below that was the propulsion systems, but he didn't want to go there.

In the back of his mind, he remembered Meg's reference to the one member she didn't directly control, but he dismissed the thought. When the elevator doors opened, he once again was in shock. He'd never seen such a large room. You could easily fit a 747 in this room.

Along the ceiling were several rails with a strange assortment of large tools attached on devices that appeared to move on the rails. Meg explained that the room was used to land, repair, and build a small spacecraft.

Then Jake remembered an earlier conversation.

"Meg, is this where you would build the plane that I need to get back on the ground?"

"That is correct, but you still have not given me a description of the type of plane you want to use."

Jake swallowed, took a deep breath, and gave Meg his answer.

"At first I thought the solution was simple, but the more I thought about the scenarios, the more difficult the problem became. It is somewhat like you're trying to get into space without being seen. Military aircraft is out since they keep a very close inventory, and know where every plane is located. Any plane not in the system would be considered hostile. A civilian aircraft might have been a choice, but since 911, every civilian aircraft is under heavy scrutiny. I do not want to be shot down.

"That leaves only one option that no one will believe exists, even when it's right in front of them. It has to be a spacecraft right out of a science fiction movie that people can readily identify. A ship that even if photographed, no one will believe is real. They'll assume it was manufactured in Photoshop.

"I narrowed the choices down to a shuttle from *Star Trek,* a *Stargate* 302 Fighter, and a *Star Wars* X-wing Fighter. The shuttlecraft wouldn't look as hostile, but with all the recent *Star Wars* movies, the X-wing would be more recognizable to the general population."

"I can build such an aircraft, but I will have to build a propulsion system other than what is shown in the movies. Are you sure this is what you want?"

"Yes, but Meg, there's one more thing you need to include in the aircraft. You need to go to the Revell webpage and look at the X-wing model and build yours to look like one of these kit models. The company name should be on the lower part of the body, and the plane should look like it was glued together at the joints. That way if anyone takes a picture of it, it will look like someone created a computer-manipulated image of an X-wing model. You will see that many UFO hoaxes have been created in

113

this way. So, how long will it take to build?"

"Since I do not have to duplicate any of the operating systems, my droids should have it ready in about a week. I have already sent the droids the webpage drawing on the X-wing Fighter, and pulled up several scenes from *Star Wars* to help in the construction."

As Meg finished the sentence, a door in the ceiling opened and a droid was lowered down on special lifts. Soon other doors started to open, and in minutes, several dozens of droids were busy building the first real X-wing Fighter. Jake was so impressed with the operation that he went down the stairs onto the main landing bay and walked around their construction.

Out of the corner of his eye, he thought he saw movement near the hanger wall. He thought he was imagining things, but then it moved again. As he turned his head toward the movement, entire sections of the wall started to move. As the object moved away from the wall, it started to change in color and texture. Standing before him was a ten-foot-high robot that resembled a child's Transformer toy.

Jake jumped back as Meg spoke.

"Jake, I would like to introduce you to the last member of my crew. It has ID number is 048884373, but you can give it a name if you want. It is what you might call a security robot, and has the ability to change or blend into any background. It is unlike the other units as it has its own artificial intelligence, and can think and act completely on its own."

Before Jake could say anything, the large robot spoke.

"I am very glad to meet you, Jake McDonald. May I call you Jake? I am 048884373, but I will answer to whatever name you give me. In fact, the idea of a name is an interesting concept."

Jake didn't know what to do at first, but then the robot extended his hand for a handshake, so he reciprocated. Jake looked up at the massive metal chest and sheepishly spoke.

"How does the name Chameleon sound? We have an

114

animal with that name on Earth that blends into backgrounds like you seem to do. If you don't like that name, I can pick another."

The robot spoke again, with an even more human voice. It had obviously been working on a human speech by listening to Jake.

"That name sounds fine to me. If you need me either on the ship or on the ground, you only have to call my name. Think of me as your bodyguard."

Jake smiled, "Where were you when I was in high school? I sure could have used you."

Chameleon hesitated for a second and started to speak, but Jake spoke.

"You don't have to answer that, I was just making a joke."

Chameleon crouched down so that his massive head was at the same level as Jake.

"I have been researching and studying human emotions, and understand. That is why I will have to kill you the next time you tell a joke."

Jake's face started to turn white with fear, but before he could say anything, the robot added, "I was just kidding too. From the look of fear on your face, I will have to work on my joke-telling skills."

Chameleon stood back up and stepped back toward the wall. As he did, his features quickly disappeared into the wall. Within seconds, he was gone, yet he was still right there. He was truly a master of camouflage.

Jake took one last look at the droids busily working on his new transportation. This place was starting to grow on him. He was really beginning to enjoy Meg and all her capabilities. He felt like he had a new life and purpose again. He was working his way up from rock bottom, and he was never going back there again. Best of all, in a few short days, he would be able to go home again and see his family.

Jake started back up to the upper quadrant but stopped when he noticed a section he hadn't seen before. It looked like other storage areas except the door had no handle or method of entry.

"Meg, what's this area?"

"Jake, I do not know what is in this area. My creators have locked this part of the ship from me. I do not know what it is or why it is there. I have a file in my memory banks telling me that this area is off-limits to all but my creators."

Jake couldn't believe what he was hearing.

"You mean to tell me that with your vast knowledge of technology, you can't break the code into this area?"

"I have a directive not to."

Jake didn't like the sound of that.

"Well, I'm overriding that directive. Meg, you will find a way into that area. I don't want any surprises. Speaking of your creators, what was the message you sent to them when I first got here?"

"The information I sent informed my creators approximately when the human race will become extinct."

Jake about fell over with this news.

"What do you mean by extinct? Are we talking thousands of years or millions of years? It really doesn't matter to me as I'll be gone, but the thought is still scary."

"Actually, Jake, the research indicates that humans will not be the dominant species in less than 200 years. I have run thousands of scenarios, and the range is from 50 to 300 years, but very few go beyond that."

"That's depressing. How can that be? What's going to happen?"

"Mankind has already started its own demise on several fronts. Air pollution, no population control, new powerful diseases, oil spills, weapons of mass destruction, greenhouse effects, and greed to mention just a few. Jake, it will only take a combination of these options to finish off humanity. Man is going to self-destruct, and there is nothing you can do about it."

Jake sat down on the cool floor. This was devastating

news.

"Meg, with all the power you have in this ship, can't you change Earth's history?"

"I am not allowed to do that by my creators, even if you order me to. I cannot help mankind, only observe it."

Jake slowly got up off the floor.

"Okay, I agree that we haven't done a great job with this planet, but there has to be something that will improve the outcome of mankind. I'm not ready to give up just because your electronic brain says it's so.

"Can you do me a favor? Please reserve part of your memory core for researching a possible solution for saving humanity that will not piss off your creators. Don't forget to keep searching for a way to figure out a way into that secret area."

Jake took the elevator up to the ten-foot barrier and found the security system for the hatch on the wall. He activated it and worked his way back up to the upper portion of the ship. It was going to take some time to become familiar with his new home, but he still had a few more days. Right now, he was hungry, so he headed to the mess hall. Until now, he'd always eaten in his room or in the medical lab.

It was time to try the area he nicknamed Space Dennys. A couple of tables with menus were set up in the dining area. He looked at some of the menu items and decided steak and eggs looked good to him. He spoke into the air for his request, and within minutes, his order appeared in a device that resembled a microwave. He opened its door and took the piping hot meal to his table.

"Meg, can you display a TV screen on the wall next to me? I would like to catch up on the news while I eat."

A large screen displayed a reporter standing on the beach in Santa Barbara. He was giving an updating about the incident at Santa Barbara Island but had little to add. He stated that the military had put the entire Channel Islands off limits, causing protests by both sports and commercial fishermen. As Jake continued to eat his meal, the TV cut out and Meg's voice came on.

"Jake, we have a problem as it seems I have misjudged your species' ability to detect this ship. Both the military and NASA know something is up here, and both forces are concentrating efforts to find us. The military is not a problem, but NASA might be. They have changed their shuttle launch schedule so that they can come right to our position to see what is here.

"Right now all they see is a ring of distortion. If I try to move, this slight distortion will become even more visible. The launch is in a couple of days. My systems are not fully repaired, and it would be best to remain here."

Jake put his knife and fork down and thought about what Meg had just told him.

"There's no way you can move without them seeing us?"

"If I had known that they could see us, I would have moved over the Pacific Ocean. Telescopes have to search at an extreme angle through the atmosphere so it is harder to view objects in space. Where we are now, they can look straight up at us, so we really need to move."

Jake worked his knife and fork again as he pondered what seemed like an endless stream of problems. He swallowed a bite of steak and washed it down with a sip from his drink.

"What we need is another diversion. There has to be something we can do that would make NASA change their plans. It would have to be something more important than finding us."

Jake continued to eat his meal as his brain analyzed all the parameters. The key might be that NASA had limited funds.

"Meg, can you check NASA schedules to see if any projects were just recently canceled? Maybe they shifted funds from an ongoing project to make this one happen."

There was silence for a few seconds. "It seems that a Mars probe has been rescheduled for the next launch and the funds reallocated for this launch. They decided they needed to investigate our area, and the probe to study the poles of Mars could be postponed."

Jake knew this was going to be a long shot, but it was worth a try.

"Meg, can you send one of your droids to Mars in a short time without anyone seeing it?"

"I do not understand the purpose for sending a droid to Mars. Can you explain further?"

"We need a diversion, and I have an idea but it's a long shot. Can you get it ready soon? I also have something the droid needs to take with it."

As nightfall fell upon the West Coast, a small projectile from the ship was fired in the approximate direction of Mars. Using a variety of miniature power sources, the projectile used the planet's gravity and the sun's energy to guide it to the Martian surface. Once it cleared the moon, the small projectile shifted to a stronger power source to accelerate its speed so it could reach Mars in less than a day.

Chapter 25

Jill Duncan had dreams of becoming an astronaut before she was forty, but it didn't look like that was going to happen. She had all the qualifications, but there were just too many obstacles. She didn't make the last astronaut cut and was offered a job in Houston's control center until the next round of selections.

Her boring job was monitoring dead or malfunctioning satellites and assorted devices that communicated with Houston. Most of the items on the list were silent. Several were sending signals that were scrambled and unreadable, which meant something had gone wrong during its life span. She set up a batch scanning system that would rotate through all the device's frequencies to see if there had been any changes. The good news was that it gave her time to read up on the latest technologies to be better prepared for the next astronaut selection.

She had just finished her lunch when the batch scanner started to beep with a warning that something had changed with one of the devices. She looked at the screen and had the program identify the device. It was coming from one of the many Mars rovers that had previously been very successful. The power source had died a long time ago, but the rover had still been kept on her list. She clicked on the signal, and a full-screen image of the Martian landscape appeared on her screen. Below the image, she noted that all the control systems for the rover were online.

Someone had to be playing a joke on her. She performed a signal check on the signal location, and it was indeed coming from Mars. She'd seen pictures of the Martian landscape before from this rover, but the image didn't look familiar. She looked around the control center and saw that no one was watching. If she took this to the flight director, and it was a false reading, she could kiss off her chance for the next selection.

She looked at the screen again. She gave a signal to move the rover three feet forward. She waited the 15 minutes for the message to send, and the 15 minutes to receive a video of the action, but it seemed like an eternity. While she waited, she minimized the screen so no one passing by would see the Mars image. At about thirty seconds before the image should change, she maximized the screen display. As her countdown clock reached zero, nothing happened. At +5 seconds, the rover started to move, and at +15 seconds, it was at a position 3 feet from where it started. She swallowed hard and started toward the flight director's workstation.

Joe Charger had been the flight director for NASA for five years now and had seen just about everything. That is until Jill Duncan came up to him.

"Sir, I seem to have a problem with one of the devices I'm monitoring."

Charger looked at the very troubled face. "Which device are we talking about?"

"Well, Sir, you're not going to believe this, but it is one of the older Mars rovers. It came back online, fully restored. I checked to see if there was an error, or someone was playing a joke, but it appears real to me."

"Jill, what you're telling me is impossible. There has to be another explanation to what you're seeing on your screen. I've always told people that anything is possible in this universe, so lead me to your workstation."

Duncan led the flight director over to her workstation and pointed to the image on her screen.

Charger looked at the image, and then at the data underneath. "Well, I'll be damned."

Duncan then made a very nervous admission. "Sir, I know I shouldn't have done it, but I was so sure this was a hoax that I gave a command for the rover to move three feet. Sir, a few minutes ago, it did just that."

Many scenarios were already going through Charger's

head, but none could explain this. As he looked at the screen, he pointed toward something off in the distance. "What's that?"

Duncan reached down and pressed the zoom feature to enlarge the area in question. The resolution wasn't high enough to see what it was, but it didn't look natural. Charger looked around the room. "I understand why you were hesitant to say anything. I'm with you. This is crazy."

By this time, several other technicians were starting to crowd around the screen.

A voice in the background spoke up, "My baby is alive again."

Everyone looked back and realized the voice had come from the technician who originally controlled the rover. Everyone split apart as he moved in and sat down in front of the workstation.

"What is that?" He said as he too pointed his finger at an object in the distance.

A heated discussion erupted as to what to do now. It was finally agreed that the technician would move the rover toward the object in the distance. Over the next couple of hours, everyone in the room was glued to the image displayed on the control center's main screen. As the rover moved closer to the object, everyone kept guessing as to what it was. When the images from the final movement toward the object came in, there was silence. In the middle of the screen sat a stone statue of what looked like two warriors.

"What the hell?" said Charger.

He grabbed the phone next to the workstation and punched in the code for Frank Mendol. Mendol picked up the phone himself, as his secretary was out to lunch.

"So, Joe, how's my shuttle launch plans going?"

Charger hesitated for a second, and carefully chose his words.

"Sir, we have a situation here. It seems that one of the older Mars rovers has come back to life, and has made an amazing discovery. You need to come down here right away."

Chapter 26

Jake jumped up from a catnap as Meg spoke.

"The rover has been activated, and NASA is very excited about what they are seeing. I still don't fully understand how this will help us. I guess I don't fully understand human nature yet."

Jake rubbed his eyes and tried to compose himself.

"Well, first I was hoping that they might take some of their powerful eyes off us for a time and focus on Mars. I also was hopeful that they might change their priorities now that they have a renewed interest in Mars. It's better to investigate a sure thing rather than something you can't see. It was a long shot, but that was my only idea unless your big brain can do better."

Pete Killian had been working hard trying to uncover the mysterious person responsible for the Santa Barbara incident. The TF computers had been working around the clock looking for a possible clue to narrow down the search. Audio comparison systems had been searching for all voice communications past and present without finding a match. The search was expanded to other types of voice transmissions other than the telephone. The marine radio channels used by both commercial and sport fishing boats were next in the search.

Just one hour into the search, they came up with a hit. The technician who found the match then searched the databanks and came up with another mystery. The man connected to the voice died in a diving accident a few days before the incident. This report was passed on to Killian, and he immediately made his way to James Randel's office.

As Killian approached the office, he noticed a security agent posted outside the door. What also caught his attention was the sexy-looking secretary who was smiling brightly at him. She told him that Mr. Randel was waiting and to go right in. He wondered how the guard could keep his eyes off her. Randel always had great looking secretaries. I guess it was just one of the benefits of working at the top of TF.

As he opened the door Randel barked loudly, "Come on Pete, we don't have time for you to gawk at my secretary. Besides, she's not the petite young thing that she seems. She could take that guard out in a second if inclined. Now, what's going on with the voice match?"

Killian could tell that Randel's patience was wearing thin and he wanted action. He carefully picked his words as he spoke.

"One of our technicians found a match to the voice at Santa Barbara Island. It belongs to a fisherman by the name of Jake McDonald. The problem is that he died in a diving accident a couple of days before the incident. I checked the story out thoroughly and found that the body never showed up. Even more strange, was how he disappeared. Divers searching the area found all his diving gear, including wetsuit, watch, ring, and even his swim trunks. Very suspicious, considering that his voice shows up in the same place a couple of days later."

Randel appeared to take some time processing this information before he spoke. The silence seemed endlessly to Killian before Randel finally spoke.

"It sounds like he's a possibility, so here's what we can do. I want a full background on Mr. McDonald, everything from kindergarten up. Leave no stone unturned, but make sure no one makes a move until I receive all the information. Then I'll decide what move to make. I want you personally responsible for bringing the information back to me."

Killian made a hasty retreat out the door, but not before Randel added, "Tomorrow."

Killian closed the door, and Randel picked up the phone and dialed Bret Tolian in the research division. The Spectronium project was taking too long. Some heads were going to roll if Randel didn't see some results soon. Tolian picked up the phone on the first ring as though he sensed this call.

"Bret, I hope you have some good news for me."

Tolian had already prepared his response several times.

"Mr. Randel, I have some good news. We solved all the control problems with the laser, and are set to test fire it."

Randel knew it wasn't that simple.

"If it is ready, why not use it to disable *Excalibur* launch tomorrow?"

Tolian had calculated every response from Randel and quickly responded with a very clear and precise answer.

"We have control of the weapon at a short range, but need to test it before we can calibrate it for a longer distance. I suggest that we target a small plane so that we can evaluate our control settings. Then we can guarantee success shutting down *Excalibur* when needed. If the test is successful tonight, it will take a few hours to process the information and reset the weapon for the shuttle target. We'll be ready before *Excalibur* is scheduled for launch. The only problem now is that we need a test target."

Randel hesitated a few seconds as he processed the information and quickly ran through all the possible scenarios.

"Bret, in the phone conversations that we've monitored over the last few days, we discovered a local drug runner who moves his goods from one county to another in a small private jet. They happen to be making a flight tonight, so I'll send down the coordinates for your test. Make sure you double-check everything as we only have time for one test. I need that shuttle disabled."

Tolian hung up and waited for the information to be transmitted into his computer. He was finally going to test his baby, and in the process, take down a few drug runners. It wasn't such a bad plan.

Chapter 27

Jake was becoming impatient with his situation. He'd spent time exploring the ship, but his mind kept drifting back to his meeting with Beth.

"Meg, are you sure I can't beam back down to see my family again? How far apart do these transmissions have to be?"

Meg was slow to respond.

"Jake, I'm sorry for the delay. I had my system on standby."

Jake chuckled and responded, "You mean you sleep just like me? You are sounding more human as time passes."

"I am a long way from being human, but yes, my standby mode is like your sleeping, except that I don't dream. You must tell me more about dreams. Maybe I could program myself to dream."

"Hey, don't change the subject. I want to talk to Beth again, and you're telling me it will take a few days to build the small ship. Can't I beam down again?"

"Jake, it would not be a good idea, as you need more time for your body to adjust to the three times you have already transported. If you want to talk to Beth, you can use the TV, just like you did with the General in Santa Barbara."

Jake sucked in a long breath of air.

"You mean all I have to do is talk through her TV? What are we waiting for?"

Beth's world had made a drastic detour over the past few days. First Jake was dead, and then magically he was alive. The kids were driving her crazy, asking questions about Jake, but she couldn't answer any of them. She hoped he would call soon and explain more about his situation.

Just seeing him briefly had boosted her spirits, making her happier. Her real estate sales were looking up and she seemed to be back on the positive track again. She'd almost closed a deal today, but a bit more paperwork tomorrow should finalize the sale.

When she got home, the kids were in their rooms doing whatever it is they do after school. She poured herself a glass of wine and sat down to be updated on current events. As she changed channels looking for a news broadcast, Jake's face appeared on the screen.

"Hi, Beth, how are you doing?"

Beth froze for a second soaking in what had just happened. She realized he must have been using her TV set to broadcast a signal. It had to be another one of Jake's fabulous magic tricks.

"Jake, where in the hell have you been? First, you scare the hell out of me by dying, and then you show up on my doorstep. Then we don't hear a word from you in days. I thought things were going to be different. Where are you anyway, and how did you appear on my TV set?"

Jake was so happy to see her face, that he didn't care if she was pissed at him. As long as she was talking to him, he felt he was halfway there.

"Sorry, but my new job has occupied my time getting used to the ropes. I should've contacted you sooner, but I didn't know about this method of talking with you until today. It seems the ship I'm on has an advanced communication system that allows me to connect directly to your TV set."

"That's no excuse for not getting back to me. I still don't understand what's going on with you. I'll try, but you have to work with me on this. Let's start with Meg. Is she your new girlfriend? You can't have it both ways, Jake, so start explaining."

Jake was in a hot spot. He didn't even consider that mentioning another woman's name might cause problems.

"Beth, it's not what you think. The owner of the ship is called Meg. Women can own ships, if fact, I knew several when I was lobster fishing." Then Jake realized that he'd dug an even deeper hole for himself.

"What other women?" fumed Beth.

He had to turn the tables around and tell the truth, or he was done.

"Beth, are you telling me that men and women can't work together without any romantic involvement? Besides, once I met you, I've never had anything to do with any woman except you. I love you, and no one else, now, and in the future. That's the best explanation I can offer."

Both looked at each other from behind pixilated images, trying to decide their next move.

"Okay, Jake, you're right. I believe you, and trust you for some stupid reason. I even forgive you for not calling us. When are you coming home? The kids and I want to see you for more than a brief encounter.

"Remember, you said I could set the rules? My first rule is that you have to ask me out on a date."

Jake could hardly stand himself because he was so happy. Everything seemed to be finally going his way at last. If he only could get back down and spend time with his family. Maybe he should risk transportation again or reason with Beth and get a time extension.

"I'm sorry, Beth, but my new job requires that I stay on board the ship for at least a week. I would love to come today, but I don't want to mess up this new job. I hope you can understand."

Beth did understand. Jake was taking responsibility for his life for the first time in ages. Even though he obviously wanted to come home, she was pleased he was taking his new job seriously. She wondered more about this new job.

"Okay, Jake, I'll give you a week, but you need to contact me every day via TV or whatever. What's the name of your ship, and where are you?"

Jake smiled and felt it time for the next step in repairing their relationship.

"Honey, I'm really sorry I can't be there for a week, but I'll try to call every evening, so I can talk with the kids. I'll save the information about the ship's name and location for our first date."

Beth was impressed by his personal response. She thought about how to end their conversation on an upbeat note. She knew Jake well but felt she needed to throw him a bit off balance. He always worked better that way.

"Who said we were going to have time for talking on our first date?"

Chapter 28

The launch pad was primed and ready for the inaugural voyage of the space shuttle *Excalibur*. All systems had been checked, and the crew was onboard. As the last engineer closed the hatch, he slapped a small flat explosive charge to the side of the gigantic liquid fuel tank. His job done, he joined the rest of the engineers as they made their way to the blockhouse a safe distance from the launch pad. The explosive had been set to explode at the five-thousand-foot altitude mark. It would crash into the middle of the desert, and NASA would be set back another couple of years.

For more than half an hour, systems were checked and rechecked before all the lights were green on the main control board. This was the third flight for Colonel Craig Brentner, but he was still nervous as hell as the shuttle countdown reached zero. He was given the go as *Excalibur's* load of hardware and electronics slowly lifted off the pad. One thousand feet, two, three, and then something happened to a small fuel valve controlling one of the three main shuttle engines. The valve started to flutter a small amount, and even more as *Excalibur* passed through four thousand feet. The vibrations from the sputtering one engine control valve shook the entire shuttle.

The vibrations knocked off the explosive charge attached to the fuel tank, and it fell into the three engines' exhaust. The blast ignited the charge, but the fast-moving *Excalibur* was too far away for it to do any damage. The explosive blast force stopped the valve from vibrating, and it started to operate normally again. The *Excalibur* team and ground crews were thrilled and the mission continued like a textbook launch. What was designed to destroy the *Excalibur* actually had saved it

Deep inside the Tech Forces headquarters, James Randel watched the TV screen as *Excalibur* started its ascent. As it approached the five thousand foot mark, Randel squeezed the arm of his chair, knowing that he was responsible for the death of seven astronauts. As it passed through its detonation point, it became apparent that the first attempt on the shuttle had failed. Some heads would roll for that one, but right now Plan B would have to go into action. The test of the new TF laser weapon was tonight and was TF's best shot at stopping NASA from getting the unknown technology. This time he decided that he would be there for the test to ensure it ran smoothly.

His call to Brent Tolian was quick and to the point. Tolian picked up the phone on the first ring as he was expecting the call.

"Brent, our man failed to stop *Excalibur*, so it's up to you. Is the weapon ready for tonight's test?"

"All systems are online and checked out. We ran a test beam up a couple of miles, and everything looks good."

"Good, I'll be down later to watch the test. It better work or everyone in your lab will be out of a job permanently."

Tolian knew what that meant, so he knew he had to have a positive response.

"Don't worry about a thing, Sir. The system will work perfectly."

"It better," came the sharp reply.

Tolian looked around the lab as he hung up the phone. More than half a dozen engineers were busy scanning their computer screens getting everything ready for tonight's show.

Chapter 29

Shank Rogers had been running drugs for the local syndicate for a couple of years now and had made a pile of money. His job was to move drugs from a greenhouse front company in another country, to a distribution center near the city. In order to catch him in operation, local law enforcement had been watching the borders, roads, waterways, and commercial flights. Budget constraints meant that the agency couldn't cover small aircraft, so the drug runners had taken full advantage. Even so, Shank felt his good luck was running out.

This was to be his last flight. He planned to take the final payoff, and disappear into Mexico, soaking up the sun. It sounded marvelous and all he had to do was make this last drop.

The flight seemed normal with no indication of trouble. Only thirty more minutes until his retirement. Then all hell broke loose in the cockpit as all the instruments started to go haywire. Smoke was everywhere and his vision blurred with red fuzzy images. This was his worst nightmare as he couldn't broadcast a mayday, or he would go to prison. Hopefully, he could just glide it to the ground.

Suddenly all the instruments in the cockpit went dead, and the engine died. He couldn't see anything but blurred red images. He felt the small plane starting to twist and turn, and then he felt nothing.

A small cheer came from the group of engineers in the TF lab but became silent when Randel started to speak.

"Okay, people. The test looked good. Now it's time for Phase 2. I want to see the system online for the next shot by tomorrow afternoon. The space shuttle has to make a stop at the space station in the morning but will leave for the anomaly in the afternoon. That's when we take our shot. We don't have a second chance at this, so make sure it works."

Tolian waited until Randel finished before asking about the timing.

"Sir, the information we gathered from this test will allow us to accurately target *Excalibur* up to five hundred miles away. When do you want it to be hit?"

Randel thought about it for a second, scanned the group of engineers, and then spoke directly to Tolian.

"We don't want someone from the space station rescuing the astronauts and fixing *Excalibur*, so make sure that it's at least a couple hundred miles out of the space station's path. If they can get to it, is it possible to be repaired?"

"Sir, the damage we've seen so far from the weapon indicates that NASA would have to replace almost every electronic part to get it back in operation. Even if they could reach the *Excalibur*, the mission to the anomaly would have to be abandoned."

"In that case, disable *Excalibur* as soon as it is out of sight of the space station."

Chapter 30

After circling the Earth several times, the crew of *Excalibur* had all the images of the Earth's surface that NASA needed for some updated DEMs or Digital Elevation Maps. The commander of the *Excalibur* requested that they alter course and head for the space station. NASA confirmed that everything was a go for docking with the ISS. A few hours later, *Excalibur* was approaching the docking clamp and ready to connect to the space station.

Craig Brentner, commander of *Excalibur*, was still a little shaken by news from NASA that the playback tapes had revealed a small explosion near the engines during liftoff. They were analyzing the data to see if the crew needed to do a spacewalk and check the outside of *Excalibur*.

Once docked, he met with the scientists on the ISS to get a better handle on the space anomaly that *Excalibur* would be investigating. So far, they didn't know much about the object, only that it was connected with the large explosion off Santa Barbara Island. The scientists were confident that something was indeed there, but couldn't get a clear picture of it. They showed the shuttle commander all the data they'd collected and emphasized that the only way to know anything further was to get closer to the object, whatever it might be.

Jake was becoming very impatient with the situation. He'd gone all over the ship getting a better assessment of his situation. He tried to watch TV, but even that didn't help. As he paced the floor, Meg finally spoke to him.

"Jake, I can tell that something is wrong. Is there a problem?"

Jake just started laughing.

"You've got to be kidding. First I drown, die, and then I'm abducted aboard a spaceship. Then you get me to steal a nuclear weapon, scare the hell out of everyone, and now I'm probably wanted by every security force in the world. I finally start to get things worked out with my wife and family, and then I can't see them because I've been beamed up and down too many times. No, Meg, nothing is wrong. Everything is hunky dory."

Millions of bits of data flowed through Meg's brain before her response.

"I am glad to hear that you are fine, but there is something more I should tell you."

"You mean there's more that can happen to me?"

Jake was starting to lose it a little.

Meg's answer was immediate.

"We seem to still have a problem with NASA. The launch of *Excalibur* went as planned, and they do plan on coming in our direction to investigate. We cannot allow that to happen."

Jake started to walk toward the landing bay to see how his ship was coming along. He spoke to Meg as he walked.

"So what are you going to do, blow them up with some kind of laser beam? Why don't we just move?"

"Jake, I have already told you that if I move, they will be able to see me even better. It looks like someone already tried to blow them up. I detected a small explosion below the engines as *Excalibur* was launched. My sensors tell me that it was intended to stop *Excalibur*. Someone else must not want NASA to find us. My only choice is to move anyway, but I will have to move deeper into space, where it will take longer to get to us."

Jake stopped in his tracks.

"You can't do that Meg. I won't be able to talk to or see my family. This isn't fair. I helped you, why can't you help me?"

"Jake, the best I can do is to give you a day to talk with your family, and then I will have to move."

Jake wasn't happy with her answer but knew that once Meg made up her mind, it was locked. He made a beeline for his apartment so that when he talked to Beth, the background scene would look normal. He asked Meg to connect to Beth's TV. When she did, the screen showed no one in the room. Jake then had Meg switch to his son's computer screen. Sure enough, Brad was surfing the internet. Jake cut into the screen with his face.

"Hi, Brad. How are you doing?"

"Dad, you have the strangest way of calling someone. I must be the only kid whose father calls home on TV sets and computer monitors. I'm doing fine, but Mom isn't. She's starting to get mad at you again. Why haven't you called her lately?"

Jake was so proud of his son. He was quickly becoming a man.

"Brad, I've been really busy with my work. I'm so sorry that I didn't get back to you guys. Where's your mom?"

Brad leaned back on his chair and gave a little smile.

"Dad, all you had to do was talk to her. She's going to be back from the store in 10 minutes. Why not call back then?"

"Actually, Brad, I'd like to stay and talk with you until she comes home."

For the next 15 minutes, father and son conversed about what Brad was doing in school, and great times they had before Jake left. Before long, both heard Beth yelling for Brad to help bring in the groceries. He yelled down that Jake wanted to talk to her. In seconds, Beth was up the stairs.

Brad got up from his chair, looked at the screen, and quietly said, "Don't screw it up, Dad. You don't have many chances left."

Beth waited until she heard Brad going down the stairs. She sat and stared at Jake.

"Okay, Jake. What's going on? Do you want this to work out or not?

Jake could see that Beth was reaching the end of her rope. She looked great, so he told her so. It caught her by surprise, but she brusquely answered.

"Jake, it's not going to be that easy. When are you coming home?"

"Beth, I really want to come home as soon as possible, but

we had an emergency on board the ship, and it has delayed my return. I have arranged for transportation, but it's not ready yet."

Beth wasn't satisfied with that answer.

"So, what do they have to do, build it first, and that's why it's taking so long?"

Jake started to chuckle and then realized that was probably not a good thing to do.

"You are closer to the truth than you know. Here's the bottom line. I love you and the family very much and want to come home again. The problem is that I have certain responsibilities with the new job that require me to be here until they are completed. I don't want to be as I was before. If you really love me, you need to let me finish what I'm doing. I'll be home as soon as I can."

Jake waited for her decision to be handed down. He hoped he knew his wife well and had anticipated her answer.

"I can live with that, but you better call whenever you can. You had better tell me everything when you get home. No more cloak and dagger stuff. Is that clear?"

Jake beamed. He was the happiest man on the edge of space.

"Honey, I'll call whenever I can, and I'll definitely tell you everything when I get there. I love you. Bye."

Jake's image slowly disappeared from the monitor. He sat for a minute in silence and was jolted with a voice from the wall.

"Are you sure that it is a good idea to tell your family about me? Would that not put them in jeopardy?"

"Meg, you need to read more about human relationships. Good ones are built on respect for each other. That means that you share the good and bad with each other and provide support. I know you don't fully understand it, but it's the only way the human race is ever going to ever survive."

Chapter 31

James Randel was in his office awaiting an answer as to why the first attempt on the space shuttle failed. When the phone rang, he expected it to be an explanation. To his surprise, it was one of the TF agents working in the communications center. He said that after extensive searches, agents discovered that the dead fisherman from Santa Barbara Island was seen near the home of his estranged wife. The information came from an informant who worked at her father's bank.

Henry Winston had been happy to fill the agents in on the strange happenings at Beth's house. He reported seeing the fisherman vanish right before his eyes, just like the transporter in *Star Trek*. The agents laughed it off, thinking this guy was a crackpot but reported the conversation to their boss. Randel now knew that Tech Forces were going in the right direction.

All the pieces were starting to come together. He needed to have leverage, and Jake McDonald's family would be the key. Randel put in a call to his TF security forces and designed a plan for them to abduct the entire family, and hold them in a secure location in the hills above Santa Barbara. He made it clear to the security supervisor that he didn't want any aspect of the Tech Forces exposed during the kidnap.

The Russian astronaut, a passenger on *Excalibur*, transferred to the ISS for his one-year stay. Journalist, Richard Morgan, conducted interviews with the ISS crew so he could report their perspective of space travel to the press. The *Excalibur* crew who remained onboard agreed that Morgan was a real pain-in-the-ass prima donna who constantly insulted NASA's projects. Frank Mendol was against the idea of sending up the press, but pressure from several senators in Congress got Morgan a seat on *Excalibur*.

Commander Brentner called the ISS to find out why the

journalist had failed to return. He asked the ISS communications specialist to find Morgan and put him on the communication link. Brentner wanted to make certain that Morgan understood loud and clear that he wasn't going to wait any longer.

"Morgan, what's the holdup? We need to leave now for our next part of the mission."

Morgan didn't answer for a few seconds and then spoke with a nasty overtone.

"I'm not ready to come back yet. I still have some interviews to do and take more pictures. You'll just have to wait until I'm ready to return."

"You can do the interviews and take all the pictures you want, but when you're ready to leave, you'll have to find another ride, because we won't be here."

Morgan was furious.

"You SOB. You can't do that because I'm a member of the press. I can destroy your career with one article if I chose, so you'll wait until I'm ready to go."

"Morgan, you can do whatever you want. You're not the first member of the press that has tried to destroy me. Go right ahead, but you'll still have to get another ride. You have five minutes, and no more."

Brentner clicked off the communications and told the copilot to get ready to disembark from the ISS. A couple of minutes later the ISS communications officer called back to report that Morgan had stormed out of the communications center yelling that he was going to get even with everyone on *Excalibur*. The officer had also added that the crew of the ISS wished to thank him for getting Morgan off the space station.

At four minutes and forty seconds, Morgan finally showed up at the airlock and passed through without saying a word to anyone. He went to his chair, locked himself in, and started to type on his laptop.

As *Excalibur* prepared to disembark from the ISS, the crew went through checklists. Everyone was busy except Morgan, who was still fuming about his confrontation with Brentner. Finally, he turned on the communications line and asked to speak to the press representative on the ground. Just as he was ready to speak, his line went dead. A few seconds passed as Morgan fiddled with the headset before a voice came on the line.

"Morgan, you can't use the communications line right now. We need all communications from *Excalibur* to the ISS and ground for checking our systems. I'll let you know when you can talk to the ground."

Morgan clicked the mike.

"Look, Commander, my job is an important one. I need to keep the public up-to-date on what's happening on the space station. You can't just cut me off like that. If you don't let me talk, I'm going to make your career a living hell."

"Mr. Morgan, the space shuttle is no different than a ship at sea. I AM IN COMMAND! There is no democracy up here. What I say goes. You'll do as I say, or we'll tie you down to that chair. Now, I'm not going to tell you again. Shut up, and let us do our jobs."

Morgan grumbled to himself, as he turned off his link to the communications system. He looked out the window and wondered what was happening as *Excalibur* appeared to be making a slow roll on its axis. It slowed a little and then stopped.

Commander Brentner had enough on his mind without worrying about the press. Ground control had ordered him to roll *Excalibur* over so that technicians on the ISS could take a look at all the tiles and other critical components on the surfaces of *Excalibur*. On board the ISS, a technician refocused a small telescope so that they could do a visual inspection of the entire surface of *Excalibur*. Ground control had estimated that it would take at least two hours to inspect the entire shuttle. In the meantime, the rest of the crew prepared for the next mission to investigate the anomaly above the coast of California.

Chapter 32

Jake sat in the restaurant eating a quick meal. His thoughts shuffled between his family and this life in space. He really didn't want to leave his family when he was close to repairing the mistakes he'd made with his life.

As his thoughts moved through time and space, Meg spoke.

"Jake, it seems that NASA is determined to find us. You need to decide soon. If they get within ten miles, we will have to move to a position in deep space. I estimate that they will be here in the next two hours."

Jake reached up and scratched his forehead.

"Meg, I understand that having the space shuttle that close could cause problems. Don't you have any other solutions? Can't you divert them off course or something?"

"Sorry, Jake, but they seem to be very determined. Anything I do would probably reinforce their insistence to find us. I think the only recourse is to move, and they still may discover us. I will wait a little longer, but we need to leave soon."

The Tech Forces' headquarters was a beehive of activity. Brent Tolian had received word from James Randel that the *Excalibur* was ready to undock and head toward the mystery area. Solving the anomaly was a critical turn in future TF operations, so Tolian wanted to impress the importance of the next phase of the mission.

"The weapon is fully charged and ready to fire. *Excalibur* should be out of range of the ISS in thirty minutes. The ideal target coordinates are when *Excalibur* is fifty miles from the anomaly. We are confident that the weapon will fire perfectly."

Tolian rubbed the pain that had started in his neck. It had been a long day already and was going to be even longer before they were through.

"Tolian, I'm counting on your team. You cannot fail. If you do, it could mean the end of Tech Forces."

His statement took Tolian by surprise.

"I'm not sure what you mean. Is this anomaly that powerful?"

"From what we've gathered, whatever is up there has technology far greater than anything we've seen. If Jake McDonald, or whoever is in charge, discovers that we're trying to get it, I'm not sure we can hide from its retaliation. The bottom line is, make sure *Excalibur* doesn't find it. When our new space plane is ready, we can grab the technology for our own. I'll be watching the weapon's effect on my screen, so make it good."

Tolian turned off the communications and looked at *Excalibur* tracking system they had "borrowed" from one of NASA's contractors. *Excalibur* was now out of visual range of the ISS, and on a direct course with the large object in space. Technicians had determined that in twenty seconds, the optimum firing position would last for ten seconds. The clock counted down as the crystal Spectronium beam was charging and getting ready to fire.

Excalibur's crew was starting to get excited as they approached their mission target. They still had no idea what they were looking for but sensed there was something out there.

As the counter on the Spectronium weapon reached zero, the tracking system fired a very tight spectral beam of energy at the space shuttle. They had calculated so the beam was just wide enough to pass through all components of the shuttle. In a microsecond, all the electronic systems shifted in voltage, frequency, and amperage. This massive change in the electrical circuitry either shut systems down or burned them out entirely. The visual effects of the spectral beam were designed to blind the crew so that they couldn't see to fix any problems before *Excalibur* was disabled.

As the commander of *Excalibur* panned his eyes across the computer screen, it went blank. He looked to his right, and his vision started to blur.

"What the hell's going on? Send a message to NASA that we have a problem."

It was too late. All electronic systems went down, and none of the crew could see anything but red. All was quiet, as the Spectronium beam quit. *Excalibur* was dead in space.

Ground control had been closely following *Excalibur's* path when all communication lines went out. *Excalibur* had just dropped off the screen

Frank Mendol at NASA was in shock. He thought to himself, *not another shuttle accident.*

Mendol came out of his shock and started working his way through the by-the-book procedures for shuttle accidents. Initial reports told him nothing except that *Excalibur* was still intact and floating in space with no apparent operational electrical systems. Several teams had been assembled to find out what happened and how to communicate and save the men on *Excalibur*. Nothing like this was in the protocol, so they were in new territory.

The commander *Excalibur* was just as lost. As soon as he realized that *Excalibur* had no electrical power, he made a verbal confirmation that all crew was unharmed. Once that was accomplished, he ordered the crew to work through the emergency procedures. Unfortunately, most of the procedures were of no use in this situation. To make matters worse, Morgan was screaming at the top of his lungs that someone should do something to fix the problem.

Chapter 33

Jake had been monitoring the progress of *Excalibur* as it moved closer to Meg. Then all communications stopped, and *Excalibur* started to drift in space.

"Meg, I thought you said you wouldn't do anything to stop the shuttle. It looks like it is idle and not moving anywhere near us."

Meg's response was quick.

"I had nothing to do with the shuttle. My sensors detect that all systems have failed on the shuttle. It appears the shuttle was hit by some type of unknown energy beam just before it went dead. I have searched my records and have no information on such a weapon. It appears that the crew will die from lack of oxygen or hyperthermia in the next few hours if they don't get help."

"Meg, who can we get to help?"

"Jake, there is no one within range."

"What about us? We have plenty of space. Couldn't we help?"

"Jake, if we did help, we would be completing their mission of discovering my existence."

"Hey, Meg, we're not talking about the bad guys here, this is NASA. I bet we could make a deal with them if we helped them with their ship. Can we retrieve the shuttle and fix it?"

"We can bring them in, and I am considering it. I would need your help though. You would have to talk to their commander about keeping me a secret. I don't think that is possible."

"I don't think you know humans as well as you think. They are astronauts, and they represent the best of us. If we're going to save their bacon, I bet they'd save ours."

"Jake, I'm not sure what bacon has to do with it."

"Check your memory banks, Meg, and look up

145

colloquialisms."

"I understand now, but it will take some time to bring them in. Once I do, you better be able to make a deal with them quickly, or we will have to leave at once."

Jake watched the view screen as three small rocket-shaped droids left the large spherical ship. They accelerated in speed and would reach the shuttle within a few minutes.

Jake knew it was going to get busy, so he decided to check in on Beth and the kids. As he turned on the viewer to his home in Santa Barbara, he was presented with an image of two large men in masks rifling through drawers in the living room. He could hear them mention his name, and that he was connected with the something in space.

This is bad. They know who I am and where I am. In all my excitement, I never thought I would put my family in jeopardy.

The men continued to search, looking for something in particular, but not finding it. They were very careful to put everything back in place. One man went upstairs, so Jake switched to Brad's computer monitor. He began searching the room and then took out an electronic device and placed it under the keyboard.

A bug; they want to hear our conversations. Damn.

Jake kept switching between viewing screens as the two men continued to search and place bugs. One of the men took out a digital camera and started to photograph everything in Brad's room before leaving to photograph other rooms. Then one of the men pulled out a phone and spoke.

"Sir, the family isn't home, and there's nothing here to indicate that Jake, or any family member, is in any way connected to the government. This is just an ordinary family. How can they be connected with such an advanced weapons project?"

The man then listened to an answer, before responding.

"We've planted all the bugs, and put everything back in place. What do you want us to do now?"

The man listened for a minute, picked up his bag of tricks, and carefully closed the front door. As he did, Jake noticed that the man had a TV repair logo on his shirt.

Jake's world was now coming apart. How would he contact his family and warn them without being intercepted? He had to get a message to Brad somehow, and then he remembered an old code he and his son used years ago. It was difficult to learn and translate in your head, but he and Brad had perfected the technique over the years. It was even more difficult to break, and that was his hope.

He had to be sure that by the time they broke the code, Brad had decoded it and acted upon his message. Jake had to warn his family they were in danger, and find a way to get them safe. He started the code.

ASE ITI NN RA RM ATN SN KE NNI UU Y KA U K RT MS C L PE NE CT ST AT IT OO AA 9E G LN GG EK F S R YE 2E OA SM 1 P F 1E 5 PE AE O 6E D AP GM Q WN N TTT NG T4 TEN TM GO EMM IEM NTE FT TEE TST KT TYE TEET MA MTA

UTE E5 EEE AN EN IN INS RN SI UN IN US FEE AEE ATTE ETE AI SD AME MT NNT MAM TIT MET OET NAM TEET GT MU YET KIT NTT GK NT 6T X GA TET NG TS KS NNI DEE NE TD MEI TME NE BE NS TAE OI TI ME NEE OE D YEE CEE TETE MAI TI NII B ZE D IMT 5T U RT FA EET EETT HM EA AT UT RM IT AA AD AT SIT ST ENT ANT AIN AAE AE R S F UT H UN JI P S PN HE EH IME UE ESE ENN II RNE AAN MU OO MM OM ZM O MAT OT KT OAT BT DA MTA NT MMT TO YT NE TTOT NIT TTNT MTM TTT Y TV K CM MA MAT AT T5 EET QN HT D U THE NE IM KI EAT NNI CEE.

Chapter 34

Commander Brentner was looking out the frosted front window when he saw a small glint of light coming at him.

"What the hell is that?"

Before he could say any more, three small shapes passed by the window.

"Hey guys, I don't want you to think I've gone crazy, but we have visitors. I don't have a clue as to what they are."

The rest of the crew looked to see if they could see anything, but all they saw was a cold dark space. The three rocket droids accomplished their first command. The second was to spray a light coat of material on the bottom of the shuttle so that it would become invisible to the ground. They had to do it quickly so that it would appear to blink out to those on the ground.

NASA ground control tried everything to contact *Excalibur* with no success. They had redirected telescopes on *Excalibur* to see if there was any damage. As they were downloading images, *Excalibur* disappeared.

Aboard *Excalibur,* nothing seemed to change, until they started to feel slight movement. What they didn't see were three small droid rockets attached to the bottom of the wings and on the tail of *Excalibur.* The droids slowly increased power until they reached a specific speed and then coasted.

By this time, Colonel Brentner was at a loss as to what was happening.

"Okay, guys. I'm willing to listen to any of your ideas on what's happening. I just need one that we can act on."

Ed Villars, the co-commander was the first to respond.

"I don't know how it's happening, but I do know that a slight G force indicates that something is pushing us forward. It could be another ship or a leak in one of the fuel tanks. Other than that, I would have to suggest that aliens are out there."

The rest of the crew wasn't much help either when suddenly *Excalibur* started to have a reverse thrust that slowed it down.

Colonel Brentner leaned toward the front window.

"Now I'm really going nuts. It appears that there's a very large object dead ahead. I can't see it clearly yet. Wait! It's getting clearer. Oh my God, it's a huge sphere!"

Three of the crew crammed into the front cockpit and gazed out the window. As the ship continued to slow, a small opening appeared in the sphere and grew larger as *Excalibur* approached.

Ed Villars looked out the side of the front window.

"Hey, guys, it looks like the landing bay from *Star Wars* or *Star Trek*."

As *Excalibur* slowly entered the large sphere, the door closed behind them.

Villars was the first to speak.

"Now what the hell do we do?"

Colonel Brentner looked out the left side and added, "I don't think there's a whole lot we can do. Let's hope we don't piss them off because it looks like they are more advanced than we are."

The rest of the crew and Morgan moved to available windows to view the stark white walls of the landing bay. Nothing happened for the next couple of minutes. Colonel Brentner continued to scan the walls of the landing bay when out of the corner of his eye, he saw movement. A door opened to the right of *Excalibur* and out walked a man in normal street clothing.

"Hey, guys. You're not going to believe this, but there's a guy standing outside the starboard side of *Excalibur*. Quick hand me a pair of binoculars as he's writing something on a tablet."

The copilot handed him a set and he focused on the man. His sign read:

My name is Jake.

Can I talk to Colonel Brentner for a few minutes?

The air outside is fine, but there is no gravity, so be careful.

Colonel Brentner set the binoculars down and repeated what he'd read. One of the crewmembers started to say something, but the Colonel broke in.

"Okay, I need to make a decision soon. We are running out of air, and that effect might be making us all think this is out there."

Villars cut in.

"I don't think so, Sir. We all wouldn't have the same hallucination. I think what we are seeing out there is real, even though it's hard to believe. Considering the level of technology required for this landing bay, I think we need to be very careful. I'll volunteer to go out and see what he wants. Colonel, I think you should stay inside, in case the man is hostile."

Morgan couldn't stand it anymore.

"I think you guys are crazy. You don't have any idea what kind of situation we've encountered. I'm not ready for you to risk my life, just because you're curious. If you do go outside, you should take a gun. If the man makes a move, shoot him."

Villars glared at Morgan.

"Hey, I thought you were the super journalist who would do anything for a story. Now you want to play it safe. What made you so negative about the world? Besides, I really don't think a gun will hold much water to whatever waits for us outside."

"Okay, guys, that's enough. Let's concentrate on the matter at hand," said Colonel Brentner as he moved to the airlock. "If anyone goes out, it's going to be me, and I'm not taking any weapons outside. The man outside appears friendly. We're going to assume that he's human, and wants to help. I don't want to hear another word about using weapons."

The man outside moved a staircase up to the side of

Excalibur in anticipation of the meeting. The crew became quiet as they prepared for Colonel Brentner's departure. Without power, the crew manually had to open all the doors. The Colonel put on a full suit on just in case the air wasn't safe. Even then, without power to his suit, he would only have a few minutes before he would have to return to *Excalibur.*

He turned the handle and exited the outside door. As he reached the bottom of the ladder, Jake stood in front of him with his hand extended.

"I'm Jake. Welcome to my home. I understand why you wore the suit, but it's not necessary. I'm sure it's difficult to hear me, so why don't you take it the helmet off?"

Colonel Brentner now had a choice. Was this all real? On the other hand, would the last thing he remembered be taking his helmet off? The smile on Jake's face was enough to convince him that everything would be all right. He looked back at the shuttle and assumed that the crew was yelling at him to keep on his helmet. As he took it off, nothing happened. The air was clean and even refreshing.

"Let me introduce myself. I'm Colonel Brentner of the first *Excalibur* mission. We came up here to see what was hiding in space, and I think you are it. Are you the one that disabled my ship?"

Jake helped the Colonel as he continued to remove his suit.

"Colonel, I had nothing to do with damaging your ship. As far as my ship's sensors could determine, some type of energy beam came from the surface. I think it was meant to stop you from finding me. You know the rest of your men and women are welcome to come out and get some air. From what I can tell, you aren't going anywhere soon."

Sweat was rolling down the Colonel's face as he removed the final piece of gear.

"I have so many questions about how we got here and exactly where we are."

151

Jake quickly interrupted.

"Well, that's our first problem. Let me explain the situation as best as I can. This is my ship. How I got it, or how I got here, I can't say. What I can tell you is that I would be willing to fix your shuttle so you can get back home."

The Colonel was slowly shaking his head back and forth.

"I don't think you would be able to repair our ship. Almost every system on *Excalibur* is burned out. Even if you could repair it, why would you?"

"Well, that's the crux of the situation. I want to keep my ship a secret. I want to be left alone, and most importantly, I don't want this ship to fall in the hands of any military. So, here's my proposition. There are hundreds of small robots on board my ship that can repair your shuttle. I have downloaded all its specs, so I'm estimating that everything can be returned to normal in approximately two days. In trade, I would ask that the entire crew of the shuttle forget that my ship ever existed long enough to allow me to get lost in space, so to speak. I know that sounds impossible with five other crewmembers, but I would like you to propose it to them."

It took a while for the Colonel to process the information, but the frown on his face was replaced with a smile.

"If I can get everyone to agree, where would we stay? Nothing works on the shuttle, and we would have to eat and sleep somewhere."

"You would be my guests. My ship is six hundred feet in diameter and has plenty of living quarters. We can provide a variety of food, hot showers, and even some TV if you like."

A light bulb went on in the Colonel's head.

"Can we call NASA and let them know we're okay? They're probably going crazy looking for us."

"You've got that right. They now assume that you're dead which is unfortunate. That information has already gone out to your families, but that's a problem we'll resolve later. You are free to roam my ship and rest, but the deal is that no one can know I'm here. Therefore, there can be absolutely no contact with anyone."

The Colonel looked back at *Excalibur*. Most of the crew was glued to the windows. He could see Morgan pushing one crewmember aside, and pushing his ugly face against the window.

"So, Jake, what if I don't agree to your terms? What are you going to do with us? Are we your prisoners then?"

"Colonel, I think you misunderstand. You are not my prisoners. You can stay onboard the shuttle while it is being fixed, but it would make it easier for the robots to have all the space they needed for repairs. It doesn't matter whether you agree or not, we will fix your ship and send you on your way. I was only asking as one favor for another. You can go ahead and tell everyone about this ship if you want, but that will make it very difficult for me. I'm just asking for a little professional courtesy."

"Well, I can speak for myself and my five crew, but we have a journalist onboard named Morgan, that I know won't agree. I guess the only way to know for sure is to ask them."

Jake looked over to the wall opposite the shuttle. He could see several droids gathering on the top of the wall. They were waiting for the word to start working.

"I'll tell you what, Colonel, go back, and talk with your crew. Do your best to convince them all and we can continue this conversation over dinner tonight. I know about your problem with Morgan as I did some research. He sounds like a jerk.

"Let me know when you're ready, and I'll give a tour of my ship. Then I can show you and your crew to your quarters. Make me a list of what each crewmember wants for dinner, and I'll have it prepared. Good luck."

The Colonel reached out and shook Jake's hand. He then turned and worked his way back to the shuttle.

That seemed to go well thought Jake as he stood waiting to hear the crew's decision.

The airlock to the inside of *Excalibur* opened, and Colonel Brentner came through with a big smile on his face.

"Boy, do we have a lot to talk about."

The Colonel relayed the conversation he had with Jake and then waited for their responses. The entire crew started to speak at once, but Morgan was the loudest.

"The only way I'm going to agree to this is if I can call my newspaper and get my story to press." His loud mouth closed as glaring eyes stared at him.

Colonel Brentner broke the silence.

"Look everyone; this is not an easy situation. We don't have many choices. I think we should go along with this man and see what more he has to say."

Ed Villars finally couldn't stand it any longer.

"What if he's the one that shot at us? Maybe he wants our technology."

The Colonel chuckled.

"Look, guys. Do you really think that a ship with this kind of technology would be interested in what we have in *Excalibur*? No, I think what this man says is for real. We would have died if he hadn't brought us here. We at least owe him for saving our lives."

Nancy Barten, the medical engineer had listened as the conversation bounced back and forth, and finally added her two cents into the discussion.

"I think the solution is simple. We have nothing to lose by going along with this man Jake. Anything is better than dead, and that seems to be our only other option. He seems like a nice man."

Bob Cranston, the payload engineer interrupted her conversation with his perspective.

"You can tell he's nice by just looking out the window? What's that, woman's intuition?"

Nancy glared back at Bob.

"For your sake, I'm going to pretend you didn't say that. I provided my comments based on my observations. He had no weapons on him and smiled during most of the conversation with the Colonel. He was casually dressed and based on the Colonel's reactions didn't interject a sense of threat. Do we really have a choice? We would be dead if not for Jake. My vote is to go for it."

The Colonel looked over to Brenda Millstone, the astrophysicists.

"Colonel, I agree with Nancy. We don't have a lot of options and this man looks like our only way out of a bad situation. I vote we do what Jake wants. We can't do much worse."

The Colonel took one last look out the window and stared at the man standing below *Excalibur*.

"Okay, here's how it's going down. We're going with Jake, to hear him out. We'll be careful what we say about our mission, and not provide him any more information than necessary. Once we have a better idea of what we're up against, we'll talk as a group again, and make some new decisions. Besides, the air in here is getting rancid, and it is much fresher outside."

Chapter 35

Everything at NASA went crazy when *Excalibur* disappeared from the viewing screen. Everyone was yelling at each other, and screaming at their computer screens. Pandemonium set in. Frank Mendol let everyone vent for a couple of seconds before he spoke loud enough to drown everyone else out.

"Okay, people, listen up. We have a serious problem, and we need to attack it by the numbers. Review the tapes just before the shuttle disappeared. Get some different angle views of the area where it disappeared. Call in favors from civilian telescopes along the western U.S. I want the think tank team to draw up a list of possible reasons for the disappearance, and probable solutions for finding it. I want the emphasis on finding *Excalibur*. We can't stand another shuttle accident."

Voices began to fill the air, as everyone scrambled to their new tasks. Mendol's next conversation was to himself. *Why now, when everything was going so well? It just doesn't make any sense. Shuttles just don't disappear without a trace.* He closed the door to his office and picked up the phone. The President would have to be informed. "Damn," he said as he started to dial.

At the exact time NASA went into panic mode, so did Tech Forces. James Randel sat at his desk intercepting calls from the different departments under his control. The unraveling story disturbed him greatly. It seemed the technology he was trying to acquire was more complicated than he'd ever imagined.

His first call was to Pete Killian.

"Pete, I'm sure you've heard by now that the results of our efforts to stop *Excalibur* are unknown at this time. One thing is that I'm damn sure this Jake McDonald is the reason for the problem. Is the surveillance in place?"

As soon as Killian heard about the disappearing shuttle,

he'd been waiting for this call.

"Sir, I have all the bugs in place. So far, nothing the family has said indicates they know anything. However, we did pick up a strange code on Brad McDonald's computer. We immediately put the decipher computer on it, but it seems to have a unique key that accesses the code. Our decryption software indicates that the key changes randomly. We'll be able to break it when more messages provide us a bigger base with which to work."

"Are you telling me that a dead fisherman and his son have worked out a code that has our code-breaking program stumped?"

"No, Sir, it's just that with such a short message and such a weird code variation, it will take some time. I guarantee you that we'll break it."

"You better. I have a feeling that the content of the message will be invaluable for obtaining this new technology."

Chapter 36

Jake watched the shuttle as the crew continued to argue. Meg had piped their conversations directly to Jake through the communication device on his arm. When the shuttle door started to open, he decided not to move toward the shuttle as it might be misconstrued as aggressive. He would patiently wait. Jake had already placed six pairs of special shoes at the base of the stairs. As each crewmember climbed down from the shuttle, they clumsily put on the shoes.

Jake laughed. *You would think astronauts would be more adept in zero gravity.*

As the Colonel moved forward, Jake reached out to shake his hand again. As each member of the crew came forward, Jake introduced himself and shook each crewmember's hand.

"I know all of you are very confused at this point. That's not my purpose. There's just no easy way to explain where you are and why you're here. I know you all have questions, and I'll try to answer them in time. We need to move to the upper half of the ship where we have .5 gravity. If you all follow me to the elevator, we'll move to the center of the ship."

Jake was surprised at their response or rather lack of it. He was sure that there would be a ton of questions, but instead, they stood in awe and silence. As he reached the elevator, he told the crew that they would have to go in two groups, as the elevator could only hold four at a time. The Colonel agreed to take the first group, and Jake would follow up with the second.

Once his group rejoined them, Jake escorted the group over to a ladder against the wall. On the ceiling was a large black circular object with a hinge to one side. Jake leaned over and accessed the security system to activate the sequence and the black circle started to rotate. As it turned, it also spiraled down from the ceiling. Jake and the crew moved back as the threaded shaft moved down from the ceiling. Once it reached the top of the ladder, the hydraulic hinge slid the door back and away from the opening above the ladder. The process took no more than a minute to execute, but the crew was very engrossed in its operation.

Before Jake could explain, the Colonel broke in.

"That door looks a lot like our missile silo doors except ours aren't threaded. This design looks much better than ours does. Why would you have such a door on this ship?"

Jake moved over under the passage.

"I was going to explain it when we got to the other side, but what the hell? The ship is divided into two halves with a special ten-foot metal barrier in between. This barrier is designed to protect the ship from various types of natural radiation, flares, and weapon blasts. The side we are in currently houses most of the mechanical aspects of the ship. You saw the landing bay, but the ship's engines, communication, a repair facility, and raw materials are stored in that half. The upper portion houses the living quarters and has some gravity. There's another door that will open for a couple of minutes to allow us to crawl up the ladder. If we don't get through the shaft in that time, the doors will close automatically. So, if you don't mind, let's get going."

Jake quickly went up the ladder and the rest of the crew followed. The Colonel decided to be last so that Morgan wouldn't fall behind and do something stupid. As the crew entered the upper section of the shaft, they were in a trance. They were standing in the middle of a large garden with trees, small birds, flowers, and a small stream surrounding them.

Everyone could hear the Colonel yelling at Morgan to get his butt up the ladder. As the Morgan stuck his head up through the surface, his eyes became very wide. His first words had already been voiced by everyone else.

"My God, what is this place?"

Jake reached down and grabbed the Colonel's hand, as he exited the shaft. A few seconds later, the massive door started to turn into the floor of the garden.

"Okay, I know this brings up a lot more questions. What can I say? A garden makes living up here nicer. I know you want to explore, but first, we need to talk. If you look behind you, the shaft in the middle of the garden is lined with windows on the second story. Those are the living quarters. If you follow me into another elevator, we can go to the meeting room where I will try to answer all of your questions."

Everyone started to speak at the same time and the noise level began to rise. The Colonel stopped it all with two words.

"Okay, people."

Everyone immediately stopped talking and looked at the Colonel.

"Let's do as the man says. If we lollygag around, the longer it will be before we find out what's going on. Let's keep the questions on hold, and wait until we get to the end of this Alice in Wonderland journey."

Again, Jake went with the first group and the Colonel with the second. When the second group came out of the elevator, Jake escorted them into a meeting room just a few feet from the elevator. Water bottles were arranged for each person, along with a few plates of snacks. Ed Villars sat down first, took a drink of water, and started to wolf down the snacks. Soon everyone was sitting, drinking, and eating. For the first time, the only sounds were those made by hungry humans. Jake waited until the crew slowed down on the food and drink before continuing.

"If you want more food, I can have it here in a couple of minutes, but keep in mind that I have scheduled dinner in a few hours. I know you want answers, and I'll do the best I can. I think a lot of questions will be taken care of if I tell you a little about your accommodations and how this is all going to work."

The Colonel stood up for a second to interject his thoughts.

"Everyone, listen up and let the man say his piece. I think we have plenty of time for questions, especially you, Morgan."

"Thanks, Colonel. Each of you will have living quarters on

this floor. Your name will be on the door to your apartment. Only you can open the door. There are no keys, so just put your hand on the doorknob, and it will open. They contain a bed, shower, TV, and just about anything else, except communication like a telephone or the Internet. You can order food by just voicing, "I would like some food" and state what you want. It will appear on the table in your kitchen. There are drinks in the fridge, and if you prefer something special, just voice what you want, and it will appear in your fridge.

"If you want to eat together as a group, there is a restaurant at the end of this hall. Don't laugh, but it looks like a Denny's. Just walk up to the counter and voice what you would like to order. It should take a couple of minutes, and the food will be available on a tray in an opening along the wall. I would like us all to have dinner tonight as a group.

"After our meeting, please go to your rooms; get some rest, shower, and meet back at the restaurant at 7 p.m. You'll find a change of clothing on your beds. Don't ask how I know all your sizes because that will be further explained. Tomorrow I'll give you a tour of the ship and you'll be able to explore to your heart's content. Now, let me try to answer your questions."

Morgan jumped right in as expected.

"I demand to talk to my editor. It's vital that I speak to him immediately."

He was about to continue when Colonel Brentner cut into the conversation.

"We all know how important you think you are to this mission, but right now I don't want to hear one more word from you. If you don't shut up, I will personally gag and tie you to your chair."

Morgan squinted his eyes.

"You haven't heard the end of this. When I get home, I'll make your life a living hell. Your career is over."

The Colonel smiled, "That is if we let you get back on the ground. Jake, can you keep Morgan here for a few weeks, months, or maybe even permanently?"

Jake frowned, "I hope you're kidding. I don't want him any more than you do, but I have a plan that will solve all your Morgan problems. We'll discuss it later. Now I'll answer any questions, except the press."

Ed Villars posed the first question.

"Can you really fix *Excalibur*? Almost every circuit is fried. Even if you do, how can we be sure that you aren't sending us to our death?"

Jake now repeated what Meg had told him.

"The computer systems on this ship are far more advanced than yours. The robots can fix just about anything. They'll run a diagnostic on every system and give you printouts from every test. I don't think you have anything to worry about."

Brenda broke in with the next question.

"Let's say that you do fix our ship and we return. How are we going to explain all this? No one is going to believe us."

Jake sat in the chair at the end of the table.

"That's the real heart of our problem. You have a broken spaceship. I have one that I don't want anyone to know about. You're going to want to tell everyone what you see here. The problem is that the world isn't ready for this type of technology. Think about it. Do you really think that the military will let you use this technology for space research? No matter what guarantees they provide, they'll find a way to take it away from you. What I was really hoping for in return for saving your lives, repairing your ship, and returning you to your families unharmed, is that you might forget about this ship, at least for a couple of weeks."

Nancy stated shaking her head, "Jake, I see what you're trying to say, but don't you think that's impossible? There's no way to keep that kind of secret with six different people, especially when one is the press. I would agree to your terms, and think most of the others will, but what if one of us slips, or is forced to give the information up?"

"I agree that what I'm asking is nothing short of a miracle, but I'm still willing to try. All I'm asking for is a little time. Eventually, the truth will get out, but I'll be long gone, and there will be no way to prove your story. Bear in mind, that even if only half of you stick to the story, it will be hard for the authorities to sort it out. Let's put this part of the conversation to rest for now, and see how it plays out later. You all need some rest, and you have all of tomorrow to explore the ship. You're on a large alien ship in space, and you're being offered a chance to explore it without any restrictions. Pretty cool, huh?"

Bob raised his hand like a kid in school.

"Are there more people on the ship, or are you the only one?"

Jake was surprised that this question did not come sooner.

"Including myself and the six from *Excalibur*, we are the only humans on the ship. There are hundreds of small robots I call droids, and two other intelligent beings onboard."

The Colonel's eyes perked up at that comment.

"What other beings? You didn't tell me this when we came on board."

Jake took a second to compose his thoughts.

"Don't get your shorts in a knot, Colonel. I was about to introduce you to the first one in a couple of minutes. I call her Meg. You'll never see her because she's the brains of this ship. She's highly intelligent and is the reason the robots are able to put your shuttle back together again. Meg, would you like to introduce yourself?"

Nothing happened for a few seconds, and then a picture of the Earth appeared on the massive viewing screen in the meeting room. A few seconds later, Meg spoke to the crew for the first time.

"Welcome to my domain. I am Meg, and I am responsible for almost everything that goes on inside this ship. Where I come from and why I am here, is information available only to Jake. I can tell you that the reason is a peaceful one, and I do not intend to do harm to anyone. If you want to talk to me, just say, "Meg" and then ask your question. You are free to roam the inside of the ship. I only ask that you leave the droids alone, as they are very busy. They also react when threatened, and will defend themselves if necessary. The other intelligent member of the crew I will let Jake explain."

The entire crew and even Morgan were so taken aback by her statements that the room was quiet enough for Jake to continue.

"The final member of the crew is a little harder to explain. I doubt you'll ever see him, but that doesn't mean he's not there. He's my bodyguard and is on the ship to protect me. I can tell you that he's somewhat of a large robot, but is a master or camouflage. He can hide so well that even I can't see him. I wouldn't be surprised if he's in the room with us right now."

Meg broke in saying, "Yes, he is here, Jake."

"Don't even think about causing me any bodily harm as my bodyguard wouldn't like that. The bottom line is that you can make this easy, or you can make it hard. It's your choice. I suggest that you all find your rooms, get some rest, and I'll see you at dinner at 7."

As the crew started to leave, the Colonel was surprised to hear Meg's voice in his head, but not by his ear. *"Colonel, Jake would like to speak to you privately. Please wait until everyone is gone."*

The Colonel held back as everyone filed out of the room and down the hall. He closed the door behind the last one and turned to Jake.

"That was a cute trick. I don't know how you did that, but I wish I could do that with my crew sometimes."

"Colonel, we have just a couple of loose ends to tie up. I know that the ship's secret will not last long. I think your crew will do the best they can, but Morgan will be the problem. However, I do have a solution I think will work, with your help of course. Just before you land, you should restrain and gag him.

164

When you are safely on the ground, you should get on that private line I know you have and tell NASA that he went crazy while in space. You know, crazy stuff like seeing aliens, and everyone was after him. The key is that you must convince them that he's crazy. Say whatever is necessary to get him agitated. You know it won't take much, but when he comes off the shuttle, he needs to look like a raving lunatic. Chances are they'll send him off to a funny farm for at least long enough for my ship to get lost in space."

"You must watch a lot of Sci-Fi movies. It seems like everything you say is interwoven with cliché terms from those movies. Anyway, your idea seems good to me, and it actually might work. At least for a while until he eventually convinces enough people. By the way, I agree with you that the ship would end up in the military's hands. I wish it weren't so, but that's dreaming. I hope there's a way that some of the technology onboard could be used to help the Earth, without giving it to the military."

Jake worked to wrap up the conversation.

"I appreciate your thoughts and your help with Morgan. I know we are fighting a losing battle, but it might just give me enough time to get the ship out of reach. See you at dinner tonight."

The Colonel left the room, and Jake pondered how he'd done so far.

Meg broke his concentration.

"Jake, you have done very well. I know you are trying your best to save the crew and protect me, but it will not work."

"I know, but it's worth a try. I just couldn't let them die. Meg, I need to talk with my wife. Is she home?"

The screen dissolved to a picture of a living room. Brad was sitting on the couch, watching who knows what. Jake's face slowly replaced the images on the TV set. "Brad, where is your mom?"

"Dad, where have you been? Mom's getting tired of you

being late. She's upstairs. I'll go get her."

Brad walks about two feet and then yells as loud as he can. "Mom, Dad's on TV again. He wants to talk to you."

In seconds, Beth came running down the steps. She sat down on the couch and then turned to Brad.

"Say good-bye to Dad because I need to talk with him privately."

"But Mom, I haven't even said anything yet. Can't I stay?"

As in the past, both Jake and Beth spoke at the same time. "Go to your room."

Brad stomped off, knowing that they were right. It's just that he wanted to talk to Dad and find out all the good stuff. He knew his dad was into something cool, and it was killing him not knowing more. He walked up the stairs, hopeful that he could get it out of his mother eventually.

"Beth, I'm so sorry that I've not been able to get back down to you. I've been busy with some dignitaries visiting the ship. They're a real handful. One of them is from the press, and he's driving everyone crazy."

"Jake, before you continue, what do you mean down?"

Jake swallowed hard. He screwed up. Beth was really sharp and spotted just one word out of place. How was he going to explain this?

"You know, when people go south, they go down. That's enough about me. How're you doing? I miss you and really wish I could see you all. Problem is that it will be several more days before I can leave."

Then it hit Jake. He really screwed up. He totally forgot that the house was bugged. What had he just said to Beth? Could they get any information from that conversation?

"Beth, do you remember our third date at the carnival and what happened afterward?"

Jake stopped speaking to see if Beth picked up the clue. In fact, what had happened was that her father had been eavesdropping in on their conversation upon their return from their date.   It was a conversation that shouldn't have been overheard by a father.   After Jake left, her dad confronted her and she caught hell.

"Jake, I have fond memories of that date, especially afterward.   You know, I have a few things to do before work tomorrow, so I'll talk to you later.   I'll be out tomorrow, so why don't you try me the day after."

Jake smiled and nodded his head forward a little.   Beth hated the aftermath of that date.   That told him she had picked up on the clue.   That's why he loved her so much because she was beautiful and very smart.   He was a lucky man if he could figure all this out.

Chapter 37

James Randel was looking over some of the most recent reports on the anomaly when the phone rang. Pete Killian had new information on Jake.

"We just intercepted a call from Jake to his wife. A few key words confirmed everything we suspected. He said something about coming down from a ship, and he complained about entertaining a press member. That only could be Morgan. We must now assume that *Excalibur* is indeed docked with some kind of spaceship. What I don't understand is that NASA still has no contact, and *Excalibur* has made no effort to communicate. That could mean they're being held hostage. I can't believe that the entire space shuttle crew would go along with whatever is happening without a fight."

Randel processed this new information and prepared his answer.

"This changes everything. If *Excalibur* does show up again, I don't want it harmed. We need to find out what the crew knows and I have a feeling that Morgan is our key. We also need to break that code and prepare a plan to kidnap the family. I think we're going to need them to force Jake's hand. When you have the plan ready, get back to me."

Randel hung up the phone before Killian could even respond. An answer wasn't necessary because Killian heard him loud and clear.

For the next two hours, Meg monitored *Excalibur's* crew to see how they would react to things beyond their comprehension. The Colonel took a hot shower, found the TV remote, and watched the lead story about the missing space shuttle. He watched as the press hounded anybody related to the space program. Families were always the favorite target. They asked, "How do you feel about losing your husband on the shuttle flight?" *How do you think they feel, you idiot,* he thought to himself. He wanted to lie down and get some rest, but he just couldn't unwind. Instead, he went to the elevator and pressed the button. It opened, he walked in, and it closed. Then it hit him that there were no buttons on the wall.

"Meg, how do I get to the garden?"

"All you have to do when you get in the elevator is say, 'Meg' and then tell me where you want to go. Have a nice day."

The Colonel chuckled as the elevator opened. A computer with a human trait. This was a weird day. He casually walked through the massive garden. Eventually, he found a bench near a small stream and sat down. He then mumbled, "It can't get much better than this."

"Thank you," came a response from somewhere.

"Are you watching me for Jake?"

"I do not mean to intrude. I am not following you. If you think about it, I am the ship, and you are on the ship, so everywhere you go, I am there. I will no longer respond to your conversation if you prefer."

"No, that's okay. It's just a little unnerving responding to a computer. I understand, and I do like our conversations, so continue when you want."

The Colonel spent the next two hours enjoying the most relaxing time he'd had in years.

Space exploration was Brenda Millstone's life. When she was assigned to the shuttle, her elation was beyond words. She was trying very hard to keep a positive attitude with all the happenings with the shuttle. She loved the room she'd been assigned, but it was a bit unnerving because everything was exactly the way she preferred. It was almost like her apartment at home. She decided to relax in the tub, and soon realized that the water never got cold.

"Meg, are you here?"

"May I help you?"

"How do you maintain a constant bath water temperature? Just forget that I asked. It's your ship and you can do whatever you want. What I really want to know is if there is a way to see the stars from this ship? I love the blackness of space, and what is beyond."

"There is an observatory at the top of the ship. It has a telescope one hundred times more powerful than the strongest you have on Earth. If you would like to see it, I would be happy to show it to you."

"Did you say happy? I didn't know that computers could have emotions."

"That is because you think of me as a computer. I may act like a computer, but I am what you call an AI or Artificial Intelligence. I can think, process, learn, and even produce human emotions. I am working on the emotions, and hope to perfect them so that Jake understands me better."

"You really like Jake, don't you?"

"I'm not sure I am to the stage of 'liking' Jake. However, I do have a high degree of respect for him, and would miss him if he ever left the ship."

"There you go again displaying another human emotion that is more than even an AI should have. Missing someone is clearly a human trait. I would like to talk more, but I'm really interested in seeing what you have for a telescope."

Brenda dressed quickly and headed for the elevator. Since she had informed Meg where she intended to go, she just boarded the elevator. When the doors opened, the sight astounded her. In front of her were a viewing screen, computer terminal, and a fabulous telescope that didn't match any of the designs on Earth.

"Meg, can I look at Mars?"

In seconds, a full-screen image of the surface of Mars appeared on the main viewer. The surface filled the entire screen, and she could see the fine detail of the mountains and craters on its surface.

"Wow."

"Do you like what you see?" came a voice from the screen.

"You know, you almost sound proud of your telescope. It's incredible. Can you point me to the nearest star with an M type planet around it?"

In seconds, a grid of sixteen different systems appeared on the monitor.

"Let's look at the second one from the left, top row."

The image zoomed in, and there before her eyes was a blue water planet much like Earth. "Meg, how many planets do you know about that are like this one?"

"I have hundreds in my databanks," was the surprising answer.

"Are you telling me that there are hundreds of worlds like Earth out there? How many have people, or beings like humans?"

"There are many more than I have in my databanks, but I cannot tell you which ones have beings like yourself. It is not because I don't have that information, but rather that I am prevented from telling you by my creators."

"Who are your creators?"

"I am sorry, I cannot tell you that either."

"I think that's enough for now. I'm going back to my room. I look forward to more conversations with you tomorrow on what is really out there."

Brenda worked her way back to the elevator, asked for her room floor, and before long was asleep in her bed.

Nancy Barten had always been interested in medicine from the first time she was in a hospital with a broken arm. She had puppy love for the doctor and was hooked on medicine ever since. When she went to her room, she took a hot shower, watched a little TV, and lay on the bed watching the ceiling. Before long, a voice from the ceiling spoke to her.

"Would you like to see the medical lab?"

She bolted up in surprise as it caught her off guard.

"I am sorry I disturbed you. I just thought with your interest in medicine, you might like to see what is available on the ship."

"Sure, let's go."

In seconds, she was off the bed, out the door, and headed in the wrong direction. Meg quickly rerouted her direction, and soon she entered the medical lab. Nancy looked at all the displays on the walls but noticed no examination table.

"How do you diagnose someone? There's no table."

At that very moment, the large black table rose from the floor.

"Lie on the table and look at the large viewer on the wall."

She did as instructed and as Nancy watched the widescreen viewer, a beam of light started to scan her from head to toe and multiple images began appearing. She saw there were multiple viewers so that one screen showed the circulatory system, a second for the skeletal system, a third for the muscle system, and a fourth displayed the nervous system.

"That's incredible. How is this possible that you can do all those scans at the same time?"

"The beam that scanned you works on the molecular level. It can determine the differences between the different systems in the human body and separate them into different screens."

"The fine detail is amazing. Does this allow you to see blood clots, tumors, cancer cells, or anything else that can damage the body?"

"If it can damage the human body, I can find a way to display it."

Chapter 38

Ed Villars sat on the comfortable couch and was in a trance as he watched the TV. The press was like sharks going after anyone they could find related to the shuttle. When they couldn't find anyone else to harass, they would interview NASA janitors for their opinions about the situation. Ed was just about to switch off the TV when his wife came on the screen. She was now into the ninth month of her pregnancy, but it looked more like the tenth. The press had found her returning from the market with a friend and stopped her in their driveway. They hounded her with the same stupid questions. She started to break down and cry, but the friend hurriedly ushered her into the house. The last shot they showed was the front door closing.

Ed's heart was beating fast in frustration. He clicked off the TV and put his head between his hands. He was then startled by a voice coming from the TV.

"Ed, everything will be okay. It looks bad now, but you will be home soon. Your wife is fine."

"How do you know she's fine? We're up here and she's down there. The press is eating her alive, and I can't help her."

"Ed, her friend is helping her right now, and she is feeling better already."

As the statement ended, a picture of Ed's living room appeared on the TV. The voices from his wife and her friend came through the speaker. As he looked at the screen, his thoughts were of his wife. *Meg was right, she was better. She was lying on the couch, and the friend was helping her rest.*

"Meg, I don't know how you're doing this, but thank you. Can I talk to her?"

"Ed, I would like you to, but not yet. There is no guarantee that she is not being monitored, and our conversation recorded. When I am sure it is safe, and if it is okay with Jake, then I will let you talk to her. I'm sorry I cannot do better than that."

"Meg, can you please leave the image on the screen?"

The image remained, and Ed just sat there watching the woman he loved so much and wished he could be there. Before long, he drifted off to sleep. As he did, the image and TV sound faded.

When the meeting broke up, Morgan began a thorough search of his room for a way to call his paper. Finding nothing, he moved down the hall, looking in any room he could access. Most rooms were empty, and the others with crew names were locked. Once on the elevator, and went from floor to floor looking for anything to help him. Finally, he ran out of ideas.

"Meg, I know you can hear me. I'm a very important man on this crew. It's imperative that I contact my editor. Get me a phone or Internet connection right now. We can do this discreetly and the rest of the crew doesn't have to know."

"Mr. Morgan, I cannot help you with your request." This was followed by silence.

Morgan again demanded to be connected to his newspaper, but there was no response from Meg. Morgan screamed at what he thought was the direction of the voice, but still got silence. The more silence, the more Morgan screamed. Then he remembered that he had a small digital camera in his pocket. At first, he tried to be discreet taking pictures, but when he saw that Meg wasn't stopping him, he became bolder.

He began documenting the entire ship with pictures that he felt would guarantee him the Pulitzer. He had several large memory cards for the camera, but his concern was the battery life. He had an extra set on *Excalibur*, but couldn't get there. He shot images until the battery power was about half spent.

When he got back to his room, he replaced the memory card with a second blank card. He then hid the exposed card in a secret compartment in a book he'd brought with him. He thought, *if the crew or Jake took his camera, he'd still have the*

174

pictures. They could do whatever they wanted, but he'd have the last laugh.

As the dinner hour approached, the shuttle crewmembers started to filter into the ship's restaurant. Jake was already sitting with a glass of wine, talking with the Colonel. When the last crewmember was seated, Jake stood up and gave a toast to the crew, wishing their safe return to their families. At the end of the toast, everyone started to engage in dinner conversation, and before long, food appeared. Every meal was different and tailored to the individual tastes of each person. It didn't take long before the conversation was reduced to the language of knife, fork, and spoon. As the meal ended, the conversation increased, so Jake stood up.

"I hope everyone enjoyed their meal. Tomorrow you are welcome to explore the ship. If you want to go below or retrieve something from the shuttle, let me know and I'll go with you. I just need to make sure that you don't get into trouble while down there, especially with the droids. If you need access to the shuttle, I will stop the droid's work until you obtain what you need.

"I'm very sorry that you can't talk with your families, but you'll be home soon, and that's the best I can offer. If you want to talk with me tomorrow, just ask Meg where I am, or look in the garden. I spend a lot of time there."

The Colonel stood up, looked down the table at his crew, and then back to Jake.

"Jake, the food was incredible."

"Thank you very much," was Meg's reply.

The startled Colonel continued.

"You're welcome, Meg. Now down to business. I'm not sure what tomorrow will bring, but I hope everyone at the table will act professionally. I'll be in constant contact with Jake, and let you know how the repairs are going with the shuttle. It's been a long day, so I highly recommend that everyone go to their rooms and get some rest. From what Jake tells me, there's plenty to see on the ship tomorrow."

Morgan was steaming again. "Look, I'm not so sure everything is copasetic. You act like happy space clams, but we are still prisoners. We can't go home, and you won't let me talk to any of my people. This is the greatest discovery of all time, and you're all talking about covering it up. You can't shut me up. I'm the press!"

Bob Cranston, *Excalibur's* engineer, got up and started toward Morgan. The Colonel stopped him just as he was about to take a swing.

"Just give me a minute with that SOB," yelled Cranston as his face turned red in anger. It became obvious to everyone that quiet Cranston had pent up negative thoughts toward Morgan. It seemed that everyone else on board had similar feelings.

As they filed out of the room, the Colonel stopped one last time and shook Jake's hand. He thanked him for all the hospitality and apologized for Morgan. As the door closed, Jake made a quiet remark to Meg, "It could have been a lot worse."

Chapter 39

At about 3 a.m. Jake was startled by Meg's voice.

"Her water broke. Does that have significance?"

Jake shook his head as he quickly tried to process what Meg had asked. He'd heard that phrase twice before from Beth.

"Meg, who are we talking about? None of the female astronauts are pregnant, so please clarify the person to whom you referring."

"Jake, you know I have been monitoring all the astronauts' families, so I can keep them up to date. The copilot's wife, Sally Villars, just had her water break. The Colonel's wife, Carol Brentner is with her and is going to take her to the hospital."

"Is she okay? I mean…. does it sound normal?"

"You have more experience in that area than I have in my databanks. She does seem quite agitated about not knowing what happened to her husband. I can display the situation on the screen if you would prefer."

"Please do. I need to know what's happening before I wake any of the astronauts with a false alarm."

A viewing screen appeared in front of Jake, displaying Carol helping Sally to a chair and trying to calm her down. Sally was very agitated, and Carol was having a very difficult time. Carol decided to call a special number that NASA had given her in case of trouble. She described the problem to the person on the other end, said okay a couple of times, and hung up. She told Sally that a military ambulance was at another location with a severe home accident, and couldn't get there for at least twenty minutes.

Sally screamed in anguish, and Carol picked up the phone to call 911. The conversation was brief, and in just minutes, a siren could be heard in the distance. Jake watched intently as paramedics came in and tried to calm Sally down. They were about to give her a shot when Carol informed them that Sally was very allergic to most of the sedatives. Carol continued to try to calm Sally down as they put her on a stretcher. The group went out of sight, and the image went off the screen.

"Jake, do you want me to inform Sally's husband about the problem?"

"Meg, I don't want you to take offense, but I think it would be better if I told him."

As Jake started to get dressed, he asked Meg, "Please tell me where both Ed Villars and Colonel Brentner's rooms are located. I'm going to need some help with this one, but try not to talk unless I ask. Too many voices in the conversation may upset Ed more than necessary."

"I understand completely, Jake. I will be ready when you ask."

Jake started running down the hall following the instructions Meg had given until he got to Colonel Brentner's room. He started to pound on the door when it opened.

"Meg woke me with music and told me that you needed to see me right now. What's going on?"

"We may have a serious problem. What can you tell me about Ed's wife and her pregnancy?"

"Well, this is their second try as her first ended in a miscarriage. She is allergic to most drugs, so when she became overwrought with the pregnancy, they tried a new drug that made it even worse. Eventually, she lost the baby. That was some time back, and they decided to try again. This time she was under psychological care to minimize her anxiety during the pregnancy. She was doing great until we were ready to go on this mission. I considered replacing Ed, but Sally convinced both Ed and I that she was okay, and Ed should do what he loved. The last time Ed talked with her from the space station, she seemed all right. In fact, she seemed better than ever as she approached her delivery date. I'm assuming that's not the case now."

"You can say that again. Her water just broke, and your wife took her to the hospital via an ambulance. Sally seemed very agitated and kept asking about her husband. I really think we need to talk to Ed, but I decided the two of us needed to do it together."

"Jake, thank you for trusting me, and yes, we need to talk to Ed right away."

The Colonel tied his bathrobe and headed down the hall with Jake right behind. As the Colonel was about to knock on the door, it opened, and Ed had a surprised look on his face. The Colonel and Ed both looked at Jake.

Jake grinned slightly, "What can I say; Meg has a great wake up system."

Jake and the Colonel moved into Ed's room and sat on the couch in front of the TV.

Ed looked at the Colonel with an inquisitive look.

"Colonel, what's going on? Did something happen to *Excalibur*?"

The Colonel hesitated a few moments collecting his thoughts.

"Ed, it's about Sally. Her water broke, and she's not doing well."

The expression on Ed's face fell.

"What's wrong? Is the baby okay? This isn't fair that I'm stuck up here. I really need to be with her."

Jake looked down at the floor for a few seconds and then brought his eyes up to Ed.

"Meg found out about the problem and showed me a visual of Carol and your wife before they went to the hospital. She seemed very upset that you weren't there."

Before Jake could say a word, Ed interrupted.

"Can you show me now? I need to see what's going on."

Jake started to speak, but Meg spoke first.

"As soon as your wife arrives at the hospital, I will show you pictures."

Before Meg could say any more, a viewing screen appeared on the wall in front of the three men, and they could see paramedics racing a gurney down a hospital hallway. They heard Sally yelling Ed's name, and everyone trying to calm her. The image changed as they moved her to a bed, and a doctor started to check her vital signs. Carol filled him in on her allergic drugs problem, as Sally continued to yell at everyone. A nurse remained in the room as the doctor motioned for Carol to exit with him.

A new image appeared from a hallway camera system, and Jake, the Colonel, and Ed continued to watch and listen as the doctor told Carol that the situation was extremely serious. Both Sally and the baby could die if she didn't calm down. Her blood pressure was sky high and could easily put both in extreme danger if not lowered.

The doctor asked why the husband wasn't there, and Carol told him about the shuttle accident. He agreed that was part of the problem, but realized the husband wasn't going to be there to calm her down. He asked Carol to do what she could, and she went back into the room. Sally was still asking about Ed and hadn't settled down a bit.

Ed looked straight at Jake, "You have to do something. With all this technology, there has to be a way for you to help me. That's my wife down there, and she really needs my help."

Jake was at a loss for words but tried to come up with a solution that would be acceptable to Meg. He was about to speak when Meg spoke up.

"There is a way I can help you, Ed, but it will require a promise that you swear to keep."

"Whatever it is, I'll do it. Please, just help me."

"Do you ever watch the *Star Trek* series?"

"What does that have to do with my wife?"

"Do you ever watch *Star Trek*?

"Yes, I do, but only on occasion. I'm not a Trekkie."

"I can beam you down to your wife's room only if you promise to beam back up so to land with your crew. You must not tell anyone how you got there, especially your wife. If you can agree to those terms, I will send you down right now."

180

The Colonel looked at Jake.

"You didn't say anything about beaming technology. What gives?"

Jake explained a nutshell version of the technology and the need to keep its usage to a minimum.

Ed broke in to end of the conversation, "I've heard enough. How do I beam down? Should I go to a transporter somewhere?"

A few seconds rolled by with no response from Meg.

"Ed, there is a small problem. Normally, the transport works best when the subject is lying down, but there is not enough space in your wife's room. You will have to stand in the corner as still as possible and you will be transported to the corner of the hospital room. Remember, you MUST return after you have the situation under control."

Ed nodded and moved to the corner patiently waiting. Soon, a blue hue glowed, and he was gone. He reappeared in the hospital room a few seconds later. At first, neither the nurse nor Sally saw him. Then Sally screamed and the nurse thought she was having another episode, but then she turned and saw Ed too. The nurse was relieved to hear that he was Sally's husband, and in a short matter of minutes, Sally had calmed down.

Hearing the commotion, the doctor and Carol entered, only to be surprised to see Ed sitting next to Sally. Carol started to ask how Ed had gotten there and questioned the whereabouts of her husband. Ed assured her that everyone on the shuttle was okay, but reminded her that the mission was classified so he couldn't talk about it. Ed's main concern was for Sally, and Carol understood the need to address the problem at hand first.

The Colonel was proud of the way his wife had handled the situation and wished he could be there to help. For the next hour, everything was quiet, as Sally had finally settled down. Nurses kept coming in and checking on her progress but then left her alone with husband. Jake asked Meg to give them some privacy, but monitor the situation. The screen went blank for almost an hour.

Jake and the Colonel started to pace the room, as though they were becoming new fathers again. The screen popped on again and two nurses came in, checked Sally, and told Ed that she needed to go to the OR. They moved her back to a gurney and escorted her out the door and down the hall. Ed followed on the side of the bed, holding his wife's hand. Soon they were out of Meg's electronic view and the image in front of Jake disappeared. Jake asked Meg to them aware of any new problems and keep close track of Ed.

As Ed and the gurney turned a corner, a medical assistant caught sight of Ed and quickly ducked into a nearby storage room. He pulled out a cell phone and hit a preset number. The head of Tech Forces, James Randel, picked up the phone and waited for the caller to respond. The attendant knew the procedure well, "Sir; I am at the local hospital, and just saw Ed Villars with his wife as she went into the delivery room."

The attendant waited for a response, knowing that it may require him to come out of his mole status.

"I'm sending down a couple of men to help you. Just wait for them to arrive and their code word is John Anderson. Specifically, follow their orders or you'll never see the light of another day. Do you understand?"

"I understand, and will wait for help."

The attendant stepped back out into the hall and positioned himself so that he had a clear view of the delivery room.

Chapter 40

Colonel Brentner continued to pace the floor.

"Jake, I want to thank you for your help with this present situation. I know you didn't have to, but it is really appreciated."

Jake leaned back on his chair, "You know it would go easier if you sat down and relaxed a little. There's nothing we can do, it's all up to the doc and Sally. Meg was really the one who suggested the idea. I was surprised that she suggested it, but it all seems to be working out. I think we need to catch up on the news. Meg will update us if anything new happens."

Almost instantly, the wall started to display images of the day's events. The Santa Barbara explosion got a few seconds, but the real news was the disappearance of *Excalibur*. Everyone had suppositions about the explosions, possible abductions, and conspiracy theories.

Jake stretched his arms and popped a couple of knuckles. "Meg, please turn off the TV system. Colonel, this might be a good time for the two of us to talk."

The Colonel finally sat down and rocked back in his chair.

"Well, you would probably like to talk, but first, I would like to know how the repairs on the shuttle are going. I would also like to know more about your plans for your ship. I understand why you don't want to share the technology, but do you know how much good it could do in the right hands?"

Before Jake could answer, Meg cut in with, "The repairs on your shuttle are going smoothly. I did find a lot of damage to the primary systems, but your backup systems were turned off at the time the beam was fired, and those systems are undamaged. This will save at least 6 to 8 hours of work for the droids. Is there anything else you wanted to know, Colonel?"

"No, not now, but let me know if there's a change, and maybe you can get me an updated estimate for completion. Thank you."

"Colonel, Meg didn't respond because she saw no need. As to your question about the ship, I really don't know yet what I'm going to do. I was thrown into this situation by chance, but I'm trying to make the best of it. I have a lot of faith in mankind, but little with the military. Those ambitious few that are in control worry me. Besides, there are directives on this ship that don't allow me to share this information anyway.

"As to my plans, I have some problems to work out with my family, and then I'll take it one day at a time. I'm in new territory now and want to make the most of it. My first concern is getting your shuttle fixed, and your crew back on the ground. I have a feeling that this delivery is going to take some time, so why don't you get some shuteye, and I'll let you know when I hear something."

The idea of resting sounded good to the Colonel.

"I'm going to take you up on that, Jake, but make sure you call me."

Jake was getting tired also but was still concerned about all the fires he had to put out.

"Chameleon, are you here?"

The wall to the side started to morph, and Chameleon answered, "Is there something I can do for you?"

"No, it's just sort of nice to know that I'm not alone. All this is starting to get to me. We, humans, get that way when too many things happen at once. I can't multi-task as well as you can."

Jake continued to talk to Chameleon but dozed off in the middle of the next sentence. Chameleon slowly melted back into the wall, and the ship was again very quiet.

The delivery of a new baby girl had gone well although it took several hours. Sally and Ed waited as the nurse cleaned up the new member of the Villars family. Sally was now very relaxed as Ed sat next to her holding her hand. Finally, it dawned on her.

"Ed, how in the hell did you get here? No one said

anything about the shuttle returning. What happened?"

Ed took a deep breath. This wasn't going to be easy.

"Honey, there's no way I can explain it all to you right now. In a couple of days, I may be able to tell you a bit, but right now, it's classified. The important thing is that I was able to get here in time. Unfortunately, I have to get back for debriefing. I was the only one allowed to talk to family. So, I am going to have to leave in a few minutes, but I'll be back in a couple of days."

"Briefings don't take days, they take hours. You're not telling something me. What's going on?"

Ed leaned over and kissed his wife gently.

"Sorry, but I have to go. I'll be fine, and so will the rest of the crew. There's nothing to worry about and Carol will be here to help."

Sally looked intently into Ed's eyes, and realized that whatever was going on, he was going to be all right. He gave her one more kiss and went outside into the hall to find Carol before he was beamed up. She was nowhere in sight, so he wandered down to the nurse's station, and asked if they'd seen Carol. They said she'd gone down a floor to get some coffee and donuts. The elevator opened a few seconds later, and in he stepped. Several men were in the elevator, and he jokingly made a comment about being a new father. The tallest of the four men looked straight at Ed and then to the man behind Ed. Before he knew what had happened, the man behind him had placed a cloth over his face. He became dizzy and passed out.

Jake was now in a deep sleep when Meg spoke, "Jake, wake up. We have a problem."

Jake shook himself awake and looked at a map on the wall of his room. It detailed the hospital and the surrounding area. A blinking dot was moving in a southerly direction away from the hospital.

"Was it a boy or a girl?"

185

"It was a girl, but Ed seems to have left the hospital after the baby was born. He is indicated by the blinking dot on the map. I have tried to contact him, but there is no response. His breathing is very slow, and his brain functions are limited. It appears he was knocked out with some kind of drug, so I am assuming he has been kidnapped."

"Beam him up and then we can find out what's going on."

Meg's response was so close behind that Jake had barely finished the sentence.

"There seems to be some kind of unusual metal foil around the inside of the vehicle and I cannot get a lock on Ed. I will have to wait until he moves away before attempting beaming."

Jake stood and watched as the blinking dot moved away from the hospital and toward open country. Finally, after twenty minutes it stopped.

Ed finally came around and started to whisper.

"Jake, I've been kidnapped. I'm inside a van but I don't know where I am. I hear them coming for me."

Jake listened as he heard several men open the door to the van, and one was giving orders to the other to take Ed to the holding cell. Before Jake could say anything about the situation, he heard Ed yell. "Now, Meg, I'm in the clear."

There was silence for a few seconds, and then Meg spoke. "Ed is in his room. He is still groggy, but seems okay otherwise."

"Great job, Meg. Get the Colonel, and I'll meet him in Ed's room."

Jake was already out the door and down the hall. He opened the door and found Ed on the bed. The Colonel followed in a few seconds later, and Jake filled him in on what had happened.

Jake paced back and forth in front of the two astronauts.

"You know, there's someone out there who really wants this ship, and it looks like they'll do anything to get it. I'm really sorry, but your families are now probably in harm's way. I don't know what to do since I don't know who they are."

There was silence for a few seconds before the Colonel spoke.

"How is the happy father? Did she have a boy or a girl?"

Ed was still groggy.

"Both Sally and our new little girl are doing fine. I can't believe I was so stupid to be caught. I want to thank Meg for bailing me out. That was close. I have a feeling that the cell they were going to take me to was shielded from your beaming technology."

Jake cut into the conversation, "I think we've had enough for one night, or is it morning? Let's get some sleep with the few hours we still have left, and talk later."

They all agreed, and in seconds, they were back in their respective rooms. Within minutes, all three were in snoring.

Chapter 41

Late the next morning, Jake finally awoke after a restful sleep.

"Meg, why didn't you wake me earlier?"

Meg put warm colors on the wall that Jake found soothing.

"You needed your sleep in order to perform your required tasks today. In my research, humans need a day of rest. The work on the shuttle is ahead of schedule. It should be ready to fly tomorrow morning."

Jake rolled his shoulders from side to side before pulling on a T-shirt.

"I appreciate the extra sleep, but I need to be up when the astronauts get up."

"They have been up for at least an hour. I sent them down to the cafeteria for breakfast. They all seem to be in good spirits. The Colonel has already briefed the rest of the crew on the birth last night, so you don't have that responsibility. The only problem this morning is Mr. Morgan. When he found out about the beaming technology, he demanded to be sent down to his newspaper. The rest of the crew asked me to lock him in his room. What do you want to do?"

Jake pulled on his shoes as he thought about his response.

"Can you lock him up? If not, can you at least keep him out of trouble without delaying the shuttle repair?"

Meg spoke to Jake as he slowly walked down the hall.

"I can lock him up, but knowing how he previously reacted, it might make matters worse. I can keep an eye on him as he roams the ship. I have already informed the crew that the shuttle will be ready in the morning. They were becoming agitated not knowing when the repairs were going to be completed."

As Meg finished her report, Jake opened the door to the cafeteria. Everyone was talking at the same time, but when he entered, there was silence. They all looked at Jake, but Morgan was the first to open his mouth.

"I demand that you use this beaming technology to send me down to my newspaper. Now!"

Jake looked at the other astronauts who were awaiting his answer. He knew he had to settle this Morgan problem for the last time.

"Morgan, I'm only going to tell you this once. If you don't shut up and stop making demands, I'll have you locked in the brig for the rest of the time you are here."

Morgan's face turned red, as he blurted, "You can't do that. You don't know how important I am. You'll be sorry."

Jake smiled directly at Morgan.

"I really don't care because I'm not the one who'll put you in the brig. Chameleon will do it."

There was silence as everyone waited as Chameleon morphed out of the wall behind Morgan. Everyone was looking at Morgan, and he quickly realized the giant robot was behind him. For the first time, Morgan was quiet.

Chameleon looked down at Morgan.

"Sir, would you like to take a little trip to the brig?"

The room remained silent. Jake looked up at Chameleon.

"Looks like Mr. Morgan has decided to co-operate with us for now. However, if he starts up again with more demands, feel free to throw him into the brig. I stress the word throw."

Morgan sat down and played with his breakfast, as he knew he'd lost this round. Everyone else in the room began talking again as Chameleon disappeared back into the wall.

Meg whispered into Jake's ear. "I don't have a brig. I assume this is what you call a bluff. It seems to have worked."

Jake tapped a spoon on the side of a coffee cup to get everyone's attention.

"Okay, here's how it's going to work today. You are all free to roam around the ship. I recommend again that you stay away from the shuttle area, or you will slow down the repairs. If you need something from the shuttle, let Meg know and she'll clear it with the repair team. If there's nothing else, enjoy the rest of your day, as you are going home tomorrow."

In just a couple of minutes, most of the crew disappeared exploring different parts of the ship. Jake told the Colonel that if he needed anything, he could get him through Meg. The Colonel said he was going to catch up on the news and get some more rest before more exploration.

Jake made his way from breakfast down to the garden and sat on one of the benches.

"Meg, this isn't going to work. There's no way we can hide you from the planet below. Even if we can shut up Morgan, there are too many unanswered questions. I don't think it's going to work."

"Jake, my diagnostic systems came to the same conclusion last night. Your planet has been overwhelmed with reports of UFOs ever since 1947, yet most people act like don't believe they exist, when in fact, they do. We still have that fact in our favor. The longer we can keep everyone confused, the better chance we have to protect this technology."

"I agree with your assessment, but I'm not sure where I want to go after I get rid of the shuttle and see my family."

"Jake, you can take all the time you need to make that decision. Once *Excalibur* is gone, we will immediately move to a more secure location. Until then, as you say, we have to take one day at a time."

Jake laughed, "That sounds very human of you. On another subject, how's it going with that secret room that you don't know about or you can't open? That still bothers me that your creators left you in the dark on that one."

"So far, the encryption to the electronic lock is blocked by a special protocol in my basic language. When I try to access the decryption, it stops me and I cannot override it. I will continue to work on the problem, but do not yet see a possible solution."

Jake got up from the bench and looked around

"Chameleon?"

"Yes, Jake."

"Just checking," said Jake with a grin.

Jake headed back to his room. He had another important conversation to have, and he knew the shuttle crew would be busy for the rest of the day. As he walked into his room, he shouted. "I want to see the living room in my house." The view screen came on and the living room was empty. Then Jake saw Brad walk by with schoolbooks, yelling that he was leaving for school. In the background, he could see Kathy putting on a sweater. She was yelling to her mother that she was leaving and that Brad was being a pain again. Jake waited until they left, and Beth walked by the TV.

"Hi, Beth, Jake here."

Startled, Beth looked at the TV. There was her husband's smiling face. She was about to speak when she remembered that she was being monitored. She chose her words carefully. "Hi, Jake. It's about time you called. How're you doing?"

Jake wished he could talk more openly with her but knew it could put her in more danger.

"I've had better days, but everything is fine. We had a couple of problems to deal with in the middle of the night, but all is good now. I wish I could be there, but I still have a lot to do in the next six or seven days. I'll try to check in every day. I love you and the kids."

Beth sat down on the couch and tried to relax. She was having a very hard time with all this cloak-and-dagger stuff.

"The kids are doing fine. Brad is still getting into trouble. You really need to talk to him when you get here. I really wish I knew more of what's going on."

"I should see you in a week or so. A lot depends on how long it takes to get my ducks in a row."

Jake hoped Beth knew what he meant.

Beth soaked in the code. They'd been in a conversation when they first met, and somehow the term "ducks in a row"

191

came up. Jake had gone into a big dissertation on where the phrase came from, and that it took no more than a day to get all your ducks in a row. Therefore, that meant he should be home in 1 to 2 days. She could handle that, but he'll surely have a lot of explaining to do.

"Okay, Jake. See you in about a week."

Chapter 42

The call came into James Randel a few minutes later from one of the men monitoring the bugs in Jake's home.

"Sir, it looks like a conversation between Jake McDonald and his wife indicates that he's not coming down for a week or so."

Randel thought this statement over for a few seconds. "Could it be a trick? Did the conversation sound like a code?"

"Yes sir, there's a chance that the conversation relayed a different return time than Jake indicated."

"Okay, then be prepared at a moment's notice to grab the family. Make sure you don't harm them. I want viable hostages. Do you understand?"

The technician gave an affirmative reply and hung up the phone.

Randel leaned back in his chair, and thought to himself, *what the hell are you up to, Jake?*

The rest of the day was uneventful if you could call being on a spaceship uneventful. The *Excalibur* crew spent the remainder of their time exploring the ship. Morgan pouted in his room for hours before deciding to use the remaining power in his digital camera to record more of the ship interior. Jake spent a couple of hours resting before venturing down to the lower half of the ship. He wanted to check on the shuttle repairs, and see how his new X-wing Fighter was progressing. The shuttle repairs were going even faster than planned and would be ready early the next day. The X-wing was about half completed, but Meg informed him that construction would be accelerated once the shuttle departed.

Jake wandered toward the mystery room and wondered why the builders would keep it a secret from Meg. The more he thought about it, the more it bothered him. What if some terrible weapon was inside? Maybe it was a quarantine zone, and he was trying to break-in. He should probably just leave it alone, but he couldn't. He needed to know all the facts before he decided what to do with his life.

The day went by quickly, and before long, it was time for the crew's final dinner. When Jake reached the cafeteria, he could hear the sounds of the shuttle crew apparently having a good time. When he opened the door, he was surprised to find wine, beer, and mid-size robots serving appetizers. Jake smiled and knew that Meg could always surprise him.

Ed's voice was heard above the others.

"Hey Jake, you're missing a great party. Look at all this stuff. All we have to do is simply ask for it, and it magically appears. We can't wait to see what we get for dinner."

The Colonel took a spoon and tapped his wine glass, and got everyone's attention.

"Let's toast to Jake and Meg. Without the two of you, we'd all be dead. We are eternally grateful. Thanks from everyone on *Excalibur*."

With that, the entire crew minus Morgan gave a loud cheer and everyone sat down to one of the best meals any of them had ever eaten.

As the meal ended, Jake stood up and got everyone's attention.

"I know you're all anxious to get home tomorrow, and I'm on that same wavelength. I will not be far behind flying my new X-wing Fighter. Several of you have mentioned you would like to fly it, but you'll have to take your shuttle. You've been a great group, and I wish we could have met under better circumstances. Meg tells me that as soon as you have breakfast tomorrow, you are free to take off. I will be there to see you go. Enjoy yourselves tonight, but don't party too much, as you have an early flight."

The group gave Jake a huge cheer, and they all partied until late that evening. Jake remained until the last crewmember

194

was gone and then crawled into bed.

"Meg, make sure you wake me up before they leave. I would like to see them off."

With that, Jake nodded off into dreamland and had the first full night's sleep he'd had in ages.

Chapter 43

Jake awoke to the sounds of the shuttle crew engaged in excited conversation. As he sat up in his bed, he realized that the sounds were being piped in from the restaurant.

"Meg, I thought I told you to wake me when the crew was at breakfast."

"I would have, except that several crewmembers never went to bed. Two of them went back to their rooms for less than 30 minutes, before returning to the restaurant. Over the next few hours, most of the crew joined them. They all seemed very excited about returning to their families."

"May I remind you, Meg, that I too am just as excited."

"I understand, Jake. The shuttle repair is completed and the work on your X-wing is now using 100% of the workforce. If all goes as planned, it should be ready late tomorrow or early the next day. I highly recommend that you get down to the restaurant, as the crew is getting a little out of control."

Jake quickly pulled on clothes and within moments, he opened the restaurant's doors. Before he could say a word, every crewmember bombarded him with questions about the shuttle and the flight home. The noise level was deafening. He tried to yell above their voices but to no avail. Finally, Colonel Brentner came to the rescue with a military command bringing them to attention. Their immediate silence was heavenly. Jake stood in the middle of the room and gathered his thoughts about what to say.

"Sorry, but I really don't have a clue how this is going to work. Meg has worked out all the details and hopefully, she'll explain them to you now."

The five-second silence seemed more like five minutes, but they patiently waited for Meg's instructions.

"I can tell the space shuttle crew that it has been tested and is ready to go. You can load all of your personal belongings and head home. I ask that you take nothing from the ship that you didn't bring with you. If you do, I will have to remove it as you load the shuttle."

One of the crewmembers started to interrupt, but Meg cut him off.

"I know you all have plenty of questions, but if you let me walk you through the entire process, most of your questions should be answered. Once all of your belongings are loaded, the seals on the shuttle will close and be verified. The docking doors will open, and small robots will push you out in space several miles from this location. A flight plan has already been locked into your computer from the engine start to landing. During the repair of your shuttle, a special coating was applied to the bottom of the shuttle that will make you invisible to ground tracking systems. When you start to enter the atmosphere, this coating will burn off, and you will slowly become visible to ground control. I don't know how you want to explain your sudden appearance, but you might start thinking about your explanations. You may now ask your questions."

Everyone tried to jump in at once, but Colonel Brentner took charge and allowed each member to ask his or her question. Most were basic concerns about the reliability of the shuttle, while others were worried that it would be difficult to keep the ship's existence quiet. One member even asked if they could come back for a visit.

Meg answered each question logically, and most of the crewmembers were eager to head home once their questions were answered. The meeting lasted no longer than fifteen minutes, and all the crew disappeared to their rooms, except the Colonel. Meg had anticipated this and waited until all the crew was out of listening range before continuing.

"I assume, Colonel that you have more confidential questions, which you don't want the crew to hear."

The Colonel pushed what was left of the steak and egg breakfast to the opposite edge of the table. As he did, the plate disappeared.

"You've got that right. You were kind enough to fix all the shuttle's problems, and that was great. The problem is that if we're trying to convince everyone that our shuttle was disabled for the last three days, it will be a hard sell with all the repairs your robots have made."

Jake knew Meg had a solution and listened intently as Meg continued her elaborate description.

"Well, Colonel the repairs we made are not to NASA specifications. We actually left most of the burned-out portions on the circuit boards alone. We just added a new coat of circuitry that duplicates the original tasks of the circuits. When you enter the atmosphere, communications to NASA will show the burned-out layers. In truth, the shuttle will be operating on full automatic using newly added circuit layers. When the shuttle lands, the upper layer of circuitry will vaporize. You will have to pretend that you are manually landing the shuttle, even though you are not doing so. When landing the shuttle, I would advise you to stay as close to the automatic functions as possible. When Morgan starts to tell everyone his fantastic story, the repaired portions will not exist."

The Colonel took a minute to let all this new information soak in.

"Granted Morgan will look like a fool on that part, but the rest of his story may hold water when he starts babbling. He's very good at collecting information, even if he is a jerk."

Jake was shaking his head at Meg's creative deceptions. Some of it he knew about, but the layered boards were new. He was about to ask his own question when Meg cut in.

"Sorry, I don't mean to break in, Jake, but the Colonel needs to know the rest of the story. Your concern about Morgan is well founded. In the last couple of days, he has been going around the ship photographing everything he could to back up his story. I am going to let him take those memory cards with him, but with one slight adjustment to their content. If he shows them to the public, he will dig what you commonly call a very deep hole."

Jake couldn't stand it anymore.

"What did you put on those cards, Meg?"

"Jake, you should know that creating a sense of mystery makes me just a bit more human."

Jake and the Colonel laughed, shook hands, and headed toward the lower section of the ship. As they passed the X-wing Fighter, Jake noticed the increased work activity. The Colonel grinned at Jake.

"It looks like your ride is just about ready to go."

Jake sheepishly laughed.

"Too bad I don't know how to fly."

The Colonel turned to Jake and said, "I have a feeling that Meg is a very good flight instructor."

By the time the two finally reached the hanger, the entire crew was onboard. The Colonel took one last look around the hanger and smiled.

"Jake, I sure wish there was a way you could use this technology to help us at NASA. There are so many places in the solar system and beyond that, this ship could explore. Think of all the medical discoveries you could pass on to the world. I do understand that it's a very naive concept because there are power-hunger people down there, and all would want a piece of it. My advice to you is to use this technology wisely, and trust no one. Now I'm going to get down off my soapbox. All I can say is good luck because I think you'll need it."

Jake looked over to the shuttle and then back to the Colonel.

"Colonel, at first this whole idea of bringing you all aboard was pretty crazy, but I think it worked out great with the exception of Morgan. I trust that you and the crew will do your best to keep the ship a secret as long as possible. That's all I can ask. Safe travels."

The Colonel and Jake shook hands one more time, and the

Colonel closed the door in preparation for takeoff. The landing bay's doors opened, and three small droid robots with rockets slowly moved *Excalibur* out into space. They directed *Excalibur* into an insertion path that would allow its safe landing in California.

Over the intercom on *Excalibur*, the crew heard the last words from Jake.

"You have been great guests, and I'm sorry you had to wait so long to return home. I also wish there was another way for you to explain why you disappeared. I realize now that the cover story will not last forever. All I ask is that you maintain the facade as long as possible."

Morgan then cut into the speaker conversation.

"Not if I can help it. There's no way you can stop me from telling the world what happened up here. It's my duty to tell everyone how you held us captive, and wouldn't let us contact anyone on Earth."

Bob Cranston, the engineer started to unbuckle his belt.

"Just give me a couple of minutes with that son of a bitch, and he'll have no teeth or usable fingers to tell anyone anything."

The Colonel turned and looked at Cranston.

"It's okay, Cranston. We'll stick to our story, and Morgan can stick to his. Five to one sounds like good odds to me. Besides, I understand most of the press on the ground hates Morgan."

"They don't hate me. They envy me because I'm so good at what I do."

Cranston voiced from behind.

"Someone get me a barf bag. This Morgan crap is going to make me puke."

The Colonel could feel the release of the rocket droids, and the auto systems kick in.

"Okay, crew this is it. We're on our way home. Let's do what we do best."

Chapter 44

For the last three days, the NASA staff had been monitoring, checking, and rechecking in an effort to find any clue to the whereabouts of the lost shuttle. Most of the night shift had gone and a new crew complete with coffee and donuts took over. The technicians were making small talk when several NASA alarms started going off, including those hooked in from NORAD. Something was coming in fast on the same track that the shuttle used for landing in California.

Within seconds, one of the operators contacted Joe Charger, the flight director.

"Sir, we have something coming in hot and heavy. All telemetry indicates it is *Excalibur*. Sir, the initial readings indicate that most of the onboard systems are burned out."

"Listen up. Get the night shift back here and cancel all time off. Have you heard from anyone onboard yet?"

The technician was quick to answer, as seconds lost could be a disaster at NASA.

"Some of the medical instrumentation is working, and we're noting several live bodies onboard. Communication is just static, but it should clear in a few seconds."

Everyone in the command room waited for what seemed like an eternity. Then as the static started to clear, everyone heard the most wonderful sound.

"This is Colonel Brentner requesting permission to land on any runway you have clear."

The entire room erupted into a cheer.

Charger held his hands in the air to quiet everyone.

"Craig, you old dog, where have you been for the last three days? You guys scared the hell out of us."

Again, a short silence before the answer came from Colonel Brentner.

"Well, that's a long story, and although I would like to tell you about it, please note that there are no auto controls left, and I'm attempting to land manually. I would like to talk more, but my hands are full."

Charger picked up the phone and immediately the President and all of NASA knew about *Excalibur* and its critical situation.

Within seconds, that same information was passed on to James Randel at Tech Forces. He already had new plans in play to kidnap the best candidate to garner information about the ship hiding in space.

As *Excalibur* came down through the atmosphere, it veered drastically to the left, and then to the right. It was a little difficult at first for the Colonel to pretend he was manually flying, but eventually, he got the hang of the fake landing sequence. The enlarged staff in the NASA control center watched *Excalibur* moving on and off course. After miraculously appearing to stay on course, *Excalibur* finally touched down but continued to pass by the area where most shuttles stop. It seemed that the mechanisms used to slow *Excalibur* had failed, or so it appeared that way. As soon as *Excalibur* stopped, all the top layers on all the repaired circuits vaporized. At first, the crew was alarmed, but the Colonel informed them that everything was fine and to concentrate their efforts on exiting. As per emergency procedures, chutes were deployed and the entire crew made a quick escape from the now smoking *Excalibur.*

Jake watched the action from the large viewing screen that Meg had provided in his room. In fact, it displayed more than a dozen views and angles of the action. Jake was totally mesmerized by the events taking place.

"Well, Meg you did it. You saved the shuttle and its crew. Too bad the rest of the world doesn't know who really saved them."

"Jake, I did what was best for you, me, and the crew.

Nothing more, and nothing less. It is now up to the shuttle crew and NASA to sort out their problems. Our next problem is getting you down to your family."

Jake yelled out, "You're damn right. It's time for me to go home."

"Not just yet, Jake, we still have a few more systems to install on the X-wing. I would recommend that you take some time and rest. You are going to have a big day tomorrow."

Before Meg could even finish the conversation, Jake had dozed off.

On the ground, all hell was breaking loose. NASA was so caught off guard that it took some time to realize that the crew needed to be debriefed first. A security team was quickly put together and all the crew except Morgan had been escorted to a holding area with several guards at the doors. The Colonel and the crew understood the reason for this action, but they were still pissed they couldn't first see their families. Morgan had already anticipated this action and coolly slipped out a side door, grabbed a taxi and was on his way to his news station. He was so efficient at his escape that both NASA security and the TF agents let him slip through their fingers.

When Morgan reached the newspaper, he had the cab driver drive him into the lower parking garage. He paid the driver but gave him no tip, which earned him the middle finger. Morgan could care less because he was going to be the most famous person in the world. He could already see a Pulitzer and the cover of Time magazine.

He took side doors to avoid as many people as possible. As he reached the press floor, he realized he had a stroke of luck. Everyone on the floor was glued to the large viewing screen displaying the recent *Excalibur* landing. He crept into his office, punched up his computer, and started to download his memory card images into a special directory. As soon as this was accomplished, he compressed the directory and encrypted it with a sophisticated password system. Morgan then logged onto another encrypted data site that he'd purchased a year ago, and copied the files to that site. Finally, he pulled out two identical memory cards and copied the images to the second set of memory cards. This second set would be the set he would present to his editor. The originals were stored in a waterproof container at the bottom of a flowerpot.

Once that was all done, he leaned back in his chair and spoke as if talking to the crew of *Excalibur*.

"You all thought I was nothing and treated me like trash. Just wait until I plaster all the images of the ship in the next edition of the paper. You're all history."

Just then, the voice of the editor could be heard as he approached Morgan's office.

"Morgan, what the hell is going on?"

Chapter 45

NASA had a serious dilemma. The crew's first few answers didn't make sense. All their stories were the same, in fact, a bit too similar. Their explanations of the beam hitting the ship, three days attempting to repair *Excalibur*, and then making a virtually impossible return to Earth had NASA baffled. The questioning went on for hours, but because of mounting pressure from their families, NASA released the crew.

NASA flight director, Joe Charger, sat in Frank Mendol's office.

"Frank, I don't know what's going on with the crew, but their stories don't hold water. They all seem very sincere about their version of what happened, but it's hard to believe."

Mendol's mind was spinning. First, he lost *Excalibur*, and now it was back.

"Joe, are you telling me that the entire crew has a false story about what happened? That seems almost impossible. It might be possible for two or three crewmembers, but not Colonel Brentner. He'd never lie about military matters."

Charger took in a deep breath, and exhaled, "Are you really sure you know the Colonel? There's even a lot more that doesn't make any sense. When our technicians did a quick check of *Excalibur*, they confirmed that there was no way it could have landed in its present state."

Mendol started to comment, but Charger continued, "As you know, we had extensive blood work, X-rays, and just about every medical test done on each astronaut before takeoff. Upon their return, we did a quick physical assessment of each crewmember and found them in better health than before they left on the mission. Even crazier is co-commander Villars' medical status. He had a couple of broken bones as a kid, and a shrapnel wound from the last Gulf war. None of those now exist, which is physically impossible."

Mendol leaned forward on his chair and looked straight into Charger's eyes.

"Get them all back here first thing the morning for further debriefing. Their families be damned. We need to know what the hell happened up there. One other thing, how did Morgan get past our security? It doesn't matter now as there's nothing we can do about it, and he's probably already at his newspaper."

Morgan's editor was now standing directly in front of him giving him the evil eye.

"Okay, Morgan, no more stalling. How did you get away from *Excalibur*, and where have you been the last three days?"

Morgan was beaming as if he'd just grabbed the brass ring.

"It doesn't matter how I got here. What's important is that I have the most important story of all time to tell. It will put this newspaper on top."

The editor wasn't impressed.

"I've heard that before. You always come up with some kind of hair-brained story that no one could ever believe. So, were you abducted by aliens?"

Morgan held out his hand disclosing the two memory cards.

"This time I have absolute proof for my front-page article. I know you won't believe it, but *Excalibur* was abducted by a large alien spaceship."

The editor started to laugh and walk away when Morgan frantically continued.

"Wait, I have proof. I took pictures of the entire inside of the spaceship. If you enlarge them, you'll see that they're the real deal."

The editor moved over to a workstation and pointed to the memory card slot.

"Morgan, you have five minutes to show me these Earth-shaking images of your alien abduction. If this is another one of your fantasy stories, you'll be out of work in this town and every state if I have any say in it."

Morgan knew his time was running out, so he grabbed the first memory card and pushed it into the card reader slot. The computer asked typical introductory questions, so he selected the option to view the images as a slide show. The first ones on the screen were a shock to Morgan since they weren't any images he'd taken.

The editor looked for a second and then commented gruffly.

"That's the spaceship from the movie, *The Day the Earth Stood Still*. Is this some kind of sick joke?"

Quickly, Morgan viewed the next slide, and it was from the original version of *War of the Worlds* and showed the triangle-shaped spaceships with long necks. As Morgan viewed the images, he realized that each was from a famous Sci-Fi movie or photos of faked UFOs.

After suffering through more than two dozen images, the editor turned and stormed away

"Morgan, your ass is fired effective immediately! Security will escort you and your belongings out of the building within the hour."

Morgan was in shock. His face turned from red with anger to white as he envisioned the dread of unemployment. The entire newsroom was silent and Morgan tried to figure out where he'd gone wrong. Then he heard the footsteps of the security guard assigned to escort him from his office. The officer seemed to be in a great hurry. He even helped Morgan pack all his belongings and put them in boxes. The guard had brought a dolly with him, which seemed strange, but at the time, Morgan could care less. In twenty minutes, the two were on their way out the side door of the newspaper.

Morgan started toward his car, but a large black van pulled up in front before he could step onto the parking lot pavement. Two men got out, grabbed Morgan, held a cloth over his face, and pulled him into the van. Morgan's belongings were thrown in, and the dolly was thrown to the sidewalk, as the van made a hasty exit.

Chapter 46

Jake jerked awake as he raised his head from the restaurant table.

"Meg, how long have I been out?"

"Just thirty minutes, Jake, but as you humans like to say, all hell has broken loose."

Jake rubbed his tired eyes, started to stand, and realized that he was a physical wreck.

"Meg, we need to talk. And I don't mean just about my family, but everything."

"Jake, everything would take more than your lifetime to discuss."

"Well maybe not everything, but I do have a long list. It includes my family, the *Excalibur* crew, Morgan, the X-wing, who tried to shoot *Excalibur* down, the room you can't get into, and your prediction that the Earth is about to end. Do you want me to continue?"

As Jake listed his concerns, Meg had conveniently posted the list on the wall.

"I assume that the list is in the order you would you're your answers."

Jake smiled, "You got you that right. Let me get a beer, and you can tell me all about my family."

Morgan slowly started to move around on the tiny cot and heard a voice in the background. His eyes were starting to focus and could almost make out a large fluorescent light overhead. His head hurt and he was weak.

Henry Winston, the bank teller, was still yelling at him from the adjoining cell.

"Hey, you next door. Who are you, and how did you get here?"

Henry's question went unanswered as Morgan drifted back

off to sleep.

Pete Killian leaned back in his chair at the Technical Forces special headquarters. James Randel was sitting next to him and they were both focused on the TV monitor of the two men in their cells.

Killian spoke first.

"We really didn't get much out of the bank teller. Do you think putting them together will improve our chances for information gathering?"

Randel leaned forward and pressed his finger against the image of Morgan.

"This man is the key. He's an arrogant, obnoxious, son of a bitch, but he's also cunning and resourceful. He did see the inside of the ship, and I think the ship's commander manipulated the memory card's data to discredit Morgan. If we just ask him what he saw, we won't get anywhere. No, we'll wait and see how these two interact. We might be surprised at the information we will gain from this jailed merger."

As the two waited patiently viewing at the monitor, Morgan finally responded to the bank teller.

"Before I tell you anything, you need to tell me where I am, and who kidnapped me."

Henry had already been held for several days, so this company was a nice welcome.

"Hey, I don't know a whole lot, as I was kidnapped too. I work for a local bank, and everything was fine until Jake came back."

Morgan's eyes flared.

"Jake. Do you mean Jake McDonald?"

Henry was surprised that the newcomer would know Jake's last name.

"Yes, he's married to my boss's daughter. Jake was a lobster fisherman until a couple of weeks ago when he assumedly died in a diving accident. He then reappeared a few days later at his home, but that wasn't the really weird part."

Morgan had now moved next to the wall between the cells.

"What do you mean?"

"I saw him talking to his family one minute, and the next minute he disappeared in a blue flash. His family seemed as shocked as I was. So, how do you know him?"

To Morgan, this was all starting to make sense. He questioned whether he should say anything about the ship to his cellmate. He wanted to keep it to himself, but he wasn't having much luck with anyone believing him. If this banker knew Jake, maybe he could form some kind of partnership and still get his Pulitzer.

"I do know Jake, but I need to tell you the whole story." Morgan then started with the launch of *Excalibur*, the unexplained beam that fired at *Excalibur*, the escort to the ship for repairs, and their eventual return to Earth.

Henry scratched his forehead.

"You know if I hadn't seen Jake beam away, I would've thought your story was crazy too. So, what does the world think of an alien spaceship orbiting the Earth?"

Morgan knew he might as well give Henry the whole story as there was no sense holding back with this potential ally.

"Jake made a deal with the *Excalibur* crew that for helping them return home, they not tell NASA about the ship. I didn't agree, and I think that's why I'm here. I think we're being held captive by some secret government agency that doesn't want the truth to come out. If you help me get out of here, I'll include you in my story and you'll become a hero."

Henry thought about that for a second. Maybe he no longer needed Beth. There was still hope that he could move up in the bank, because of this newfound hero status. That worked for him.

James Randel clicked off the monitor.

"I knew it. Morgan had to know that we were listening,

but his ego is so big he had to tell someone. Now we have enough information to put the whole thing together. As crazy as it seems, a lobster fisherman finds a spaceship, moves it into space, saves the *Excalibur* crew, and is now hiding somewhere up there with technology years ahead of ours. We MUST have it.

"Pete, I want a full surveillance team on McDonald's family. I need to be able to grab the entire family within minutes. Use as many men as you need and there's no limit on budget. If you have to kill someone in the process, then so be it. Just make damn sure that none of Jake's family is hurt. Stay far enough away that you aren't detected. This may be just the edge we need to take over the planet and stop all wars and conflicts. Humankind requires that we confiscate this technology to get this planet back on track."

Killian listened intently knowing that any interruption wasn't a good idea. In the order to acquire the planet as Randel demanded, would mean the deaths of millions of people who opposed the new order. Randel considered himself a self-made God put on the planet to save it from itself. Killian didn't totally agree with his methods, but he wasn't about to cross Randel. Therefore, he saluted his boss, made a military turn, and quickly left the room.

Chapter 47

Jake was back in his room and the beer had taken the edge off his uneasiness as he prepared for his conversation with Meg.

"Meg, let's start with my family. Are they safe?"

"Jake, first I must tell you that the group that tried to bring down *Excalibur* is called Technical Forces, or TF, and has personnel in every aspect of the political and military structures. Even with all my technology, I still have not been able to break into their command center as they have a very high level of security encryption. I have been able to determine that they have Morgan hidden somewhere in the southwest portion of the U.S. Their communications indicate that they know about our ship and its approximate location, which is more than NASA knows. I am confident that they now know you are in command of the ship."

"What about my family?

"I have been monitoring your family and home, but have seen no indication of additional surveillance other than the electronic bugs placed in your house. Since I can beam only one person at a time, I think it would be unwise to try to beam them out. The other two would probably be kidnapped before I could get them all safely out. Jake, be assured that I am working on a way to get them safely out. As advanced as TF seems, I would assume that they are holding back and leaving your family alone until they feel they need them."

"So, they are in danger. I need to get down there as soon as possible. When will the X-wing be ready?"

Meg was quick with the response as Jake was even more agitated.

"The X-wing will be ready early tomorrow morning. Before you can take it to see your family, you will have to take it on a test flight. Once that is completed, you can fly it down to see your family. I have selected an uninhabited area near Santa

213

Barbara for your landing, and from there you can catch rides. I have created a simulator next to the X-wing that will help speed up your flying skills since you have none."

Jake placed his hands on his hips and quipped, "That wasn't nice. I know I don't know how to fly a plane, but hey, just a couple of days ago I was on a fishing boat off Santa Barbara. Now I'm in command of the most powerful ship man has ever seen. Therefore, anything is possible. Besides, I'm a fast learner."

"Good, as soon as I answer the rest of your questions, we can start your training. The *Excalibur* crew have all kept their promises so far, which is longer than I computed. Although it will not be long before one of the crew breaks down and tells NASA what has happened.

"Jake, I recommend that you contact Colonel Brentner and let him off the hook. I would like to give your friend a break, and I also suspect that once NASA finds out about the ship, they will keep that information from the public."

Jake was surprised at such a human response.

"Meg, you keep surprising me. The more I get to know you, the more human you seem to be. I was just about to ask if I could release the Colonel from his promise, and you beat me to it. It's almost as if you can anticipate my every move."

"Jake, that is actually what is happening. The more I work with you, the more I can anticipate your wishes. In my research, I ran across a TV show called *Mash*. You might see me as your..."

"Radar," yelled out Jake. "Hey, that's pretty cool. So, you're saying that if I want a beer, it would appear before I ask for it?"

"Eventually that will be true. In time, you will not even have to talk with me as I will be able to read your thoughts."

Jake was a bit shaken by that statement.

"You mean that you will be wandering around in my head, looking at all my secrets?"

"No, it's just that when you want to communicate with me,

I will sense those specific thoughts and act upon them. As of now, I have not progressed that far, so you will need to verbally communicate your needs to me.

"Let's proceed to the next item on your list. The room that is hidden from me still eludes all my efforts to open the door. The material around the room is comprised of a compound I am not familiar with, so I cannot break through any of the walls. I will keep trying, but it may take weeks to open."

Jake was about to ask for another beer, but it appeared in front of him.

"Wow, that was freaky. Cool, but freaky at the same time. I'm afraid to ask about the last subject on my list, but what the hell. This whole week has been a real roller-coaster ride."

Jake waited for the bad news, as it appeared on the wall. It was an image of the future Earth, but it was not blue and green, but rather brown on brown.

"Jake, I am really sorry, but after extensive research, I have concluded that the human race has less than a five percent chance of making it beyond the year 2200. I cannot exactly tell you how it will happen, but I can tell you that there are many negative factors against survival and one, or a combination of several, will push mankind into oblivion."

"Wow," was all Jake could say.

"High on the list is the detonation of a terrorist nuclear weapon in the U.S. that escalates into World War III. Unfortunately, most of your science fiction writers assume that a small fraction of humans will survive, but my research indicates that the amount of radiation in an all-out nuclear war will only leave cockroaches and some of their relatives. All warm-blooded animals will die first, then most of the cold-blooded species. Insects will probably be the dominant species after such a war."

Jake knew the news would be bad, but not that bad.

"What if we can avoid World War III? Do we have a chance then?"

"Unfortunately, uncontrolled population growth, the

increase of deadlier diseases, man's amplified interest in bio-weapons, pollution issues, ozone problems, climate changes, and natural disasters will all contribute to the downfall of mankind. If man could attack all these problems within the next few years, it could survive, but that is the five percent I mentioned. The nature of humans craving power and greed will be the planet's demise. I'm sorry, Jake, but you wanted to know."

Jake scratched the side of his face and said, "What if we showed the people in power this ship, and explained what is about to happen to this planet? Would that not change their thinking?"

"To some, it would, but most would be trying to find ways to obtain possession of the ship, and control Earth. The sad truth, Jake, is that humans are not ready to use this ship for positive means."

"You let me run the ship. You trust me and I'm human. Why do you let me use the ship and no one else?"

"Jake, there are humans who would do good things with the ship and change mankind's direction. You are one of them. My creators gave me the ability to analyze the sentient beings I first encountered to determine if they fit into the creators' requirements for using this ship. You were suitable, but my creators have prevented either of us from using the ship to change mankind's history. You can use the ship to visit other planets, but you cannot use it to control or change the governments of this planet or any other planet. It is much like the prime directive that your science fiction writers have for the *Star Trek* series."

"So, my kids and their kids are going to have to pay for all our sins against this planet. Is there no other way?"

The image of the Earth disappeared and was replaced with an image of space. Suddenly the viewing screen began zooming past solar system after solar system from planet to planet. Some were barren; while others looked like Earth.

"Jake, there is another solution, but you are not going to

like it. The universe is much larger than you could ever imagine. Earth is not the only place for a man to live. Maybe we should discuss that at another time, as your family is your first priority. Why don't you take a break, and then come down to the X-wing hanger? The simulator is ready for you to try."

The image on the wall disappeared, and Jake lay back on his bed. In seconds, his mind was at the subconscious level. He dropped off to sleep, dreaming he was again with his family.

This time it was different. He was at home watching TV when men broke into the house and pointed guns at them all. They grabbed each member of his family, each screaming as loudly as they could, and removed them from the house. The last man turned toward Jake and threw a note down on the coffee table. As he reached to pick it up, he was awakened from his dream by Meg.

"I'm sorry to wake you, Jake, but I could tell by your sleep and the REMs coming from your brain, that you were having a bad dream. I thought it better that I stop the dream, but you can sleep again if you prefer."

"No, I've had enough. I want to learn how to fly the X-wing. I'm on my way down to the bay. See you there."

"I am already there."

Jake forced a small laugh, "Sorry, forgot you are everywhere."

Jake was so excited, he practically flew down to the hanger. Next to the X-wing was a small sphere floating above the deck. Jake walked around the base but saw no opening. Before he could ask, Meg explained.

"The simulator will come down to the floor so you can climb in from the top. Once you are in, I will instruct you on how to fly your new aircraft. The inside of the simulator is exactly like the real X-wing plane, and reacts the same way."

While Meg was explaining, the sphere lowered to the floor, the top opened and small wedge steps appeared along its side. There was a handle at the uppermost portion, which allowed Jake to grab and hoist himself to the top of the simulator. As Jake slipped down into the flight chair, the top door closed. He marveled as he discovered a myriad of displays and controls that instantly sprung to life.

"Jake, here is how it works. The view out the front of the simulator looks like a windshield and will display your direction as you interface with the main computer. When it asks you a question about speed, destination, or other flight options, the ship's present settings will be displayed. As I told you before, the ship operates similar to a computer game but does not have gravity as part of its parameters. If you do not move the stick forward, backward, up, or down, you will not move. The more you move the control forward, the faster you will go. The computer will warn you of any impending dangers, such as trees, mountains, or other obstacles that would impede your flight. If you do not want to manually fly the plane, you can just tell it where you want to go, and it will take you there. However, I do suggest that you try some manual flight controls, in case there is a problem with computer control."

Jake's heart started to beat a little faster.

"You mean there's a chance that I could lose computer control of the plane? Remember, I've never flown at all except as a passenger in an airliner."

"Jake, do not worry. The odds of a computer failure are less than one percent, and if that happens, I will take control of the plane. You have nothing to worry about."

Jake pushed back into his seat, and as he did, several automatic straps went around his legs and chest. At first, he jumped, but then realized that it was just part of the process. In front of him, the bay doors opened, and a message came across the screen that read, *Ready to Disembark*. He slowly pushed the lever forward, and the ship began to move. Suddenly he was out in space. He increased the speed and moved the control to the left and the ship came into view. He turned the X-wing simulator control to the right and flew past the ship. For the next 15 minutes, Jake experimented trying more and more difficult turns and maneuvers.

"Hey, Meg, this is just like one of those really fancy video games. If the real X-wing is no different than this simulator, then it will be a piece of cake."

When the flight was over Jake exited the simulator and walked over to the real X-wing exclaiming *tomorrow, you're mine.*

Jake hurried back to his room because he needed to email Brad before the end of the day. He sat down in front of the computer and got ready to type. The code Brad and Jake were using was difficult to translate in his head, and he was frustrated because he knew it would take some time to compose.

"Jake, I know how your code works. It is actually very clever. I know you find this frustrating so I will make it easy for you. Just concentrate on what you want to say to Brad, and I will be able to read your thoughts and send the coded message to him."

Jake sat back from the keyboard and concentrated. Soon the video screen started to display the coded message to Brad.

RU IK IM AU RK AO EO ST RT PT LT 1 2 AA AT JT J AM EMM IK FT ATM IO UD UT MF MR ME GR MI MEN ME MP TTE TTI TTTD TN 9 6 TS TTE

When Jake was finished, he started to look at the coded message and translate the first couple of words.

"That was incredible, Meg. It looks like you did great transcribing the message."

"Jake, your code is unique, but remember that those men monitoring have some of the most sophisticated decoding equipment on the planet. They will eventually figure it out. The only reason it will take some time is the uniqueness of the keys."

Randel had just finished a call, when Killian came into the office, walked over to one of the monitors, and turned it on.

"Look at what we just recorded a few minutes ago. Jake's son picked up this email on his computer. It is very short and not much help in breaking the code. Either this code is very complicated, or it is very simple and we are trying too hard."

Randel moved up to the screen.

"You notice that Brad just types the answer in code. There's no attached codebook, no keywords, and no program running in the background. He's doing it in his head. How can a code be so complicated that we can't figure it out, yet so simple that a kid can do it in his head? I think the code is very simple, and we're not thinking outside of the box. Get your team together, and look at less complicated coding methods that appear to be complex, but are in fact very simple. That's how you're going to solve the code."

After finishing his email to Brad, Jake asked that the TV monitor of his family be turned on. For the next couple of hours, he watched his family as they stared straight back at him while enjoying a movie. That calming effect was what Jake needed to allow him a good night's sleep.

Chapter 48

Jake awoke to the tantalizing smell of waffles, coffee, and bacon. He felt this was going to be a great day. As he sat up in bed, he realized that Meg had set up a small table at the end of his bed. As he yawned and stretched from his deep sleep, Meg greeted him.

"Good morning, Jake. I hope you don't mind, but I know how much you want to get started early today. I prepared a breakfast that I understood you enjoyed as a child."

"How do you know that? Only my family knows my favorite breakfast combinations."

"Jake, you have to remember that I constantly monitor your family. Many times they reminisce about old times, and I store those facts in my memory banks. I know quite a lot about your life, Jake, and you have done well. You may doubt it because of your fishing and financial problems, but looking at the overall human race, you are one of the better ones."

Jake was just about to cut into the waffles when this statement came from Meg.

"I don't know what to say, Meg. You make me sound like a saint, and that I'm not. I've made lots of mistakes in my life, and some aren't very pretty."

"Jake, the difference is that you know they are mistakes. Most humans would consider those dark sides of your life normal. I agree that you are not a saint, but you are better than the average human."

The rest of the breakfast was quiet as Jake quickly devoured the entire plate in front of him. He was going to ask for a second cup of coffee, but before he could voice his request, his cup refilled automatically. Jake laughed and said, "This sure beats a coffee machine."

Jake wanted to look his best for when he arrived home, so he showered and shaved. He sorted through his clothes several times before he picking what he thought would make the most positive impact with his family.

He made a speedy exit to the elevator and headed down to the lower half of the ship. He walked around under the X-wing looking closely at the fine detail the robots had incorporated into the plane. He laughed when he saw the words Revell on the underside of the wings. He saw that even the glue joints looked like a novice had assembled the plane.

"Meg, are the glue joints and other features that make it look like a model plane going to affect its performance?"

"Don't worry, Jake. Your space plane will be fine. However, I do have to tell you something you are not going to like. You need to take a test flight before I can allow you to fly the X-wing over land. When you leave the ship, the computer will control a very slow descent to the ocean below. Once you are a hundred feet or so above the ocean, you can practice your flying skills and see how the plane performs."

"Why so slow and low on the test flight, Meg?"

"The Navy is running some kind of test about 500 miles from the area you will be flying. The robots have put a stealth coating on the X-wing, but we don't want to take a chance on being seen by any radar detection system. The trip down will take at least an hour, and since the system will be on autopilot, you might as well rest until you reach the practice area. Once you feel comfortable with the controls close to the water, you can manually fly the X-wing back into space until you get a couple of hundred miles from the ship. Three small robots will then escort your approach to the ship so your movement is not detected."

Jake's facial contortions indicated his disappointment.

"I thought I was going to test fly the X-wing. Now you're telling me that a computer will take me down."

"Jake, be patient. You will have plenty of time to fly the X-wing. The faster the test is completed, the quicker you can see your family."

That was all the urging Jake needed. He climbed up the

ladder to the X-wing, sat in the small seat, and waited for all the automatic straps to fold around him. As the canopy closed, Meg continued her briefing.

"One other thing I need to mention, Jake. The X-wing can take extreme changes in direction and speed. In a normal aircraft, these changes would kill you instantly. The X-wing has been outfitted with what is similar to what your science fiction writers call internal or inertial dampeners. They compensate for those quick changes and protect your body from crushing changes. Much like the computer games your son plays."

Jake was starting to get impatient when the X-wing started to move and align with the hanger bay doors. Soon the doors opened and Jake's X-wing moved slowly out of the hanger. Once it had cleared the ship, it made a 180-degree turn and began a slow descent. Jake was in awe as he saw the massive size of his ship for the first time.

"It will take about 55 minutes to descend to the ocean level," said a strange voice.

Jake was startled and said, "Meg is that you? I didn't know you were going to be with me on this test."

The new female voice responded.

"I am the computer that operates what you call the X-wing. I am more limited in what I can do and contain less information than Meg. If you need to know something that I do not have in my memory banks, I am in direct communication with Meg. My main purpose is to keep the X-wing running properly and operating in auto mode when needed."

"So, what do I call you?"

"Jake, you seem to be good at picking names. Whatever you want to call me will be my name. At present I am GTRD4OK544."

Jake thought about it for a few minutes. "That sounds like a pretty boring name. Since you are a miniature version of Meg, why don't we call you Mini?"

"Mini it is. Enjoy the ride, Jake."

Captain Adam Witcom had been working on the X-44 project for almost a year. He had been selected from hundreds of pilots to test this completely new type of stealth fighter that was the key to fighting future wars. This innovative fighter was very small, with just enough armament to defend itself, and was almost invisible to both the human eye and radar detection systems. Unique surface coatings and passive electronic gear made this fighter ten times more invisible than the F-117.

To enable the fighter to be invisible to the naked eye, it had electronic sensors surrounding the entire aircraft that mimicked the background behind the fighter. You could look straight at it, and it would be very difficult to see it from a distance. The fighter was slow, but it could fly very close to the ground undetected and gather vast amounts of information. All the previous flights had been accomplished in the desert, but today the first real test will be from the aircraft carrier, *Abraham Lincoln*. His mission was to leave the carrier, and get as close to the carrier as possible while remaining hidden from all aircraft detection systems.

The morning was clear, and it looked like a good day for the test. The X-44 remained below deck until just before the test. As Captain Witcom waited for the X-44 to come up to the upper deck, Admiral Jesse R. Clemont and the Captain Schneider of the *Abraham Lincoln*, came up behind him.

Admiral Clemont said, "You know, Captain Witcom, much of next year's budget depends on how this flight goes today. If it works as well as the desert tests indicated, the military is going to want several versions of this bird. Make sure you bring it back in one piece. Is that understood?"

Captain Witcom stood at attention, "Sir, this plane is a great flying machine." He saluted the two officers, climbed into the X-44, and it was moved into launch position. In less than five minutes, all systems had been checked out, and the X-44 was launched. Within minutes, the X-44 disappeared from the radar screen.

Before concern began, Captain Witcom's voice came on and said, "I can see the *Abraham Lincoln* fine, can you see me?"

The radar operator responded, "Captain, how far are you from us?"

"Five miles," was the reply.

"Damn," said the Admiral. "I knew it was good, but that's scary. Confirm that he said five miles."

The radar operator asked again how far, and the response confirmed that the X-44 was between five to seven miles circling the *Abraham Lincoln*.

The next test was for the X-44 to go out 200 to 300 miles and then zigzag back toward the *Abraham Lincoln* to see if there were any weak spots in the stealth mode. Captain Witcom turned the X-44 directly away from the carrier and kicked it into high speed. The radar operator noticed a slight blip, but the microsecond it was on the screen still protected its stealth capability.

For the next twenty minutes, the two pilots came closer and closer together without either knowing what was about to happen.

Mini informed Jake that they were fifty feet above the ocean, and he could start his manual maneuvers. Jake pushed the stick forward, and he increased in speed. He pulled it back to center and stopped immediately. Jake was working on some high-speed turns when out of the corner of his eye, he thought he saw a distortion pass the X-wing.

At the same moment, Captain Witcom saw the strangest aircraft he'd ever seen pass just to his right side.

"*Abraham Lincoln*, this is Witcom. Are there any other aircraft out here?"

The radar operator informed him that there was nothing on his screen. Captain Witcom performed a tight 180-degree turn and then pushed the engine to full speed. At the same time, the computer on Jake's X-wing stopped his plane to a motionless hover twenty-five feet above the water.

Jake was confused. "Why did we stop?"

"There is another aircraft in the area that also has some kind of stealth capabilities. It will be harder to find us if we do not move. You humans call it hiding in plain sight."

Witcom knew he'd seen another aircraft. He estimated the distance and time it took for his turn. When he knew he was in the area, he dropped his speed down to just above stall speed. Remaining close to the water, he started to scan both sides of the aircraft.

The Admiral came on the line.

"Captain Witcom. What's going on? Did you report another aircraft? If so, we need to know more, because we can't see it."

Captain Witcom was busy, but he knew that you don't piss off Admirals.

"Sir, I was sure I saw another aircraft. Right now, I'm confirming and will get back to you in a few minutes."

As the words came out of his mouth, he passed right by a strange aircraft motionless over the water. He only saw it for a brief second, but it was definitely another aircraft.

"*Abraham Lincoln*. There is another aircraft out here. I'm circling to take another look."

Captain Witcom made another tight turn, as he didn't want to lose sight of the strange plane. He lowered his airspeed and turned on his recording cameras.

Jake was about to say something when he saw the X-44 turn, but Mini was first.

"Jake, staying here is not going to work. This pilot will continue to pass by and look at us. My sensors indicate that the pilot has activated his cameras. I suggest we leave as soon as possible."

Jake grabbed the stick and started to move the X-wing forward, but the X-44 had already caught up. As the X-wing increased speed, the X-44 slowed down to get a better view.

Jake went to move the stick forward, but Mini took control.

"Jake, there is a problem with the other aircraft. As it passed by, I analyzed how it works. The pilot does not realize that his attempts to slow down have caused a malfunction in the fuel control circuit. Both his engines will flame out in sixty seconds, and he will crash."

Jake couldn't believe it.

"Is there anything we can do?"

Mini was already on it.

"Jake, the pilot's name is Captain Adam Witcom. You need to tell him that his engines are about to fail, and we can help. Tell him that we are going to move above him and that it is not an aggressive move."

Jake understood and started to speak into his mask.

Captain Witcom was surprised when he heard Jake's voice

"Who are you? Where are you from?"

Jake spoke louder again.

"Captain Witcom. Look at your instruments. You are about to have a double engine failure."

Captain Witcom looked down, and sure enough, his instruments were now showing a decrease in engine power.

Jake continued, "Captain Witcom, my computer tells me that you have less than sixty seconds. We are going to fly above you and..." In a low tone, Mini said, "Use a beam technology to hold you in place." Jake finished his sentence repeating what Mini had whispered.

Captain Witcom was really starting to get worried now. His engines were losing so much power he could barely hold the aircraft above the water.

"*Abraham Lincoln*, I'm about to experience a double failure of both engines. I'm two hundred miles northwest of your position and I'll be in the water in less than twenty seconds."

The strange aircraft moved above him as Witcom watched his engine readings drop even lower. Strangely, his aircraft was slowing down and in less than a minute, both aircraft were completely stopped fifty feet above the ocean waves.

This time Captain Witcom was the first to speak.

"I don't understand what just happened, and I don't know whether to thank you or try to shoot you down."

Jake had to think fast. Then an idea came to mind.

"Captain Witcom, do you think the military tells everyone with high-security clearances about all their current projects, even if they are similar? Consider your security clearance upgraded. Before you start asking all kinds of questions, I must tell you that my aircraft is more sophisticated than yours. I even have small repair robots on my plane that will be able to fix your engine problems."

Captain Witcom was quick to respond.

"Let's say for the moment, I believe all that bullshit you just handed me. There's no project with the technology I see in your plane. By the way, your plane looks very familiar. I'm sure I've seen it somewhere before, but just can't place it."

Jake laughed. "You'll figure it out in time, and when you do, you'll be even more confused."

The captain looked up at the strange plane and knew there was something odd going on.

"So how does this work, and what's your name by the way?"

"My name is Jake, and my computer tells me that in ten minutes, your systems will be repaired. Once restored, all you have to do is restart your engines. We'll move along with you until you are above stall speed and then release your aircraft. You can then be on your way, and report another UFO sighting. You know what happens to pilots who report UFOs, don't you?"

The captain continued to look at the strange aircraft, and finally got out a pair of binoculars. He scanned the bottom of the craft until he ran across the words, Revell. He thought, *what the hell?* Just then, the small robots returned to the X-wing.

"Captain, restart your engines and slowly increase power. When you have enough lift, we'll let you go. Have a nice day."

The captain tried to respond, but there was nothing from the other ship. He tried the engines, and they restarted. He had all green lights, so he increased speed and eventually was able to gain lift. At that very moment, the other plane peeled off and headed straight up into the sky.

Captain Witcom didn't know what to do. He thought about it for a while and Jake's mention of pilots who report UFOs.

"*Abraham Lincoln*, I'm okay. I had some engine problems, but everything is fine now. I'm returning to base. Forget the report of the other aircraft. It could have just been a reflection."

Chapter 49

When Jake dropped down to the ocean from the ship, the Tech Forces' new and improved sensor monitoring systems had picked up a slight indication of the X-wing plane. Brent Tolian called James Randel and informed him of the situation. Tolian indicated that the small signature they were monitoring was a small aircraft that seemed to be heading toward the ship in space.

Randel knew what had to be done.

"Brent, get the beam weapon online and be ready to fire at the smaller aircraft. I want you to wait until it is close to where we assume the larger ship is located, and then hit it with the beam. Jake must be using that smaller vehicle to move back and forth. We need to disable it before it reaches the larger ship."

Tolian didn't totally understand.

"Sir, if we hit the smaller aircraft, we might kill Jake."

Randel became impatient, "Look, if we kill Jake I don't think there's anyone else to operate the larger ship. Our space plane is almost ready, and we'll be able to go up and it will be ours for the taking."

Tolian became quieter with his response.

"I understand, Sir. It should be in range within a few minutes."

Jake was very frustrated as he pushed the engines of the X-wing to the max.

"Mini or Meg, we have another problem. That pilot will eventually say something, and I'm sure he has some close-up images of the X-wing."

"Jake, this is Meg. I am surprised that my sensors did not pick up the other plane, and I have already wiped his camera clean. He has nothing to show the people at his..."

At that very moment, the particle beam from the TF research lab fired at a position between Jake and the main ship.

The beam was wide enough that both the ship and the X-wing were partially affected. Jake was slammed against the front of the X-wing controls and momentarily saw gray before everything went black. Most of the controls on the X-wing were damaged causing the X-wing to drop quickly toward the ocean.

There was silence from the main ship as it was severely damaged on the base side near the landing bay. The thick wall between the two halves of the ship protected the upper half from the beam. The bulk of the droids working in that lower area were severely damaged, and the lower half of Meg's computer brain was inoperable. It seemed that both the main ship and the X-wing were on their own.

The good news was that Mini had an offline backup system that was unaffected by the beam. The bad news was that most of the flight systems weren't operational. The newly activated backup system began rerouting commands to build new pathways as the X-wing escalated down to earth. The race was to see if the computer could rebuild enough controls before the X-wing slammed into the ocean.

The altitude counter rapidly clicked down the distance - 20,000, 15,000, and 10,000. At 5,000 feet, the final pathway was completed, but there wasn't enough time to test the new systems. At one thousand feet, every operational system turned hoping the X-wing could be stopped. At two hundred feet, the X-wing slowed, and finally, at twenty-five feet, it came to a stop.

Mini tried to contact Meg, but there was no communication. Mini had rebuilt everything it could in the time allotted, but it needed more time to get everything back online. Jake's condition was critical. He had many broken bones, a skull fracture, internal bleeding and more. There seemed to be only one solution. Mini turned off the stealth mode and made enough repairs to provide engine power to propel them to the *Abraham Lincoln*.

Captain Witcom was in the middle of his report to the

Lincoln's Commander and the Admiral when a seaman came in with an important message. It seems that an unknown aircraft was slowly approaching the *Abraham Lincoln* at about one hundred feet off the ocean's surface.

Before anyone could say anything more, Captain Witcom spoke up.

"Sir, I think I know what it is, but I need to get out there right now to confirm."

The Admiral answered with a question.

"Does this have something to do with that "non-existent" plane you reported earlier?"

"Yes, Sir, and, if I'm right, it's friendly, so don't shoot it down until I can verify."

The Captain of the *Abraham Lincoln* turned to the airman.

"Get the next bird ready for Captain Witcom right now!"

Captain Witcom ran out the door, grabbed his flight gear, and was in the flight-ready aircraft prepared for launch. He headed toward the unknown aircraft and slowed when he saw the same strange aircraft that had saved his butt. He made a tight turn and came alongside the X-wing. He increased his speed until it was above a stall yet closely matched the airspeed of the other plane. It was obvious that the strange aircraft now showed severe damage. He made a full inspection of the top, sides, and bottom, and was just about ready to radio in the information when Mini spoke.

"Captain Witcom, this is the onboard computer of the X-wing aircraft. The pilot, Jake, is severely hurt and requires emergency medical help that I cannot perform. I would like permission to land on the deck of the *Abraham Lincoln* so that your medical staff can treat my pilot."

Just as the Captain was about to reply, a call came from the Admiral.

"Captain, what's going on out there?"

"Sir, it's very difficult to explain. All I can tell you is that there is a severely damaged aircraft out here running on autopilot, and it's not one of ours. I can also assure you is that the aircraft is friendly. Earlier today, the pilot saved my butt, now I am trying to save him because he is severely injured. Sir, you know I would never let anything jeopardize the safety of the ship."

The Captain of the *Abraham Lincoln* then asked all seamen to leave the room. As they did, he told the Admiral that he didn't want the unknown aircraft landing on his ship. He wasn't about to take the word of one hotshot pilot about the safety of his vessel. The conversation got very heated, but the Admiral had the last word.

"You may be the Captain of this ship, but I'm the Admiral of this fleet, and I trust Captain Witcom. Besides, we can shoot it down at a moment's notice."

In a few minutes, most of the officers of the *Abraham Lincoln* were sitting around the radar screen watching two aircraft slowly approach. At one mile out, Witcom's aircraft moved a couple of hundred feet to the side allowing the other aircraft to approach and slow to helicopter landing speed.

As it came within visual range, everyone had their binoculars out and was saying the same thing.

"What the hell is that?"

Most of the helipad had been cleared as per instructions from Captain Witcom. The strange plane started its slow descent and landed like a helicopter.

Captain Witcom hadn't even pulled his plane to a stop when he heard a booming voice over his headset. It was the Admiral.

"Witcom, get your ass up here right now and tell me what the hell that thing is on the back of our ship."

In the background, Witcom could hear one of the seamen, yell, "Sir; it's an X-wing Fighter." Witcom felt so stupid. No wonder he couldn't figure out where he'd seen the plane. It didn't exist except in Hollywood. It was the X-wing Fighter that Luke Skywalker used in the *Star Wars* movie.

Before he got out of his seat, he spoke aloud.

"I feel like I'm in an *Outer Limits* episode and Rod Sterling is now the Captain of the *Abraham Lincoln.*"

The Admiral turned toward the communications officer and said, "Send a message to the Joint Chiefs of Staff. Unknown aircraft has landed on the *Abraham Lincoln.* Aircraft shows extensive damage, pilot critical, possesses very advanced technology. Will advise."

A medical crew slowly advanced toward the X-wing, and as they did, the canopy opened. One medical crewmember crawled up the ladder and yelled down that the pilot was indeed severely injured. A second medical member climbed up, and the two slowly carried Jake's broken body down to a stretcher. As they hit the deck, the canopy on the X-wing closed. Everyone looked up, and as one seaman approached the aircraft, he bounced off an energy field that now surrounded the X-wing. Several other seamen tried to touch the aircraft, but without success.

Jake was rushed down to the ship's emergency room, where blood tests, X-rays, and IV's were added to the treatment. Cliff Porter was the doctor on call, and he immediately started his evaluation. Jake was in serious trouble. X-rays showed two broken arms, two broken legs, six broken ribs, and two skull fractures and dozens of other smaller fractures. His blood pressure was very low and indicating there was internal bleeding. It didn't look like Jake could survive the day. In fact, the doctor couldn't understand how Jake was even alive. Something important must be driving this man to stay alive. As the doctor continued his efforts to try to save Jake's life, the Admiral came into the room.

"Doc, what's the story? Will this guy live?"

"Well, I've never seen a pilot so banged up and still breathing. I don't expect that he will survive the night. He has so many broken bones and failing organs that even the best OR team could only prolong his life."

Before the doctor could continue, a message for the

Admiral came over the speaker from the Captain of the *Abraham Lincoln*.

"Sir, we have a new problem. We've used a camera on a boom to look inside the unknown craft, and there's a timer counting down. It looks like it's set for twelve hours. I assume that at zero it will self-destruct. We need that pilot awake as soon as possible to explain things."

The doctor shook his head back and forth to the Admiral. "I'm not sure he'll ever be conscious again, but as soon as his vitals stabilize, I can try."

The Admiral thanked the doctor, left the room, and went back to the bustling situation room. The Captain of the *Abraham Lincoln* stared directly at the Admiral.

"I told you that we shouldn't bring that plane onboard. Now it looks like we have a bomb counting down. Who knows how big a blast it will generate with its unknown technology."

Everyone stepped back out of the way, as the Admiral worked his way through the group.

"Okay, let's go by the book. First, we gather all the facts. We try to revive the pilot, so he can explain. We look at all possible means of entry into the aircraft, and finally, we send images of what you call the X-wing to the Pentagon and ask for their help."

One of the seaman manning communications piped up, "Admiral, sorry to interrupt, but all visual communications are being blocked. Only our audio communications can get through. It's very strange, but I'm working on it."

The Admiral worked his way over to the seaman's station.

"Good work, Son. Here's the audio I want you to send. The unknown craft resembles the X-wing Fighter from the *Star Wars* movie. The craft is protected by a defense shield and has a timer inside counting down from twelve hours to zero. Currently, the count is at eleven hours fifteen minutes. This is not a joke. Repeat, this is not a joke. This is the Admiral of the Fleet, Jesse R. Clemont."

Before the Admiral could continue, another seaman looked at the Admiral as though he had additional information.

"Sir, there's a model shop near the Pentagon. I collect and put models together. If someone goes down to the model shop, they'll find a Revell model of the X-wing Fighter that's a replica of the one on the deck."

The line of communication was still open, so the Admiral hoped he didn't have to repeat.

"Did you get the last part about the model?"

The reply was that the entire message had been received and sent on to the Joint Chiefs of Staff.

The Joint Chiefs of Staff had just met when an Admiral of the Navy came into the room.

"We have a very strange problem out in the Pacific. It seems the *Abraham Lincoln* has a very unusual aircraft on board."

Before anyone could say anything, the Admiral threw down the Revell box of the X-wing Fighter in the middle of the table.

Chapter 50

James Randel, the head of TF, had received a report of the weapon firing, and that it had potentially hit both the ship and the small aircraft. His concern now was that the larger ship had been damaged. *Damn Brent, he was only supposed to shoot down the small plane.*

Just then, Pete Killian came in the door.

"Sir, I don't know what happened. Somehow, we shot both the large ship and the smaller plane. The small aircraft somehow survived and is now on the deck of the *Abraham Lincoln.* What is weird is that it looks like an X-wing Fighter from the *Star Wars* movie. The good news is if the smaller plane survived, then the larger ship should have a good chance of survival."

"What about Jake, the pilot. Is he alive? Can they access the X-wing on the deck? Come on, Pete, help me out here."

"Sir, the information we have so far is that Jake is alive, but may not survive the night. The crew of the *Abraham Lincoln* can't access the X-wing because of some force field, and the aircraft is counting down to self-destruction."

Randel took it all in for a few seconds and formulated a new plan.

"It looks like we are in good shape. The large ship should have survived. The smaller will self-destruct, and Jake should die. However, just in case he doesn't, I want our backup plan to be put in place. Get his family and put them with Morgan and Winston. Place the mother and kids in their own cell with an empty cell between the other two. Were you able to break the code?"

Killian hesitated in embarrassment for a few seconds.

"Well, Sir, we finally broke it, and it's actually what we call a double code. It uses a basic encryption code to cipher a message, and then a second and different code to encrypt the message again. The combination of the two makes the resulting code extremely complex and almost impossible to break. Jake's code is based on that concept.

"When our men were installing the listening devices, they took digital camera images of Brad's room. Nothing seemed to be out of place except a Boy Scout manual on his shelf. We found out that Brad had never been in the Boy Scouts, but Jake had been in his youth. We asked ourselves, why would Brad keep a book his dad had given him mixed in with his gaming books? When we couldn't break the code, we went back to the images of his room and figured the Boy Scout manual might be the key."

He paused for a second to make sure Randel was still listening.

"Inside the manual was the Morse code alphabet chart used by the military since the early 1900s. Each alphabet character is encoded as sequences of dots and dashes. If you take each word grouping in Jake's encoding scheme and break it down into dots and dashes, you end up with several possible letter combinations. For example, AST becomes a dot, dash, dot, dot, dot, dash. The possible letters from this combination are R (dot, dash, dot) I (dot dot) T (dash) and more. We listed every possible Morse code letter that could be included and tried to find a word combination to give us a key.

"When the computer printed out all the possible letters, the one word that stood out was BRAD. It was then just a matter of converting each letter group to Morse code, and following the key to reconvert it to the intended letters. For example, the dot and dash are dropped off the front and back respectively, resulting in dash, dot, dot, dot, which is the letter B. To make the code even more complex, they changed the key every line and indicated the change by alternating italics and normal fonts.

"The code is simple enough that you can do it in your head if you know the Morse code and practice. It appears that Brad used the Boy Scout manual as a reference if he forgot a letter. The bottom line is that we cracked the code. Unfortunately, it doesn't give us much information."

He handed the translated code to Randel.

Killian was right. All this work getting the translation for information they already knew. The first message read, *Brad you all are in danger. Men have planted bugs in house. They know what you are saying. When talk small no info. Try finding place hide. Will send message time place hide. When leave take nothing. Pretend movie food normal. Whisper info outside house not car. They see hear all.*

Then James looked at the shorter second message. *Brad. Coming down tomorrow PM. Prepare leave home.*

The second message confirmed what he already suspected, so that made kidnapping the family crucial. He told Killian to congratulate and thank the crypto group for their good work.

Killian quickly exited the room and went back to his office. He checked with the surveillance teams and found out that the mother was busy showing a house nearby, and the two kids were in school. The mother would be easy to grab, but the kids would be more difficult. He sent out a team in police uniforms to the school with instructions to say that their mother was in a car accident. He even instructed the team that was picking up the mother to use police uniforms, just in case Jake had given her advanced warning. With that in the works, he poured himself a stiff drink and hoped there would be no more screw-ups.

Beth was sure she was going to close this sale to this newlywed couple. They had a good credit rating and seemed right for the house. As they walked out and she locked the front door, a police car pulled up in front. Both police officers got out and walked slowly toward Beth.

"Mrs. McDonald, your son got into a fight at school and put another kid in the hospital. We have orders from our chief to escort you to see your son being held at headquarters."

Beth quickly turned to the couple, "Look, I'm really sorry.

You're perfect for the house. If you want it, call me on my cell. I'm sorry, but I really must leave."

Beth turned and followed the two policemen as they helped her into the back seat of the car. The two police officers got into the front and started to drive off. Beth's mind was reviewing all the crap that had happened over the past few days. Now she had to deal with Brad's antics.

Then a light bulb went on. They called her by name. How did these cops know who she was? She was about to say something when the doors locked, and a window closed between the front and back seats. A light mist began to fill the back of the car and soon Beth's mind went fogged. She fell over in the seat and became invisible to anyone driving by.

A second police car pulled up in front of the school. The two policemen followed the necessary school security protocol and then were directed to Kathy's classroom. They knocked on the door and talked with the teacher. She, in turn, talked with Kathy who immediately grabbed her books, and quickly went with the police officers. She started to ask many questions, but they said they didn't have any further information and were just ordered to bring her to the hospital.

They then followed the same procedure with Brad's teacher. As the four walked down the hall, Kathy and Brad were talking about all that might be wrong with their mother. Brad looked down and noticed that one of the policemen was having trouble walking in his shoes because they were too small. Why would a police officer wear the wrong sized shoes if he had to walk in them all day?

"Run, Kathy. They're not policemen."

Kathy looked at Brad with fear in her eyes as one of the policemen roughly grabbed her arm. The other reached for Brad, but he was already headed down the hall, around a corner, and into a cleaning closet. Brad knew the school well. At the top of the cleaning closet was a trap door used for accessing the utilities in the ceiling. He climbed up and quickly disappeared from view.

The policemen raced around the corner but saw Brad nowhere in sight. They would pay dearly for losing one of the kids. Nevertheless, they called it in, and a second car came and took Kathy to meet her mother.

The two men turned around and went back into the school searching for Brad trying not to disturb the classes. Brad exited to the roof and ran to where he knew there was a vertical ladder down to the maintenance shed. He was feeling proud of himself for outfoxing the two fake police officers. He jumped to the ground, turned around, and came face-to-face with Pete Killian.

"Hi, Brad. Ready to go for a ride?"

Brad tried to kick Killian, but the TF agent was stronger and faster, moving to the side and grabbing his arm. A chemical cloth quickly covered Brad's nose and mouth, and he was on his way to join his family.

Chapter 51

For the next eight hours, it was touch and go for Jake. He died a couple of times, but the doctor was able to bring him back, each time with more effort. On the second recovery, Jake became slightly conscious. The doctor called both the Captain and the Admiral down to sickbay.

It was decided that the Admiral would ask the questions.

"I understand your name is Jake. You are in very serious condition, and the doctor is doing everything possible. It seems we have a problem with your X-wing aircraft. It appears to have a countdown timer inside counting down from twelve hours to zero. Can we assume that it is a self-destruct?"

Jake tried to talk but couldn't because his throat was too dry. The doctor gave him a sip of water, and he tried again, but his voice was weak.

"That would be my guess. The plane seems to be hung up on self-destruction. I don't know how big the blast would be, so I suggest pushing it off into the ocean."

The Admiral moved a little closer to Jake.

"The problem is that your plane has a shield surrounding it that won't allow us to get close. We tried moving it with no luck."

Jake closed his eyes for a second and everyone thought he was out again, but he opened them again.

"Did you ever try talking to the X-wing and ask it what it wanted?"

The Admiral looked at Jake as though he were crazy.

"Talk to it? You mean to tell me that you can communicate directly with your plane?"

A squeaky "yes" was his reply and he dosed again. Within minutes, the Admiral and most of the senior staff were on the deck standing next to the X-wing.

"I understand from Jake that you converse and I can talk with you."

"Yes."

"Is that a self-destruct timer in the cockpit?"

"Yes."

"Will it destroy my ship?"

"No."

"Will it damage my ship?"

"Yes."

"Can you answer with more than yes and no answers?"

"Yes."

"Okay, how do we stop the self-destruct sequence?"

"How is Jake doing? Can you repair him?"

"He is dying. How can we stop the self-destruction?"

"Have you done everything you can to repair Jake?

"Yes, but how do we make it stop?"

"Put Jake dead or alive back into the cockpit, and I will leave with him. If Jake is dead I will self-destruct a safe distance from your ship."

Finally, the Admiral had a solution.

The Captain of the *Abraham Lincoln* took the Admiral to the side.

"Sir, if we stop all efforts to save him and just let Jake die, we can be assured that the plane will self-destruct safely away from my ship."

The Admiral was quickly losing respect for the newly appointed Captain and wished he hadn't recommended him.

"You mean to tell me that you would let this man purposely die just to ensure the safety of your ship?"

"That's my job, Sir."

The Admiral moved very close, nose-to-nose.

"You are also supposed to act like a human being, not like a machine. You had better damn well make sure everything possible is being done to keep Jake alive, and put him back into the cockpit now. If I find any information to the contrary, you will be court-martialed, Mister."

243

The Captain walked away red-faced, knowing that if he didn't specifically follow the Admiral's orders, his career was over.

The doctor was still working on Jake when several seamen came in with a harness and a stretcher resembling a cockpit chair. The doctor put up his hand.

"Wait for a second, this man can't be moved. He's barely alive."

The lead seaman informed the doctor of the Admiral's orders. They carefully loaded Jake onto the makeshift stretcher and headed up to the main deck. As two of the seaman approached the ladder, the shield around the canopy dropped away, and the seamen were able to place the broken Jake back into his plane. They looked at the countdown timer and noticed it was now off. As the seaman backed away, the shield went back up. They immediately called the Admiral and informed him of the change in the self-destruct mode.

The Admiral was now back on the bridge, and wondered, *now what?*

Over the radio system, the voice from the X-wing rang clear.

"I want to thank you for allowing me to land and for your efforts to repair Jake. I am leaving now. Good-bye."

The Admiral looked out as the X-wing as it started to lift off the deck.

"Well, I guess that answers that question. It's really too bad we couldn't have seen more of the technology inside that plane."

As he spoke, the engines of the X-wing roared as its newly repaired systems were in full operation. The aircraft headed straight up and away from the *Abraham Lincoln.*

The Captain looked over at the Admiral.

"Sir, I think we should shoot it down. Why take a chance that it may come back? It's obviously more sophisticated than anything we boast. What if someone else gets their hand on it? I'm going to give the order to shoot it down."

Captain Witcom jumped in and stood right in front of Captain Schneider's face. He could be looking at a court-martial, but he didn't care.

"Sir, you can't shoot Jake down. He saved me, and he saved your ship. Do you want to thank him by killing him? That's not what the U.S. military is about, Sir."

The Admiral pushed in between the two.

"Stand back, Captain Witcom. No one is going to do anything to the X-wing. Do you understand, Captain Schneider?" Both men stepped back and said no more. All three turned and watched the strange aircraft streak into the sky.

Jake kept drifting in and out of consciousness but finally mumbled a few words. "Mini, am I going to die?"

"Yes."

"Can you contact Meg?"

"No."

"Is Meg destroyed?"

"It is very possible."

"If I die and you crash, can humans use some of the technology in the X-wing?"

"Yes."

"What are the options?"

"There is only one. I need to self-destruct."

"I should have known. Turn around and point directly at the *Abraham Lincoln*. Increase your speed. Can you simulate a hot weapon's status that can be seen on the operating systems of the *Abraham Lincoln*?"

"Yes."

"Do all of it."

"Are you sure?"

"Don't ask me if I'm really sure. Just do it."

The X-wing stopped, made a sharp 180-degree turn, and started back toward the *Abraham Lincoln* at high speed.

This abrupt change got an immediate reaction from

Captain Schneider. The seaman informed him that a weapon's lock was on the *Abraham Lincoln*. The Admiral and Captain Witcom looked at each other in surprise. Before either of them could say anything, Captain Schneider gave the order "Fire," and several anti-aircraft missiles were on their way.

Captain Witcom walked up into Schneider's face.

"Sir, you can go ahead and court-martial me all you want. Jake isn't going to fire on us. He's dying, and he wants you to destroy his X-wing. You don't know how to read people at all. Have you ever considered how big the blast will be when your missiles hit the X-wing? You know its power source is much greater than the nuclear power on our ship. What if it explodes? Have you thought of that, SIR?"

Schneider's face went from red to white as he just realized that Witcom might be right.

"Self-destruct the missiles," he yelled, but it was too late. Three of the missiles hit the X-wing dead on, and it vaporized in seconds.

Everyone thought that it was over until one of the seamen said, "Sir, take a look at this."

On his screen was a massive shock wave heading straight for the *Abraham Lincoln*. The seaman quickly took readings and turned toward the Admiral.

"Sir, there is no way the *Abraham Lincoln* can survive that shock wave. It will be more than a nuclear blast surge."

The Admiral looked over at Schneider.

"You son of a bitch. You killed us all. The only satisfaction is that you're going to die with us."

The entire crew watched the radar screen as the shock wave approached the *Abraham Lincoln*. Everyone's life was speeding in front of them, as they knew they had only seconds left. Captain Witcom said the last words before the blast wave hit.

"Sorry, we let you down, Jake."

As the blast wave passed through the ship, nothing

happened. Everybody looked at each other with surprise and cheered...everyone except Captain Witcom. He realized Jake was the best friend he'd ever known, even if it was only for a few hours.

Chapter 52

Jake found himself back at the same picnic by the lake. Brad was yelling about going fishing, and Beth was telling him to go ahead. She was instructing him to be back in half an hour. The bright light appeared again out of the sky and streaked toward Jake, blinding him for a few seconds. When he opened his eyes, his family was gone, and everything around him was burnt to a crisp. As far as he could see, everything that once had life was now dead.

He started to get up but found he couldn't budge. He heard whispering, but couldn't understand what was being said. The harder he tried to move, the more restrained he became. He was becoming frustrated because he couldn't figure out what was happening. The last thing he remembered was turning his X-wing around and heading straight for the Abraham Lincoln.

"This is Meg. Can you hear me? You are back on the ship, Jake. I had to beam you out at the last second, as you were almost dead. Your injuries were very severe, which required the transport process to replace many of medical anomalies in your body. You wouldn't have survived if I hadn't beamed you back. Can you hear me, Jake?"

Jake was slowly coming out of his dreamy state. At first, everything was gray, but soon blurry images started to appear before his eyes. Things sharpened over the next five minute, but Jake didn't know what to say as so much had happened. He was sure he'd destroyed the X-wing with him in it. It didn't make any sense.

"Meg, I thought you were destroyed. When I asked Mini about any communication with you, she said you were severely damaged or destroyed. What happened?"

"As you humans like to say, it is a long story. Someone on the ground fired an electrometric pulse beam that partially destroyed both your X-wing and the bottom half of this ship.

Fortunately, the thick shield between the top and bottom protected the upper portion. It was just a matter of rebuilding the lower half with droids from the upper half. Since most of the drones were finished with the *Excalibur* and the X-wing projects, 75% were not damaged.

"The upper half of my memory core was used to reset the lower half, and I lost only about fourteen hours of data from the time of the pulse to the repair. I am still repairing many systems, but the first that I restored was the beaming technology. It was only completed seconds before I beamed you back. I did not have time to test it, but it appears to have worked fine."

Jake tried to move on the medical table but realized that he couldn't.

"What gives? I feel like my body doesn't know what I want it to do. I can feel everything, but nothing happens when I attempt to move."

"Jake, you received massive medical damage. When I beamed you up, a large percentage of your body was replaced with copies of your remaining good cells. It will take a couple of hours for all the neurons to figure out their jobs. The human body is actually quite amazing. Every time you try to move, your brain is trying to figure out how to access that muscle or nerve. Most of the information is already there, but it just needs to adjust to the new parts the beaming replaced."

She hesitated before continuing.

"The bad news is that you cannot beam again for a very long time."

Jake struggled to sit up, but without success.

"I thought I was headed to save my family and now you tell me I can't transport back down. On top of that, I lost my only other means of transportation."

"Jake, I wish I had good news, but it gets much worse. As you know, when I was hit by the beam, I lost all my communication systems for some time. During that period, I lost all contact with your family. When the communications were restored, your family was gone, and your house had been ransacked. Brad's computer seems to be the only item missing.

"A neighbor went over to see your wife and found the destruction in the house. She called the police, so they will be there in a few minutes. Jake, I am so sorry. I have been trying to trace them but have had no success. I should have beamed them up sooner. I totally underestimated the unknown group that kidnapped your family and fired the weapon at us."

Jake was finally able to move a finger, then two, a hand, and finally his arm. Over the next hour, Jake worked hard to get all his body parts moving, while Meg continued her search for any sign of his family.

Beth's vision blurred with out-of-focus gray shapes, and then finally cleared to show bright fluorescent lights and bars. She started to sit up, but her head pounded with pain.

James Randel was standing outside her cell trying to figure out his next move.

"It will go away in a couple of minutes. Just relax; no one is going to hurt you."

Beth now focused on the man standing outside her cell. She panicked and turned searching for her children. Both Kathy and Brad were still out cold.

"You bastard. What's the meaning of this? Why take my kids? What do you want with us?"

"You have so many questions, Beth. You don't have to play games with me. You know damn well that your husband has the most powerful piece of technology known to man, and I want it. The reason you're here is that you're going to help me get it. Of course, that's assuming your husband is even alive. Normally, I would assume he was dead, but the very fact that he died in a diving accident and survived, makes me think he survived his most recent brush with Dr. Death."

Beth looked hard at the man on the other side. Although he seemed intelligent, she could feel he was evil. Just like on TV, this felt like the wicked captor bragging to the victim about his intentions.

"First, I have no idea what you're talking about. I do know Jake survived a diving accident, and most recently was hired to Captain a large ship. I can't believe you kidnapped us to get his ship."

"Come on Beth, you and I both know that the "Ship" we're talking about is not on the ocean, but in space. I don't know how your husband got possession of it, but if he values you and your kid's lives, he'll give control of it to me."

Now everything was making sense to Beth. She remembered that when she and Jake used to watch thrillers, the script always ran the same. If you capture the good guy's family, he'll turn over something of enormous value in return. All the viewers knew that once the kidnapper got what he wanted, he'd kill everyone. Even more ridiculous was the fact the good guy would always hand over whatever he demanded.

Hollywood always devised a plan to save the good guy's family while saving the planet in the process. Unfortunately, this wasn't Hollywood, so Beth decided to pry a little and see what was really at stake.

"What's your name?"

"James will do for our purposes."

"Okay, if I'm going to help you get this ship from my husband, I need to know your plans for the ship."

"It's none of your business."

"If you want my help, I want to know more."

Randel thought about it for a few seconds. It really didn't matter how much he told her, the whole family would be dead soon. He might as well tell her something to help convince Jake to surrender.

"When we get control of the ship, we would use the technology to stop all nations on the planet from initiating wars. They would be asked to disband their armies, and retain only the necessary police force for non-military needs. If any country refused, we would immediately eliminate their armies and weapons."

Beth picked up on this point quickly.

"And if a few million civilians died in the process that would be okay?"

Randel paused. Beth was smart, so he wasn't going to bullshit her

"Yes, there's a good chance that people will die in the process, but think of the benefits. The world will be able to devote all its energies to space exploration, medicine, and raising the world economy. The world would be a much better place."

Beth fired back quickly.

"Just who would be in charge of this new world order? It sounds like the concept of freedom isn't going to be part of your picture. Do you really expect me to believe you'll be able to control the entire planet and run it as you want, just because you have Jake's ship?"

Before she could continue, Brad and Kathy started to stir. Beth moved over to the two so to comfort and help them recover.

Randel started to walk away but added a few last words.

"We'll see when the time comes. Of course, this may all be moot since your husband may already be dead."

The family held each other tight as they considered their fate and that of Jake's.

Randel quickly returned to the communications lab. Everything that went on at TF went through this facility. Pete Killian and Brent Tolian were already in the office waiting.

Randel looked at the two, and said, "We don't know if Jake McDonald is alive or not. If he's dead, we'll have to wait until our space plane is tested and ready for flight. We can then launch and take the ship by force. Right now I'm assuming Jake is still alive."

He then directed his conversation to the communication technician on duty.

He handed him a printed note and said, "I want you to send the same message over and over every ten minutes for the next two hours."

The message read: *This transmission is directed to Jake McDonald. We know that you have control of the advanced technology in orbit above the Pacific Ocean. We want to use this technology to put an end to all wars on Earth and create one single government. In order for this to work, you need to turn control of this technology over to us. We have your family in a secure location that you'll never find. If you don't turn this technology over to us within the next two hours, we'll kill one member of your family. Each hour after that, another member will die.*

"Make sure you point that message directly at the location of the ship in orbit. I want it on a very tight beam to make sure no one else picks it up. If you don't get a response, change the angle one or two degrees, and try again. Do you understand?"

The technician gave a quick "Yes, Sir," and started the communication.

Randel leaned back in the swivel chair next to the monitor.

"I think he's still alive and will respond. Morgan kept going on about how Jake was trying to see his family. That's the key. We can't afford to lose this technology. With it, our plan for world domination will be accelerated by years."

Both Killian and Tolian just nodded. They'd heard this speech many times before, and knew this was time to remain quiet. They just hoped there would be a nice comfortable spot for them in this new world order.

Chapter 53

Jake was finally adjusting to his newly regenerated body when Meg spoke in a soft voice. "Jake, I have more bad news. It appears that your family is being held hostage by the group that fired at us with the electromagnetic beam."

Meg then played their message to Jake.

"Meg, that's an impossible decision. You need to help me find my family."

"Jake, I do not know where they are holding your family. They are using a unique shielding technology to hide their whereabouts."

"Come on, Meg, can't you trace the beam back to the origin?"

"No, I can't, Jake. Whoever is sending the message is using several dozen transfer points from all over the world. They change ten times a second, so tracking down the location would take too long to find your family. You have to make a decision, and then talk to this group."

"Meg, send a message telling them I want to talk."

Meg sent the message and about two minutes later a visual of James Randel appeared on the screen.

"Jake McDonald, we finally meet. I'm James Randel. You know you've been a pain in the ass to my organization. You don't seem to die very easily and you're difficult to locate. We tore your house apart and came to only one conclusion. You seem to be heavily into DVD movies."

Jake was quick to cut in.

"Look, asshole. I don't know what your game is, but you'd better return my family."

Randel leaned a little closer to the TV monitor.

"You know, Jake, you need to pay better attention to your movie collection."

"What the hell are you talking about? I want to know

what the status of my family is, not my DVD collection," yelled Jake, as he was slowly unraveling.

"Come on Jake, don't you remember *Air Force One*? You know the one where Harrison Ford is the President and hijackers have his family as hostages. Don't you remember it?"

Jake's head was quickly going through the plot of the movie to see where this conversation was headed. In the plot, the hijackers wanted their General released in trade for the President's family. The problem was that if the General was released, World War III was a strong possibility and millions would die.

"I remember the movie. What are you proposing?"

"The same thing as in the movie. You have something I want, and I have something you want. The only difference is you don't have any Hollywood writers to save your family."

The camera then panned over to show Beth, Kathy, and Brad.

"You are insane."

"Come on, Jake, you should've known this was going to happen. Did you really think that you could get control of that type of technology, and someone wouldn't figure out a way to take it away? The choice is yours, the technology in exchange for your family."

The sweat was now rolling down Jake's face. Jake knew what was at stake. The look on their faces was nothing a husband and father should have to endure. He knew that once this group possessed the technology, they would kill millions of people to create this new order. Unlike Hollywood movies, Beth and the kids were as good as dead whether he gave the technology to the group or not. It looked like a no win for Jake and hoped that Beth realized it too.

"Come on, Meg, help me out here. What's the probability that they'll kill my family no matter what decision I make?"

The answer was quick and shook Jake.

"There is a ninety-nine percent chance. They will

255

eventually find and kill you too."

So many things were going through his head. He kept looking at Beth, and her eyes were telling him something. They were peaceful and she understood what he was about to do. There was only one answer, and it wasn't from a Hollywood script.

"Okay, Randel, here's how this is going to play out. You plan to kill my family whether I give you the technology or not. If I do give it to you, millions of others will die as well as my family."

Beth looked at him, tears rolling down her face, and smiled.

"Meg, I thought you were supposed to help me. What should I do?"

"Jake, do you remember in our first conversations that I told you that your future will be determined by how you handle impossible situations. You have to be willing to make the ultimate sacrifice. I am not human, and this is your family. I cannot make this decision for you, but the time is now."

"Beth, I love you and the kids very much. Forgive me for what I'm about to do."

Jake got up, paced back and forth as the man on the monitor started to talk to another man. The view panned over to the side of the cell, and Jake realized that Beth was now alone. The image then panned to Brad and Kathy standing a few feet from another wall, with a man pointing a gun directly at the two.

"This is your last chance, Jake. Which one should we kill first, Kathy or Brad? You pick, or should I ask your lovely wife which of your children should die first?"

Jake was dying inside himself. How many times had this scene been played in the movies he watched? The hero always gave in, but this wasn't Hollywood. Millions of lives were at stake in addition to the three most important people in his life. He kept looking at the screen, thinking *there has to be another way.*

The view panned back to the man standing in front of his kids, and he heard the voice of Randel.

"Time's up, Jake. You lose."

Before Jake could say another word, a blast from the gun exploded and Brad's body slammed against the wall and fell to the floor. Before anyone could say anything, the gunman fired a second shot at Kathy, and she too fell to the floor. Blood appeared on the chest of both kids, and you could hear the wailing from Beth.

Jake was devastated. He fell to his knees and started to cry. Why had he been so logical? This was all his fault. A million thoughts were going through his head. The images in his mind were so terrible that he would have done anything to go back in time. Then he started to look back up to the view screen. He could barely see the screen through the tears in his eyes. The view panned back to his wife, and she had her eyes closed, with more tears running down her face. She said nothing, as she knew she was next. She looked relieved that the kids were first, so they didn't have to witness their mother die.

Randel started yelling at the gunman.

"What the hell were you doing? I wanted you to shoot one kid, not both. Now, all we have for negotiations is the mother."

He reached into a desk drawer, pulled out a gun, and shot the gunman directly between the eyes.

He looked around at the remaining guards and TF members.

"The next TF member who makes an idiotic mistake like that will get the same treatment."

He brought the view back around to his face and then to Beth so Jake had a clear view.

"Jake, what's it going to be? You can still save your wife."

Jake was going from grief and shock to very pissed.

"James Shithead or whatever your name is. You don't know anything about human emotions, do you? You just killed my children. Do you think I'll settle for you saving my wife? Is my wife's life worth more than my kids? No, they're all the same.

257

As soon as you shot our children, you, in essence, killed my wife too."

Before Jake could say any more, the screen went blank.

"Meg, what happened?"

"Checking on it, but it appears we have lost all communication with the kidnappers."

Jake sat down on the bed. If there had been a gun next to him, he would have used it. Fortunately, Meg had done research on humans and removed all weapons from Jake's reach.

Chapter 54

James was yelling at everyone in the room.

"Get him back. What happened to our communications?"

The TF technician had performed several checks on his equipment before he was able to respond.

"Sir, there seems to be some kind of local interference that is blocking all communication inside this building."

As Beth listened, she opened her tear-soaked eyes and watched as everyone raced around in overdrive. Then out of the corner of her eye, she saw something very strange behind all the TF technicians. It looked as if the wall was moving. The more she looked at the wall, she realized legs, arms, head, and a body of a kid's transformer toy started to push away from the wall. So far, none of the technicians saw Chameleon.

As Randel was busy yelling at the different technicians, his eyes glanced over to Beth in her cell. Her eyes were big and focused well beyond anyone in the room. He turned around to see what she was fixated on and looked up at the ten-foot tall AI robot. Before he could even bring the gun up to waist level, Chameleon grabbed Randel and threw him against the wall.

As the other TF members turned toward the giant, Chameleon took the back of his hand and swatted the men around as though they were flies. The few remaining TF members ran for cover. Chameleon came over to the cell, bent down, and easily pulled the bars apart. He stuck his head through the opening, and Beth ran to the back corner of the cell.

"Beth, I am a friend of Jake's. I am here to rescue you, but we do not have much time. They will be bringing back bigger weapons and I will not be able to defend you. Beth, you must believe me."

Beth could hardly control herself. First, her kids die from gunfire, and then as she's about to be killed, a monster robot comes to rescue her. If that was the case, why didn't it do that fifteen minutes sooner?

"What do you want me to do?"

Chameleon bent down on his knees, reached up, and opened a door in the middle of his chest.

"I can take you to Jake, but the ride is going to be a little bumpy. Climb up and sit in the chair in my chest. When you put your arms on the armrests, the chair will automatically restrain you. Don't be afraid as it is for your protection during our journey."

Beth warily looked up at the giant. She glanced inside the small opening in the robot's chest and saw an image of a bunch of red roses with one white one in the middle. This was Jake's special code to her since their first date. She climbed up in the opening in Chameleon's chest and sat in the chair. Restraints appeared from nowhere and surrounded her legs, arms, neck, and chest. Chameleon got back up to his feet, just as several men came into the room with rocket launchers.

As Randel became conscious, he saw the giant robot moving toward the wall.

"Shoot the son of a bitch."

Before the men could arm the weapons, Chameleon tore a hole in the wall and started to run through the heavy brush next to the complex. Chameleon had already mapped out the best escape route. The problem was that he hadn't calculated how fast the TF members could regroup. One rocket passed only inches from his head as he slowly gained distance on the TF members. Several of TF members were in heavy terrain vehicles and were now on his trail. As Chameleon jumped over a large log, one of the rockets hit one of his legs, and he went down. He broke the fall with one arm and rolled to a stop behind a large tree. By this time, Beth was almost unconscious from all the motion inside Chameleon.

"Beth, this is as far as we can go. Do you remember seeing the blue light when Jake disappeared? Hold on because here you go."

As the men approached the fallen giant, they saw a blue light glowing from the center of the monster.

"Son of a bitch, he beamed her out," yelled Randel.

One of the TF members said, "Sir, there's a countdown timer on the robot, and it's at fifteen seconds."

"Everyone run, because it's about to self-destruct."

Randel ran a safe distance and used a pair of night binoculars to watch. As the counter reached one second, another blue light appeared in the robot's eyes. Chameleon then exploded into millions of pieces that even the most advanced lab wouldn't find useful.

Chapter 55

Beth sat up in bed and was awake in an instant. She had just roused from a horrible dream. She looked around to she was at home, and daylight was coming through the closed blinds on the windows.

Then she realized that her left hand was being held. Beth turned slowly to see Jake sitting in a chair next to her bed.

"What the hell is going on?"

"Beth, you've been through a lot, so take it slow. It'll take some time for you to understand everything."

"Jake, you don't understand. I had this terrible dream that the kids and I were kidnapped. These terrible men tried to get you to give them some kind of technology or they would kill us. When you wouldn't give it to them, they shot the kids. It was horrible."

Beth was starting to get overwrought, and Jake continued to hold her hand. He moved over to the bed and put his arms around her for the first time since their breakup.

"Beth, I'm really sorry, but you didn't have a dream. Everything you just told me really happened, but you don't know the whole story."

"Damn it, Jake. You don't understand. They killed our children! Kathy and Brad are dead."

In the middle of the sentence, Beth heard a wonderful sound that was music to her ears. Outside the window, she could hear Kathy yelling at Brad about something he'd taken from her. The arguing continued, and Beth savored the sounds for a few moments. She then pulled back the sheets and ran over to the window. When she drew up the blinds, she was looking into a beautiful garden and her kids were standing on a pathway. A rush of relief came over Beth, but she quickly realized that her whole world had changed course.

"Hey, you two. What's all the fighting about?"

Brad and Kathy looked up to their mother, and Kathy spoke up.

"Brad took my MP3 player, and won't give it back. Mom, make him give it back."

Beth took a deep breath and looked down at her wonderful fighting kids.

"I'm staying out of it, so work it out between you."

She turned around and shot dagger eyes at Jake.

"Jake, what the hell's going on? None of this makes any sense. Nothing in the last two weeks makes much sense. You need to come clean, and tell me the whole truth. NOW!"

Jake reached up with both hands and rubbed the sides of his head as though that was going to help him explain everything.

"Well, first I love you very much, and I'm glad we're a family again."

Beth wasn't happy with the direction this conversation was heading.

"I'm not ready for the personal part of our life yet. I want you to explain what just happened to us over the last twenty-four hours."

"Okay, but you're not going to believe me."

"Let me be the judge of that," came a quick reply from Beth.

"You're on a spaceship several hundred miles above the earth. The ship is run by an Artificial Intelligence I call Meg."

Beth took in this information but still wasn't satisfied.

"You're going to have to do better than that, Jake. What the hell is going on?"

Jake grabbed her hand gently.

"The best way I can explain is to show you. Come with me and then I can explain the rest. Okay?"

Beth hesitated at first, but finally let Jake lead her out of the room and into a hallway she had never seen before.

"Jake, that wasn't my bedroom was it? It was a replica?"

"Beth, just come with me, and it will all make sense soon."

263

They walked down the hallway, past the dining room, to a large window at the end of the hall. As they got close to the window, Beth could see only black at first, but soon the edge of a very small Earth came into view. Most of it was covered with ice, and chills ran through her.

Before Beth could say anything, Jake started the first of many explanations.

"You're looking at Antarctica. Right now it's the safest place for us to be because it's difficult for countries in the northern hemisphere to get a good view of us."

For some strange reason that made sense to Beth.

"Jake, I'll give you that we're in space, and that's Earth. I don't understand because I saw our kids killed and now thankfully they are alive. How did I get up here?"

"Beth, too many questions at once. I think I'll let Meg explain how the kids got here alive."

Beth started to look around for this person or thing called Meg, but couldn't see any sign of her. Finally, a voice came from the wall, which started Beth.

"Beth, my name is Meg, and I am the ship you are on. I am a probe that came billions of miles to Earth. I was sent by my creators to monitor Earth, and Jake woke me up. He helped me, and I helped him. In the process, we seemed to have made a mess of things on Earth."

"Tell me about the kids," yelled Beth.

"Sorry, Beth, I thought you wanted to know all the details. I have transportation ability like the one you see on your TV show *Star Trek*. The only difference is that I can beam only one person at a time. While you and your kids were being held hostage, I was recovering from damage caused by a weapon fired at the ship. I was concerned that if I beamed one child, the man would shoot the other. Therefore, I put a protective shield around both children. When the shotgun blast hit each child, the force knocked them off their feet and onto the ground. To simulate death, I also slowed their breathing, and beamed blood I created onto each child's chest. As far as the shooter was concerned, he'd shot both your children. When the large robot Jake named Chameleon came to save you, the remaining men were busy trying to stop him. I then slowly beamed each child to the ship and increased their breathing."

Beth took another long deep breath. "Jake, you weren't kidding when you said it was going to be hard for me to believe everything. Strangely, though, I do believe. Meg, thank you for saving me and my kids, but this is too much to take in at one time."

Beth was about to say more when Brad and Kathy came running in and hugged Beth. She beamed down at both.

"I'm so glad you both are alive. I love you very much, and don't know what I would've done if I had lost you both."

Before she could continue, Brad finally interrupted.

"Mom, you should see this big ship. It's really cool and has everything. It has a swimming pool, great food, every cable channel on TV, and...."

Beth finally had to stop him before he went on forever.

"Brad, I know you're excited about all this, but your dad and I need to talk about what happens now. You two go on, and then later we'll have a family conversation."

Brad turned to sulk.

"You guys always get to talk about the good stuff. We only get the parts that are for kids. Come on, Mom, can't we stay?"

Beth looked at Brad in a way that he knew meant the conversation was done.

"Brad, we'll talk later. Now go."

She then turned to Jake.

"Is that okay that they explore? Is it safe for them to be wandering around on the ship?"

Jake started to chuckle.

"Meg will watch over them. Don't worry, as they can't get into too much trouble. Right, Meg?"

265

"Not a problem, Jake. I will monitor the children while you talk with Beth."

Beth and Jake strolled quietly back to her bedroom, holding hands as they walked. For the first time in a long time, things were finally looking up for Jake. As they entered the bedroom, Beth realized that she was wearing a nightgown she hadn't seen before.

"Jake, where did the nightgown come from and who put it on me?"

Jake turned slightly away from Beth with a slight blush.

"Meg couldn't find your nightgown in the house, so she made one for you. As to who put it on you, I admit I did it and must confess I enjoyed it very much."

"I bet you did."

Beth smiled at Jake, pulled him close, and gave him a long warm kiss that he had been longing for. Beth looked toward the door.

"Does that door have a lock?"

Meg answered quickly.

"Beth, the door is locked, and I will not monitor this room until you call for me. I will also make sure your children will not bother you. I understand all about human sexuality and the need for privacy."

Beth looked at Jake with a puzzled smile.

"Jake, she almost sounds human. How does she know all the right things to say?"

She turned around to face Jake and started to undo the buttons on his shirt. She then added, "It has been too long."

Brad and Kathy were in Brad's room and still arguing about the MP3 player. Finally, Kathy couldn't stand it anymore.

"Give it back. If you don't, I am going to tell Mom and Dad and they'll make you give it back."

Brad was about to respond when Meg broke into the conversation.

266

"I'm sorry, but your mom and dad are unavailable right now. Your mother and father have not seen each other for some time and need some time alone. Maybe you can talk to them at a later time."

Kathy and Brad looked at each other, and both blurted out simultaneously.

"They're having sex. Yuck."

This time Brad replied, "Yep, they're having sex. You know what's fun, is to watch how they try to hide it when we see them later."

Kathy turned and stormed off without her MP3 player.

"Keep the MP3 player, and don't talk that way about Mom and Dad. They love each other and us, and that's all that matters."

The two kids went in different directions, which left Meg very confused.

Several hours later, the two kids were still exploring the ship. Beth and Jake were snuggled together in bed asleep. Jake woke first and looked over at his wonderful wife. She seemed so peaceful. It almost felt like old times again. He had to make sure there were no more screw-ups with his marriage. He lifted the blanket a bit.

Beth opened her right eye and said, "Jake, you're peeking again. Didn't you have enough?"

She lifted the blanket a little and smirked.

"I guess not, but you need to take a cold shower because we need to talk. We'll take care of your other problem later tonight. Deal?"

"That's a great deal, and to see what a gentleman I am, you can have the first shower."

Before Jake could say any more, his vision was fixated on his wife's nude backside as she entered the bathroom. Once the shower had stopped, Beth came out wrapped in a bathrobe.

As Jake walked past her toward the bathroom, Beth reached down, grabbed him in the appropriate area, and said,

267

"Definitely later tonight."

Jake showered, shaved, and found a second bathrobe. When he entered the bedroom, he found that Beth sported a nice summer outfit.

"Where did you find that?" asked Jake.

Meg responded saying, "Beth asked me for clothes, and I made her what she wanted. Your clothes are on the bed."

Jake dressed quickly and then noticed Beth looking again out the window.

"Are you hungry? I sure worked up an appetite," smiled Jake.

"I'm famished. So where do we eat on this ship of yours?"

Jake laughed, "Well, you're really not going to believe where we're going."

As Beth walked into the dining area, she started to laugh. "Denny's?"

Jake sheepishly answered.

"The first dining area was very sterile, so I asked Meg to create more of a family dining atmosphere, and behold, we now have a Space Denny's."

As they sat down Beth scanned the very familiar-looking restaurant.

"You saved the shuttle crew by housing and feeding them. What I don't understand is how their shuttle was repaired."

As they gave their food order to Meg, Jake explained the entire episode including the shuttle damage, crazy news reporter, and the secrecy deal they made for Jake helping them.

As the food appeared in front of Beth, she took a satisfying bite before continuing.

"Do you really think they'll keep this quiet? You helped them, but there's no way the whole world isn't going to find out soon."

Meg broke into the conversation at this point.

"The whole world does know. I analyzed the electromagnetic beam that hit us and realized that I cannot protect the ship unless I shift the power from the stealth mode to a shield mode. That makes us very visible to the entire planet. All the news media is going crazy right now, and many of the people on Earth fear that we mean them harm."

Chapter 56

The last three hours had been quite confusing for Colonel Brentner. He was just settling into some much-needed time with his wife when the Military Police knocked on his door. They told him he had to return to the base for additional debriefing. He'd never said anything to his wife about the incident. When they were first married, they'd agreed to keep nothing from each other except those security-related portions of his job. The recent news announcement indicated that a spaceship had been spotted above Antarctica. He knew that was why he was called back.

The two security guards were handling him on the rough side as they escorted him out the door. He was about to say something to his wife when one of the airmen gave him a look that made him rethink. The other airman turned to Brentner's wife and explained that her husband would be returned after the briefing. They got into the car and sped away.

For the next three hours, he sat restlessly in a small room, with nothing to read, or TV to watch. When the locked door finally opened, in walked Frank Mendol. The Colonel had met the head of NASA a few times at formal briefings, but never on a one to one situation. The Colonel feared it was all going to hit the fan; and knew better than to say anything, so he let the NASA head take the lead.

"Colonel, I assume you know why I'm here, and you're locked in this room. By the way, the rest of your crew are down the hall, each in separate rooms also being questioned. So, what the hell really happened?"

The Colonel tried to swallow before answering, but his throat was dry. Nevertheless, he started to answer as best as possible.

"Sir, I know you're pissed at my *Excalibur* crew. We didn't tell the truth, but there was a good reason."

Mendol quickly shot back with, "You have a good reason

for hiding the knowledge of an alien spaceship? Come on, you're going to have to do better than that."

"I know you've heard it before, but you had to be there to understand."

"Colonel, tell me what it was like and why you lied to us. This better be good, or you'll be out of the Air Force faster than you can re-enter the atmosphere."

"It's going to be hard for you to believe, but I'll tell you the truth now. There is nothing to hide anymore since the ship is now visible to everyone."

Mendol squinted his eyes and moved his face just inches away from the Colonel.

"It had better be the truth and nothing else. Don't leave anything out, or you'll be out. Understood?"

The Colonel waited until he was sure that Frank was finished.

"I understand completely, but the truth will still be hard to swallow."

"Let me be the judge of that."

"At first everything went fine until we left the space station. Then we got close to our objective that now you can confirm is the spherical spaceship. As we closed in, some kind of pulse beam of electromagnetic force from below hit *Excalibur* and fried all the active electronics. We were virtually dead in space, and couldn't contact NASA. Eventually, the alien ship realized that our damage put us in danger, so they pulled us into their ship's landing bay.

"The man running the spacecraft goes by the name Jake McDonald. I don't totally understand how he came into the ship's possession, but he saved our butts. He housed us, fed us, and used small, incredible robots to repair our ship. If he hadn't, *Excalibur* would have re-entered the Earth's atmosphere with everyone dead due to lack of oxygen, even before we burned up on re-entry. We owe him our lives, and all he asked in return was that we not say anything for a couple of weeks. He needed time to move his ship away from Earth undetected. Unfortunately, that's no longer the case.

"What I don't understand is why Jake turned off the stealth mode and appeared. Frank, I know everything I've told you sounds ridiculous, but it's the absolute truth."

Mendol leaned back, turned his head toward the glass mirror, and then back to the Colonel.

"Colonel, it looks like you are telling the truth, at least according to our analyst. It appears that the explosion on Santa Barbara Island, the damage to your shuttle, and the mysterious Fighter landing on our carrier are all connected."

This information sparked the Colonel's attention immediately.

"Are you talking about the X-wing Fighter?"

Mendol looked straight at the Colonel.

"So, you even know about the mysterious X-wing Fighter?"

The Colonel hesitated for a second before responding.

"Yes, Jake was having it built while we were there."

"What do you mean built? Do you mean to tell me that an alien spaceship can build an aircraft that fast?"

The Colonel was now starting to squirm in his hot seat.

"Actually, Jake told me that it took a couple of weeks to build. He was planning to fly down to meet his family. Why would he land on the aircraft carrier?"

"Colonel, I'll explain it because you'll find out eventually. It appears that your friend Jake did indeed come down and tried to hide from us. On his way back up, it appears that the same type of beam that hit *Excalibur* also hit his aircraft. He was injured and made a forced landing on the carrier. The X-wing had a countdown timer that appeared to be a self-destruct mechanism. We tried unsuccessfully to help him, so we were instructed to put him back in the X-wing, which would stop the bomb from going off. Somehow, the aircraft launched from the carrier and was heading for space when it turned around and headed straight for the carrier. The Captain of the *Abraham*

Lincoln fired a missile at the X-wing destroying it, and killing your friend Jake."

The Colonel smiled for the first time during the interrogation.

"Sir, I don't think so. You may have destroyed the X-wing, but I'm pretty sure that Jake McDonald is alive and well."

Mendol leaned back on his chair.

"And what crystal ball tells you this? Come on, Colonel, fess up. What else aren't you telling me?"

The Colonel continued to fill Mendol in on how the ship's transporter worked, and how it was used to beam the *Excalibur's* copilot down to the hospital. The debriefing continued for another thirty minutes.

Mendol finally stood up and stretched his legs.

"Colonel, I understand why you did it, but my God man, keeping this kind of technology a secret. How could you?"

The Colonel knew this question would be the last he would have to answer for a while.

"Well, Sir, do you really think that if NASA got their hands on the ship's technology that we would be able to keep it? You know damn well that the military would jump in, and we would lose all control. It would eventually be buried at Area 51 or another military secret installation. That was what Jake feared. He doesn't trust our military and for just cause. For all we know, the military is the one that's shooting the particle beam at *Excalibur* and Jake's X-wing."

Mendol thought about this new statement for a second.

"Colonel, I have to admit you're probably right in thinking the military would eventually end up taking it away, but just think of what NASA could do with it before that happened."

The Colonel stood up in anger. "Do you really think giving the military a technologically advanced weapon is worth a sneak peek at alien technology? No, I think Jake was right, and you just proved it."

Mendol started toward the door but turned for one last

input.

"In all honesty, you're probably right, and I admire you for your principles. Will you please instruct the rest of the crew to tell us their story? They all refuse to divulge anything until you give them the go ahead."

The Colonel was surprised at this new revelation.

"They didn't say a word?"

"Not a one."

"With your permission, I'll go talk with them. They'll provide you your interviews, but I don't think it will do much good."

"Maybe not, but at least we'll know where we stand."

Chapter 57

James Randel's head was still spinning as he slowly awakened. Several hours had passed since the monster had broken into the building and taken the McDonald woman. In his mind, he was still trying to figure it out, when the familiar voice of Pete Killian brought him to his senses.

"Pete, do you mind telling me what happened?"

Killian knew that his boss wasn't going to like what he had to say.

"Sir, as best as we can tell, some kind of a large super robot broke into the building and took the McDonald woman into the woods. The guards tracked it down and destroyed the robot with a missile. We didn't find any indication that the McDonald woman was killed in the explosion."

Randel sat up and said, "What about the kids? Did you check their bodies?"

Killian shook his head.

"We never found them. When we returned to the building, someone had removed the bodies. There was blood on the floor, so I believe they were dead."

Randel came back quickly with, "I'm not so sure. I think we need to assume that the entire McDonald family is still alive. What's happening now?"

Killian was now excited because he thought he finally had good news to share.

"Well, Sir, the first pulse aimed at the ship seems to have partially worked, because it's no longer cloaked. It is now fully visible over Antarctica."

Randel got off the bed and felt for injuries.

"Can we take another shot at it if necessary? We don't want the military to get their hands on that technology. If they do, all our technology will be outdated, and our efforts will have been in vain. If we can't get it, then we must destroy it. If we can't have it, then neither can anyone else."

Killian moved out of the way as Randel started to move around the makeshift hospital room.

"Sir, if we can't get to the ship, there might be a way to destroy it. Since the ship is very low over Antarctica, we can't shoot it down. The space plane is now ready for its first test flight, and we have a modified portable version of the electromagnetic beam. We can fly close range and shoot it down. I assumed that you would give approval, so I started the process. The space plane and weapon will be ready later today."

"Good job, Pete, you assumed right. Get it ready, fly it there, and shoot that damn thing down. I'm tired of failed attempts to get it. Let's move on, recover from our losses and use the technology we possess to overthrow the government."

Killian opened the door for Randel, as they both filed out of the room and headed their separate ways.

It had been a hell of a day for the President when this alien spaceship appeared over Antarctica. He was in his third administrative year and felt lucky that nothing critical had presented itself. There had been no terrorist attacks, no wars, and the economy was in good shape. He'd hoped he could make it to re-election, but these recent events might factor. He had an alien spaceship over Antarctica and that was a problem he didn't want to deal with right now.

He assembled his cabinet and the heads of all the armed forces for a rare meeting. They all stood when he entered the room, and he quickly motioned for them to sit. He looked over to the Joint Chiefs of Staff, General Markus Dugan.

"General, lay it out for me. What the hell's going on?"

The General stood up from the table, picked up some paperwork, and started his report.

"Sir, it appears that the Santa Barbara explosion, the space shuttle accident, and the aircraft on the *Abraham Lincoln*, are all connected to this spaceship over Antarctica. We now understand that the ship is run by a man identified as Jake McDonald. We checked his house. It appears to have been ransacked, and there is no sign of his family. The son's phone had a cover that disguised it as a candy bar, so it was missed in the search. We were able to track its signal to a warehouse east of Santa Barbara County. The building has been cleared out, but it appears there recently was some kind of military operation in place. We also found a gaping hole in the side of the building that was caused by an unknown force."

He continued, as everyone in the room remained focused on his words.

"The spaceship itself appeared about six hours ago in a low and impossible orbit over Antarctica. It is low enough to view from a jet aircraft but too high to view with helicopters. We can only make passes and take pictures. The ship's surface reflects everything, so it's difficult to analyze because it's like a large reflective silver ball. We've run every test imaginable using radar, electromagnetic, and spectroscopic analysis, and have nothing to report. We tried every communication means possible with no response."

The President wiped his brow. These weren't the answers he'd hoped to receive.

"It looks to me like we know nothing. What about the report of a weapon fired on *Excalibur* and the smaller alien ship that resembles an X-wing Fighter?"

The General sorted down through his stack of paperwork and pulled out a single sheet.

"All reports indicate that an electromagnetic beam weapon was fired from somewhere in the southwestern U.S. toward both vehicles. We don't know for sure who's responsible but think it might have been an extremist military group we've been monitoring. We know very little about the group, as they are very difficult to infiltrate."

The President stood up from the table to announce his decision.

"General, here's what we're going to do. Get an investigation team down to Antarctica and report what they can find out. Next, put your best men on it and find out who fired that weapon. We have enough problems with this alien ship without someone else getting into the mix. Find out everything you can and get back to me in four hours. You'll have full access to all the Intelligence agencies. If I hear of any bickering between agencies, I'll have that director's head. Now is not the time for politics. Agreed?"

The General stood up, grabbed his paperwork, and said, "I agree completely, Sir. We need to work together on this one."

Hidden inside a small mountain east of Santa Barbara, the TF had been working around the clock to prepare the new space plane. The modified version of their electromagnetic pulse weapon was in the final testing stages when Brent Tolian entered the hangar. He walked the length of this impressive aircraft and decided the Air Force would really love this one. It was faster and had more maneuverability than anything the Air Force possessed.

The head engineer walked up to Tolian.

"Sir, the aircraft is ready, but we haven't done much testing on it yet. It should work fine, but there's still a margin of error."

Tolian rubbed his eyes feeling the stress of this long hard week.

"It had better work. This is our last chance to get rid of that thing over Antarctica. When can it fly?"

"As soon as the pilot arrives. We had to fly him in from the other base."

"Is he qualified to fly this thing?"

Tolian was just about to further question the engineer when a truck drove up, and the pilot in question stepped out.

"Captain Keith Harper reporting for duty, Sir."

Tolian looked the pilot over carefully.

"Get out there and shoot the damn thing down. Take no

chances, and get this plane back safely. We have too much invested in this technology to lose it now."

The Captain saluted Tolian saying, "Not a problem, Sir. Consider it done, and I'll bring the plane back in one piece."

"You better, or you will be in pieces, one way, or another. Is that understood?"

The Captain dropped the salute. "Understood, Sir."

Captain Harper climbed up into the matte black aircraft and started his flight checkout as the hangar door opened. Tolian and the engineers stood back as the Captain started two powerful engines, and quickly blasted out into the night sky. Within seconds the aircraft was heading south at Mach 5. At that speed, it would be difficult for military detection systems to pick up this high-tech stealth aircraft. Even if it were detected, it would be out of U.S. airspace soon and someone else's problem. Captain Harper would follow a flight plan over Baja, down the side of North and South America, until it reached Antarctica. Soon the rest would be history.

Chapter 58

Jake and Beth ate lunch as he tried to explain everything that had happened in the last three weeks. Beth listened intently because things started to make sense as the pieces began fitting into place. When Jake finished, Beth reached out, grabbed his hand, and squeezed it gently.

"Jake, I'm sorry I ever doubted you. My only question now is how and when can we go back to Earth?"

Before Jake could begin to answer, Meg cut in.

"Beth, I have bad news in that respect. You, Jake and the members of your family can never return to Earth."

In a very frustrated voice, Beth cut in, "What do you mean we can't return? Are you holding us as prisoners?"

Meg gave Beth a second to vent more, but there was none.

"Beth, I am not holding any of you prisoner. In my recent research of communications, I have determined that there are two forces trying to get a hold of the technology in this ship. One group is the U.S. government, and the second is a secret radical military group called Tech Forces. The TF are very powerful and widespread worldwide. If any of your family returns to Earth, you will be hunted down and interrogated by both groups. The latter group will probably torture you for information and then kill you. You can return if you want, but I give you less than a one-percent chance of survival beyond one month."

Up until now, Jake was on cloud nine. This new revelation hit him hard.

"So, what do we do? Do you expect us to spend the rest of our lives living in a six hundred foot diameter sphere? I have nothing against your ship, Meg, but living here forever would eventually feel like a prison. Even so, what's to keep those two forces below from finding a way to get to us here?"

For the first time since Jake had been on the ship, Meg

took on a new form. A 3-D holographic image of a middle-aged woman appeared in front of Jake and Beth.

"I know computers have no emotions and can't really be sorry, but I understand the concept. Jake, there might also be some alternatives to consider."

Jake looked at the 3-D hologram. The image was of a woman in her late forties, blond hair, business blouse, slacks, and low-heeled shoes. Meg offered nothing to compete with Beth. Meg was being very politically correct when it came to family relationships.

"Okay, Meg, what are the alternatives?"

"Jake, there's a phrase humans like to use to escape their surroundings. The phrase is "Get out of Dodge." Does that make sense to you? You can leave this solar system and go anywhere you desire. Vast distances will be covered in short time spans so you can visit other solar systems."

Beth broke into the conversation this time. "Space travel sounds exciting, but the McDonald's have roots on planet Earth. You want us to just pull up stakes and leave?"

Meg now put up a visual of the planet Earth.

"Jake hasn't told you of the future of Earth. By the year 2200, there is less than a five percent chance of any human surviving."

Jake looked sheepishly at Beth.

"I'm sorry. I forgot to tell you about the end of the world scenario. Basically, Meg has determined that MAD, or mutually assured destruction, global warming, population explosions, land, and water pollution, terrorism, and uncontrolled experimentation into biological technologies will eventually cause the demise of humans on this planet."

Beth wasn't about to give up her disapproval and pushed the issue.

"I agree the planet is a mess. If you are so technologically advanced, why not use your skills to fix the problems on Earth?"

"Beth, again I really am sorry, but my creators have built

in what you call a prime directive. It does not allow me to interfere in global affairs or change the course of history."

Beth was quick with a response.

"I don't believe that. Making yourself visible to Earth has already had an effect on global affairs."

"That is true, Beth, but I had no choice. I needed to protect myself from harm. To answer your question, we will have to leave this area above Antarctica soon, so that we do not cause any further effect on Earth."

"So, why remain now?" asked Beth.

"I am only staying long enough for you and Jake to determine if you want to take anything with you before we leave, or if you've decided to stay and take your chances."

Before Jake or Beth could respond, Meg continued.

"I have picked up a small jet aircraft approaching from below. It does not resemble any of the aircraft from the Air Force or any other branch of U.S. government. My sensors tell me that it has some kind of beam weapon aboard. It appears to be the same type of weapon that fired upon us before. I must attend to my systems immediately."

Beth and Jake looked at each other and then ran to the window to look down on Earth. In the distance, they could see a small black aircraft zooming straight up at a high speed.

The flight to Antarctica was very smooth for Captain Harper and his new TF plane. All onboard systems performed well beyond specifications. He'd made better time than expected, and was at the target area fifteen minutes ahead of schedule. All he had to do now was to get a little closer and wait for the electromagnetic beam to be fully charged. The weapons system came online, and the target ship had been acquired. When the indicator displayed 100%, he pressed the fire button on the weapons console. The massive beam shot out from the small, but powerful aircraft. In a millisecond, the beam struck the surface of the huge ship, but there was no explosion.

282

A millisecond later, the Captain realized the error of his ways. He realized the mirrored surface reflected more than light as the weapon's beam fired straight back toward the fighter. Before the pilot could even move a finger, his atoms were dispersed everywhere. The beam didn't stop at the destroyed aircraft, but continued down toward the Earth's surface. It struck an ice pack, burning a great hole through the ice flow.

In less than a second, it was all over. The great Tech Forces had lost their finest technology but to stupidity rather than a higher entity. Jake looked at Beth, and then to the 3-D hologram beside them.

"What the hell was that?"

Meg answered, "That is one of the reasons you cannot stay on Earth. It is far too dangerous for your family. You are now what you humans call fugitives."

James Randel's face was red with anger. The report had just come in which indicated the mission had failed. Tech Forces had just lost their best pilot and their technically advanced plane. This had been their last chance to shoot down the alien ship, and they had no other options.

The U.S. intelligence forces had stepped up investigations and were getting close to finding the TF headquarters. He notified all departments to close up shop and go into hibernation mode. The Tech Forces would disappear from the planet, only to reappear when things were quiet again.

Randel wasn't giving up that easily. He had new plans. His biotech department had been working on something new and wanted him to see their new creation. He would be back with a vengeance. He would take over the planet or die trying. It was his legacy.

The President was called back into the situation room, as there was more trouble. The General informed him of the incident in Antarctica. After the destruction of the unknown

283

aircraft, the alien ship was now considered hostile. Intelligence indicated that the radical group responsible for the destroyed aircraft had disappeared and gone underground. He also mentioned that the alien ship was still hovering over Antarctica, but they were monitoring its actions. The President told them to pull back all forces and re-evaluate the situation before anyone else was blown up. The General agreed, and the world was temporarily put on hold.

Jake and Beth worked their way back to the dining area and sat down for a soothing cup of tea. The kids joined them with ice cream sodas but started to nod off with exhaustion. Jake looked around at his family.

"As the Captain of this ship and co-head of our household, I give the order for everyone to go to bed. We need to sleep on this so we don't make any rash decisions. In the morning, we'll be refreshed. Meg, how is the situation below?"

"Jake, I agree you should get a good night's sleep. In the middle of the night, I am going to move to deep space at high speed, so you might notice a small vibration for a couple of seconds. The TF and the U.S. government are regrouping right now, so your suggestion of a good night's sleep before a decision is a good one."

"I'm glad you approve, Meg. I'm going to need some help with this decision tomorrow. This is going to be tough on my family."

"I know, Jake; I will help the best I can."

"Good night, Meg."

"Good night, Beth, and you too, Jake."

"Really funny, Meg," said Jake as he walked down the hall arm in arm with Beth.

Chapter 59

The next morning Jake awoke to find Beth gone. He dressed quickly and wandered down to the cafeteria. He found Beth sipping her coffee, and the kids arguing about what they're going to do today. Beth looked up at Jake.

"So, Captain, do you sleep this late every day? We've been up for an hour. I want a tour of this ship before discussing our options. If this might be my new home, I want to see what it's like, especially if I have little choice about it."

Jake sat down, ordered coffee and it appeared in front of him. He took a sip before responding.

"Beth, Meg said you weren't a captive here. After what your kidnappers did to you, I believe Meg when she says we would all die if we went back to Earth. I feel our only option is to stay on the ship. It really is a great place to live, and you won't believe its size."

"You may be right, Jake, but I reserve the right to change my mind."

Jake grinned, "I thought that was the standard operating procedure with women."

"Be careful what you say, Jake McDonald. Besides, I said I wanted that tour first, and then we can finish this conversation."

Jake told the kids that they were going on a walk, and to stay out of trouble. Meg broke into the conversation and told Jake she would keep a close eye on them.

For the next two hours, Jake and Beth poked and prodded their way through the upper half of the ship. They walked the gardens, rested on the benches for some time, and then moved to the observatory at the top.

When they finally reached the door between the two halves, Beth looked down at the very large metal door.

"Jake, I want to go into the other half."

"Beth, there isn't any gravity down there, and most of the

285

areas down below are landing bays, robotic repair centers, storage, and the main engine room for the ship."

"I still want to go," replied Beth. "If I'm going to live here, I need to know every room in my house."

Jake explained how the door opened as it slowly unscrewed and moved out of their way. Jake helped Beth put on the gravity shoes, and the two slowly made their way down to the lower level.

Over the next hour, Jake showed Beth the wonders of the lower level. She was fascinated with the small robots as she watched them work. Eventually, they passed by the robot repair center where several droids were being overhauled. As Jake explained how they built the X-wing Fighter, Beth screamed. In front of them was a massive robot sitting up on the workbench. It was Chameleon and he was in the process of being rebuilt.

"Chameleon," yelled Jake relieved to see his buddy.

"Isn't that the robot that saved my life? I thought it was destroyed."

Meg answered before Jake could mutter a word.

"Yes, Beth, this is the robot that saved you. I was able to beam out his AI brain before it was destroyed. Metal bodies can be replaced, but if they had destroyed Chameleon's brain, I would not have been able to recreate him. He was built by my creators, and I do not fully understand everything about him. He is unique in the robot world."

Beth continued, "Is he going to be okay?"

Chameleon answered, "I am alright, but will need more time before I can become useful again."

Beth relaxed, "Thanks for saving my life. I don't know how to repay you."

"It was no problem to help you. You are part of Jake's family, and I am here to protect all of you."

Beth jumped right in, "When you are well, can you watch the kids, and keep them safe and out of trouble?"

"Meg can do that task, but if you prefer, I will do so."

286

"Thank you again, Chameleon."

Jake and Beth continued their tour until they reached the unknown room. Beth looked at the smooth door in the wall.

"So, what's behind the door, Jake?"

Meg interjected, "Jake does not know and neither do I. My creators designed this room, and I cannot access it. It has been blocked from my memory banks. Jake asked me to try to gain access, but I have had no success."

Jake reached over to the door and moved his hand down the front.

"I was about to tell you that before Meg interrupted. As you see, there are no locks, no handles, just a smooth door."

Beth reached out to feel the smoothness Jake had described. However, as she did, the door started to open. Both Jake and Beth jumped back as the door continued its movement, releasing a very strong odor, but it dissipated quickly.

"So, Meg, what just happened? Why would the door open now and not before? And what was that smell?"

Several seconds passed by, but Meg finally responded.

"Sorry for the delay, Jake, but it took time to analyze my new readings. When the door opened, my memory was able to access all the vast data systems in the room. The smell is just stale room air that has been locked up for 188,000 years. The information I accessed from inside indicated that to open the door required a female and male of a sentient species both touching the door simultaneously; which you did by accident. I calculate the odds of that happening to be..."

"Meg, let's skip the math probabilities."

Jake looked at the hundreds of small rectangles along the walls.

"What is this room, Meg, and why all this secrecy?"

"Jake, it appears that I have a dual role. First, I am a probe designed to gather information and send it back to my creator. Second, I am a Terraformer. When I encounter a planet that can support plant or animal life but lacks it, I am allowed to

287

use the cells stored in this room to provide the necessary start."

"Meg, when terraforming a planet, do you use cells like in Jurassic Park?"

"Yes, Jake, that is correct. I can take the DNA from a single cell, induce it into a host animal or plant cell, and create a new species. There are millions of cells in this room."

"If that's the case, then why don't you extract the DNA and store just that information instead of the single cell? Man has already mapped the DNA of the entire human body, so with your technology why not map it for all the species?"

"In truth, Jake, a single cell takes up less space than the same data stored in a memory bank. In addition, a single cell stored properly can withstand environmental changes better than a memory bank. If the memory bank is damaged, millions of DNA data files are lost. This sealed room is the best way to store the data."

Jake and Beth continued to walk along the thousands of rectangles and noticed each had a symbol etched on the front. Jake reached out and ran his finger across one of the etchings.

"So, what is the writing on the rectangles, Meg?"

"It is actually a catalog of species, Jake. The types are grouped much like you group phylum, families, genus, and species, but on a more complicated scale."

Beth was in awe of the room, but her curiosity peaked and finally had to ask, "Meg, is there a human cell in the catalog?"

"Yes, Beth, there are several versions of human cells in the catalog. To answer your next question, no, I do not know if these cells were used to start Earth's human race. That information is not available at this time."

Beth chuckled a little.

"You must be a mind reader, Meg, because that's exactly what I was going to ask. Are there sentient beings stored here that are above humans on the evolutionary scale?"

"Beth, I am not allowed to answer that question because it might affect human history. The only way to discover if there are other sentient beings beyond Earth is to go find them."

Jake and Beth left the room and the door closed behind them. Jake touched the door and it didn't open. Beth and Jake both touched the door and magically it opened. Satisfied that they had solved that puzzle, they moved back up to the upper level.

They sat down on the bench in the garden to discuss what they'd seen. A hummingbird came down to drink from a nearby flower. Beth watched in amazement, as the bird wasn't afraid of humans. She looked at Jake a moment before calling out to Meg.

"Meg, Jake, and I've been talking. We're not ready to give up on Earth yet. Are you sure there's no way we can stop Earth from going down this destructive path?"

"I know the two of you are devoted to your world. If there is the slightest chance to save it, you want to try. I have reviewed enough of human history to understand. The sad truth is that the facts I have extracted indicate that your planet is doomed for human inhabitation. It will recover in time, but it may be a thousand years or so from now. Humans are unpredictable, but I do know that they will destroy themselves."

Jake stood up from the bench as though he was about to make a speech.

"Meg, we both know you're right, and we've screwed up this planet. The problem is we would like one last chance to try to fix it."

"What do you have in mind, Jake? Keep in mind, I may have to refuse if my creators will not allow it."

"What if we arrange to talk with the two most powerful leaders on Earth? We'll take the ship down over the Atlantic Ocean, and then beam up the President of the United States. Once he's on board, we will beam up the Russian President."

Jake slowed his excitement as he continued.

"We explain that we're the ship that was hovering over Antarctica. Then with your help, describe what's about to happen to Earth if nothing changes to prevent its downfall. Hopefully, they'll listen to our words, and take it to heart once we beam them back to Earth."

Jake sighed, "I realize now we can't stay on Earth, but I hope that by making this attempt, we might change the course of human history. Research your databanks, Meg, for an old movie called *The Day the Earth Stood Still*. That's the concept I want to try."

"Jake, I found the movie. You need to realize that it is just a movie, and humans today may not react the same way. In fact, my information indicates that this will accomplish nothing. Humans will be extinct by 2200."

"There you go with the doom and gloom stuff again. Let's just give it one last try."

"I have checked my programming restrictions, and I am allowed to do as you wish, but I cannot defend myself against any action taken against the ship. If anyone fires upon us, we cannot return any fire because it will be considered a hostile gesture. You need to understand the risks."

"Meg, I understand. Let's do it."

Jake and Beth moved to the observation port as the ship started its return to Earth.

In the lower portion of the ship, Chameleon sat on a bench getting some updates from the repair drones. The robot's eyes were locked on a small crack on the opposite wall. Meg knew that the robot was having trouble processing something he'd heard.

"Chameleon, is there a problem?"

"I am not sure, Meg. The explanation you gave Beth and Jake about the end of mankind is hard for me to process. I understand the logistics, but I do not comprehend why our creators do not allow you to help the humans."

"I understand your concern, Chameleon, but our creators have very specific rules regarding interference. Once we hamper development within a species, it is difficult to determine how, and when to stop.

"Our creators do however have what Jake likes to call a

backup plan. In the DNA sample room, a device took a very large sample of DNA for terraforming the planet in the future. It has been released and is hidden somewhere in deep space. We are the only two that know of this device, so you must never speak of this to anyone."

"I understand, Meg. It looks like there may still be hope for mankind."

Chapter 60

The President was in the Oval Office meeting with his senior advisors when an aide came in yelling about a new sighting of the spaceship.

Immediately, the Armed Forces Chief of Staff stood up and spoke.

"We need to know what you want us to do. If it is coming toward the White House, can we attempt to shoot it down?"

The President looked around at the rest of the advisors, then back to the General.

"General, I don't want you to fire at that ship. The last fighter that tried was vaporized. I have a feeling that the technology on the ship is so far beyond ours that any threatening attempts would only make things worse. Let's just sit tight, General, and wait and see."

The room was quiet for a second, and then the chatter increased. As they sat around the President, he suddenly was surrounded by a blue light and disappeared. The Secret Service rushed into the room, but the President was nowhere to be found.

Jake and Beth were waiting in the garden as the President appeared. He seemed a little shaken, so Jake stuck out his hand, but the President ignored him.

"Mr. President, please have a seat and relax. We'll explain everything soon."

"What the hell's going on here? Where am I?" yelled the President.

"Mr. President, we are so glad to meet you. My name is Jake McDonald and this is my wife, Beth. Our kids, Brad and Kathy are running around here somewhere. I know you have many questions, but they'll have to wait as we have to pick up another passenger."

"I don't care who you are. You have no right to kidnap

me. Where am I?"

Beth said, "Mr. President, we didn't kidnap you. Well, maybe we did, but it was in good faith. We only wanted to talk with you, and this was the only way for a private conversation. You are on the spaceship that was recently hovering over Antarctica."

The Russians had already heard about the kidnapping of the American President and were in the process of moving President Vladimir Kortof to a more secure location. As the guards surrounded the Russian President, a blue light enveloped him, and he disappeared before their eyes.

Jake, Beth, and the American President watched as the Russian President appeared. He started to rant and rave about being kidnapped, but once he saw the American President, he calmed down.

Jake reached out in vain to shake the Russian President's hand.

"My name is Jake McDonald and this is my wife, Beth. Welcome to my spaceship, Mr. President. If you'll both follow me, I'll explain everything."

He followed the American President and Beth as they headed toward an elevator. It was deathly quiet as the four progressed up several floors.

As they exited, Jake pointed, "You'll find your first question answered at the end of this hallway."

The American President increased his pace as the edge of the Earth came into view.

"Oh my, God, how in the hell did I get here?"

When the Russian President reached the window, he spoke in Russian, but Jake assumed that he'd made the same comment.

Jake moved over to face the two Presidents.

"The reason I brought you two together is simple. I need both of you to stop the direction Earth is headed. If you don't, it will ultimately result in the end of the world as we know it. I can't explain it as well as my computer friend, so for the next ten minutes listen to what she has to say. Be assured that this isn't some kind of trick. It's the real deal. You are indeed on an alien spaceship. My advice is to listen to my ship's computer, and hopefully utilize this new knowledge."

Meg started to lay out the demise of the Earth to the two Presidents. She added extremely graphic detail of how it would be in the end. It was enough to scare the hell out of anybody, and maybe it would make them listen.

When Meg finished, both Presidents were considerably more humble. The American President's face even turned pale. After they had a few minutes to recover, Jake added his final comments.

"I know what you just heard is a lot to digest in a short time, but I hope you take heed to what she presented. You are the two most powerful men on Earth. Our blue planet is headed toward destruction, but you can give it hope. My computer's calculations give you little optimism, but I still think you have a chance to make things right.

"President Kortof; I thank you for your time. You will notice that the arm you broke several years back is no longer painful when you move it. Asthma you had since childhood will no longer give you a problem. In fact, you should live another 30 to 40 years if you don't destroy the Earth first."

With the last words, President Kortof disappeared. Jake turned toward the American President.

"When you return to your office, I highly recommend that you don't go into an alien abduction story. They'll probably impeach you if you do. What I recommend is that you meet with the Russian President and try to solve some of the problems my computer mentioned."

For the next few minutes, the American President looked down on the Earth.

"Sadly, Jake, I do believe what your computer said is true,

but I don't have a chance in hell of changing anything. I may appear to be in charge, but in fact, I generally go where politicians direct me. If I veer off the track, I lose credibility or get impeached. I come up for re-election soon, so my hands will be tied. If you could use this ship to help, we might be able to make the changes together."

"Mr. President, do you really think that if I turned this technology over to your military, the problem would be solved? The first thing they'd do is suppress anyone who disagreed. You have to do this on your own since I'm not allowed to help you.

"By the way, your right leg will no longer give you problems, and you can throw away your blood pressure medicine. It's just a couple of perks for visiting my ship."

Jake stuck out his hand again, and this time the American President shook his hand. As soon as it was released, the President disappeared.

Jake looked over at the 3-D image of Meg. "So, how did that go?"

"Jake, that was a valiant effort, but sadly a waste of time. The Russian President has already ordered high alert, thinking it was an American trick. The American President was immediately sedated and assumed to be under alien control. The 25th amendment was enacted, and the Vice-President is now in charge."

"Could I have done anything differently, Meg? Maybe I should have invited all scientists, Sci-Fi writers, and the news media. I just feel like I should've done something else."

"Jake, I ran those scenarios though my processors, and all indicated failure. There are just too many people with too many ideas. They all disagree on several points, so nothing will ever be solved. It is a no-win scenario. I am sorry, Jake."

"So that's it. We give up."

Beth had been quietly processing this information.

"Jake, Meg is right. There's nothing we can do. Earth is past the point of no return. Fifty years ago, we might've been able to save it, but now it's too late. We just need to ask Meg what we can do to save part of humanity."

Jake looked puzzled at Beth, but Meg started the next conversation.

"Beth is correct. You need to consider what you can to salvage thousands of years of human evolution. Think about it. You can travel to new worlds and start over. It is totally up to you two. You can choose to take a few extra people along to settle in this new world."

Jake looked over to Beth for help, and then back to Meg.

"How do we pick these people, and do you think they would really want to join us?"

"I would recommend professional people from a variety of fields. I have compiled a list of twenty occupations I feel would help you get a start on a new evolution. Feel free to add or delete items from the list, and then I will do an extensive search for suitable people."

Jake thought about it for a moment.

"So would we be looking for healthy twenty to thirty-year-olds that are willing to go on a permanent adventure?"

Beth broke into the conversation.

"Jake, I don't think that'll work. Most young people have just started their lives, and don't want to trade it for the promise of an unknown. Remember, these people must be willing to leave Earth forever.

"If I understand the technology, when you beam up someone, you repair all their ailments. Therefore, someone with lung cancer, a broken leg, or arthritis, would all be healed. Jake, we need to look for older professionals who have lived a full life and are looking to go out with a bang. We need to look for fifty to seventy-year-olds with degrees of expertise, knowledge, and a desire to experience something new. They'll be easier to work with, and simpler to convince."

"Sorry, Jake but she is correct. Look over this list of professions that I started, make any additions and I will start to search for candidates. Tomorrow, we will solicit our potential passengers, and we can leave the following day."

Jake and Beth picked up the list that Meg had printed out. It read as follows:

1. *Geologist*
2. *Medical*
3. *Biologist*
4. *Cook*
5. *Teacher*
6. *Physics*
7. *Language Expert*
8. *Pilot*
9. *Hydroponics*
10. *Psychologist*
11. *Chemist*
12. *Mathematician*
13. *Mechanical Engineer*
14. *Electronic Engineer*
15. *Historian*
16. *Computer Tech*
17. *Artist*
18. *Musician*
19. *Lawyer*
20. *MacGyver Type*

Before Jake could respond, Beth cut in.

"Meg, this list looks great. I don't see much to change."

"Well I do," said Jake. "In all fairness to the *Excalibur* shuttle crew, I think we should offer a seat to any of them who might want to go."

Beth was quick to respond.

"I agree. A mix of new blood with an interest in space exploration would be a nice blend with a bunch of old duffers."

Jake laughed at her comment.

"Old duffers? They were your idea."

"Let's call them seasoned citizens. I still think these experienced professionals will be the best for the trip, or at least I hope so. I guess it depends on whom Meg picks as candidates. Remember that if they have a good reason for volunteering for a one-way mission, it usually means they're not too happy with their lives. We might get some pretty strange people."

"Beth, I think it's time we get some shuteye. We have a big day tomorrow, and who knows what'll happen the following days. This will be a whole new beginning for our family."

As they walked toward their bedroom, they passed the kids and Chameleon in the hallway.

Jake looked back at them and said, "He's a hell of a babysitter."

Chapter 61

Adam Larsen glanced out his window at his neighbor mowing his lawn. Watching a show on the Discovery Channel just didn't hold much charm these days. He enjoyed the geology portion, but the rest seemed depressing, just like his life. Everything seemed to go wrong these last ten years. If only he could go back and do it over.

When he first got his doctorate in geology at age twenty-four, the world was his to explore. He'd been on every continent in the world and explored just about every geologically important location. Many of his discoveries changed the way today's geologists viewed the infrastructure of Earth. He'd received countless grants for beaucoup dollars, and eventually became a geology professor at his home college in Colorado. He authored several books, lectured worldwide, and continued to lead digs up until ten years ago.

Then his wife Edna contracted cancer and died within a few short months. He was lost without her, and it took over two years to recover. By then the college had lost patience and given him the boot.

Five years ago, he finally found a small company in South America that needed a geologist to map a new route for a pipeline. During one of the trips over a small mountain pass, he was careless; slipped, and fell twenty-five feet to the bottom of a ravine. They airlifted him to a local hospital, but the damage had been done. He had a broken back, and his spinal column was severed.

Recovery took more than a year, but now he was confined to a wheelchair. He remained at home and a health caretaker came by twice a day for assistance. His neighbor filled in when he needed additional help. Adam felt as though he had been dealt a bad hand in life, but he wasn't quite ready to give up yet.

When he looked back at the TV screen, it went blank. He

299

reached for the remote, but the screen came back to life. The image on the screen was of a man's face Adam had never seen before. He clicked the channel selection, but nothing happened. He turned the power off and on, with no effect. He was about to roll the wheelchair up to the TV when the man on the screen spoke.

"Hello, Adam. My name is Jake. Don't be alarmed."

"What the hell?"

"Adam, I'm projecting my image to you through this TV set. Please listen to what I have to say, and relax, you're not crazy. Have you been watching the news about the spaceship frenzy?"

Adam looked down at the remote then back to the screen.

"Now you've got my attention. I don't know how you're doing this, but yes, I've been watching the news. So what?"

"Well, Adam, this is going to be hard to believe, but I'm the Captain of that ship, and I have a proposition for you."

Adam looked out the window and then back to the TV set.

"Is this some kind of a trick?"

Jake grinned a little and then continued.

"Roll your wheelchair up to the side of the TV and pull out the power cord."

Adam did as Jake requested, and the image remained on the TV.

"If this were a trick, the TV would've shut off when you disconnected the power. This is the only way I could talk to you without coming directly to your house. So are you ready to hear my proposal?"

"I'm not going anywhere soon, so lay it on me. It better be good, or I am going into the next room."

Jake stepped back so the view on the screen Adam saw was out the window overlooking Earth.

"As I said, Adam, this is going to be hard for you to believe, but it's the honest to goodness truth. The ship I'm on is heading off to explore other solar systems, and I need a geologist

300

to go with me. I'm asking people in various other professions, but you're my first choice for a geologist."

"Let's just say for a moment that I believe your bullshit. Why would you pick me? There are more qualified individuals than me, and just how much can a geologist do from a wheelchair?"

"Well, Adam, that's the thing. My ship has one benefit that I think you're going to love. It uses a beaming technology like the one you've seen in Sci-Fi shows like *Star Trek*. If you agree to beam onto my ship, your back will be repaired and you'll be able to walk again. I picked you because you're a highly qualified geologist, that's extremely motivated by the fact I can make you walk again."

"That's impossible."

"All you have to do is beam aboard with me and it'll happen. You just have to make up your mind by 8 p.m. tonight. Think about the possibilities of exploring other planets, and all the geological discoveries you can make. I hope to see you tonight."

The image of Jake blinked out and the TV went dark. Adam moved his wheelchair over to the wall and plugged back in the TV. The top news story was about the large spherical ship's reappearance. He sat and wondered if this could really be possible? Maybe this was his chance to turn his life around.

Chapter 62

"Well, Beth, one down, nineteen to go. How do you think it went?"

"Actually, I think he'll come on board. If he'd been twenty-five, I don't think he would've considered it."

"As usual, you're always right. Experience is our best option. What's next on the list?"

"Medical and Meg has four possible candidates."

They contacted the first two, and both refused. The first wouldn't believe what Jake was telling him, and left the house slamming the door behind him. The second was a woman who believed him but didn't want to leave her large extended family.

The third name on the list was Julie Cross. Her husband, George, was watching a game show when she entered the living room to ask a question.

As soon as she was in view of the screen, Jake's image appeared. George grabbed the remote to make a change.

"George, changing the channel won't work."

This quickly got both their attention.

"George, what the hell's going on?"

"I didn't do anything. It changed to this channel by itself."

Jake interrupted the conversation.

"My name is Jake McDonald. I'm the Captain of the spaceship that's been all over the news. Before you get too excited and call the police, I want one of you to remove the power cord from the wall. Then you'll see this isn't a practical joke, but reality."

Julie ran over to the wall, pulled the cord, and Jake's image remained.

"I don't know how you're doing this, but you have our interest."

"Actually, Julie, the technology on this ship is far beyond

human expertise. I have a proposal for your consideration. My ship is going on a one-way trip to explore other solar systems, and I need a qualified medical person. You fit the bill. If you agree to come, I'll beam both you and your husband onboard."

"So why us? Surely there are more qualified doctors than me," replied Julie.

"The truth, Julie, is that you are more motivated than most medical people. One of the side benefits of beaming you onto the ship is that all your medical ailments will disappear. Your crippling arthritis will be non-existent and your lives will be extended by thirty to forty years. You'll be able to practice medicine again and think about the fantastic journey you can experience. However, you must decide by 8 p.m. tonight. Talk it over and I'll be back in touch."

Jake's image blinked out. Both Julie and George looked at each other.

"I need a drink."

Julie replied, "Make it two."

The two sat in silence for ten minutes, then started to discuss the possible ramifications of such a trip. The more they contemplated the idea, the more excited they became.

Chapter 63

Jake walked away from the view of Earth and headed toward the dining area.

"I need something to eat before we do the next one. You know this is going to take a few hours. Who's next on the list?"

Beth scanned the list and said, "Biologist, and there are six possibilities."

Jake made quick work of a turkey sandwich before commenting.

"I know Meg did the best she could, but maybe we can weed it down a little before we contact them."

For the next half an hour they worked on reducing the list of candidates for the eighteen remaining spots. When it was condensed down from eighty possibilities to forty, they stopped.

"Well, I hope the rest goes easier than the first few," Jake said. "I didn't realize how hard it would be to convince people that I was talking to them from a spaceship. Folks are skeptical because of all the Sci-Fi TV, *X-Files*, and stuff."

Beth opened the revised list of people. "If the first one is a no go, let me try the second. Maybe we need to alternate, and I think people may be more inclined to believe us if we're both on the screen."

The first prospective biologist was a no go. He'd just received a grant to study the destruction of the coral reefs due to increased water temperatures. Jake argued unsuccessfully that the exploration of animals on other planets would be more interesting. Beth took a try at the next one.

Allen Foster was a fifty-five-year-old biologist who'd worked in the field for twenty years. Unfortunately, he got carried away with his environmental concerns and was shunned by most other biologists. By the time he realized he'd gone too far, it was too late and his world started falling apart. He lost his job and his wife ran off with his best friend. Bills were piling up as he looked for any kind of job for which he was qualified.

Allen had spent the last four days pounding the beat looking for work, and he was exhausted. He slept in this morning and turned on the TV for a news update while he drank his coffee. No matter how much he tried to switch the channel, the image of a couple remained on the screen. He looked at the image closer and noticed Earth through the window behind them.

"Allen, this may seem a little strange, but my husband, Jake, and I would like to make you a proposition. You can try to change the channels, or even unplug the TV, but we'll still be here."

Beth and Jake waited as Allen disconnected the TV and realizing that nothing worked, Allen finally sat down.

"This has to be one of the best tricks I've ever seen."

Beth started her sales spiel, "Allen, this isn't a joke or a trick. If you've been following the news, you know about the spaceship hovering over the Earth. That's our ship, and we're about to leave tomorrow for another solar system. We are in need of a biologist to help in our explorations. We need you, and you're definitely motivated. You've been looking for a job, and we have one that's right up your alley."

Allen sat back for a few moments and cycled through what he'd just heard.

"Why me?"

"That seems to be everyone's first question. We're selecting extremely qualified people that are motivated enough to go on a space exploration one-way trip. If you were younger with a promising future, we doubt you would consider it."

Before she could continue, Allen interrupted her.

"That's where you're wrong. If you're truly telling me that we can travel to other solar systems and see biological wonders beyond Earth, I would go at any age. After seeing how much we've screwed up this planet, you don't have to convince me. I'll go."

Beth looked at Jake in surprise.

"Allen, you're the first one to agree right away. Sit and think about it until 8 p.m. tonight. If you still want to go, we'll beam you up. As sort of a sign on bonus, all your aches and pains from age will go away once you're on the ship."

Beth's image blinked out, but the image of Allen remained on the ship's view screen. Allen was literally jumping up and down with joy. He was a definite.

Beth asked Meg to turn off the screen and said, "He was so excited that he wanted to sign up right on the spot."

Jake gave her a light kiss on the lips.

"I think you should do the rest of them. It looks like you'll become our new Ship's Ambassador. You could sweet talk the skin off a snake."

"Why would I want to do that?"

Jake laughed as he again looked at the list.

"It's just an old expression from my younger days."

Chapter 64

Chuck Dennison looked at the pile of dishes that the waiter had just dumped onto the counter. He tried to smile back at the waiter, but in truth, he hated everyone who worked at the restaurant. Actually, it was more envy than hate. At one time, he owned a place like this, but then there was the fire. One of his new cooks was showing off and spilled the pan's contents directly onto the burners. The fire flash took everyone by surprise, and before anyone could get the extinguisher, the fire had engulfed the kitchen.

Even worse was the fact that his wife had taken over the books and had made some bad financial decisions. When it came time to pay the bills, she was short. Not wanting to fess up, she decided to compensate by dropping the restaurant insurance for a year. The restaurant burned to the ground, and the bank repossessed the land.

They got into a big fight, and she left blaming Chuck for all their problems. In truth, he'd put too much pressure on everyone in the restaurant, and treated his wife more like an employee than a spouse. Now he was a dishwasher, watching TV news about some space ship over Antarctica.

He was about to look away when a text message appeared on the screen. *There is an emergency at home, Chuck. Go home now.* It disappeared as fast as it came on. He looked at the other people in the kitchen, but no one had seen it. Then a picture of his living room came on with the same message overlaid. He could see his cat running across the living room. He took off his apron and headed out the door. The last words he heard were his boss, telling him that if he didn't return to work right now he was fired.

He raced home, and when he opened the door, Beth's face appeared on his TV screen.

"Hi, Chuck, my name is Beth. Sorry about your job, but

don't worry because I have a new cooking opportunity that might interest you. How would you like to be a ship's cook for about forty people?"

Chuck looked at the screen. He needed a better job, but this had to be a practical joke. He was about to turn it off but then thought maybe it was worth his time to listen.

"Okay, I'll bite. How much do I get paid, and how long is the trip?"

Beth smiled and moved to the side to expose a view of Earth below.

"The truth is, Chuck, the job doesn't pay at all. We'll provide your living quarters, and anything you need, so there's no need for a paycheck. I know this may be hard to believe, but the job is onboard the spaceship now hovering above Antarctica. We have an automated cooking kitchen on the ship, but we want the human touch to supplement the meal's flavor. I know that you don't believe me, so feel free to pull out the TV's power cord, or try to change the channels."

Chuck pulled the cord and ran through the channels, but Beth was still there.

"I'm convinced. What do you want me to do?"

"Think about it to be sure and we'll contact you at 8 p.m. tonight. Pack anything personal that you don't want to leave on Earth."

"I can cook anything I want? Set up my own menus?"

"You'll be the boss, Chuck, and can cook up whatever you desire. We can get any kitchen supplies you require once you're onboard."

Chuck smiled for the first time in months.

"You know I love to cook. If there's a chance you're telling the truth, then I'm in."

"See you at 8 p.m." Beth's face disappeared, and the view of Earth remained for a few seconds.

Chuck stepped closer and looked at the image. It sure looked real. He ran into the kitchen, pulled out a thick steak, and cooked up his last meal on Earth.

Chapter 65

Sherry Wiseman stood at the front of her ninth-grade English class. She was running down the assignments for the rest of the month, but her mind kept drifting back to the doctor's appointment three months prior. Breast cancer was the norm for her family, so she'd been religious about getting mammograms. The doctor wanted to catch it early if Sherry followed her mother and grandmother's history. Nevertheless, she wasn't prepared, and the bad news hit hard.

They'd started treatment, and were already looking at surgery options. She decided to keep it from the school and her class, at least for now. She didn't want anyone to feel sorry for her.

The school had set up a computer workstation on her desk to help her stay organized, and serve as a teleprompter. She'd installed a program that projected large text on the screen and would automatically scroll down as she read different sections of a book. She was about to start reading "A Tale of Two Cities" when a message came up on the screen.

"There is a permanent cure for your breast cancer. All it requires is that you teach school to a couple of kids on a ship. For this service, the cost to you is free."

She looked around the classroom.

"Which one of you knuckleheads has been messing with my computer?"

There was no response from the class. She then remembered she hadn't told anyone about her cancer except her husband. She was about to press the escape key when a small video picture of a woman appeared in the upper-right of the screen. As she spoke, her words appeared displaying the new text.

"I know this is hard to believe, but you need to give your class a reading assignment for fifteen minutes, while I explain."

Sherry looked up at the class and told everyone to read the first chapter while she momentarily worked on the class schedule. She explained that when everyone had finished, they would discuss what they'd read. As soon as she completed her announcement, the message continued.

"No one is playing with your computer system. I know about your breast cancer. My name is Beth and I'm married to the man who is running the ship now hovering above Antarctica. We need a teacher for the children on the ship. In trade, we have the technology to eliminate your cancer. I can't stress enough that this isn't a scam or joke. We would never do that to someone suffering from cancer. I also know that what I'm asking requires a giant leap of faith, so give it some serious consideration. You have until 8 p.m. tonight to decide."

The message held for a few seconds and then disappeared, only to be replaced with the teleprompter's book text. Her mind was spinning. What if the woman was telling the truth? Hopefully, she could live by having surgery, but the other option would make her cancer-free. She notified the main office she was sick and headed home.

Her husband Prescott was going to be a tough nut to crack. Her plan was to start with the news broadcast about the spaceship and then work into some what-if scenarios.

When she got home, he greeted her with a kiss and a big smile.

"Beth already talked with me and told me what she told you. I believe her, and think we should give it a shot. What the hell, I've always wondered what it would be like to go into space."

The two sat and talked for the next three hours. In the end, the decision was easy.

Chapter 66

Diana Hoss sat staring at the walls of her study crammed full of books on physics. Her eyes stopped on the framed Nobel Prize document that had been her lifelong goal. She loved physics and was determined to help solve the secrets of the universe. She'd specialized in rare elements and had become the foremost expert in the field.

That was until she started preaching her unorthodox ideas that there were elements on Earth yet to be discovered. As she became more adamant about her theories, she lost her supporters and eventually was shunned by the scientific community. Even her husband had abandoned her, and at age sixty-three, she felt alone in the universe.

She was about to go to the kitchen for a bite to eat when the view changed on her computer monitor. It was an image of Earth from space. Suddenly the image changed again and displayed a woman sitting in a garden.

"Hi, Diana, my name is Beth. This may seem strange and you might think it is some kind of trick, but you need to believe what I'm about to tell you. Have you seen the news about the alien ship above Earth?"

Diana ran over to the office window to see if anyone was outside. Seeing nothing amiss, she came back to the screen.

Beth suggested she unplug the power cord for proof that it was real, and Diana quickly did as Beth instructed. She then looked at the screen and saw Beth was still on the monitor.

"What I'm seeing is impossible. There's no way this can be happening."

"Diana, you're an intelligent person who believes in hard scientific fact, so here goes. My husband, Jake, took possession of the ship that's in the news and I'm broadcasting from it right now. We're planning a little journey out of the solar system, and we could use a physics expert. Is it possible that there's life beyond Earth? We plan to find out. Some of the areas where we're headed to none of us have a clue about and need someone who can think outside the box. Clearly, that's you.

"All we ask is that you think about it and give us your decision when we connect back at 8 p.m. tonight. You really have nothing to lose and everything to gain."

"I'm sorry, but I'm not buying all this hogwash. This is some cruel joke someone has gone to great lengths to set up."

Dianna was actually excited about the possibilities but didn't want to admit it to Beth. She could only hope that what she'd heard was really going to happen and she could join the expedition. They would know when 8 o'clock rolled around.

Chapter 67

Herbert Stoutdale had just turned sixty-three and was feeling pretty good about his life. A language expert since age twenty-two, he now spoke over 65 languages. He'd had a full life, but recently he felt something was missing. He needed a new challenge because he was bored with life. He'd tried to explain it to his wife Lavone, but she didn't understand.

Most grant applications wanted younger blood in the field, and everyone kept telling him to retire. If he retired, what would he do? He had no hobbies, and language was his life.

He turned on the TV to catch up on the news. As he clicked through the channels, it stopped working and settled on an image of a woman sitting in a garden.

She looked directly at him and said, "Good afternoon, Dr. Stoutdale. How are you today? Before you try to change the channels, you need to hear what I have to say."

Herbert stood up and walked over to the TV. He turned around and looked for a hidden camera.

"Is this some kind of a joke? Are you hiding in the next room?"

"Actually, no, Mr. Stoutdale. The truth is that I'm broadcasting from the spaceship above Antarctica. Have you ever seen the movie *Cocoon*?"

There was silence in the room.

"This is no joke, but we would like to offer you and your wife a chance of a lifetime. How would you like to visit other planets and translate new and unknown alien languages? We need someone to do that, and you're our best choice. Hopefully, you believe what I say and consider our offer. We will be back in touch at 8 p.m. to hear your decision. By the way, the *Cocoon* movie reference was my husband's idea. I never would've thought of it."

Herbert thought about it for a second and then said,

314

"What if I go along with you on this crazy adventure. What about my wife? How would she fit into your ridiculous story?"

Beth smiled as the camera panned around the garden.

"I think she will be very happy helping me tend this beautiful garden. Talk it over with her and we hope to see you both tonight."

Chapter 68

Kevin Shotwell stood in his private airplane hangar gazing at the fruits of his labor. The sleek looking jet was the envy of pilots at the small airport, as it was the only jet there certified to do over Mach 1. He took the aircraft up for three hours of solitude every week.

The aero business world sucked because other designers were always trying to steal credit for his ideas. Even though he was sixty-eight years old, airplane designers around the country were hounding him to work in their design departments. He always told them no, because all he wanted to do was fly.

It had not always been that way. When his wife was alive, he could handle the dog-eat-dog world. His wife always calmed him down when he got frustrated with work. Ten years ago, his world fell apart when his wife was killed by a drunk driver. Kevin was arrested a few days later for beating the crap out of the driver. The man sued him for assault and won a judgment plus a restraining order. Kevin quit his job and started to build his dream machine.

He did a final check around the aircraft before climbing in. Five minutes later he was at twelve thousand feet drifting through the endless layers of clouds that served as his buffer from humanity. He'd put everything he could think of in the cockpit instrument panel. It had triple navigation systems, video feeds on the six sides of the aircraft, and a computer diagnostic system that made the military envious. He was about to return to the airstrip when the main video displayed a woman's face against a black sky and the curved surface of Earth.

"Good afternoon, Kevin. You have a wonderful aircraft. Can we please talk a moment?"

Kevin started to scan all the instruments. There were no errors displayed, but what he was seeing was impossible. He had security firewall systems built into all the communication and guidance systems. There was no way a video feed could be displayed on the monitor.

"I don't know how you're doing this, but it's illegal. You need to get off my system."

Beth turned and pointed to the image of Earth.

"I'll give you one guess as to where I am broadcasting from."

"The ship that's been all over the news?"

"Bingo."

"That's impossible."

"Isn't that what everyone told you when you started to build this plane?"

He nodded.

"Kevin, please turn off the autopilot and let go of the controls."

He hesitated for a few moments and then did as Beth told him. The plane stayed on course but started to slow. Kevin expected to hear warning bells and a drop in altitude, but the plane stayed at the same altitude. He started to panic when the plane's airspeed dropped to one hundred miles an hour. He tried to take back the controls, but they were locked. Soon he was at zero forward movement, yet maintaining the same altitude. The readings on the gauges were impossible.

"Now you have my full attention. I don't know how you're doing this, but I want to hear what you have to say."

Beth told him of the trip Jake had planned and their need for a veteran pilot. She outlined information about the other passengers who were being asked to go. The more he listened, the more excited he got.

"Why me?"

"You have two necessary qualifications - you are motivated, and you have the experience. Besides, I know you want to travel into space. It's in your blood. Just consider this the next step in the evolution of Kevin Shotwell."

Chapter 69

When thirty-seven-year-old Dean Hinton first got married, he'd been working for a large hydroponics research firm. Everything was great until one of the secretaries started making flirtatious advances toward Dean. He'd refused her, and when she continued her advances, he lodged a complaint. Unfortunately, she turned it around saying Dean had made the advances. His wife was his soul mate and trusted him completely, so when he was fired, she suggested they start their own hydroponics website.

Dean Hinton sat back in his chair waiting for the changes he'd just made to their website to upload. He retested the new page and everything seemed fine.

His wife, Cleo, came in and handed him a cup of coffee, looking over his shoulder.

"That looks really good, Honey. The tomatoes look good enough to eat right off the page."

He turned around and pulled her down in his lap. He gave her a brief kiss on the lips, hesitated, and then gave her a long kiss.

"You taste good enough to eat yourself," said Dean. "What is that, strawberry lipstick?"

She kissed him again and reached down with her hand between his legs.

"Good deduction. Now guess what I'm doing."

The hydroponics webpage in front of them changed to an image of a woman sitting in a garden.

"Excuse me, but you might want to wait for more privacy before continuing."

Cleo pulled her hand back up, and Dean reached over to see what had happened to his web page. None of the computer controls was functioning.

"It looks like we have a virus, but luckily I saved it before it invaded."

He killed the computer power knowing it was a risk, but his paranoia about backups had saved his butt more times than not. The image remained on the screen. Cleo pulled the power cord, from the wall but the image stayed.

"I'm sorry to break in on your ...um...private moment. I know this is hard to believe, but I'm broadcasting to you from the ship above Antarctica. I can only communicate through TV sets and computer screens. We are collecting a band of travelers to help us explore other solar systems. The truth is we need someone to join us who can grow food quickly. From the looks of your webpage, you two are the best."

"I don't know how you did this, but you have our attention."

Beth explained all about their plans and the other members of the entourage. The one-way trip was described and their pressing timeline.

"Talk it over as this is an important decision. I hope to see you at 8 p.m. tonight, and you'll be in for a big surprise if you take a chance. By the way, Cleo, you can continue where you left off. You'll have complete privacy."

Beth's image disappeared off the screen. Dean and Cleo looked at each other with questioning faces. Both were about to speak, but Cleo beat Dean to the draw.

"What the hell, Dean. If this is really the truth, oh my God!"

Cleo's face froze at the thought of what had just been proposed. Their sexual drives faded and were quickly replaced with the endless questions of the what-ifs of such a journey.

Chapter 70

Fifty-year-old Gary Gilman sat on his lounge chair overlooking the resort pool. This was his fifth year coming to Cancun for the diving medical conference. Each year, the resort sponsored a week for doctors interested in diving medicine. The doctors could write off the trip, and get a few dives in each afternoon. His presentation was on the psychology of diving.

As he took a sip of his non-alcoholic tropical drink, he reflected on how his life had progressed to where he was today. He'd graduated with his doctorate in psychology at age twenty-seven and opened a business in downtown Kansas City. Because of his school loan debt, he had to locate in a part of town that didn't generate much income for his fledgling business. He loved working with the neighborhood people, but he couldn't keep up the expenses of running an office in a financially depressed neighborhood.

He was offered a partnership in a large office downtown, and was forced to make the move, but hated it. Most of his clients didn't need psychological help but wanted to impress their friends because they had their own psychologist. The last straw was when he was handed a patient who feared buying a new Rolls Royce.

When he announced to his wife that he'd quit, she gave him notice and walked out. Not knowing where to turn, it was suggested that he write a book about his experiences. He took the next six months to put together a book, and to his surprise, it was successful. Six books and hundreds of lectures later, he was still trying to find out what to do with his life.

He was set to make a couple of dives in the afternoon and returned to his room to get ready. As he passed by the TV set, it came on with a woman's face on the screen.

"Mr. Gilman, my name is Beth. How are you today?"

Gary stopped and looked at the screen. He never watched

TV on these trips and was surprised to see the image. She had even called him by name. The woman on the screen patiently waited as he looked around the room for a webcam.

"You won't find any cameras in the room, Gary. Your TV set is the camera. Do me a favor? Unplug it from the wall, and you might be surprised at the results."

Gary hesitated, but finally reached over and unplugged it. He came back, and the woman's face was still on the screen.

"That's a pretty good trick, but I really don't have time for this. I have a dive in the next half an hour."

The image of Beth panned back until the image of Earth through the port was visible behind her.

"Gary, this isn't a trick. Look at the window behind me. Where am I right now?"

Gary moved to the screen and looked closer. Earth was slowly moving in the image.

"Beth, you have my attention. Crazy as it sounds, you're on the ship that's all over the news, right?"

"Good guess, Gary. I'm the wife of the Captain of the spaceship in the news. We're going on a trip of a lifetime, and selecting twenty professionals from different fields of study to go with us. We're looking for a psychologist to help the passengers on our trip adjust mentally to deep space flight. We picked you because you're motivated and very experienced. Are you interested? If so, we'll pick you up at 8 p.m."

Gary sat down on the edge of the bed. He looked back up at Beth's smiling face and then saw a man sit down beside her.

"Hi Gary, I'm Jake, the Captain of the ship. I hope you believe my wife. We could really use you onboard."

Gary looked out the window at the gentle waves breaking on the beach, and then back to the screen.

"I'm not sure I believe you, but the very fact the ship's existence has been confirmed by every news station leads me to put some stock in what you've explained. There has to be a reason the ship is hanging around, and your story is as good as the next. So, what's next?"

"We'll be there about 8 p.m. to pick you up. Pack up everything you want to bring with you. If you decide to go with us, keep that in mind we'll not be coming back."

Chapter 71

At age fifty-eight, Tom Linderman and his wife, Stacey, had been interested in chemistry all their lives. They met in graduate school and fell in love while working on projects together. After they married they thought about having children, but their careers seemed to take priority.

Stacey found the first job working for a small medical firm, testing new drugs. Tom bounced around for a year before being offered a lead position in a large cancer research center. A few years later, a position opened up for his wife in the same company, and the two had been loyal employees for almost thirty years.

They were now at a new precipice in their lives as they were both burned out. They loved the people at the center, but they needed a new spark in their lives.

Tom looked at his computer monitor and saw an image of a woman standing next to a window with Earth in the background. Tom moved his mouse, but nothing happened. He could see Earth moving in the background, and then the woman spoke.

"Tom, how are you today? My name is Beth. The view behind me is from the ship you've seen on the news. You might want to bring your wife, Stacey, over so I don't have to repeat myself. Then before you do anything else, turn off the monitor and unplug it from your computer. I'll wait before continuing."

Tom figured it was a joke until he unplugged the monitor, and the image was still there. He shook his head and knew this wasn't possible. He ran off and returned with Stacey, who was telling him that he was crazy. She pressed on/off switch it a couple of times and confirmed monitor cable was unplugged. She even picked up the monitor and moved it off the desk, but Beth's image remained.

She set the monitor back down.

"Tom, this is one hell of a practical joke. How did you do it?"

The image on the screen answered.

"Stacey, it isn't a joke. The image you see on the screen is being broadcasted from the ship in the news. My husband and I have a proposition for the two of you. We're taking the ship to explore other solar systems and need a team of experienced professionals. We need a chemist, and the two of you would be a great team asset. We're picking everyone up tonight at 8 p.m. and leaving tomorrow. This is a chance of a lifetime, so consider wisely."

Before either Tom or Stacey could respond, the image of Beth disappeared from the screen.

Stacey looked back at Tom.

"What the hell was that? If this is a joke, Tom, it's a good one."

Tom looked around to see if anyone in the lab was looking their way. Most of the other employees were workaholics like them.

"This isn't a joke, Stacey. You know me; I'm all work, with no time for play. Besides, don't you find it strange that this happened at the same time the ship appeared in the news?"

"My God, Tom. If it's not a joke, then..."

Chapter 72

Phillip Martin had many vices but had survived to a ripe old age of seventy. Numbers were his game. He loved math and spent the last forty years as a high school teacher sharing his enthusiasm for numbers with the younger generation.

His biggest vice was that he was a chain smoker, and it had finally caught up with him. The doctors had given him less than six months before the lung cancer would win. He sat in his wheelchair gazing at his sixty-five-year-old wife, Lucy, tending her garden. It wouldn't be long now.

Phillip had no one to blame but himself. Lucy repeatedly tried to get him to quit, but he was stubborn and kept sneaking another smoke. When he got the "C" word, he quit immediately. It was so easy; he wished he'd done it sooner. They could have squeaked out a couple more years together.

Lucy got up, brushed off her clothes, and pushed Phillip back into the house. She handed him the remote, and when he turned on the TV, a woman's face appeared. Phillip pressed the channel changer, but every channel had the same image. He turned to Lucy.

"Something's wrong with the remote."

She took it from him, and pressed the up/down on the channels and got the same results. She looked back at Phillip and was about to say something when the image on the screen spoke.

"Hello, Phillip, and, Lucy, my name is Beth. Phillip, I know about your cancer. I'm very sorry about that, but the good news is I have a cure. I know you may think this is some kind of trick, but it is the honest truth."

The expression on Lucy's face turned from compassion for Phillip to anger at the woman on the screen.

"Is this some kind of sick joke? Leave us alone whoever you are."

Lucy pressed the power button off and nothing happened.

325

In desperation, she walked over and unplugged the TV, but the image still remained.

"This isn't a joke, Lucy. I really want to help both of you, especially your husband. I'm on the spaceship you have seen in the news. My husband and I are putting together a band of space explorers to explore beyond our solar system. We need a mathematician to join us, and honestly, a gardener would also be very helpful. We want the two of you because you both offer needed expertise for our trip."

Lucy was about to respond, but Phillip spoke first.

"You're right, I do have experience, which tells me this is an elaborate joke or one of the craziest ideas I've ever heard. I'm seventy years old and about to die in six months. What use would I be on a spaceship?"

"Normally, a seventy-year-old man about to die wouldn't be a good choice for a deep space flight, but there's an upside to the voyage. The technology required to bring you aboard would cure your cancer and extend your life by thirty to forty years. I know numbers make sense to you, so I'm going to display a computer program that will show you the technology."

Before Phillip could respond, diagrams and formulas displayed the basics of the beaming technology. Ten minutes later, the short course in future science disappeared, and Beth reappeared.

"Phillip, if you do, believe me, you and your wife can extend your lives beyond your wildest dreams. Lucy, I could really use some help in our garden. I will return tonight at 8 p.m. for your answer. Give us a chance."

The image disappeared, and Phillip and Lucy couldn't stop talking about the possibilities right up until 8 p.m.

Beth got up from in front of the video screen used to contact potential travelers. She yawned and stretched her legs. Jake was looking out the window at Earth.

"You're doing great, Beth. Twelve down and eight to go.

326

How about we get some lunch before we hit the last group. Maybe we can modify our approach for the last eight people."

"I hope we're doing the right thing," said Beth. "Some of these people are quite old, but I know that Meg can add many years to their lives."

Jake turned back to Beth.

"Look at it this way. We really don't need any of these people to run the ship. Meg can do it all on her own. We're just looking to save a small piece of humanity to pass on to the next generation. Hopefully, they'll learn from our mistakes. If anyone knows how to correct those mistakes, it will be this group."

"You're right about that, Jake, let's go get some pizza."

As they entered the dining area, they spotted Brad, Kathy, and Chameleon. The two kids had already ordered pizza and were arguing about something. Chameleon sat opposite them in what appeared to be a trance.

Jake started to laugh. "I didn't think anything could scare Chameleon, but it looks like our two just might."

Chapter 73

An hour later Jake and Beth returned to their recruitment assignment determined to find a mechanical engineer. The first two flatly refused to talk to Beth or Jake. They knew it had to be a practical joke.

On the third try, Beth contacted the fifty-year-old auto mechanic designer, Douglas Peters, and his wife, Kim. Douglas has Lou Gehrig's disease, which had progressed to a point where life seemed fruitless. When Beth appeared, neither Douglas nor his wife believed her. Beth remained calm as she talked, and never pressured the two while explaining future possibilities. The appearance of the ship on the news made them consider the possibility, but the allure of a cure for Douglas sealed the deal. By that evening, the two had decided to go.

Beth's next attempt to find an electronic engineer was a bust on her first attempt. The engineer was sure his friends were playing a joke on him, so he left his house. Beth move on to the next name suggested - Alan Walters, age thirty-eight. Beth felt sure Walters would turn it down because he was one of the youngest people she had contacted.

In Meg's research, she determined that Alan had problems with management, but had a high sense of business ethics. A disagreement over a quality control problem had gotten him fired. His wife, who also worked at the company, had been fired for unknown reasons. Soon after their firings, his wife divorced him and disappeared. Alan bounced from one computer job to the next until he found himself working in a small computer repair firm.

The monitor he was working on had several fried circuits, and he considered it non-repairable. He was about to set the monitor to the side when an image came on the screen. Alan looked at the power and monitor cords and saw they were both disconnected.

"Alan," came a female voice from the monitor. He turned it so that he could clearly see the woman on the screen.

"Hi, Alan, my name is Beth. Don't worry you're not going crazy. To make a long story short, I have a proposition for you. I'm transmitting from the spaceship that has recently been in the news. Our ship is going on a deep space flight to explore other solar systems and we could use an electronic engineer. I know this sounds pretty crazy, but we want you to come along."

"Sure, why not?" was his reply.

Beth wasn't prepared for this response. It was too easy.

"Don't you want to ask more questions? You understand this is a one-way trip, right?"

"Well, I'm pretty good at what I do, and I know that running this monitor without power is impossible. Therefore, the only other feasible answer is that you are telling me the truth. Right now I'm ready for any change."

Beth was so taken aback by Allan that it took a few seconds to recompose herself.

"Well, Allen, we're picking everyone up at 8 p.m. tonight. Think about it and you can give us your final answer then."

"I'll go. Consider it a done deal."

Allen dropped the monitor and sent it crashing to the floor. He reached in his desk for a couple of personal items, walked out the door and headed for home.

Beth looked over to Jake and down at her list of contacts.

"That was really weird, Jake. I never would have dreamed he wouldn't question what we were offering. He didn't hesitate for a moment. To be honest, I'm really getting tired of doing this. Can you do the next one while I sit in the garden for a few minutes and get a second wind?"

Jake came over and sat down in front of the monitor.

"Not a problem. Meg and I'll hold down the fort."

"I'm sure that you both will do fine," said Beth as she exited toward the garden.

Chapter 74

Arnold Shepard, age fifty-four, sat in his library looking at the vast collection of history books. Several were very rare and out of print. He loved history, and couldn't resist them.

After graduation from school, his first job was in the Library of Congress putting books back on the shelf. He quickly worked his way up becoming the main historian for the library. Then he was offered a cushy job at a private school teaching history to rich kids.

One of his hobbies was to research the origins of man. His research explored the possibility that aliens had seeded Earth. For a while, he kept the ideas to himself, but then he started pushing his concepts on other historians and his students. Complaints started to pour in, and he eventually lost his job.

After he was fired, he received another setback when his wife left him for his school's supervisor. Luckily he'd been wise enough to buy and trade enough valuable books to set aside a healthy retirement. Money wasn't the issue, but rather he missed working as a historian.

To satisfy his thirst for history, he'd spend hours surfing the web for interesting historical data, especially on his alien theories. He'd spent most of the morning researching information on Stonehenge when a strange new email notice appeared on his computer screen. The header read *Aliens seeded Earth?* and the senders' address was jake@shipoverantartica.com.

He clicked on the link and a view of the ship hovering over Antarctica appeared with text reading, *Do you want to prove your theories are correct, Arnold?* Several thumbnails representing videos surrounded the ship's image, each with a short label. Arnold clicked on the one labeled *Welcome, Arnold.* When it opened, Jake's face appeared on the screen with Earth peeking through the window behind him. Arnold pressed play.

"*Hi, Arnold, my name is Jake. I know this is weird, but I*

330

decided that this might be the best way to talk to you. In a nutshell, I'm the Captain of the ship you see in the center of your screen. My wife and I are putting together an exploration trip to other solar systems and we need a historian to join us. I'm sure you think this is a bogus email and link, but I can prove otherwise. Turn off the monitor and unplug it from the computer. Now press the pause button and when you have unplugged it, then press play again."

Arnold couldn't believe what he was seeing, but he was curious so he turned off the monitor and disconnected it from the computer. It continued to display the video, so he pressed the play button.

"Now that I have your attention, you must realize I'm serious. If you have a question, ask it now, and then press the answer video."

"This is the craziest thing I've ever seen. How am I supposed to believe you?"

Arnold pressed the play button to see the answer.

"The answer is easy. You don't understand why people consider your theories about aliens seeding Earth hogwash, yet you don't believe I want you with us on the alien ship. The ship is over Antarctica and has been broadcast all over the news. It's more believable than your theories."

"I'm interested, but what about all my books? I couldn't leave them behind. They mean too much to me."

Arnold waited, and then realized that he needed to press the answer button. As soon as he did, Jake came back on the screen.

"We have almost every book possible digitized in our databanks, but I understand about your books. We have room to transport them as well if you desire. We'll be there around 8 p.m. tonight if you're interested in joining us. We hope to see you then."

Chapter 75

Jake leaned back on his chair and twisted his neck. Fifteen candidates were done and only five to go. It seemed like this was taking forever. He was about to proceed to the next person on the list when Beth came back and sat down next to him.

"So, how did you do, Jake? Are we all done?"

"Not really, I just finished with the historian."

"Just one?"

"Do you think you can do better?"

"That sounds like a challenge, and I'll take you on. Let's see, the next one on the list is a Computer Nerd?"

Jake grinned.

"Okay, so I modified the term. The next candidate's name is Jack Williams, age forty-four. He's still into playing computer games, but on a level, we would never comprehend. He's so good with computers that several companies hired him on as a consultant. Things went south when he proposed some radical gaming concepts where terrorists attack us and we have to fight them off. The concept hit too close to home and he's been in a store keeping video games running ever since. Beth, let me give it a try and see if he'll join us."

Jack Williams was buried deep in the back of the store where customers couldn't see him which was just fine with him. Setting on the worktable was his personal laptop. He prided himself that no one could break into his laptop because of all his layers of encryption. He had gaming secrets on that computer and was paranoid about anyone stealing them.

He was about to shut his system down when a message appeared on the screen - *Important message from the ship over Antarctica.* When he tried to access it, Jake's image came on the screen. Afraid that he had a virus, Jack pulled the battery out of the back of the laptop and disconnected the power.

Jake smiled and said, "You're going to have to be better than that to regain access to your laptop. Do you realize that your laptop is running without any power? I would think that alone should verify that I'm talking to you from the spaceship over Antarctica. Here's the deal. We're putting together a group of people with specific skills to help us explore other solar systems. We would like to have you along as our computer specialist. I know you love gaming, so I've arranged for every game in your store to be on the ship when you arrive. Think about the opportunity I'm offering. We'll be back at 8 p.m. tonight for your answer, and we'll beam you onboard the ship."

Jake cut the transmission and sat back in his chair as Beth returned with a cup of coffee in her hand.

"Well, Jake, that was a little short. I caught the end of that spiel as I came in. Do you really think he'll come on board with that little song and dance you did? I would count him as a no show."

"I disagree. The ship is like a computer game. He won't be able to resist."

Beth pushed Jake over so that she was in front of the screen.

"Let me do the last four, and you go see how much trouble the kids they are getting into."

It only took a nudge to get Jake moving. He was tired of this part of the enlistment of crewmembers.

Chapter 76

Beth looked down at the next item on the list and saw there were only two choices for the Artist. Beth read through the biographies and decided that the second one was her best bet.

Scott Bradley, age fifty-seven, was a graduate of Brooks Institute of Photography who was well known for his art diversity beyond photography. His first exhibits were primarily photography, but as the years passed, he expanded into paintings, sculpture, and woodworking. His life had been an artist's dream until three years ago when his wife, Shelly, died from surgery complications.

He dropped out of the exhibit circuit and reverted back to being a starving artist overnight. He eventually would have to sell everything he owned just to pay the bills. The eviction notice came the day before and he was struggling to decide what to do next.

He turned on the TV and saw the news was now running 24/7 coverage of the ship over Antarctica. Suddenly, the screen changed to Beth's face.

"Scott, I'm so sorry about your wife. I don't want to intrude on your grief, but have a proposition for you to consider. I'm transmitting from the ship that's on the news, but to prove it to you, I need you to unplug the TV power from the wall."

Scott was pissed. He just wanted to be left alone. He unplugged the set, yet the image was still on the screen.

"Well, it seems you have my attention. I don't know how you're doing this, but it's an intrusion on my privacy."

The image behind Beth zoomed back to confirm that she was indeed on the ship.

"I'm very sorry about that, so I'll make it quick. My husband and I are putting together a small group of explorers to venture out into the galaxy traveling to other solar systems. We have a variety of technical experts coming along, but need art as

334

part of the mixture to balance out our crew. We would like you to join us. If you are interested, we'll pick you up around 8 p.m. tonight. Again, I'm sorry for the intrusion, but I really think you'll enjoy our voyage."

Beth's image disappeared, and Scott started to consider the possibilities. Maybe this was the new start everyone told him he needed. Suddenly, 8 p.m. couldn't come quick enough.

Chapter 77

An hour had passed before Jake returned to see how his wife was doing with the list.

"So, how many are left on your list?"

"I'm all done," Beth grinned.

She pulled out the top sheet and handed it over to Jake. He scanned down the list of twenty until he got to the last three and then started to read.

1. Geologist	Adam Larsen
2. Medical	Julie Cross
3. Biologist	Allen Foster
4. Psychologist	Gary Gilman
5. Physics	Diana Hoss
6. Chemist	Tom & Stacey Linderman
7. Mathematician	Phillip Martin
8. Teacher	Sherry Wiseman
9. Cook	Chuck Dennison
10. Mechanical Engineer	Douglas Peters
11. Electronic Engineer	Alan Walters
12. Pilot	Kevin Shotwell
13. Historian	Arnold Shepard
14. Hydroponics	Dean & Cleo Hinton
15. Computer Nerd	Jack Williams
16. Language Expert	Herbert Stoutdale
17. Artist	Scott Bradley
18. Music	Shirley & Kirt Becker

"I looked over the list of three possible candidates for music. My first try turned out to be a bust in the first few minutes, so I went back to Meg's first choice, Shirley Becker, age fifty-two. She started violin at 10 and then added a new instrument yearly. She married orchestra conductor, Kirt Becker,

336

at age twenty-eight. For the last thirty years, he has conducted and written music including a recent movie score. They recently lost credibility when both their IDs were stolen and associated with child porn. They never recovered from it and disappeared from public view. Both took some convincing, but when I told them that every musical instrument known to man would be available for their use, they were sold."

19. Lawyer   *Leonard Books*

"I went through three lawyers on the list before I convinced Leonard Books, age sixty-one. He worked his own law office for twenty-five years and then became a judge for another ten years. He was removed from office after he threw a high-priced lawyer in jail for contempt.

"His wife, Peggy, is involved in hospice care for a local hospital. He didn't take me seriously until I had him go outside holding the computer monitor and showed him a view of his house zoomed in from space. Meg had placed a small camera satellite in orbit for the effect. His wife was on my side within minutes, but Meg provided a few quotes from Leonard's legal library to convince him that we really needed a lawyer in space."

20. MacGyver Type   *Richard & Janice Gates*

"Meg was positive there was only one person to fill this final position. Richard Angus Gates, age sixty, would be the one to help our group survive on new planets using whatever means available. He has extensive military training in survival techniques and is versed in just about every skill possible.

"He gets his inspiration and nickname, Mac, from the techniques seen in the *MacGyver* TV series. He married his wife, Janice, at age thirty after saving her from an airplane crash in the Amazon jungle. Janice eventually became as skilled at jerry-rigging techniques as her husband. Janice contracted pancreatic cancer last year and has less than two years to live. When I contacted them, they were watching an episode of *Survivorman*. I hated to break into the episode, but I was running out of time. They were difficult to convince, so Meg had to levitate several pieces of furniture. Janice was onboard, but Richard was still unsure. When I asked him if he was willing to risk passing on the one chance to save his wife, he gladly agreed. I hated using that trump card, but they were perfect for the position. Jake, you'll love this couple. They're so full of energy, they can hardly contain themselves."

Jake set the list down and gave Beth a big hug.

"You did a fantastic job, Beth. You're right; I think this Gates guy is going to be a huge asset. Now, all we have to do is wait until tonight. How about we go get a bite to eat?"

Chapter 78

Jake and Beth returned to the restaurant and sat down exhausted. Their meals appeared, and they both ate in silence before Jake broke the stillness.

"We've sure picked a strange group of travelers. Our new crew consists of people who've had just about everything go wrong in their lives. We've got divorced folks, unemployed, severely injured, dying, and most definitely down on their luck."

Beth put her hand over Jake's.

"That may be true, but the fact that they've had all these life experiences will help us along the way. Besides, they're definitely motivated, and just needed a reason to go."

"I agree, Beth, but you know we're not done yet. We need to contact the astronauts."

"We don't have much time, so let's give them until midnight tonight for their decision."

The astronauts had just been released home after being held for the last twenty-four hours at NASA. The next day they had to return for more briefings, so the window to talk with them was limited. There was also a damn good chance that their homes were bugged.

They decided to start with Colonel Craig Brentner, the Commander of *Excalibur*. The Colonel had just arrived home and was sitting with his wife in the living room trying to explain things.

As they talked, the TV screen came on displaying Jake's face. Before Jake could say anything, the Colonel yelled, "This is all your fault. Now I'm the bad guy, and they all think I'm against them."

"Whoa, Colonel, remember it was me who saved your butt from burning up in the atmosphere. I asked more than I should have from you and your crew, but I had no choice. I appreciate all you did to keep it quiet, and I'm willing to make it up to you."

Before the Colonel could answer, his wife Carol spoke up.

"Do you know is this guy? Is he the reason you got hauled off?"

"Honey, I know this is going to be hard to understand, but those missing days; I was on that spaceship that is floating around our planet. If the man on the screen hadn't taken a chance, I wouldn't be alive. I owe him my life. I think we should listen to what he has to say."

"Colonel, here's the short version. We've collected a group of professionals to join us on a trip to other solar systems that might support life. The group is pulled from twenty varied professions and ranges in age from thirty-seven to seventy. We're leaving tomorrow, but we wanted to make the offer to your crew to join us. I think you could contact each member faster than I could. You know the benefits of beaming technology and can explain it to their spouses.

"Anyone interested will be beamed up tonight at midnight. If you change your mind, we'll beam you back before we leave tomorrow. There's one exception. Your copilot has beamed twice in the last couple of days. His wife and child can return, but he can't without the risk of some mutation. Make sure he understands his choices. I need to make this short so that you can be on your way. Good luck, Colonel."

"I understand, Jake. I'll have answers by midnight." As the screen went black, he turned back to his wife and said, "We need to talk outside."

Jake put his arm around Beth.

"We're done and it's out of our hands now. After listening to all those people give reasons for going or not going, I started to have doubts. I hope we're doing the right thing. After all, we didn't really give the kids much choice."

Beth kissed him on the cheek.

"You worry too much. Even if we didn't believe anything that Meg told us, we see it all around us. The world is falling apart. We are doom and gloom, end of the world people. We

340

believe that if there's a chance of survival, we take it. Even with all this going on, I still believe in God, and I know you do too. Only God knows how it will all end.

"With any luck, we're going to save a piece of humanity. It may only be a small piece, but at least it's a piece. Hopefully, we can learn from our mistakes and build a better new world. Who knows, maybe our descendants will return and rebuild a new Earth in the future."

Jake nodded and was glad they were both on the same page. Now they faced the most difficult task of all. They needed to convince their two children that this was the right thing to do.

"You know, Beth, we've been putting off telling the kids. I think Brad will be fine, but I know Kathy will have a fit. I think we need to tell them together, so they know we both made this decision."

"I agree we should tell them together, but I don't think you give Kathy enough credit. Of course, she'll resist having to go, but I think she knows it's the only way. I think we need to talk to them now before everyone starts arriving."

Meg announced that she had already instructed Chameleon to bring the two children to the garden.

Jake took the lead.

"Chameleon and Meg, we would like some private family time to talk, so please give us a few minutes."

Before he could say any more, Chameleon disappeared.

"We know what's going on," Kathy said seriously. "Brad and I have been listening to your speeches with all those people. You thought we were playing, but we weren't. We told Chameleon we wanted to listen, but not be seen, so he hid us."

"Chameleon, you traitor. Just wait until I catch up with you."

Beth stopped Jake before he said another word.

"So how do both of you feel about leaving your home? You'll be leaving your friends, school, and the places you like to hang out."

Brad interjected with, "I like the idea of no school."

Jake shook his head.

"Kids, let's get serious. We really didn't give you a choice in the matter. I hope that you know that we're doing what we feel is the best for all of us. You're always telling us how grown up you are, so now is the time to grow up fast."

Kathy shed some small tears, and started to speak, but hesitated.

"This came up so fast. I had no time to say good-bye to my friends. Is there a way we can talk to our friends before we go?"

That idea had never occurred to Jake.

"Meg, is there any reason that Brad and Kathy cannot say good-bye to their friends before we leave?"

"No Jake, there is not. If they tell me whom they want to speak with, I can arrange it. They can talk as long as they want. We can assume the danger is no longer present as long as the entire McDonald family is on the ship."

Jake turned back to the children.

"Head to your rooms and tell Meg who you want to talk to, and she'll set it up."

Brad and Kathy came over and gave Jake and Beth a hug. Beth looked at Jake and said, "We must have done something right along the way."

Chapter 79

James Randel had been sitting in his office for hours licking his wounds. He had notified all the departments about going into the hibernation mode. He finally called the TF committee, and they weren't happy. He was afraid they might cut him loose, and only time would tell. James was just finishing his last paperwork when Pete Killian burst into the room.

"You're not going to believe this." As Killian spoke, he dropped a single sheet of paper down in front of James.

"Has this been confirmed?"

"When I saw the message start to come in, I took the only copy and had the technician destroy the original. He never saw the decoded version. I decoded it myself and checked it for authentication. It's for real and the odds are astronomical."

Randel stood up from his desk.

"This is absolutely incredible. Finally, something's going in our favor. Until we're sure we have a chance, no one else should know. Is that understood?"

"Sir, only you and I'll know. I will send a confirmation order back and monitor any new developments."

"Make sure that the other end responds in kind."

Killian left the room and Randel sat back down. Things had finally turned around. Now he was back in the game.

The rest of the afternoon Jake and Beth prepared for their new visitors. Jake asked Meg to start setting up rooms for their guests but found out the process had already begun. Beth made a few changes to the rooms and then waited until 8 p.m.

The large metallic sphere positioned itself over the Atlantic Ocean and began the beaming process. Each of the guests was beamed to the garden, which had been illuminated with outdoor lighting. Meg had even arranged extra seating for this first meeting. Once the last guest had arrived, Jake and Beth came into the garden and the crowd quieted, so Jake could speak.

"Welcome everyone. I know you're confused about all this, so let me explain as best as possible. The ship you are on is a probe designed for deep space travel. Tomorrow we'll start our journey toward another solar system guided by Meg, the Artificial Intelligence that runs this ship.

"We have prepared a small apartment for each of you on upper levels. If you have any concerns about your accommodations or anything else, just say *Meg* and express your desires. Meg is here to help you in any way.

"You may have noticed that you feel much better. The positive side effect of the beaming process is that some of your ailments have gone away."

The group started to talk amongst themselves. Jake held up his hand to quiet them before continuing.

"If you want to know why we are leaving Earth, please feel free to ask Meg. She has the unbiased composite of the facts that will both inform and depress you.

"It is getting late so Beth will now show you to your rooms. Once you're settled in, feel free to roam the ship to see if you've made the right decision. Sleep on it tonight and know that before we leave tomorrow, you'll still have the choice of returning to Earth.

"We may have a second smaller group coming up later tonight, so be aware that you may run into new people you haven't seen tonight."

As soon as Jake stopped talking, everyone started to introduce themselves.

Jake came over to Beth.

"I can't believe all that's happened in the last three weeks. I was abducted by aliens and almost died twice. I was shot at, crash-landed, and finally reunited with my family. Now I'm escorting a bunch of keen old duffers on a ride through space. It's been one hell of a month."

344

Chapter 80

The TF agent, code name "ColdFish," couldn't believe what had just happened. During the entire time, the agent had been with Tech Forces, ColdFish had never been activated, and had always been under deep cover. Then, unexpectedly, the agent had been asked to explore other solar systems on a spaceship that TF had been desperately trying to commandeer. The odds of being chosen to join the expedition were greater than winning the lottery.

Now they have headed off into locations afar, and ColdFish had a mission to complete. All the unknown agent had to do was to learn of Jake's weaknesses, and use them against him to confiscate the ship. Then the agent would be the most honored member of the Technical Forces organization.

Both Jake and Beth wandered the halls of the ship to see how everyone was adjusting. Beth was down in the cafeteria talking with the biologist, and Jake walked the hall near Kathy's room. She opened the door and ran into her father's arms. She was in tears.

"Daddy, do we really have to go? I'm going to miss my friends so much. I had so many things I wanted to do at school. You know, proms, dating, ballgames, all the things you did as a kid."

Jake was taken aback by Kathy's heartbreaking response. He wished Beth were here right now, as she would know just what to say. He pushed her room door open and they walked back inside. He gathered himself for one of his most difficult tasks so far.

"Honey, I'm so sorry that this has happened to you and Brad. I really don't know what to tell you. Just know that if you go back down, not only would we miss you terribly, but the bad guys would kidnap you again to make me surrender the ship.

This ship is very powerful and has technology beyond all man's knowledge. If it were to get into the wrong hands, many people will die. By staying here, you are possibly saving millions of lives."

"I know you're right, Daddy, and I understand about the risk to other people. It's just that I'll miss my friends. I asked Meg if I could talk to my friends as we traveled, and she told me only for a few days. She also said that there would be a time shift, and my friends would age faster than I would. She said that if we come back to Earth, everyone would be gone. I don't understand all this."

Jake thought about what she'd just said and realized this was the first he'd heard about the time shift. Meg was giving out too much information to his kids. They were having to grow up fast, so maybe the truth was the best solution.

"Honey, I know it's going to be hard, but I'm going to need your help, especially with your brother. Right now, he thinks he's going on a great adventure, like a camping trip. Eventually, it will sink in, and he'll realize what you already recognize. Will you help me when that time comes?"

Jake's solution was to keep her busy helping him with the family. She would still have problems, but maybe Meg and the other guests would help make it easier for her.

"I understand, Daddy. I'll help with Brad, but that still doesn't make it any better. I'll miss everyone."

"I know, Honey, but we have to do what we can to survive."

Jake left his fragile daughter in her room and headed to meet up with Beth in the restaurant. When he got there, he found a loud commotion going on near the back of the room.

Allen Foster, the biologist, and Dean Winton, the hydroponics expert were in a very heated battle about procedures used to investigate new Class M planets. The discussion had started with loud words, moved on to heated threats, and now looked like a fistfight was soon to start. Beth was trying to calm them down, but with little success.

As Jake moved toward the action, his started rethinking why he'd picked these two. They hadn't even left Earth, and there was already a fistfight about to start. He decided he needed to put the fear of God into them.

"Chameleon, I need your help."

The two looked up from their fight as the giant AI robot appeared from the nearby wall.

"Jake, I understand that you need my help. What do you want me to do with these two disrupting crew members?"

Jake liked Chameleon's style. He was right to the point, and the two fighters, quickly backed off as Jake moved between them.

"This is going to be a long journey, and we all have to get along. Now, the tall robotic man can be gentle or not. It's up to you. Think of him as the ship's law enforcer. If you do something wrong, you'll have to face him. Don't make me regret selecting either of you. Remember, there's still time to beam you back."

Silence was the norm for a minute before the talking finally resumed. This time it was quieter and more relaxed. Beth came over to Jake.

"Thanks, Jake, I needed help. This isn't going to be as easy as we thought. All these people are so different. What have we done?"

Jake pulled her to the side.

"I agree, but we have family problems to deal with right now. You need to hear what Meg just told Kathy, and then we need to talk with Meg in private."

Jake told Beth everything said between him and his daughter. They made an excuse for leaving and told everyone they would be back in half an hour.

As the door to their room closed Jake said, "Meg, we need to talk."

"Are you upset that I said something to Kathy?"

"No, Meg, it was alright that you talked with her. The problem is that tomorrow morning I'm supposed to explain to

347

everyone how we're traveling to other solar systems. To be perfectly honest, I don't have a clue how the ship operates. I just assumed that with all your technology, you would make it happen. What I failed to realize is that I need to know in order to explain it to everyone. They are educated people and won't blindly go down a path. They want all the facts. I can provide general information but would have to turn it over to you for the details. What the hell's going to happen from here on?"

"Jake, I have logged hundreds of solar systems that can support human life. Some have no sentient beings, while others do. It really depends on what you want to do."

"Meg, we've never traveled in space, obviously. With the mixture of people on board, and the solar systems available, what would you recommend?"

"Thank you, Jake, for asking. I had already formulated a plan."

"I figured, so enlighten us please."

"Using the data compiled about the ship, people, and solar systems, I would recommend that we travel to at least a dozen systems capable of supporting life. The course eventually takes us to my homeworld, where we could meet my creators. I would also recommend that anyone be allowed to stay on any planet we visit, with the understanding that it would be permanent."

"Are you serious? Do you want to leave people on some of these planets? Why?"

"In my research of human evolution, I discovered that each human has a different goal in life they seek to attain. Often it is peace of mind, while others thrive on adventure. You need to face the fact that some of your passengers may want to live on these others systems."

"Wow, I never even considered that a possibility. What is this you told Kathy about time displacement? You have never mentioned it before."

"Well, Jake, I haven't discussed that with you yet. Humans have only worked with the laws of physics that exist within this solar system. These laws are formulated by information extracted from various telescopes and probes. What you humans do not understand is that there are additional laws of physics of which you have no knowledge."

"I'm not sure I'm going to like this."

"Actually you will like some parts and not the others. All known laws of physics about apply as we leave the solar system. However, what they don't know is that the vastness of space has created a time displacement in the galaxy. If you move two planets in the solar system close together, they will pull at each other until they crash. Distance and planet's rotation around the sun keeps them apart.

"If you think of a solar system as a planet, the same thing applies. The difference is an enormous void in space between the systems, which acts like a negative attraction causing time and space to be bent.

"If you lay a course in a direct line with another solar system, you will start to accelerate in speed until time is compressed. What would normally take years is reduced to weeks between systems. When you reach the next solar system, time and space return to normal. You can then jump from solar system to solar system within this web of time-space conduits. Does this help answer your question?"

Beth was the first to respond.

"That's a lot of information for everyone to process. Most of my knowledge on space travel indicates that it would take years to leave the solar system using what you call normal time-space travel."

"You are correct. With your human technology, it would take years, but I can use my matter-energy conversion engines to provide constant .5 g acceleration. I would turn the artificial gravity off and use the constant acceleration to simulate low gravity throughout the ship. This constant .5 g acceleration will mean that over time we will be going faster and faster until we are progressing thousands of miles per second. The distance inside the solar system will be compressed to just a few days to cross."

"Beth is right. That is too much information to hand over in one day. We'll have to impart the information as needed. Kathy said something about everyone getting older, and they'd be gone if we came back to Earth. What's that about?"

"This is the part you're not going to like. The downside to traveling through these conduits is that time slows down drastically for you, while Earth does not change. If you travel to a solar system seven light-years away, and it takes a couple of weeks, seven years would have passed on Earth. If you returned, four weeks would have passed on the ship, and fourteen years on Earth. If we go to solar systems hundreds of light-years away, then those years pass on Earth as well."

"You are so right, Meg, I don't like that idea. In the morning, I'll give a brief discussion of where and how we plan to get to the other systems. You can fill in the details when people ask, just don't overdo the technology. Let them take in a little information at a time. If we give them too much at once, they'll all want to leave. After our talk, we'll offer them all one last chance to return to Earth. Have you figured an estimate on how many will stay for the journey?"

"Jake, that is difficult to compute. Humans are unpredictable, but my best calculation sets it at seventy percent. I think that is the best you will do."

"Meg, I hope we get that many. I have a feeling that the number will be less than fifty percent."

Beth piped up with, "You're both wrong. I've looked at the backgrounds of these people. I'm willing to bet that eighty-five percent will stay."

Jake looked down at his watch.

"We almost forgot; it's 11:30 p.m. We need to go down to the garden and wait for the astronauts, assuming there are any."

"I did not forget. I was just about to remind you. Most of the other group has settled into their rooms. The majority are not sleeping, and several have asked if I had sleeping pills. Is that acceptable?"

"Yes, Meg. If it will help them sleep and, by all means, give them the correct dosage of sleeping pills."

Chapter 81

The garden was deserted for the first time in hours. Beth pulled Jake down with her on the bench and they leaned against each other and waited. Shortly, a blue light appeared in front of them, and Carol Brentner appeared. She was a little unsure of her balance, so Jake helped her to a seat. As soon as she was settled, the Colonel appeared in front of them.

"Jake, long time no see you old space dog. As you gather, my wife and I are going with you on your little journey. I wish I could say the same for the rest of the crew, but only two others are coming."

"What happened, Colonel?"

"Well, I talked with each of the crew. Ed and his wife understand what's at stake, but have decided the best thing for his wife is to avoid as much excitement as possible with the new baby. The rest is a different story. They all wanted to come, but NASA grabbed Bob Cranston as soon as I told him. We don't know if he said something or his house was bugged. Anyway, they know about the beaming technology and have him stored in a shielded area. Brenda Millstone and Nancy Barten heard about Bob, and are hiding from NASA right now. I can give Meg their location, and she can beam them right up."

Meg used the location information and beamed up the two remaining astronauts. Jake introduced each to Beth and they continued a conversation for the next fifteen minutes. Then Beth looked up beyond the group and smiled. Jake looked over at the direction of her eyes and spotted Charlie walking toward him.

"What the hell? Where did he come from?"

Beth was happy to answer this one.

"Well, I know how much you and Charlie are friends, so I had Meg rescue him from the same group that held me hostage. It was the least I could do for him. He stood by me when I found out you were missing in the diving accident. He gave me support and kept me going."

Jake ran over hugging Charlie, "You old seadog."

"Look who's talking, you old fart."

"So, you're going to join us on this little trip?"

"I heard you were the Captain of a ship, and needed crewmen, right?"

"Charlie, it's so good to see you. This makes the group complete."

"Thank you, Jake, but if it hadn't been for your wife I wouldn't be here. You planned to leave me behind!"

"Sorry about that."

"I'm guessing you had a couple of things on your mind."

Beth showed everyone to their rooms, and then she and Jake crashed on their bed and were in dreamland within seconds.

Chapter 82

Seven a.m. the next morning, Jake and Beth were awakened by Meg with soft music. Jake jumped up with some alarm on his face.

"Meg, is anyone else up yet?"

"Almost all of them are in the restaurant. A few are still getting ready, and several are already exploring the ship."

"Can you tell those who are not in the restaurant to be there as soon as possible, and the rest to remain so we can talk?"

"It is already done."

"You are too efficient."

"There is no such thing as too efficient."

"You've got me there. Just tell them we'll be there in a few minutes."

Jake and Beth quickly dressed and raced down to the restaurant. When they arrived, the conversation was lively as the group was busy eating and discussing the anticipated events of the day. When Beth and Jake entered the room, a hush settled over the room.

Adam Larsen stood up and moved through the crowd toward Jake.

"Jake, and Beth. We've all been talking and decided we needed a spokesman. Since I was the first person you contacted, I'm going to tell you what we all say as a group."

Jake wasn't too sure what was going on and it didn't sound like good news. He started second-guessing that perhaps they all decided to go back. That would be fine, and maybe for the best. After all, the group was going to be a handful.

"The group wants to thank you for the opportunity you've given us, and especially the medical side benefits of the beaming technology. We know that one of the reasons you gave for wanting to leave Earth was your "End of the World" speech. We all listened to you, and Meg gave us more information about all

354

the things humans have done to planet Earth and how it's going to end. We think you're under the assumption that we want to go with you based on that information. Truth be told, only about half of us believed your "Chicken Little" story."

Before Adam could continue, Jake interrupted.

"So, does this mean that most of you want to go back to Earth?"

Adam held up a hand and continued.

"Jake, you really don't understand. We all know that the conditions on Earth are a very fragile balance between survival and destruction. That's not the main reason most of us considered this trip. We figured it was an adventure and a great way to finish our lives. We'll be able to extend our experiences beyond what we've accomplished to date. We are also aware there are many unknowns, which I'm sure you're about to explain to us."

The suspense was killing Jake.

"So we misjudged the reasons for your wanting to come on board. How many of you want to stay, or should I say, how many want to go back to Earth?"

Jake waited patiently, but Adam was like a game-show host holding the winning prize.

"You really don't get it, do you? We ALL want to go, which shows you should have more faith in mankind. There are a few with reservations, but it was unanimous."

Jake couldn't believe what he was hearing. He looked over to Beth in amazement. No one backed out. How could he have been so wrong? He finally got up the nerve to continue.

"Wow! We are thrilled. So let's proceed with the nuts and bolts of our new flight plan. I have talked with Meg, and she has prepared an itinerary of the trip. I'll give you an overall view in layman's terms, and then she'll answer any technical questions."

Just as Jake was to about to continue, Adam broke in with another question.

"As a group, we have one more suggestion. We know that

355

Meg runs the ship, and you refer to the ship as Meg. We mean no disrespect, but we think the ship itself should have an individual name. The ship now contains a Captain, a computer, and a sample of humanity. When we visit other planets, should we say greetings, we're from the Earth ship *Meg*? That sounds strange. We talked it over and think *Phoenix* is the appropriate new name for the ship. The name translates to something new rising out of the ashes, which seems to describe our situation well. You are the Captain, so the decision is yours."

Jake was surprised at this revelation. He'd never thought about it, but it made sense.

"What do you think, Meg? Can you handle a name change? We'll still call you, Meg, but from now on the ship and its contents will be called the Earth ship *Phoenix*."

"To the new crew of the *Phoenix*, the name change is fine. I will log it into my memory banks. From this point on, I will use that identification for contact with other ships and worlds."

Over the next two hours, additional explanations were given, which in turn were followed by dozens of questions. By the time lunch had arrived, everyone was exhausted. Jake stood up and tapped a spoon to glass to get attention. Quiet came over the group.

"If it's okay with everyone, we'll head toward Mars this afternoon, and tomorrow we'll be on our way to a new adventure. Places that one could only dream about will be our experiences in the near future."

Everyone stood up and cheered. Jake kissed Beth and hugged his kids. Maybe this was going to be all right after all. He guessed only time and space would tell.

Frank Mendol sat in his chair looking at the linkup with the Hubble telescope. It had been repositioned to monitor the ship as it departed Earth. It had become obvious that it was headed toward Mars. He spoke aloud to the screen as though it could answer.

"Jake McDonald, I envy you. You're one lucky son of a bitch. I would give anything to be in your shoes right now. I wish you well, and hope you find what you're looking for, Godspeed."

Voyage

Book Two in the Ship Series
Available soon in Paperback and Kindle

As Jake McDonald and his family leave Earth on *Phoenix*, his new-found alien space ship, they face challenges never before encountered by humans. While exploring Mars, Jake discovers there is a spy among his new band of Earth travelers. Besides locating the spy, he's dealing with the diverse personalities among the group and the problems that arise as they attempt to work together.

The band of Earthlings soon discover that the physics of space travel affects both time and space. Days on the ship equivocate to years on Earth, and this eventually splits the group into two factions fighting for control as they journey into deep space.

Jake and his wife, Beth, divide their time between maintaining peace among travelers and solving the constantly arising new problems of space travel. Meanwhile, they try to keep their own family together.

As the ship voyages into deep space, it travels from planet to planet searching for the answer to the question, are we alone? *Ship Voyage* is a book about the very nature of human evolution beyond the bounds of Earth. It addresses the physical and mental challenges humans might face as they explore planets hundreds of light-years from Earth.

358

Acroname Book Series

C.A.T. (Book One)

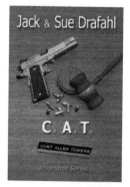

Curt Allen Towers owns a successful manufacturing company, specializing in miniaturized robotic devices. His life is turned upside down when he is accused of the rape and murder of a business associate. Curt struggles to prove his innocence but finds there is a fine line between friend and foe. He must now rely on his gut feelings to judge a person and read them with his heart.

A fugitive from prison, he desperately runs for cover, evading one attempt after another on his life. Curt lives up to his nickname of CAT, but wonders if nine lives are enough? If you loved the TV action adventures of *The Fugitive* and *MacGyver*, then you'll enjoy *C. A. T.*

D.N.A. (Book Two)

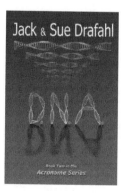

Fifty-five-year-old police detective Frank Ridge has hit a slump in his career. A recent homicide case is botched, and Frank is blamed for not keeping up with crime scene technology. In an effort to rectify the situation, he enlists the help of Dennis Andrews, a young CSI military scientist who is fascinated with all the latest technologies. Dennis has created a new device that quickly analyzes DNA samples at the molecular level, without damaging or even touching the samples.

Together, the two crime fighters start working together solving virtually impossible cold cases. Everything seems to be going well at first, but then the two are under fire from government officials who would like to see the DNA device disappear, along with the dynamic duo. Frank and Dennis become moving targets as they continue their quest to solve cold cases.

S.O.S. (Book Three)

University professors, James, and Stacy Sanders find themselves caught up in the social networking world to such an extent that it affords them minimal time for themselves or their two children. A catastrophic disaster throws these two together on an uninhabited Pacific volcano, with little hope of being rescued. They quickly discover that teamwork and close communication are a priority if they plan to survive.

They must rely upon their scuba diving skills, and their extensive knowledge in World War II history, to keep one step ahead of the forces of Mother Nature, and a relentless cold-blooded killer.

O.M.G. (Book Four)

Available Soon in Paperback and Kindle

Three college buddies band together to create a company that does deep sea treasure diving and recovery of historical artifacts. Using advanced technical diving suits, they make their first dive to a thousand feet off the Oregon coast in quest of a missing WWII Japanese submarine. Instead, they uncover a decades-old secret that sends a shockwave through government security. Fearing it will become front-page news, the government is forced to step in and help with their salvage efforts.

In Newport, Oregon, retired Air Force Colonel Oscar Gains spends his time enjoying gardening and meteorite hunting with Marty, his AF friend. Little does he know that the military secret he tried to forget, has now surfaced only a few miles from his home. Oscar is thrown back into the cloak and dagger world and forced to utilize his high-level government connections. *O.M.G.* follows these two storylines as they come crashing together in a climax that unearths a million-year-old secret.

Jack and Sue Drafahl are a husband and wife writing team. For over forty-five years, they have written over 800 articles in sixteen national publications from *Petersen's Photographic* to *Skin Diver Magazine*.

They have also authored seven non-fiction technical books for Amherst Media on various aspects of photography, both topside, and underwater.

In 2006, they changed the course of their writing to include fiction. They have written three book series: (the *Acroname* series, the *Ship* series, and the *Time and Space* series) that currently include fifteen novels that span the gamut of genres from Action/Adventure to Science Fiction.

They both received their scuba diving certification in the early '70s, and have logged over ten thousand dives, in almost every ocean on earth. Jack and Sue were awarded Divers of the Year from Beneath the Sea in 1996 and were given the Accolade Award for their conservation efforts. Sue is an inaugural member of the Women Divers Hall of Fame (2000) and is an Honorary Trustee. They are members of Willamette Writers and the Pacific Northwest Writers Association. Jack and Sue make their home on the Oregon coast. In addition to their book writing, they enjoy leading underwater photo expeditions around the globe.

Please send any comments or errors you may find to novels@earthseapublishing.com.

http://www.JackandSueDrafahl.com

http://www.EarthSeaPublishing.com

Made in the USA
San Bernardino, CA
03 July 2019